THE PRECIPICE

THE PRECIPICE

HUGH MACLENNAN

Introduction: Elspeth Cameron
General Editor: Michael Gnarowski

MCGILL-QUEEN'S UNIVERSITY PRESS

Montreal & Kingston • London • Ithaca

© McGill-Queen's University Press 2013

ISBN 978-0-7735-4267-9 (paper)
ISBN 978-0-7735-8971-1 (ePDF)
ISBN 978-0-7735-8972-8 (ePUB)

Legal deposit fourth quarter 2013
Bibliothèque nationale du Québec

Printed in Canada on acid-free paper that is 100% ancient forest free
(100% post-consumer recycled), processed chlorine free

McGill-Queen's University Press acknowledges the support of the Canada Council for
the Arts for our publishing program. We also acknowledge the financial support of the
Government of Canada through the Canada Book Fund for our publishing activities.

Library and Archives Canada Cataloguing in Publication

MacLennan, Hugh, 1907–1990, author
The precipice / Hugh MacLennan ; introduction: Elspeth
Cameron ; general editor: Michael Gnarowski.

Includes bibliographical references.
Issued in print and electronic formats.
ISBN 978-0-7735-4267-9 (pbk.).–ISBN 978-0-7735-8971-1 (ePDF).–
ISBN 978-0-7735-8972-8 (ePUB)

I. Cameron, Elspeth, 1943–, writer of introduction
II. Gnarowski, Michael, 1934–, editor III. Title.

PS8525.L54P7 2013   C813'.54   C2013-906803-1
C2013-906804-X

For Dorothy

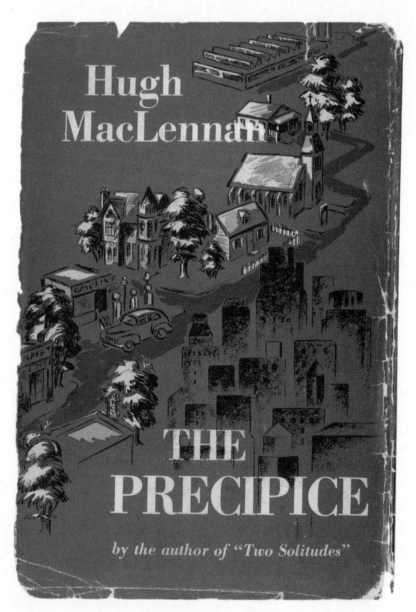

Front of dust-jacket of first Canadian edition with a collage-like
effect juxtaposing images of an urban skyline and more modest
rural dwellings and a country church

CONTENTS

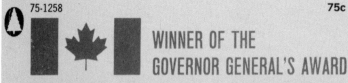

75-1258   75c

WINNER OF THE
GOVERNOR GENERAL'S AWARD

THE PRECIPICE

By Hugh MacLennan
Author of *Return of the Sphinx*

THE POWERFUL NOVEL OF A MAN AND WOMAN
LOCKED IN LOVE—AND SAVAGE VIOLENCE
"BRILLIANT"—The Saturday Review
"ARRESTING...COMPELLING"—The Montreal Star

Cover image of the Popular Library paperback edition of *The Precipice*.
Although a paperback version may have been issued as early as 1948,
this particular edition is clearly from a much later date since it identifies
MacLennan as the author of *Return of the Sphinx*, which appeared in 1967.

GENERAL EDITOR'S NOTE

The text of *The Precipice* presented here was derived by means of an optical character recognition scan of the first Canadian edition published by Wm. Collins Sons & Co., Ltd. of Toronto, Canada in 1948. Minor changes have been effected to correct typographical errors and/or spelling errors. Canadian spelling is used for this edition.

CHRONOLOGY

1907 John Hugh MacLennan born on 20 March in Glace Bay, Nova Scotia, son and second child of Katherine MacQuarrie and Samuel MacLennan, a medical doctor employed by the coal mining industry.

1915 The MacLennan household moves from Cape Breton Island to Halifax where Dr. MacLennan sets up his practice after having been invalided out of service in the First World War.

1917 MacLennan lives through the catastrophe of the Halifax Explosion, which will become the subject of his first published novel, *Barometer Rising* (1941).

1924 MacLennan graduates from Halifax County Academy with a University Entrance Scholarship and the Yeoman Prize in Latin and Greek. Enrols in Dalhousie University to study Classics, at which he excels.

1928 Having distinguished himself academically and in sports, MacLennan graduates from Dalhousie University, disappointed at not having won the (expected and hoped for) Rhodes Scholarship for Nova Scotia but is then chosen Rhodes Scholar for Canada-at-Large. Sails for England and Oxford in September of that year.

1928–32 Once settled in at Oriel College, MacLennan finds his studies in Classics rigorous and demanding. He has little social life other than sports (rugby and tennis, at which he was a champion player at the University); writes frequent letters to his family, and takes advantage of his vacations to travel modestly on the Continent in France, Italy, Austria, and Germany, where he encounters strong right wing nationalism and the rising tides of fascism and communism. Earns his BA in Classics from Oxford in 1932 and wins a Fellowship at Princeton to continue his studies for a Ph.D.

1932 Sailing home from Oxford, meets an American woman, Dorothy Duncan (1903–1957), a writer (*Bluenose: A Portrait of Nova Scotia*, 1942) as well as a graphic artist, and marries her four years later.

1932–35 Unable to find suitable employment, MacLennan, offered a modest fellowship at Princeton, decides to study there for his Ph.D in classical history. While at the University he tries his hand at writing fiction, leading to two early novels, both of which remain unpublished. In 1935 receives his doctorate and his dissertation, *Oxyrhynchus: An Economic and Social Study,* is published by Princeton University Press. He moves to Montreal and takes up a position as schoolmaster at Lower Canada College.

1936 Hugh MacLennan and Dorothy Duncan are married on 22 June in Wilmette, Illinois, returning via Boston and Yarmouth, Nova Scotia, to settle in Montreal.

1937–39 MacLennan struggles unsuccessfully to arrange for the publication of his two novels in manuscript, "A Man Should Rejoice" which is rejected by Random House and "So All Their

Praises" which is rejected by Longmans Green, both in New York. The first novel, dated 1933, was accepted by New York publisher Robert O. Ballou, but went bankrupt before the novel could be published. He reportedly reads Ringuet's *Trente Arpents,* which had appeared in 1938 and without which, MacLennan later confesses, *Two Solitudes* could not have been written. Predicts that war will begin in September of 1939.

1936–41 Continues at Lower Canada College and begins to develop a career at writing for magazines. He is prompted by his wife to turn his fiction to Canadian themes. She, having written a guide book, *Here's to Canada!* (1941), is embarked on her book *Bluenose* (1942) and is credited with MacLennan's choosing the Halifax explosion of 1917 as the focus of his novel *Barometer Rising,* which launches his career as a novelist.

1941 *Barometer Rising* is published and is well-received. MacLennan continues to teach at Lower Canada College but feels financially constrained and endeavours to supplement his income by writing for magazines.

1943 MacLennan is awarded a Guggenheim Fellowship, which provides some financial relief and frees him somewhat to work on his next novel, *Two Solitudes,* which he had apparently begun the previous year. MacLennan's declared project is to write a novel of Canadian life in the years 1917–40. Announcement of the fellowship generates a series of letters from American publishers (J.B. Lippincott; Doubleday, Doran; Houghton, Mifflin) expressing interest in publishing his next novel.

1944 MacLennan begins correspondence with Willem L. Graff, professor of German, as he tries to pin down the exact wording and location of the "two solitudes" reference in the work of the German poet Rainer-Maria Rilke. In July he dispatches a copy of the 582 page typescript of *Two Solitudes* to Blanche Gregory, his literary agent in New York, and the publisher Duell, Sloan and Pearce. A third copy will go to Collins in Toronto, who will publish in Canada.

1945 *Two Solitudes* is published (publication date is mid-January although copies had been made available in December of 1944). The book is well-received with congratulatory letters from friends and literary associates and excellent reviews and good sales. The success of *Two Solitudes* and its financial returns enable MacLennan to resign from Lower Canada College, a position that he had never enjoyed. He wins the Governor General's Award for fiction.

1948 MacLennan publishes *The Precipice*, which, while it wins the Governor General's Award for fiction is not a commercial or critical success.

1949 *Cross Country*, a collection of ten previously published essays/articles, half of which had appeared in *Maclean's* magazine, is published. The collection wins the Governor General's Award for non-fiction.

1951 With his wife's health beginning to fail and medical bills becoming a burden (there had even been a suggestion the previous year that he accept financial help from the Canadian Writer's Foundation), MacLennan accepts a part-time position in the English Department of McGill University, entering the academic profession in which he will remain until his retirement. *Each Man's Son* is published in May in spite of paper shortages. MacLennan teaches two courses at McGill, one on Canadian fiction and the other on English prose.

He keeps abreast of contemporary writing, admiring the work of W.O. Mitchell, whose *Who Has Seen the Wind* is on his assigned reading list. Similarly Evelyn Waugh's *Brideshead Revisited* is recommended to his English prose class.

1954 *Thirty and Three*, MacLennan's second collection of essays, is published and wins the Governor General's Award for non-fiction.

1957 Dorothy Duncan, MacLennan's wife for twenty-one years, dies after a prolonged struggle with chronic illness.

1959 MacLennan marries Frances Aline Walker, known as Tota, who had been a family friend for some years. *The Watch that Ends the Night* is published and wins MacLennan's fifth and last Governor General's Award.

1960 *Scotchman's Return and Other Essays* is published.

1964 MacLennan takes a sabbatical leave from the University and goes to live in Grenoble, France, where he continues writing his next novel and works hard at mastering spoken French.

1966 The Molson Prize, a rich cash award in the second year of its existence, names MacLennan as the recipient of this honour.

1967 *Return of the Sphinx* is published; MacLennan is inducted as a Companion of the Order of Canada.

1968 Alarmed at the general malaise in society and the militancy of the young – student riots in Paris; a mob marching to demand a "McGill français"; the burning of the computer centre at Sir George Williams University in Montreal – MacLennan retreats into himself to incubate the themes of personal dysfunctiion and social alienation that become strong and prophetic elements in his last novel, *Voices in Time.*

1980 *Voices in Time*, blurbed as MacLennan's finest novel, is also his last.

1990 MacLennan dies on 9 November at his country home in North Hatley in the Eastern Townships of Quebec.

Note: MacLennan won many awards and distinctions in his time. He was made a Chevalier of the National Order of Quebec, elected a Fellow of The Royal Society of Canada, and had honorary degrees conferred on him by several Canadian Universities.

SELECT BIBLIOGRAPHY

BOOKS BY HUGH MacLENNAN

Barometer Rising (New York/Toronto, 1941)
Two Solitudes (New York/Toronto, 1945)
The Precipice (New York/Toronto, 1948)
Cross-Country (Toronto, 1949)
Each Man's Son (Boston/Toronto, 1951)
Thirty and Three (Toronto, 1954)
The Watch that Ends the Night (New York/Toronto, 1959)
Scotchman's Return and Other Essays (Toronto, 1960)
Seven Rivers of Canada (New York/Toronto, 1961) (With the
   camera of John De Visser)
Return of the Sphinx (New York/Toronto, 1967)
The Colour of Canada (Toronto/Boston, 1967)
*The Other Side of Hugh MacLennan: Selected Essays Old and
   New*. Edited by Elspeth Cameron. (Toronto, 1978)
Voices in Time (Toronto, 1980)
Hugh MacLennan's Best. Edited By Douglas Gibson (Toronto,
   1991)

BOOKS ABOUT OR RELATING TO HUGH MacLENNAN

Dorothy Duncan, *Bluenose: A Portrait of Nova Scotia* (New York/London, 1942)

Robert Cockburn, *The Novels of Hugh MacLennan* (Montreal, 1969)

George Woodcock, *Hugh McLennan* (Toronto, 1969)

Paul Goetsch, *Hugh MacLennan* (Toronto, 1973)

Elspeth Cameron, "Ordeal by Fire: The Genesis of MacLennan's *The Precipice*," *Canadian Literature*, Vol. 82 (Autumn 1979): 35–46.

Elspeth Cameron, "Hugh MacLennan: An Annotated Bibliography" in *The Annotated Bibliography of Canada's Major Authors*, Vol. 1. Edited by Robert Lecker and Jack David (Downsview, 1979)

Elspeth Cameron, *Hugh MacLennan: A Writer's Life* (Toronto, 1981)

T.D. MacLulich, "MacLennan's Anatomy of Failure," *Journal of Canadian Studies* Vol. 14, no. 4 (Winter 1979–80): 54–65.

Elspeth Cameron, ed., *Hugh MacLennan: 1982. Proceedings of the MacLennan Conference at University College* (Toronto, 1982)

Three Canadian Writers, Provincial Education Media Centre (Richmond, BC, 1983)

Helen Hoy, *Hugh MacLennan and His Works* (Toronto, 1990)

Mari Peepre-Bordessa, *Hugh MacLennan's National Trilogy: Mapping a Canadian Identity 1940–1950* (Helsinki?, 1990)

Frank M. Tierney, ed., *Hugh MacLennan* (Ottawa, 1994)

Christl Verduyn, ed., *Dear Marian, Dear Hugh: The MacLennan-Engel Correspondence* (Ottawa, 1995)

Robert D. Chambers, *Hugh MacLennan and Religion: The Precipice Revisited*," *Journal of Canadian Studies*, Vol. 14, no. 4 (Winter 1979–80): 46–53.

Barbara Pell, *Faith and Fiction: A Theological Critique of the Narrative Strategies of Hugh MacLennan and Morley Callaghan*, (Waterloo, 1998)

Anne Coleman, *I'll Tell You a Secret: A Memory of Seven Summers* (Toronto, 2004)

INTRODUCTION

When Hugh MacLennan turned forty in March 1947, he took stock of his career. His first two published novels *Barometer Rising* (1941) and *Two Solitudes* (1945) had been exceptionally successful, catapulting him to the position of the foremost Canadian novelist. *Two Solitudes* especially had enjoyed huge sales,[1] a place on *The New York Times* bestseller list, and other such lists, for a year, and Canada's top literary prize, the Governor General's Award. Translations were soon underway in numerous languages.[2] This accession to fortune and fame made it possible to realize his hope that he could resign his wearisome position teaching boys at Lower Canada College and write full time.[4]

Yet MacLennan was bitter. Within six months of *Two Solitudes'* publication, he was protesting the unfairness of Canadian tax laws regarding writers. He was also complaining about the way publishing contracts were set up. "[M]y years of working in the Canadian market – and indeed in partially creating its present dimensions – are profiting almost everyone concerned [but] myself," he griped to his publisher."[4] The $12,000 he had earned after taxes would support him and his wife Dorothy Duncan for three years, he calculated. He wanted more. His protests won him his first separate Canadian contract with Collins to ensure Canadian sales for his next novel.

He had already begun that novel. He had carefully assessed what type of novel it might be. Shorter, for a start, and firmly built on a moral base, unlike the "decadent" fiction – many by "homo-sexuals" (sic)[5] such as Marcel Proust, André Gide, Christopher Isherwood, and, to some extent, Evelyn Waugh. He set the bar high. He rejected regional fiction for its narrowness. He felt caged by the notion of interpreting Canada to Canadians, the source of much of his acclaim. From the outset, he had been a reluctant nationalist. He was now determined instead to interpret Canada to the world at large. He aspired to become nothing less than a genius. His definition of genius is idiosyncratic: "nothing but a peculiar combination of will-power, tenacity, and the ability to make one's subconscious work for one."[6] Willpower and tenacity MacLennan certainly had. Yet making the subconscious work seems like an oxymoron. If the subconscious lies below consciousness, how can one *make* it work? Then, what of talent? Intuition? Luck?

MacLennan thought his best path lay through "the American branch cycle" of English fiction.[7] In his 1946 essay "Canada Between Covers,"[8] he identified the sociological novel, as exemplified in Ernest Hemingway, F. Scott Fitzgerald, John Dos Passos, and especially Sinclair Lewis's *Babbit* and Arthur Koestler's *Darkness at Noon*, as his models for *The Precipice*. These writers were either his contemporaries or a decade or so older. He did not assess the younger writers emerging at the time.

The idea for *Two Solitudes* had come from MacLennan's dream of two men shouting at one another: one in French, one in English, neither understanding the other.[9] It seems not to have occurred to him that this might have contributed to his engagement with the work and its unquestionable success. *Barometer Rising* had developed from a suggestion from his wife, Dorothy Duncan, that he write about Canada. His two early, unpublished novels had not been set in Canada, and they were rejected by many publishers.[10] Dorothy deduced their failures were because MacLennan had set them in locations he did not know well. This was to prove a problem for *The Precipice* as well, since MacLennan had not spent much time in any of the novel's settings.[11]

As he was writing his novel, Dorothy – whose heart was seriously damaged by childhood rheumatic fever – declined in health. He confided to his American publisher in March 1947 that the reason his novel was not yet finished was because, "I have had to be nurse, cook and housekeeper" to Dorothy.[12] In those days before medicare MacLennan had to pay her expensive health costs.[13] No longer employed at Lower Canada College, he took advantage of offers to lecture and write articles (though he was convinced, wrongly, that he was not good at either) to raise more money than *Two Solitudes* had brought in.

As with his first published novel, MacLennan relied on others, not on himself, for the ideas in this novel. His Nova Scotian friend Blair Fraser (1909–1968) had suggested that he turn his attention to "darkest Ontario."[14] By this, Fraser meant the puritanical outlook in the province's small towns that was so different from the earthy, life-loving Nova Scotian attitude.[15] MacLennan had every reason to take Fraser's advice seriously, because Fraser was on his way to becoming the leading English Canadian political journalist. When MacLennan moved to Montreal in the fall of 1935, Fraser had been writing for the English daily newspapers there for half a dozen years. They could have met in any number of ways, and once they did, the two Scottish Nova Scotians became close friends, debating many political and social ideas. By the time MacLennan was writing *The Precipice*, Fraser had become the Ottawa editor of the national publication *Maclean's* magazine. Fraser considered that "darkest Ontario" puritanism was different from American puritanism. This was a subject MacLennan explored at length in his essay "Discovering Who We Are" (1946),[16] published in *Maclean's* while Fraser was editor. MacLennan subsequently spent a week or so in the Ontario lakeshore towns of Cobourg, Belleville, and Port Hope chatting with the locals and getting a feel for the landscape. In Port Hope he noted a sanitary fixtures company whose products had been deteriorating after it was taken over by an American company. It would become a model for Grenville's Ceramic Company, a branch plant of the American Sani-Quip in *The Precipice*.

Fraser was not the only one to formulate ideas for *The Precipice*. As with *Barometer Rising*, Dorothy Duncan made a suggestion to her husband that was crucial. The couple had seen the New York City ballet *Pillar of Fire* in 1946, and had stood with the cheering crowd at its conclusion. They saw Anthony Tudor's ballet a second time. Both times it aroused in MacLennan "an immediate, strong, creative feeling."[17] Dorothy pronounced, "There, Hugh, is the plot for your novel right there." MacLennan's working title for his new book became *Pillar of Fire*.[18]

Hugh Laing and Nora Kaye in *Pillar of Fire*.

MacLennan had already decided – probably at Dorothy's prompting – to make his central character a woman for the first time. His electric response to this modern erotic ballet had much to do with its principal dancer, Nora Kaye. Kaye danced the role of Hagar, the middle sister of three, who undergoes a sexual awakening in a small puritanical Victorian community.[19] Kaye – who bore a strong resemblance to Dorothy – gave a performance that was passionately sexual. Hagar's Elder Sister is a rigid, church-going spinster who dominates the household; her Younger Sister is a pretty, superficial flirt. The two men competing for Hagar are generically named the Friend and the Young Man from the House Opposite.

The ballet was inspired by Arnold Schoenberg's 1899 twelve-tone composition *Verklärte Nacht* (*Transfigured Night*). Schoenberg in turn had based his lyrical, dissonant music on the 1896 poem "Weib und die Welt" (Woman and the World) by the German romantic poet, Richard Dehmel. This erotic sequence of poems – scandalous in its time – could have been familiar to MacLennan from his readings in *The Oxford Book of German Verse*, which he owned when he was a student at Oxford. The poem describes an altercation between two lovers involved in a love triangle. The woman is pregnant with a baby fathered by one man who she now believes is worthless; the other man, her true friend and love, eventually forgives her.[20]

MacLennan framed his characters on those in his sources. Lucy Cameron – who physically resembles Nora Kaye, even to her dark hair and graceful walk – became his central character. Lucy's older sister, Jane, is taken almost exactly from the Elder Sister in *Pillar of Fire*, as is Nina from the Younger Sister. Bruce Fraser, Lucy's next-door neighbour, is the Friend, especially in his decency and loyalty. Their names are suggestive of their characters: Lucy suggests "light," Jane brings to mind "plain Jane," Nina is the Spanish word for "child." The surname "Cameron" signifies the Scottish puritanism of small-town Ontario. "Fraser" is doubtless taken from Blair Fraser – a tribute to his suggestions for the novel.

That's where the similarities to MacLennan's sources end. While Stephen Lassiter resembles the unbridled seducer in *Pillar of Fire* (and "Weib und die Welt"), the Man in the House Opposite, whose casual sexual encounter with Hagar (and the unnamed woman in the poem) results in the pregnancy so central to their plots. Yet MacLennan does not have Lucy become pregnant until *after* she marries Stephen.

Why would MacLennan forego the very tension that propels his sources and stimulated his excitement at the ballet? He had already made clear his revulsion from "decadent" fiction. He wanted sales as big as *Two Solitudes*, but did not want to resort to salacious scenes to gain them. His fictional *bête noire* at the time was *Forever Amber*, a 1944 costume novel by Kathleen Winsor set in the seventeenth century. In this novel, the destitute orphan Amber rises through her sexual exploits to become the mistress of King Charles II. The novel sold an enviable 100,000 copies in the first week and was made into a movie in 1947. In sidestepping the central *raison d'être* of his sources, MacLennan ironically shows himself to be somewhat puritan at the same time that he is critical of both Canadian and American puritanism.

He had other intentions for Stephen Lassiter in addition to that of a seducer. Stephen was intended to represent the American puritanism of action in stark contrast to the stronger Canadian puritanism of repressed passivity. By refocusing Stephen's role in this way, MacLennan shifted the plane of his fiction from the close-up of an overwrought love triangle to a panoramic view of the two main North American cultures. The result feels mismatched, passionless, jarring.

In "On Discovering Who We Are," written when his novel was well underway, MacLennan tussled with how these two cultures differed. He confidently claimed that he had an insider's view of the United States due to the fact that he had spent a year at Princeton and half a year in New York, and was married to an American. The proceeds from *Two Solitudes* had bought the MacLennans a cottage named Stone Hedge in North Hatley near the US border, a popular summer spot for wealthy Americans. No doubt the couple often observed and discussed such differences with their American friends there. They had driven across the States in December 1946 (on Dorothy's doctor's advice that she find a warmer climate) to visit Dorothy's retired parents in Laguna Beach, California. Everywhere along the way, MacLennan had chatted with locals and garnered sociological and political details, which he then discussed with Dorothy. Her effect on his specific works, as well as on his overall career, has been greatly underestimated. MacLennan himself knew this full well and often acknowledged her influence. "It was my wife who persuaded me to see Canada as it was and to write of it as I saw it ... It was she who helped me discover Canada ... for she, in her own way, found another framework of differences when she came to live in my country."[21]

What MacLennan discovered about the differences between Americans and Canadians was this: "Americans are proud of what they do. The excessive puritanism of Canadians make them proud of what they don't do."[22] A weakened American puritanism had led to "mechanized feelings," a "superiority complex," and "irresponsibility." In an observation that presaged *The Precipice*, he wrote, "it seems that nothing but catastrophe can check the furious progress of Americans into a still more dangerous desert of technology."[23] The same idea is more elaborately stated by Lucy, who has come to agree with her friend Bruce:

> The other night after we heard about the atomic bomb [destroying Hiroshima] I began to think of the Americans the way you do – like a great mass of people and not as individuals. I saw them moving in a vast swarm over a plain. They had gone faster and farther than any people had ever gone before. Each day for years they had measured out the distance they'd advanced. They were trained to believe there was nothing any of them had to do but keep on traveling in the same way. And then suddenly they were brought up short at the edge of a precipice which hadn't been marked on the map. There they were with all their vehicles and equipment, jostling and piling up on the front rank. For of course the ones behind didn't know the precipice was there and couldn't understand why the ones in front had stopped advancing. The pressure from behind kept increasing on the front ranks and they were all shouting at each other so loudly nobody could hear anything. (336)

The larger-than-life athletic American businessman Stephen Lassiter embodies this blind, thrusting, dangerous progress. He has established a branch plant for Sani-Quip, the bathroom equipment business his father established in the U.S., in sleepy Grenville. The Cameron girls, particularly Jane, represent the Canadian puritanism that stifles emotion and resists any change from the ways of their severe, controlling late father, John Knox Cameron. Feelings in this family can surface only through the arts (Jane's piano music and Lucy's gardening). Lassiter is ruthless, athletic (he plays tennis), and reckless.[24] Jane is rigid, controlling, anhedonic. This scheme structures the novel at the expense of individual characterization. For example, it is uncharacteristic for Lucy to make such a long, intellectual comment about Americans. Nor is it probable that she would tell Bruce that "Stephen … made me see that what counts is not what you keep yourself from doing, but what you do" (336). These are among many examples of MacLennan's proselytizing through his characters.

MacLennan was particularly proud of the structure of *The Precipice*. He believed it had a well-constructed plot, one that resembled *Barometer Rising* rather than the sprawling *Two Solitudes*. When the novel was two-thirds written in March 1947, he wrote to his publisher Charles Duell, "the book is such a tightly knit organism, is in my belief such a great advance over *Two Solitudes* both in scope and depth, and even in construction, that every attempt to hurry it has been a failure."[25] His attempts to hurry the novel arose from his need to pay Dorothy's medical bills, the recent financial burden of the cottage in North Hatley, and from the sudden unaccustomed expectations of writing full-time. When Dorothy suffered a serious embolism on New Year's Day 1948, six months before his novel was finished, the pressure increased. She would have only nine more years to live.

What is the novel's structure? It falls into two sections of equal length. Part One, describes Grenville's puritanism and gives the backstory of the Cameron family. It introduces all of the main characters but one (Marcia Stapleton, Stephen's twice-divorced sister). The plot develops after the meeting of Lucy and Stephen, through Lucy's sexual blossoming, to their impulsive elopement to New York City. The second section includes Parts Two to Five. These parts address the dilemmas of the main characters, showing them in various combinations, to complicate what happens after Lucy and Stephen's marriage. These include the growing tensions in that marriage and its ultimate fracture. In a short unexpected (and unbelievable) reversal in Part Five, Lucy decides to return to Stephen.

The progression of all five parts of the novel are temporally and thematically linked to the larger context of World War II. The story begins in the summer of 1938, and Neville Chamberlain's trip to Munich (which resulted in the "appeasement" of Hitler and Germany's annexation of Czechoslovakia's Sudetenland) is mentioned. The futility of the Munich Agreement and the inevitability of war are paralleled by Lucy and Stephen's doomed "international" union.

MacLennan marks the passage of time with references to the war. Part Two shows the uniformed Bruce Fraser in New York in 1940. He is on leave from the RCAF and is putting in time before visiting Lucy and Stephen at their fashionable New York City apartment. In a bar, he chats with an atypical American lieutenant. Their conversation draws attention to the fact that Canada joined the war effort from the outset, whereas the United States in 1940 has not. In Part Three, the Japanese bombing of the American naval base at Pearl Harbor on 7 December 1941 finally precipitates American entry into the Allied war effort. In Part Four, the death of Hitler (30 April 1945) is mentioned at the same time Stephen begins the affair with Gail Beaumont that will break Lucy's trust. Part Five is set in the final phase of the war with the bombings of Hiroshima (6 August 1945) and Nagasaki (three days later). These horrific events parallel the shattering of Lucy's marriage. They simultaneously illustrate the cold, relentless American pursuit of technological brilliance that MacLennan believed would catapult the United States over the edge of a precipice.

This penultimate section of the novel seems more conclusive than the softer ending MacLennan seems to have tacked on without much conviction. He leaves us with an unconvincing situation in which Canadian puritanism is mollified, represented by Jane's acceptance of Lucy and her children after a long rejection. A new stronger Canadian identity has emerged, represented by Bruce, who has been disfigured terribly in the war, yet returns to Grenville and his teaching job stronger and wiser. Stephen, who has represented the blind American drive towards greater mechanization and a consumer society, drops away from the corrupt world of advertising in Carl Bratian's Madison Avenue agency, hoping to return to an engineering career that will build rather than destroy things.

Compact though it is, this structure is flawed. The two sections of the novel are as unbalanced as a see-saw with one long side and one short side. Part One is far more leisurely, detailed, and rhythmic than the subsequent block of curt, at times preachy, parts in the second half. Part One resembles *Two Solitudes*; Parts Two through Five resemble the more succinct *Barometer Rising*. Their juxtaposition is awkward, giving the impression that MacLennan was indeed hurrying the completion of his novel.

MacLennan's attempt to make his central character a woman is also unsuccessful, and he would not attempt it again. Lucy is simply too good to be true – she has no flaws at all. Unlike Hagar, she does not succumb to Stephen until they are married. MacLennan, a year and a half later in an essay called "Changing Values in Fiction," seemed to realize that something about Lucy was not right. "[A] good woman is enemy to a good plot," he wrote. "[N]othing is harder to deal with in a rapid-action novel than a good woman ... [f]or it is the nature of a good woman to absorb conflict rather than create it."[26] Had MacLennan stayed true to the *Pillar of Fire* plot that so excited him, and had Lucy become pregnant out of wedlock, the novel would have been far more dynamic. His determination to avoid "decadent" sexuality and the fact that Lucy was based largely on Dorothy and her North Hatley garden, preclude the portrayal of Lucy as a fallen woman. Cultivating roses may have been as close as MacLennan wanted to come to sensuality. His later essay "The Secret and Voluptuous Life of a Rose Grower,"[27] is playful, but it also sounds a serious note that suggests he idealized the women he loved. His loyalty to his friend Blair Fraser also ensured that Bruce Fraser would not falter in his ethical behaviour; he destroys his love letter to Lucy without sending it.

MacLennan's moral improvement of Hagar in his portrayal of Lucy is important. What flattened the effect in MacLennan's novel was part of the essential MacLennan. Decency, stability, and loyalty lay deep in him. Even a decade later, in *The Watch that Ends the Night*, he protects Catherine's reputation by having her second marriage to George occur only because her first husband, Jerome, is (wrongly) believed dead. Like Lucy, Catherine is partly based on Dorothy, just as George follows in Bruce's fictional footsteps. It was this conservative moral quality that partly distinguished MacLennan as a Canadian writer. To energize his fictions, he needed passages of strong physical action writing, such as his description of the Halifax Explosion of 1917.

The books published elsewhere by writers younger than those he used as models for *The Precipice*, offer a stark contrast to this quality. In the United States, Russian-American Ayn Rand had already published *The Fountainhead* in 1943; *Atlas Shrugged*, with its revolutionary rejection of religious faith and altruism in favour of egotistic self-interest, followed in 1957. The Kinsey Report on male sexuality appeared the same year as *The Precipice*. Five years later the companion report on female sexuality was published. These reports revealed, what seemed to many people, shockingly candid information. Yet they opened the door to more and more sexually explicit fiction.

In the United States, a new generation of creative writers was writing about illicit sexual acts and drug use while expressing these subjects in spontaneous, unrevised writing peppered with profanity.[28] One novel MacLennan especially disliked was Norman Mailer's *The Naked and the Dead*, also published in 1948. Jack Kerouac began *On the Road* in 1949;[29] it was published in 1956, the same year that Allen Ginsberg's *Howl* appeared. Sexual content fast-forwarded from the pre-Kinsey era. In 1952, J.D. Salinger's iconic *Catcher in the Rye* and John Steinbeck's *East of Eden* were among two of the early manifestations of a new *zeitgeist* that would drive American fiction in a direction far from Canada's. In 1956, Elvis Presley released his No. 1 single "Heartbreak Hotel," ushering in a sexualized popular music revolution that paralleled what was happening in American fiction.

William Golding's *Lord of the Flies* (1954) and Vladimir Nabokov's *Lolita* (1955) explored the inevitable disintegration of morality without law and the acceptability of pedophilia, respectively. Grace Metalious's best-selling *Peyton Place* (1956), which dealt with incest, abortion, and adultery in a small New England town, made MacLennan's descriptions of Lucy's sexual awakening in Grenville seem Victorian. If MacLennan hoped to join the "American branch cycle" of modern fiction, he could not write novels like *The Precipice* and expect much enthusiasm south of the border.

Just as the Beat generation with their penchant for black clothing and communist politics appeared in the United States during the mid-1950s, a new generation of British writers – the so-called Angry Young Men – began to publish their fictional rants of disillusionment against the upper classes. John Osborne's play *Look Back in Anger* (1956) gave the loosely associated group its name. The gritty realism and agitated resentments of working-class novels like John Braine's *Room at the Top* (1957) and Alan Sillitoe's *Saturday Night, Sunday Morning* (1958) heralded a radical change from the refined, elitist work that preceded them and inspired MacLennan.[30] It would not be long before the Beatles expressed these sentiments with their working-class Liverpudlian accents in popular music.

In Canada, the regional novels MacLennan disdained, such as W.O. Mitchell's *Who Has Seen the Wind* (1947),[31] and novels of more sophisticated quests for religion (Morley Callaghan's Catholic work) or Anglo-British culture (Robertson Davies)[32] were the two main strands of what was still a fledgling Canadian fiction at the time.[33]

As critics T.D. MacLulich, Robert D. Chambers, and Barbara Pell have all observed, MacLennan's central interest in *The Precipice* is not the love triangle presaged by *Pillar of Fire*, nor is it an exploration of Canadian versus American identity, nor is it a commentary on World War II. MacLulich argues cogently that the novel's main theme is failure.[34] Yet, while it is true that most of the characters "obsess about failure," MacLennan's central focus is the theme he would later treat more deeply and extensively in *The Watch that Ends the Night*. What was needed for this theme to become central was to shift away from a female main character like Lucy and to make Bruce the central character (as MacLennan did with George Stewart in *The Watch*). That central theme in *The Precipice* hinged on two questions. What is the meaning of life, once all the crutches of organized religion, political visions, humanism, and even human relationships are knocked away? What can alleviate the profound and painful aloneness of every man, and his desperate need to belong to something greater than himself?

Robert D. Chambers, in the same issue of *Canadian Literature* as MacLulich's article, gets closer to the novel's core. He sees MacLennan as delving into his vague and wavering religious belief. If "the A-bomb drop on Hiroshima ... confirmed the appalling possibility of a scientific daemon dethroning the traditional God of compassion and love," all that might be left was "[g]reed, sex and violence ... and ... a kind of horrified vision of a world without any redeeming impulse."[35] Chambers points to the notion of the buried self found in the novel, mainly in Bruce, whose near-death experience in the war brings his "buried self" to the surface and in Marcia Stapleton who moves from three divorces, through psychoanalysis[36] to become a Roman Catholic nurse. Chambers seems convinced by Marcia's conversion, but not entirely with Lucy's forgiveness of Stephen.

Barbara Pell's analysis of religion in *The Precipice*[37] makes reference to the existentialist theologian Paul Tillich's theories in *The Courage to Be* (1952).[38] He argues that "autonomy left to its own devices leads to increasing emptiness and – since there cannot be a vacuum even in the spiritual realm – it finally becomes imbued with demonically destructive forces."[39] To counter this, Tillich suggests not an escape from the vacuum,[40] but a deepening of autonomy (aloneness) until a new spiritual transcendence breaks through. Pell uses this idea to understand MacLennan's "transitional" novel. She sees Lucy at the end of the novel as representing "what the church means when it talks of Grace."[41] (It is as if MacLennan has transmuted Nora Kaye's physical grace as a ballerina into Lucy's spiritual grace.) Pell acknowledges that MacLennan neither defines this religious dilemma, nor its solution, clearly. She finds the novel and its central theme "too obviously structured and schematic,"[42] and, like most critics, she finds *The Precipice* a failure.[43]

Yet Pell draws our attention to the way MacLennan awkwardly fumbles his way into existential meaninglessness and his even more awkward struggle to save himself from it and to locate meaning somewhere, somehow. It is the "superfluous"[44] character Bruce Fraser, MacLennan's writer-intellectual-teacher alter ego, who best exemplifies this fumbling and struggling. Bruce knowingly "makes himself bare, bleak, and self-reliant again" when he reasons his way out of declaring his love for Lucy in a cold cerebral philosophical syllogism: "Lucy was married. Therefore it was impossible to fall in love with her. Therefore he did not love her. Therefore he must think of something else" (196). After Bruce's late sexual initiation – a one-night stand initiated by Marcia in New York – he voices MacLennan's deepest conflict: "he was not sure whether he had crossed the frontier of a deeper mystery or merely entered the first of a long series of empty rooms" (206). Similarly, Stephen says, "The loneliness is all there is," and listening to a jazz trio in a bar at three in the morning, senses "the vastness of the continental loneliness" (298).

This angst, this despair (realized in his next novel *Each Man's Son*[45] and more clearly in the following novel *The Watch that Ends the Night*) has a great deal in common with the existential writers

emerging in Europe. Ten years before *The Precipice*, Jean-Paul
Sartre's novel *La Nauseé*[46] dramatized what came to be loosely
called existentialism. Man must bear the intolerable burden of the
freedom to act without religious (or any other) certainty, which
meant making choices in a vacuum. English translations of Albert
Camus's *The Stranger* (1942) and Sartre's play *No Exit* (1944) soon
followed. MacLennan did not know these works. Yet his depiction
of the stripping away of all man's supports until he is alone with his
terror and his anxiety, is very close indeed to the thinking of these
existentialists. Hovering just offstage for MacLennan's characters in
the depths of despair is the spectre of suicide.[47]

In a *Maclean's* article written right after he finished *The Precipice*,
MacLennan explored his (and Bruce's) spiritual dilemma. "Are We
a Godless People?" revealed MacLennan's confusion about spiritual
matters.[48] He knew he wasn't Christian – especially Calvinist – in
any conventional sense. What were his "beliefs?" Even his readers
were confused. Although he had far more responses by mail and by
telephone to this article than to anything else he had written to date,
these responses consisted of "widely divergent views."[49] Each correspondent or caller believed MacLennan had reflected his or her
view. In his article, he traces the decline of religion in western society, concluding that there is now a "fracture with two thousand
years of religious tradition."[50] As in *The Precipice*, he fumbles awkwardly and inconsistently to make sense of the human condition.
He *wills* what is not yet convincing to him. The resolution (or "sal-
vation") he will eventually find arises from the heart, from the irrational connection between human beings through intense feeling. It
is, he will find, an inexplicable mystery.[51] In *The Precipice* this message is veiled, obscure, unfathomable, though the note is sounded.

The Precipice won the Governor General's Award for fiction. Yet
that was little cause for celebration as there was no financial reward
to accompany it. Sales of the novel were not nearly what those of
Two Solitudes had been and MacLennan believed that the three-
month lapse between the novel's release by his Canadian publisher
Collins and its American publication by Duell, Sloan, and Pearce
was to blame for decreased sales. The earlier Canadian reviews were
not as fulsome as the later American ones, partly because MacLennan
seemed to have betrayed his role as nationalist chronicler by extending his setting and characters into the United States.[52] There was no

interest in the movie he hoped might follow.[53] Two years after publication he wrote, "*The Precipice* was a gamble on which I lost."[54] Thirteen years later, after publishing another two novels, both more successful than *The Precipice*, he admitted, "I think I would have done better to have waited ... longer than I did [to submit my manuscript], but at that time I couldn't write non-fiction and thought fiction was all I could do."[55] There is also the possibility that the extraordinary effort he put into *Two Solitudes* left him too drained of creative energy to undertake another novel so soon. The same pattern would occur when, depleted from writing *The Watch that Ends the Night*, he tackled *Return of the Sphinx*, a shorter novel that also lacked forcefulness and did not do well.

Three years after *The Precipice* was published, MacLennan could no longer support himself and Dorothy on writing alone. He approached McGill University, and was offered two courses at a surprisingly small salary, which would begin in the fall.[56] Meanwhile he earned money as a consultant to the National Film Board, spending the summer in Ottawa, while Dorothy's mother tended to her at Stone Hedge in North Hatley.

On New Year's Eve, he wrote a sad and angry letter to Charles Duell telling him that he intended to leave Duell, Sloan, and Pearce, partly because they had not promoted or sold his book effectively or given him the emotional support he needed. Two American firms immediately tried to acquire him, and he chose Little, Brown and Company, with their Canadian affiliate Macmillan's in Toronto, in order to have what he needed to continue writing. This choice was excellent, for it put him into the hands of the best editor he was to have: John Gray.[57]

Though MacLennan is known, admired, and sometimes disliked for his chronicling of sweeping social and political forces, this aspect of his fiction too often resulted in didactic passages and one-dimensional characters that represent these forces. Yet he was much more. His temperament and style marked him as a writer unlike either the American or the British writers of his time. He eschewed the liberated bohemianism of the Beats, and his Red Toryism made him more sympathetic than the Angry Young Men in Britain to all classes in society. Instead, he was tolerant, thoughtful, and moral. His writing carried forward some of the aspects of Victorian fiction: the positioning of man at the mercy of larger forces, the provision of back-stories for his characters that rooted them in history, and his reliance on traditional linear plot structures. Though he would come to sense that fiction required new bottles for new wine,[58] he was reticent to experiment.

Yet his work is much more than this conservatism. He was uncannily prescient in *The Precipice* as elsewhere. Carl Bratian,[59] the Romanian immigrant entrepreneur is a case in point. His soulless life and ruthless behaviour as head of his advertising agency draws attention to a major phenomenon just emerging in the United States and Canada. It is a phenomenon that still engages us, for example, in the TV series *Mad Men*, a scathing critique of the lifestyle and business dealings of Madison Avenue advertising agencies in the 1960s.

MacLennan had read and deplored *The Hucksters* (1946),[60] a popular novel that exposed the amoral way in which ad agencies manipulated the public to want things they did not need. The book was made into a highly successful film the following year. The year *The Precipice* was published, the *American Advertising Theory and Practice* by C.H. Sandage went into its third edition. This handbook touted the creation of "wants" through the use of "desires" (unrelated to the "wants," using visuals – especially sexual ones – and radio commercials). In Canada, Ontario painter Bertram Booker had published three advertising manuals under the pseudonym, Richard W. Surrey: *Subconscious Selling* (1923), *Layout Technique in Advertising* (1929), and *Copy Technique in Advertising* (1930).[61] Only three years after MacLennan's novel appeared, Canadian communications guru Marshall McLuhan's iconic *The Mechanical Bride* also took an anti-advertising position, establishing a significant difference between the way Canadians and Americans viewed advertising for the future.[62]

The novel's title was also prescient. MacLennan treats the culmination of destructive mechanization in the American bombings of Nagasaki and Hiroshima as the final events to push the United States over the symbolic precipice. Yet even today, the desperate culmination of American self-destruction known as the "fiscal cliff" reveals a country brought to the brink of catastrophe because of consumerism, financial recklessness, and mechanization.

With his next novel, MacLennan would abandon any attempt to join the "American branch cycle." He would set it in a place he knew far more deeply than the settings in *The Precipice*. Most important, he would forego the explanations of Canadian places and social customs that he believed had been obstacles to writing the kind of "heroic" and "universal" novel he had always aspired to.[63] Ironically, the novel would be regional. With *Each Man's Son*, set in the Cape Breton mining community of Glace Bay where he had lived as a child, he deepened the quest for the meaning of life begun by Bruce Fraser in *The Precipice*. Finally, in *The Watch that Ends the Night*, after narrowly surviving his despair at Dorothy's death, he articulated it.

NOTES

1 The novel sold approximately 50,000 copies in North America.

2 Spanish, Dutch, Swedish, Czech, Estonian, Japanese, Korean, German, and Norwegian. For bureaucratic reasons, the French translation did not appear until 1963, which meant that some French-Canadians could not read about this iconic version of their relation to English Canada for almost twenty years.

3 Elspeth Cameron, *Hugh MacLennan: A Writer's Life* (Toronto: University of Toronto Press, 1981).

4 Ibid., 202.

5 HM to Bill Deacon 18 May, 7 March 1946; and "Canada Between Covers," *Saturday Review of Literature* 29 (7 September 1946), 5–6, 28–30.

6 Ibid., 212.

7 Ibid., 201.

8 "Canada Between Covers," *Saturday Review of Literature* 29 (7 September 1946), 5–6, 28–30.

9 See Cameron, *Hugh MacLennan*, 170. A similar image of incomprehensible shouting occurs in an important passage in *The Precipice*, 336.

10 "So All Their Praises" and "A Man Should Rejoice." The love triangle in the former is set in Germany, New York, and Nova Scotia between 1929 and 1933. The latter follows a young American artist to Austria and Princeton, NJ. See Cameron, *Hugh MacLennan*, 82–8 and 95–7 for more details.

11 New York, Princeton, and three small southern Ontario towns.

12 Cameron, *Hugh MacLennan*, 199–200.

13 In 1947, as MacLennan was writing *The Precipice*,
Saskatchewan Premier Tommy Douglas brought in the first
provincial hospital insurance program. Not until 1966 would
all Canadians have comprehensive health care, regardless of
ability to pay.

14 HM to author, 7 January 1976.

15 Nova Scotia was marked by Calvinism, too, and MacLennan's
doctor father was a case in point. MacLennan, however, cre-
ates minor characters ("splinter" characters) outside the community (such as Matt McCunn in *The Precipice* and Captain
Yardley in *The Watch that Ends the Night*) that represent this
earthiness. It was also an aspect of MacLennan himself.

16 "On Discovering Who We Are," *Maclean's*, 15 December
1946. This article was re-titled "How We Differ from Americans," in *Cross-Country* (Toronto: Collins 1949), 35–56.

17 See Cameron, "Ordeal by Fire: The Genesis of MacLennan's
The Precipice," *Canadian Literature* 82 (1979): 35–46. This
article contains a more detailed account of the influence of
Pillar of Fire on *The Precipice*.

18 Ibid.

19 Anthony Tudor chose the name Hagar to suggest the biblical
Hagar, Abraham's Egyptian bondswoman, sent by his barren
wife, Sarah, to conceive a child for her. Consequently, the out-
cast Hagar wanders in the desert until God gives her direction.
See Cameron, *Hugh MacLennan*, 205. Anthony Tudor, interview with the author, New York City, 7 September 1976.

20 See Cameron, "Ordeal by Fire," and *Hugh MacLennan* for
a more detailed account of these source materials.

21 "On Discovering," in *Cross-Country*, 51–2.

22 Ibid., 55–6.

23 Ibid.

24 Lassiter is partly inspired by MacLennan's North Hatley rival
in tennis, John Bassett. The blond, handsome, wealthy
Toronto businessman inherited the *Toronto Telegram*. Their
tennis matches were legendary.

25 MacLennan to Charles Duell, 5 March 1947, MacLennan
Papers, McGill University Library.

26 MacLennan, "Changing Values in Fiction," *Canadian Author
and Bookman* 25, 3 (Autumn 1949), 15.

27 *The Montrealer* (28 September 1954), 23, 25, 27, 29.
Reprinted in *Scotchman's Return and Other Essays* (Toronto:
The Macmillan Company Limited, 1960), 159–67.

28 MacLennan mentions marihuana (sic) in *The Precipice*, but
only in the context of a jazz nightclub. He was unaware of
any drug culture beyond marijuana usage.

29 Surprisingly, MacLennan observed a similar phenomenon in
The Precipice. Lucy, describing her vision of the headlong rush
of Americans towards a precipice, says to Bruce: "they were
all shouting at each other so loudly nobody could hear anything" (336).

30 Many details in *The Precipice* – the Lassiter's maid in their
New York apartment, details of clothing, and Jane's sophisticated knowledge of classical music – show that MacLennan
(whose family always had a maid) was far from harbouring
working-class resentments.

31 This novel had won the Governor General's Award in 1947,
the year before *The Precipice*.

32 Davies's Salterton trilogy was about to appear in 1951, 1954,
and 1957.

33 Malcolm Lowry published *Under the Volcano* in 1947, but he
was considered a British writer because he was born and
raised in England and his publisher, Jonathan Cape Ltd., was
British. His novel would not be fully appreciated in Canada
for many years.

34 T.D. MacLulich, "MacLennan's Anatomy of Failure," *Journal
of Canadian Studies* 14, 4 (Winter 1979–80): 54–65.

35 Robert D. Chambers, "Hugh MacLennan and Religion: *The
Precipice* Revisited," *Journal of Canadian Studies* 14, 4,
(Winter 1979–80): 46–53.

36 MacLulich rightly shows MacLennan's ambivalence about
psychology and psychoanalysis in this novel. See *The
Precipice*, 75 and 329

37 Barbara Pell, *Faith and Fiction: A Theological Critique of
the Narrative Strategies of Hugh MacLennan and Morley
Callaghan* (Waterloo: Canadian Corporation for Studies in
Religion/Wilfrid Laurier University Press, 1998), 31–43.

38 Paul Tillich, *The Courage to Be* (London: Fontana-Collins,
1962).

39 Ibid., as cited by Pell, 35.

40 In *The Precipice* such escapes include alcohol (Stephen), marijuana (the jazz trio), psychoanalysis (Marcia), the intellect (Bruce), institutionalized religion (Catholicism), work, the arts (humanism), exile (Matt McCunn), and fantasy.

41 Pell, *Faith and Fiction*.

42 Ibid., 36.

43 See MacLulich, "MacLennan's Anatomy of Failure," 65n1, for references to the eight critics who thought the novel failed.

44 Ibid., 61.

45 Where Daniel Ainslie repeats to himself, "God is dead." Hugh MacLennan, *Each Man's Son* (Toronto: Macmillan, 1951), 219.

46 *La Nausée* was published in 1938; *Nausea*, the English translation by Lloyd Alexander, was published by New Directions, New Classics Library (New York, 1949).

47 This is most clearly seen in *The Watch*. Drawing on his own extreme desolation and despair after Dorothy's death, MacLennan has his alter ego George Stewart reflect:

> Then a man discovers in dismay that what he believed to be his identity is no more than a tiny canoe at the mercy of an ocean. Shark-filled, plankton-filled, refractor of light, terrible and mysterious, for years this ocean has seemed to slumber beneath the tiny identity it received from the dark river.
> Now the ocean rises and the things within it become visible. Little man, what now? The ocean rises, all frames disappear from around the pictures, there is no form, no sense, nothing but chaos in the darkness of the ocean storm. Little man, what now? (343)

48 MacLennan, "Are We a Godless People?" *Maclean's*, 15 Mar. 1949. Re-published as "'Help Thou Mine Unbelief,'" in *Cross-Country*.

49 See MacLennan, *Cross-Country*, 132.

50 Ibid., 135.

51 MacLennan does not find a technique to express this, although he comes close with George Stewart's declaration that "Life is a gift." The sense of mystery and privilege MacLennan (and

George) feels is often apprehended through the contemplation of simple natural things, though it is not pantheistic.

52 See Cameron, *Hugh MacLennan*, 212–18.

53 MacLennan to Charles Duell, 5 March 1947. MacLennan Papers, McGill University Library.

54 MacLennan to John Gray, 27 May 1950. MacLennan Papers, McGill University Library.

55 HM to John Gray 27 December 1961. MacLennan Papers, McGill University Library.

56 MacLennan was paid $3,000, a pittance that astonished his publishers. See Cameron, *Hugh MacLennan*, 246–7.

57 Gray had admired *Two Solitudes*, which he read in Holland when he was stationed at Intelligence Headquarters with the Canadian army, and was delighted to become MacLennan's editor. Soon, they were fast friends.

58 MacLennan refers to Jesus's parable, "New wine must be put in new bottles" (Matthew 9:14–17) in *The Watch*. It is one of many references to biblical texts in his work.

59 Bratian is an unfortunate choice of name, as it was a common upper-class name in Romania. See Cameron, *Hugh MacLennan*, 393n16.

60 Frederic Wakeman, *The Hucksters* (New York: Rinehart, 1946).

61 See website: http://en.wikipedipedia.org/wiki/Bertram_Brooker

62 Marshall McLuhan, *The Mechanical Bride: Folklore of Industrial Man* (New York, Vanguard Press, 1951). This book launched McLuhan's career. It intrigued Americans because it demonstrated a detachment from and amusement about ads, rather than the seduction ad agencies expected. He and MacLennan differed in their positions: MacLennan being forcefully opposed to ad agencies and McLuhan exposing their methods in a humorous way.

63 MacLennan's publishers insisted on a preamble explaining Cape Breton and Calvinism, which annoyed MacLennan. See Cameron, *Hugh MacLennan*, 230–1.

THE PRECIPICE

Sometimes we wake in the night and know why we have become what we are. Waking alone in the night, listening to the cars rumbling under the pavement of Park Avenue, or the grain boat's foghorn throbbing against the shore of Lake Ontario, or the wail of the through-freight on the Nebraska plain, we see in a flash against the eyeballs a fragment of what has happened to us all, and lacking the brave illusion of daylight, it is easy to wish we had been born in another century, or had inherited some other time than now.

Were there nights in Egypt when the builders could not sleep? Surely there were nights when they lay on their backs and thought of the long road over the desert of which this was the end, counted the steps of the pyramids rising against the stars and wondered how many more layers would have to be added before the converging lines met at a final point and the whole could rise no higher? Did they wonder, looking at the colossal stone coffins they were building, why the pyramids were the only works that mattered in their day?

But time is more than now, more than twelve o'clock, or any particular century. It is also ourselves. It is millions of people and many nations. It is the coolie whose water buffalo pulls a wooden plow through his master's rice paddy. It is the airman handing to a girl in Cairo one of the two silk stockings he remembers buying thirty-six hours earlier on Ste. Catherine Street. It is the scientist trying to harness God.

Gaze up at the Empire State and the R.C.A. Building, watch the Skymaster circle into LaGuardia with its bellyful of executives, see the shop girls staring at rubies and pearls reposing like a mogul's concubines in the window of Van Cleef and Arpels, the roar of the fight crowd in the Garden, look at the festoons of toilet paper descending upon the hero who makes his Roman progress up the avenue, see the greatest flash of them all shoot through cloud-rings into the stratosphere. How near are you then to the end of the journey which the Puritans began more than three hundred years ago when they lost hope in themselves and decided to bet their lives on the things they could do rather than on the men they were?

Although time is millions of people and many nations, we say for the sake of convenience that this story begins in the innocent summer of 1938, when August heat brooded over the Middle West, and Germans crouched in Silesian fields with their steel helmets wreathed in sheaves of wheat, and old men everywhere fluttered their hands and looked at each other with frightened eyes.

ONE

⌢⌢⌢

IN LATER YEARS BRUCE FRASER OFTEN asked himself how it had happened that a woman he had taken for granted most of his life, had casually watched at work in her garden next door, should ultimately seem to him the embodiment of all that was essentially female – easier to sense than to understand, durable, and possessed of a kind of private beauty he felt he alone could recognize. The time came when the thought of Lucy Cameron never failed to stir him.

But no such thoughts were near the surface of his mind that August morning in 1938 as he stood on the porch of his father's house in Grenville, Ontario, and watched her trimming the edges of her patch of lawn. Bruce was young enough then to think that ideas were more important than people. And besides, those were still the days of innocence in a little town like Grenville, where Canada breathed out the last minutes of her long Victorian sleep. They were the days when the well-meaning generation everywhere – in college common rooms, in the pages of the rough-paper magazines, in smoky apartments where beer drinking was a ritual and a symbol of the times – were still so excited by the novelty of knowing the score that they could spend delicious hours proving to themselves that life was a dirty trick, measuring with logic and dialectic each year against its predecessor to prove how inevitable it was that the tide should keep flooding in. Now Italy, now Germany, now Spain, and soon the rest of us.

Bruce thought about the book he had been reading the night before, a book so full of social significance it had drugged him into a state of perverse contentment. If all the famous men in the world except a handful of Russians were knaves, fools, or conspirators, who could rightly blame him for being unsuccessful at twenty-four?

After days of rain the sun was out again and the sharp ozone from Lake Ontario was in his nostrils. Light shimmered on the water and redoubled itself, light vibrant and sensual as calling trumpets. On a morning like this, after two months in Montreal, even the old street where he had grown up seemed new.

Lack of experience made Bruce look even younger than he was, in spite of a rugged jaw which was oblong and very Scotch, bristly brown hair, and strong blue eyes. His youth showed in his tall, slim intensity and in his frequent expressions of startled surprise.

A dog barked next door and Bruce turned his head. It was a remarkably gracious house, he decided, as he did each time he came home. Massed ranks of phlox bloomed on either side of a low doorstep behind a curving border of petunias and sweet alyssum. The door itself had been painted a hue of turquoise blue and a polished brass knocker hung in the centre of it below a wide-spreading fanlight. The walls were white clapboard with outside shutters of blue; dormers on the third storey broke the slope of the roof. But more than any other one thing about it, he liked the way the house clung to the ground, facing a street as quiet as Sunday.

It was an outward expression of the personality of Lucy Cameron. Seven years ago, when her father died, there had been no gardens and no colour, the splendid British colonial style of the house browned off by blistered tan paint, its lines unsoftened, its fences wood instead of the hedges that had taken their place. In those days it had seemed exactly the kind of house old John Knox Cameron would choose to live in, and to leave to the three daughters who were his only children. He would have been horrified, Bruce reflected, could he have guessed what Lucy would do with it on the strength of four years' salary from the only paying job she had ever held.

And yet she had done nothing new to the house at all. She had merely stripped off an imposed ugliness and restored it to its proper position in time, for it was one of the oldest properties in Grenville, built by a Massachusetts judge who had been driven out of New England at the time of the American Revolution, owned by his descendants ever since. It was a Scotsman who had married into the family three generations before who had added the brown paint and the harshness, for the Scotch and Scotch-Irish who had flooded into Ontario in the wake of the original Loyalist settlers had roughened everything they touched. It would be another hundred years before any part of English-speaking Canada could hope to be rid of what they had done to it.

Bruce left the steps of his porch and began to stroll up the narrow street. A century and a half ago someone had given it the name of Matilda Lane to honour a relative of George the Third, and the name had stuck. It seemed to Bruce more absurd than quaint, but he liked the street itself better than any other in town, for the elms that lined it, planted by the original settlers, had reached a noble height. Only here, in this lane running down from the King's Highway to the common at the edge of the lake, did Grenville seem in any sense mature. The branches of the elms soared up and out, dark gray under the mass of their leaves, and joined tips high overhead to make the lane like a cathedral nave open at both ends. It was constantly rich in changing lights. This morning the sunshine struck down, tangled in the branches, and dropped such a net of shadows onto the red paving bricks of the street that he seemed to be wading through them as he walked.

He turned at the King's Highway and strolled back the way he had come. When he reached the Cameron house Lucy was working among her flowers. A shopping basket lay on the grass behind her, and without noticing Bruce she moved slowly along the border as she looked at the petunias. Suddenly she bent down, carefully snipped off a dried seed pod, dropped it into a small envelope she took from a pocket, and shook the seeds loose. She was in profile to Bruce but he could see an expression of quiet, shy pleasure touch her face. He thought with some pity and even with a faint feeling of male superiority that any pleasures Lucy Cameron would ever have would be shy ones.

The Frasers had always been sorry for the Cameron women who lived next door. Bruce's mother was a happy, nerveless woman whose only grief was an operation which had made it impossible for her to have more than one child. His father was the best general practitioner in the county. Dr. Fraser's life had been clouded by the knowledge that he could have risen to the top of his profession in any of the cities of the country, had he not been compelled to support his parents after leaving medical school by establishing a practice in the first town where a vacancy had occurred. As a result he had concentrated most of his thwarted ambition on his son and was considered by Grenville a stern and highly respectable man.

But compared to old John Knox Cameron, Dr. Fraser's life had been almost licentious. John Knox had been hard even for an Ontario small town to take, where the Scotch-Irish are chocolate-brown with Calvinism. He had been dead for seven years now, but his ghost still haunted the house where he lived. His wife had died the year after her husband, in thankful relief, Mrs. Fraser was known to have said, and now his three daughters lived there alone. Jane, the eldest, was a church organist and a music teacher, known to be well on her way toward forty. Lucy, ten years younger than Jane, kept the house. Nina was only nineteen and she knew she was considered the prettiest girl in town.

Bruce waited for Lucy to turn around, but she was intent on her flowers so he called out, "Hello, Lucy! How are you?"

She turned around, quick pleasure flashed into her face as she saw him and then was immediately checked, as though she thought she might create the presumption that he was equally pleased to see her.

"When did you get back?" she said.

"Last night."

"How was Montreal? And McGill?"

"All I can remember was the heat. If there were marshes instead of factories along the St. Lawrence the place would be famous for its malaria." He walked across the lawn to look at her flowers. "Your garden grows lovelier all the time."

She flushed with pleasure but her voice was matter of fact as she answered, "August is a dull month for gardens. I wish you could have seen it in June."

A cicada screamed from the tall grass on the common which lay between the foot of the street and the lake. Sunlight reflected from the white clapboards, and Bruce looked curiously toward an open window as he heard the tinkling of Jane's piano. He had once played the same piece himself, in the same room, and he grinned at Lucy as she read his thoughts. It was nine years since he had stopped taking lessons and Jane couldn't have been thirty at the time, but she had seemed to belong to his mother's generation then and she still did.

"You must get tired hearing those same things year after year."

"I do. Or I would if I hadn't stopped hearing them long ago. Nina complains about having to be quiet so much of the time in the house, but I never seem to notice." She bent down to pick up her shopping basket and dropped the shears and the envelope containing the seed pod into it. "If you're looking for Nina you might find her on the shore. She went down there with her dog."

"I wasn't looking for anyone. I'm lazy today."

Lucy stood with her basket on her arm. "I'm afraid I have to go along to King Street now. You're not going that way?"

"Not now. But maybe I could climb the back fence this evening?"

A trace of a smile touched her face and he thought it made her look charming and a little sad. "You won't be able to see the flowers in the dark," she said.

As she walked toward the King's Highway he watched her and wondered why he had never troubled himself to think about Lucy Cameron before. One took so many people for granted in Grenville; one accepted the stock judgments made of one's neighbours by the community and let it go at that. If Lucy would only give herself a chance, he thought, she could be an attractive woman. She moved with the quiet grace of a shy animal, yet in all her movements there was an air of conscious control, as though she hoped that whatever she did would escape notice. This same characteristic was even more marked in her face. It was an intelligent face, he thought, essentially a proud face. Her chin and the upper part of her head could have modelled a cameo, clean-cut and distant. But in the eyes and mouth unknown qualities brooded. Her large eyes were brown and widely spaced, with curving brows. Her lips were soft, warm, and sensuous. These features, together with her air of dignified solitude, combined to give her the prevailing expression of a woman who has never been recognized by others for what she knows herself to be.

Bruce turned and strolled down to the common. The grass was resilient as he walked under the trees and he felt a wall of coolness rise to meet him as he neared the lake. It was good to be back. Grenville was such a safe place, so stubbornly sure of itself and so full of humour when one knew it well. Certainly not a single one of the madmen who were making current history could support himself within its limits.

But even as the loveliness of the scene and the warmth of his returning affections invaded his mind, the restless, critical side of Bruce rose to meet them. Grenville was also a town of eight thousand people who had been stiff-necked from the day the first United Empire Loyalist had marked out his lot a century and a half ago, constantly right in its judgments but usually for the wrong reasons. Here was lodged the hard core of Canadian matter-of-factness on which men of imagination had been breaking themselves for years. Grenville was sound, it was dull, it was loyal, it was competent – and oh, God, it was so Canadian! The ferments and the revolutions of the past twenty years might never have existed so far as this town was concerned. Until the Grenvilles of Canada were debunked from top to bottom, Bruce decided, there would be no fun and no future for anyone in the country.

He reached the sand, picked up a flat stone warm from the sun, drew back his shoulder, and launched his whole body into the throw. The stone skipped over the flat blue water, splashing up a series of miniature rainbows, then tumbled, and sank. He stood on the edge of the shore for several minutes before he turned to stroll back under the trees of the common. He skirted a bandstand where once a fortnight in the summer a grocer, a hardware merchant, a shoemaker, a hotel-keeper, a freight-handler, and three clerks met to play marches and popular medleys while the children of Grenville came down to the common with their parents to listen. In one corner of the common near the foot of Matilda Lane he came to a neat, white belvedere, built two generations ago in honour of Queen Victoria's Golden Jubilee by the man who at that time had been the town's leading citizen.

Bruce climbed the steps into the belvedere and sat down for a smoke. Engrossed in his own thoughts, he forgot all about Grenville and the middle Cameron sister. Lines of poetry entered his head, were driven out by a sentence he thought he might use in an article he hoped to write for *The Canadian Forum*. He thought about Hitler and Chamberlain and the stupidity of the British tories and his own unique ability to understand so much. Then he remembered that Nina Cameron was supposed to be somewhere on the beach, so he left the belvedere and walked down to the shore again.

There was no sign of Nina or her dog. The beach was empty as far as he could see in both directions. The water stretched over the horizon into the United States. Ontario might be the smallest of the five continental lakes, but to the people of Grenville its frontier seemed at least as absolute as an ocean.

MEANWHILE Lucy Cameron was walking into town along the King's Highway where the tranquil quietness that seeped up from the lakeshore was shattered. Cars and trucks poured past steadily, for Grenville lay on the main road between Toronto and Montreal, and all of them were faced with a full-sized black and white billboard which announced, GRENVILLE LOVES ITS CHILDREN … DRIVE SAFELY OR LIVE WITH A BAD CONSCIENCE.

Lucy stopped as she reached a brown-shingled mission bungalow. She took out of her basket the envelope she had dropped into it and started up the walk to the door. Before she could reach it, Mrs. Jimmie Morse came out with a broom in her hand and her frizzy gray hair tied up in a blue and white polka-dot handkerchief.

"Now that's nice of you, Lucy!" she said. "Have you really got those seeds?"

"I think so. I had a hard time keeping the bees from ruining my plant, but I think I managed to protect it. It was a lovely one – almost a true sky blue. If I really have succeeded I'm going to try to market it."

As the Frasers felt sorry for the Camerons, so the Camerons felt sorry for Mary Morse because her husband drank. Lucy could see him in his shirt sleeves now, half hidden by the vine of Dutchman's pipe that covered the veranda. He had been out of work for a month and the whole town knew he had been drinking again, this time really hard. She tried not to look in his direction, though he seemed to be sitting quietly enough reading a paper.

"Be sure to let me know how these seeds turn out," Lucy said.

But Mary Morse had little interest that morning in flowers. Lucy's presence gave her a chance to speak her mind.

"We might have known everything would be turned upside down when the Ceramic was sold to Americans," she said. "A lot their fine promises amounted to about not making any changes! The next thing you know, they'll start bringing in cheap French-Canadian labour to take more jobs from our own men. If only old John MacDougall had stayed alive! But no, young John thinks he's far too grand to stay here and watch the business the way his father always did. He had to move to Toronto, and of course that's ruined him!"

Lucy tried to think of something to say to make Mary Morse feel better. The Ceramic Company was the largest industry in Grenville, but Grenville was not a factory town and the ups and downs of the plant affected only a limited number of people.

"I said there'd be trouble when they sent that young man up from the States," Mrs. Morse went on. "Imagine somebody his age thinking he can tell Mr. Craig how to run his business! Now that he's here, I don't like his looks, either. What do you think of him?"

"Who do you mean? I don't know who you're talking about."

"Stephen Lassiter. The American!"

"Oh. I hadn't heard about him."

"Well, I don't see why you *should* be interested. He's been here two months and it makes me uncomfortable just to look at him. He has that kind of face – you know, bold." Another pause and another sharp look. "I wonder how it makes him feel, firing men right and left? Still, you should be interested, more or less, since Mr. McCunn is his latest victim."

Lucy's face guarded itself, for Matthew McCunn was her uncle.

"What about Uncle Matt?" she said. "Is that definite, or is it just – just –"

She went no further because she realized that Mary Morse had drawn her into a trap. Mrs. Morse wanted to talk about Matt McCunn because in doing so she could draw attention to the well-known fact that the Cameron girls' own uncle drank a great deal worse than her husband. And yet, Lucy thought, she ought to know better than to compare them, even on such a plane, for nobody in Grenville had taken McCunn seriously in many years, not since he was unfrocked as a minister.

Mary Morse, watching the touch of colour appear on Lucy's cheeks, recognized the end of her conversation with the middle Cameron sister for that day.

"I was only inquiring," she said, and began to sweep her walk.

Lucy said good-bye and went on toward the shops, a prickly feeling of discomfort at the nape of her neck. So many people in Grenville, especially the women, seemed to be composed of sharp edges. In spite of the fact that she understood the reason for it, she found them no easier to live with. They were all so eager to do the right thing, but doing it made them no better. They were all fighting to retain the unity of their homes in the only kind of town they were able to understand, but their confidence was being steadily undermined by the knowledge that Grenville had nothing to offer their children, nothing to keep them from leaving home as soon as they could. Like Mary Morse, the women became bitter with their feelings of insecurity and their sense of injustice, and so they worked harder than ever, trying to sweep their worries into the gutter along with old leaves and twigs and dust.

Lucy reached the edge of the business district where the King's Highway became King Street. She passed the Presbyterian Church, grey fieldstone and gothic; the First Baptist Church, red brick and squat. Beyond the Baptist Church, a short iron bridge took the road over a limestone gully down which water poured in a heavy spate. The stream disappeared a hundred yards below at the cement wall of the Grenville Ceramic Company where Jimmie Morse had worked for twenty years as assistant sales manager. The factory had once produced church ornaments, heavily flowered vases, and ponderous earthenware spittoons decorated with pastoral scenes embossed in colour. With the passage of years the company had expanded and become more specialized. Now it made porcelain articles which the town designated broadly as plumbing fixtures.

A large corporation with headquarters in Cleveland had acquired control of the Ceramic Company several years ago, and last year had taken over the remaining assets. So far the Americans had moved slowly. They had been eager to win good will. Wages had been raised slightly. A rumour had been carefully spread that there would be no drastic changes. But this year some production men had been sent up from Cleveland and they had spent a week surveying and examining the whole plant. One of them, called by some an industrial engineer and by others an efficiency expert, had remained behind to complete the reorganization and cut out unnecessary costs. It was assumed that he was acting strictly on orders from above and had been selected for this most unpopular kind of work because he was a fairly affable character. Rumour now had it that within another few months the reorganization would be complete. A Canadian plant, using American methods and financed by American money, would be functioning legally within the framework of the British Empire trade agreements.

The failure of the old Ceramic Company had shaken Grenville, for the town had always been proud to think that its one factory distributed goods from Halifax to Vancouver. The grandfather of the last owner, a lusty, hairy Victorian, had settled many arguments with customers by the flat statement that what was good enough for the King of England was good enough for them. If the customers were unfamiliar with the story which everyone in Grenville knew, they were enlightened. Edward the Seventh had once taken a bath in one of the company's products. A bathtub, embossed in appropriate colours with the royal coat of arms, had been presented to the incumbent Governor-General in Ottawa just two weeks before Edward, then Prince of Wales, had appeared in the capital on a royal tour, and there was even a legend in Grenville that the Prince had found the tub so roomy and comfortable he had fallen asleep in it.

Lucy left the bridge and moved into the main part of town. King Street baked in the sun. It curved in a slow arc with the business buildings like two walls of a solid moat taking the curve as they went, red brick on one side and dark cement on the other, the symmetry of the curve completely spoiled by lines of not-too-straight telegraph poles, the whole area raw as the business sections of all Canadian small towns, ugly to the point of shock. Nearing the post office, she crossed streets sweetened by names redolent of British colonial history: Wellington Street, Simcoe Street, Sydenham Avenue, Duke Street, Elgin Lane. In this, Grenville was typical of its province; there was hardly a British general, admiral, or cabinet minister who had functioned between the French Revolution and the accession of Queen Victoria who was not commemorated in the name of a street, town, or county somewhere in Ontario. It was all part of the longing of a twice-transplanted people for a stable home. She reached Dorchester Square, enclosed by the courthouse and jail, a branch of the Royal Bank of Canada, and Nick Petropolis's Manhattan Pharmacy. In its heart was a patch of grass and four war memorials. The square was dominated on the fourth side by the post office, a monstrous aggression of red brick, its roof crowned by a four-faced clock shaped like a gigantic cruet. Inside this building Lucy encountered her uncle.

Matt McCunn was leaning against a desk near one of the windows, eyeing a middle-aged woman who was buying stamps. His face wore the expression of curiosity which had always enraged and mortified Lucy's father when he was alive. Under a cap of grizzled hair, two brilliant blue eyes peered out of a weather-beaten face. He looked like a cross between a Presbyterian minister of the old school and a sergeant-major of a line regiment, which was suitable enough, since during a varied career he had been both. His pepper-and-salt trousers had a clean press along the crease and he wore a spotless white shirt, but his sleeves were rolled up to reveal a pair of wiry brown forearms, with a snake tattooed on one and a dancing girl on the other.

Lucy glanced at her uncle, avoided his eyes for a moment, bought stamps, and mailed the letters she had brought. When the other woman left the rotunda she turned to him.

"Uncle Matt – tell me the truth for once. Have you lost your job again?"

He scratched his head behind his right ear. "You know what's the matter with this place, Lucy? It's a town of women and children. You ought to get out of here."

Another woman came through the door and nodded in Lucy's direction. McCunn made a face as his eyes followed her jerky walk across the floor.

"Daisy doesn't like me any more," he said, quite audibly.

Lucy went outside and her uncle followed her, blinking into the sunshine.

"She did once, though. Something might have come of it, only she was too scared." He shook his head. "I remember the first time I ever saw her. It was at a Sunday-school picnic up at the lake, and I'm telling you, all she needed was a harvest moon to make her look better'n a piece of pie. But look at her now!" He caught Lucy's arm and she smelled a faint whiff of whiskey as his free hand made a wide gesture toward the chained-in patch of grass in the centre of Dorchester Square. "You know, right there in front of you is one of the main reasons for Grenville being like it is – four bloody memorials to four bloody British wars. The War of 1812, the Crimea, the Boer War, and the real one."

"Uncle Matt, I asked you a question."

He grinned and disregarded the interruption. "I've been thinking lately – these little towns, they're prematurely old. They're like respectable women, they're old before they ever start living. Why, I can remember when this was quite a place on a Saturday night. I've seen the drunks lined up like dead soldiers on the sidewalk right here in front of the post office, and I've seen Angus McNab fight three-quarters of an hour to a finish with Mickey McQuinn and back him right across the square from here to the Royal Bank. But look at it now! It's the women are the trouble. There were twenty-five per cent too many of them when the last war ended and instead of improving themselves what did they do? They ganged up on us and tried to make us ashamed of ourselves. It's God's truth they did, and the boys back from France couldn't stand it, so where are they now? In Toronto or the States, most of them. You ought to get out of here before you get to be like Jane."

A quick flash of fear ghosted across Lucy's face as she went down the steps and began to cross the square. McCunn followed her, and they walked side by side until they reached the Manhattan Pharmacy.

"Doesn't it ever occur to you that people worry about you?" she said.

"My dear child, in this town people worry about everything. So why not let them worry about something interesting for a change?"

Lucy was uncomfortable, standing there with McCunn on the busiest spot in town. He took a pipe from his pocket and stuffed it with tobacco. As he did so, the hips of the dancing girl wiggled rhythmically over the muscles of his forearm.

"I'm going in here," she said. "Jane wants some toothpaste, and I want a cold drink."

"No harm in that," McCunn said. "I'll come too."

They sat on stools in front of the marble counter, and Lucy sighed with relief. It was cool in the drugstore. Apart from a young man at the other end of the counter, they were the only customers, except for some people at the prescription counter at the back. McCunn took a sip of his drink and laid down the glass.

"Do you really like this stuff?" He passed his hand around to his hip pocket, fondled the hard outlines of a flask, and for an instant Lucy was afraid he would produce it and pour some of its contents into his glass. Instead he leaned sideways with his elbow on the counter. "You were asking about my job. Yes, it looks as if I've lost it. This efficiency expert – this man Lassiter they sent up from the States – he doesn't think I'm efficient."

"Were you surprised at that?" Lucy asked.

McCunn eyed her for a moment and grinned again, "You know what I told Lassiter? I told him that when New York burns, efficiency will be the cause of it. He didn't get the point so I tried again. I asked him if he believed in progress, so of course he said he did. So I told him the most progressive animals the world had ever seen had been the Gadarene swine. That didn't do any good, either. He'd never heard of the Gadarene swine. So I tried again. I told him that before he came up here the warehouse at the Ceramic used to be a pleasant place, and that I didn't mind losing the job because I wanted to remember it that way. He got the point. Otherwise he's not a bad fella when you get to know him."

Lucy sipped her drink and watched his reflection in the mirror behind the counter. It pleased McCunn to know that everyone considered him preposterous, but apparently it had never occurred to him that he really was preposterous. When Lucy was a little girl he had seemed wonderful to her. He had been the war hero and the adventurer; he had told wonderful stories; he had spent three weeks in the East on a merchant ship after leaving the army. Every time he had come to the Cameron house he had made her whole world seem larger. But she had always known that her father had hated him and been ashamed of him, and as she grew older she knew that Jane's friends made a point of never mentioning his name in the presence of any of the Cameron sisters. And yet, McCunn had never been a public charge. Somehow or other, he had always got along.

He was looking past her at the waitress behind the soda fountain. The girl was at the far end of the counter talking to the other customer, a man called Ike Blackman. It gave Lucy a twinge of amusement to realize that she was now sitting between the two most disreputable men in Grenville. Blackman was supposed to be unspeakably immoral. On Saturday nights he played the drums in a dance band, and that was about all the honest work he ever did. He wore sideburns, he parted his hair in the middle and slicked it back so that it gleamed sleekly, he had made himself carefully into a model of the very kind of man Grenville most especially disliked. And of course, he was believed to have a way with women. The high-school boys said he had a different one every week, though where he acquired them they never knew.

Now he turned his oval head slowly, looked at Lucy's ankles, and addressed McCunn: "How's tricks at the factory, Matt? You got a day off?"

McCunn began talking to the other man across her, and for no apparent reason the Greek waitress let out a loud laugh. Her hips moved suggestively as she worked behind the counter, she and Mc-Cunn and Blackman were relaxed as they talked to one another, and Lucy felt excluded. It occurred to her that in a town like Grenville personal freedom could rest only on a bad reputation.

Another customer entered and sat on a stool in the middle of the counter. The girl moved to serve him, the stranger got into conversation with Blackman, and McCunn turned back to Lucy.

"You've got a nice head of hair," he said as if he had noticed it for the first time. "Why do you fix it like that?"

"It saves bother. I can't have it getting into my eyes the way Nina's does. After all, I work in a garden."

McCunn turned toward a rack of magazines standing near his end of the counter. On the cover of one of them was a carefully wind-blown blonde standing in a field of daisies, wearing a big smile, an embroidered blouse, and a dirndl skirt.

"I'd like to see you looking like that," he said. "You could if you tried."

"It costs money to dress like a girl on a magazine cover."

"Hell!" he said. After a brief pause he went on: "The only reason you dress plain is because the women in Grenville would scratch your eyes out if you did anything different." He nodded toward the waitress. "Look at Rose. She's got less money than you have, but she gets noticed."

Lucy finished her drink, laid ten cents on the counter, and got up to leave. McCunn unwound his long legs and got up too. When he opened the door the heat of the square quivered against them.

Out on the street, he said gently, "The men notice a girl like that, Lucy. No matter what you may think about her."

"Of course they do!" There was controlled anger in her face as she turned to her uncle.

McCunn grinned amiably.

"Is that the only purpose you think a woman should have in her life – to be noticed by some man?"

"Listen, Lucy – I like you. And this is the God's truth. For a woman to be considered beautiful, she's got to be bold. Most men haven't got much imagination. You've got to spell it out for them so they can be sure they aren't making a mistake. Sure – she can conceal the boldness all she likes. But it's got to be there."

They were heading along King Street toward Duke, where her uncle would have to turn north for his mile walk out of town to his own place. He lived in a small whitewashed cottage on the slope of a hill with farmed land spreading around it. McCunn had once owned fifty acres of this land, but now he owned nothing more than the cottage on the edge of one of the fields.

"You're obviously getting ready to leave Grenville again," Lucy said. "Where will it be this time?"

"Ever heard of a place called Yellowknife?"

"Aren't you too old to keep on disappearing into the bush like that?"

"What do you mean, bush? Yellowknife's turning into quite a town. And do you think fifty-one is old? I'm in good condition." They stopped on a corner while a truck filled with rattling cases of beer passed by. "Labatt's," he informed her, and went on, "You tell Jane something from me. Tell her to quit worrying."

They crossed the street and began walking under old trees, past houses which had clung to the business section for years without being absorbed by it. Next door to an undertaking parlour the high wire backstop of the tennis courts came into view.

"You know," McCunn said as another truck went past, "the whole bloody country pounds through this town every day, and people like Jane don't even see it. That's another reason why the men have to get out." He gripped her arm suddenly. "Look – there's the bastard that fired me."

A game of singles was in progress on the tennis courts, a rare sight in Grenville these days, particularly in the middle of a business morning.

"The big one," McCunn said. "That's Stephen Lassiter. Effi-ciency expert." He laughed. "Let's go over and make him feel uncomfortable. He's supposed to set an example up here and it'll make him feel as guilty as hell if he sees me watching him play tennis when he ought to be on the job."

Lucy felt she had taken about as much of McCunn as she could stand for the day. "I forgot to get the groceries," she said. "I'll have to go back." She stopped and faced him. "We're really concerned about you, Uncle Matt. Please don't leave town without telling us, the way you did last time."

He smiled at her with affection and with a look in his eyes she had sometimes noticed in the eyes of other men, but did not under-stand. As she walked back to the square a feeling of disenchantment filled her. She liked Grenville; she loved its trees and changing weather; she liked most of its people. But sometimes the town seemed to be closing in around her, freezing her into the mould of a perpetual childhood. She had no function here. Neither had Bruce Fraser nor Matt McCunn, but being men they could escape. McCunn had escaped without finding a function anywhere, but the odd thing about him was that he really believed he had lived a full life, even though his wife had left him years ago and the only gold he had ever discovered had been cheated out of him by mining pro-moters. When he had enough to drink McCunn liked to say that the secret of a good life was courage, but he meant something else by the word than Lucy did. What did he know of a woman's courage, the courage of waiting, of facing a blank wall for the rest of your life with a quiet and decent dignity? As this thought struck her, the brightness of the morning became a pain. Could she really have been describing herself?

TEN minutes later, when Lucy came out of the grocery store with a full basket, McCunn was nowhere to be seen. By the time she reached the backstop of the courts again three children were watching the game. She stopped beside them for a moment and then turned into the club grounds and entered the deep shade cast by three great pine trees which rose over the old, white-painted pavilion.

The appearance of the club had changed little since she was a small girl. As she laid her basket on the pavilion steps and sat beside it, she remembered the times she had been here as a child. When her father had been alive and active, her mother had sometimes brought her out here on Saturday afternoons as a treat, to watch him pitch quoits. In the winters there had been a Quebec heater in the pavilion and the snowshoe club had used the place every weekend. Men wearing red-and-white woollen suits with long woollen stockings and parkas and red scarves would meet on Saturday afternoons at the club, trudge until dark over the fields, and then return to the pavilion for a supper of pork and beans, hot breads, and coffee prepared by their wives. Then they would sing together and tell each other how tired they were and repeat that the blizzards had been much heavier when they were children. Always, on such evenings, someone was sure to remember the great storm that had struck Grenville on Twelfth Night, 1909, when the Anglicans were holding a social in the basement of their church. That had been a storm. The lake wind had piled the drifts so high around the church that when the first people tried to leave they had floundered in the snow and finally had lost their feet, and old Sid Townshend, who had been out West, had made a lariat out of a clothesline he found in the basement and had thrown the lasso at them, and the whole congregation had mocked the Methodists by singing a Methodist hymn, *Throw Out the Lifeline*, while they hauled them in. After that they had taken all the cushions and hassocks out of the pews and spent the night in the basement, and the next week the Presbyterians said there was one thing they were sure of, it was the first time any of the Anglicans had ever willingly spent more than half an hour inside a church in their lives.

The snowshoe club had died fifteen years ago and the Quebec heater had been removed from the pavilion. As more and more people acquired cars, they had lost the habit of making their own pleasures. The quoit beds were still there, covered with sticky brown canvas tarpaulins, but few men used them any more. There were not enough native young men even to support the tennis courts, and the clay would have gone to grass and weeds had it not been for the handful of summer people from Toronto who contributed enough to keep them going. But the old familiar smells of the place were still present as reminders that once the club had possessed life and reason of its own: pine needles hot with sun, pine cones lying on the ground, the dry odour of old tennis balls seeping out the pavilion door from the changing rooms. After skirting the building Lucy looked out at the tennis courts.

There are moments in life when quite ordinary scenes, scenes which are really none of our business, startle us without our knowing why they should. For Lucy this was such a moment. As she watched Stephen Lassiter playing tennis, the thought occurred to her, so clearly she could almost see it in print: if this man is important, then everyone else I know is not.

But as soon as she examined the thought it disappeared. She told herself that Lassiter was merely a man who had been an athlete when younger and had managed to find someone who could give him a good game of tennis. Yet, as she watched him, her original feeling returned. The game brought his aggressive facade of self-confidence into sharp focus, and as she looked at his face and movements, Grenville seemed a smaller place than it had seemed half an hour ago.

She found herself enjoying the game, realizing that she had never really seen tennis properly played before. Lassiter was probably over thirty and less than thirty-five, and his opponent looked the same age. Both wore sweat shirts with large Ps on the front and both handled themselves on the court with trained concentration. Even with nothing at stake they were playing to win. Beyond that all resemblance between them ended.

Lassiter's opponent was a wiry little man with smooth dark hair, a large nose, and an oval face which to Lucy looked foreign. He played a carefully calculated game, using a lot of slice, and waited for Lassiter to make mistakes. Lassiter was well over six feet in height, but his chest and shoulders were so powerful he seemed large rather than tall. In spite of his muscular development he was not stiff; he moved on the court with the feline precision of a natural tennis player. Neither man was in good condition, but Lassiter seemed the more fit of the two. The little man covered court like a rabbit, but Lassiter had too much power for him. Lucy watched the heavy muscles of his calves knotting as he bent his knees to hit, relaxing as the weight left them, knotting as the next ball came. They had a sort of proud, easy power, like the muscles of a horse, and his rusty-blond hair was loose on his head and flopped as he ran.

A set was finished on an odd game and they changed sides. Lassiter stripped off his sweat shirt and stood with one large hand on the heaving muscles of his diaphragm while the other clamped his racket against the net cord. His linen shirt clung to his body like a wet bathing suit. The buttons were open at the top, showing a chest dusted with brown hair.

"These shadows are bastards!" he said as he panted.

The little man wiped his hands on a towel and said nothing. Lucy had no idea who he was, but supposed from the P on his sweatshirt that he must be an old college friend who had come to visit Lassiter.

"That last shot in the corner," Lassiter said. As he panted his voice came in jerks. "I couldn't see it at all. Why the hell don't they cut down the trees?"

They walked away from each other toward the baselines. Lassiter's diaphragm muscles showed taut through his wet shirt as he stretched for his service. He threw the ball very high and reached while his heavy body pivoted on the splayed toes of his left foot; the racket hit the ball with a smack like a rug-beater on a wet sheet and the ball caught the court wide and two feet above the service-court angle. His opponent didn't get his racket within two yards of it.

"How was that, Carl?"

The little man shook his head. "I didn't see it. Take it again."

"How was that, did you see?"

With a start, Lucy realized that Lassiter was addressing her, looking straight at her from the middle of the court, and she flushed with embarrassment. She knew nothing of tennis, and couldn't have answered even if she had seen the ball strike.

"Was it good?" Lassiter said. "I couldn't see it. They ought to cut these trees down."

She heard her own voice say, "I think it was all right."

Lassiter looked at her and turned back to the baseline, and she felt a fool as he said over his shoulder, "We'd better take it over, Carl."

Lucy was self-conscious now, wondering what they would think of a lone girl who came to the club to watch them. She turned to leave, and as she walked beside the court toward the road she passed quite close to Lassiter. This was a face millions of people would recognize even if they didn't know the man himself. It was authentic

American; a product of what the United States so often does to the original Anglo-Saxon mould. It was larger and bolder than the faces of most Canadian men she knew, but somehow its lines were less decisive, and it was a difficult face for her to understand. The eyes looked boyish. The mouth, when he concentrated, looked hard. When he grinned he was very attractive. It was the face of a man who expects most people to like him exactly as he is.

THE lawn in front of the Cameron house was deep green under the noonday sun, and a girl was lolling in its centre playing with the wire-haired terrier she had just washed. She was a girl with blue eyes, golden curls, a snub nose, a wide laughing mouth, plump bare arms coloured like honey in the sun, and a short neat body that was never still. Her hair kept falling into her eyes and she laughed as the dog barked. The dog caught the end of the towel she held, braced his feet, and tugged. Both the girl and the dog seemed to understand each other, and between them they formed a full part of the summer morning.

Nina's gambolling stopped abruptly as Lucy came up with her basket.

"Where've you been?" she said. "Oh, of course, you were shopping. You've been an awfully long time. Jane was looking for you."

The dog made another convulsive movement which tore the towel out of Nina's hands. He ran with it to the edge of the steps, dropped it to bark at a cat, and stood panting with the towel on the ground in front of his forepaws, while the cat eyed him with a solemn and distasteful air. Lucy skirted the dog and sat on the top step. The dog barked again.

"Pan!" Nina said. "Shut up, for heaven's sake!"

The cat moved in against Lucy's thigh and her right hand began to stroke it. The throat throbbed with a slow, pulsing purr, the hair felt hot with sun, and Lucy's eyes ranged over Nina's head down the road across the common to the lake. The water looked cool, green, and vast, and the deckhouses of a grainboat were just nudging the horizon.

"Jane's fit to be tied this morning," Nina said.

There was another skirmish between Nina and the dog. Through the screen door of the house came the faint echo of another music lesson: *do, re, mi, fa, sol, la, ti, do* repeated six times in different keys with a few mistakes. Nina caught the towel, but when the dog suddenly stopped pulling on his end of it, he took her off balance and she collapsed backwards. She remained sitting squarely on the lawn, her legs spread flat in front of her, her arms like a pair of flying buttresses propping upright the weight of her back. She tossed the hair out of her eyes.

"What a wonderful day!" she said, as though she were the only person in the world who knew it. "You can almost taste it. I could bite a morning like this." Then, without a pause, "You know that blue chiffon dress of yours?"

Lucy looked at her younger sister.

"May I have it?" Nina said. "I want to dye it. You practically never use a party dress except for Jane's recitals. I'll have it dyed and cut down to fit. It'll look lovely on me. Don't you think it will? It never suited you, anyway."

The corners of Lucy's mouth turned up in a faint smile, but Nina had already grabbed the towel and begun playing with Pan again.

"What's the matter with Jane this morning?" Lucy said.

"Oh, it's that letter she got yesterday. She probably stayed awake half the night thinking up answers to it, and of course she won't use any of them. You know Jane."

The scale-playing had ceased, and Jane's pupil was now beginning a piece called *Sunday Morning at Glion*. From the truculent incompetence in its execution it was evident the player was a boy. Lucy waited for the mistake that usually came at the twelfth bar. It came. The playing stuttered a bar further, stopped, returned, repeated the mistake, stopped once more, then went angrily back to the beginning again.

"What letter?" she said to Nina.

"It's something to do with the library. She left it on the hall table and I read it. She probably wanted us to read it or she wouldn't have left it there. Something completely silly – but you know Jane."

Lucy continued to look at the lake. A faint scroll of smoke from the grainboat curled on the horizon with a long, sinuous gesture. A pack of cumulus cloud had risen like a vast white mountain out of a flat blue floor.

"You don't mind if I take that old dress, do you?" Nina said.

"What do you want it now for?" Lucy's voice was a quiet contralto with real movement in it. Nina's voice had rather a hard tone, though no harder than most people's in her part of the country.

"Pan!" Nina said. "Go away, you're still wet!" She turned with another backward toss of her hair. "You know – the club dance."

Lucy sat quietly in the sun. "You don't need a dinner dress for that."

"But this time I do!" Nina got up and sat on the bottom step. "It won't be just an ordinary club hop, you know. Steve Lassiter's going to be there."

Lucy smiled. "Do you know him?"

"No, but he's going to be there, and Mary Macdonnell knows him." Nina peered inside Lucy's basket and began turning over the parcels. "You didn't get any icing sugar and I specially wanted a cake for tomorrow. He's from New York, you know."

The dog made another sally with the towel, but Nina had forgotten all about him. Inside the house, *Sunday Morning at Glion* staggered to a defiant end.

"He's got a LaSalle convertible," Nina went on. "And it's perfectly obvious he thinks none of the girls here has any style."

Lucy had often wondered if Jane guessed how much difference the movies had made in her younger sister's life. Jane practically never went to the movies, and Lucy herself went seldom. But Nina, being nine years younger, had grown up with moving pictures. She would have resented it if anyone had called her a movie fan. She never read movie magazines and in her high-school days she had never gossiped about the movie stars the way some of the other girls did, but she tended to see situations in terms of movie formulae. It occurred to Lucy now that she was probably seeing Lassiter in this way: the handsome man from the big city, presumably rich, forced to spend a few months on business in a small town which contained, to his delighted surprise, Nina herself. Another vague formula which Nina shared in common with many Canadians told her that she was somewhat superior to Americans, though she never asked herself why, or expected Americans to recognize the superiority.

"He oughtn't to be allowed to think this is just another hick town," Nina said.

"And isn't it?"

A frown traced an inverted V above Nina's snub nose. It made her look about three years younger.

"You know perfectly well it isn't," she said. "We're not in the least like those American small towns. Grenville has a real history, after all. We're – well, we're different." She spun around on the step, hoisted her knees to chin level, and hugged them to herself with both hands. The frown disappeared. "The only trouble with Grenville is that people here think it isn't nice to be different. And Americans are always trying to be different and – anyway, he looks like one of the better kind of Americans."

Lucy rose and picked up her basket. Nina remained on the step.

"I think you're mean," Nina said.

Through the screen door came the sound of Jane's voice, followed by the dutiful answer of a small boy. Then the door opened and a carrot-headed youngster of twelve came out with a music roll under his arm. The expression of relief on his face at having finished his music lesson was not sufficient to counteract his disgust at having had to take one at all, or at being seen walking home with a music roll.

"Hello, Bobby," Lucy said.

"Hello, Miss Cameron."

"It's a shame having to work on a day like this, isn't it?"

The boy looked sheepish. "Well, I guess so."

He shifted from one foot to the other, and then his sheepishness yielded to an expression of superiority that made Lucy feel his junior. He strode down the steps and out to the sidewalk. He kicked a pebble as far as he could and it shot across the street and lodged in a depression by a tree root. Pan rushed after it and began nuzzling. The boy picked up a larger stone and threw it toward the lake. Pan left the tree and chased. The boy let out a whoop and ran after him, and the two faded across the common onto the beach. Lucy stood watching, her hand on the doorknob. Nina was still on the bottom step.

"It's not as if it was doing any good hanging up in your closet," Nina said. "After all – the condition your hands get into with your flowers –" She turned and looked at her sister, and her young forehead wrinkled. "You never go any place that matters."

Lucy said nothing.

"Oh, Lucy – can't you see what I mean? It's different for someone like you. But I've got to have some fun. If you'd ever go out and meet people – if you'd ever in your life met a man like Steve Lassiter for instance, you'd know what I mean."

Lucy opened the screen door and paused, holding her basket by her side. Her large eyes were calm. There was relaxation in her face, partly amused, partly affectionate, as she regarded her sister.

"I've already met him, Nina," she said, and then she went into the darkness of the hall and let the door fall shut behind her.

AS SOON as Lucy entered the house she heard the sounds of Jane's piano. The opening bars of the slow movement of the *Apassionata* broke into the stillness. Jane was playing to herself. The rich cellar tones of the first bars vibrated through the dark interior air, and the moment Lucy heard them, she knew her older sister was disturbed by something.

Lucy carried her basket down the narrow hall to the kitchen, closed the door behind her, and began to prepare lunch. She arranged the food on a tray: a bowl of salad, a plate of bread and butter, three glasses of milk, three bowls of fresh berries with cream and sugar. Jane was still playing when she opened the door, ready to call her sisters. It was strange music for a summer day, but natural enough for Jane. In spite of her efforts to appear like everyone else, to think, say, and do nothing which the better people in Grenville would not consider completely normal, Jane had always seemed to Lucy a strange woman. The music continued, and with it the revelation of a deep, indignant passion of which Jane herself was obviously unaware.

Lucy leaned against the kitchen door and listened while the sombre chords throbbed through the house. She could see her sister's back rising stiffly from the piano stool in the living room where she gave her lessons. She was a small woman, neat, very plainly dressed, and she looked considerably older than her thirty-seven years. Hearing the music, noting how well she played Beethoven, Lucy marvelled for the thousandth time that it was possible for Jane to love music so much and still to consider that in itself music was not particularly important. Sometimes she even told the parents of her pupils that music lessons were useful because they kept small boys from wasting their time in the streets.

Since the death of the girls' father, Jane had been the principal support of the family. She believed quite simply that her father had been one of the best men who ever lived, and she felt that few people had appreciated him. Yet, Lucy had always suspected, Jane's genuine love and devotion for her father were the main reasons why she disliked and despised men in general, for in her heart Jane must have known that she had more real force and practical sense than John Knox Cameron had ever had. Living in a small town, she judged the entire male sex by the specimens of it she found in Grenville, and she knew that in a contest of wills not one of them could stand up against her. Jonathan Eldridge, the lawyer; Jim Craig, the factory manager; Donald Fraser, the doctor; Dr. Grant, the minister – these and all the others had to be humoured by women, made to feel important by women, led surreptitiously by the nose for their own good by women. Yet Jane had never uttered a single word against men in general and would have condemned any other woman who did. The memory of her father remained sacrosanct with her. She was sure he had recognized her ability and put a special trust in her because the girls' mother – at least, so Jane thought – had been a frail and rather timid woman. When John Knox died, Jane felt that the family and the house had been left to her as a special trust.

She struck out the final chords. Her hands dropped to her lap and for a moment she sat erect looking up at the over-sized, walnut-framed print of *The Light of the World* which hung against the tan wallpaper above the piano. Then she laid her music aside and with a brisk movement covered the keys. She swung around on the stool, saw Lucy at the door, and rose.

"You should have told me lunch was ready," she said.

"There's no hurry. I enjoy listening to you."

"Well, you've heard me often enough." Jane crossed the floor. "Where's Nina?"

"She was outside on the lawn fifteen minutes ago."

"I must say," Jane remarked as she mounted the narrow stairs that bounded one side of the hall, "two years of college have made Nina lose whatever sense of time she ever had. She's never ready for anything any more. I don't know what Father would have said."

Jane kept on talking, but the rest of her words were lost as she rounded the corner into the upper hall.

Long before Nina appeared, Lucy and Jane were sitting in their deck chairs in the back garden on either side of a round wooden table under an apple tree. The lunch rested on the table. Heat brooded in the garden, which ran in a long rectangle behind the house, bounded by high hedges. In one corner at the back of the garden was a small greenhouse. It was in this garden that Lucy grew her best flowers, the ones for which she sometimes won prizes. White and carmine phlox dominated the beds, the yellow of hyperion lilies glowed at rhythmic intervals between them, there were clusters of snapdragon, nicotiana drooped closed against the sun, and here and there cerise splashes of clarkia balanced the blue of larkspur. In a separate bed four dozen rose bushes stood in solitude showing only a few between-season buds, and petunias bounded a modest kitchen garden near the house.

Jane's fingers drummed idly on the table. "I can't imagine what's keeping her." And then, a few minutes later, "There's terrible news in the paper this morning. I can't bear reading it." And a moment later, "We're so lucky here. We've never really wanted for anything, have we? Who would have thought one could count on having so many music pupils in Grenville?" A cicada screamed in the vacant field behind the garden. "Father was right. He knew if we stayed together we'd manage."

Lucy sat in silence. Glancing at her sister's face, she wondered with mild curiosity what thoughts had troubled her when she was playing Beethoven, but at this moment Jane's face had no marked expression, and whatever it was, she had probably forgotten all about it now. Her nose and chin were somewhat pointed, her mouth small and straight. Her features were sharp enough to give her an air of decision, though they were not gaunt. Her dark hair, severely drawn back, formed a widow's peak at the top of the forehead. It was a heart-shaped face, and a vain woman would have made much of it. But nothing about Jane invited admiration; everything about her demanded respect.

"I saw Uncle Matt today," Lucy said.

"Where did you see him?"

"In town. He's lost his job, I'm afraid."

Jane's lips pursed, but she said nothing.

"He told me he intends to go north again."

"That disgusting, dirty old man!"

"Jane," Lucy said quietly, "he's not that. You know he's not."

"I think it would be just as well if you took care not to be seen with him anywhere in town." Her voice dropped and became quite calm. She sounded like a sensible, pleasantly reasonable woman. "After all, *everybody* knows what kind of a man he is. It's not our fault that he happens to be connected with us, but it would be just as well if people weren't reminded of it. After all, my work depends to a great extent on what people think of us." In a moment, she added, "You know, Lucy, you read too many novels. I don't think it's good for you to read so much. You seem to think Uncle Matt is interesting because he's like those disgusting characters so many American writers are putting into their books these days. Real life is not like that – not even in the States."

Lucy was silent as restlessness broke over her in waves. She remembered what McCunn had told her. Incongruously, she remembered the bold expression on Lassiter's face. And for an instant, as she glanced at Jane, she thought in sudden terror that in ten years she herself might look like her sister.

"There's something I've been wanting to ask you," Lucy said slowly. "That field behind the garden – you know it hasn't been used for years. I'm sure I could rent it. It wouldn't cost much."

"What do you want it for?"

"It's good land. I've tested it. For about a quarter of a mile along this section of the shore the land is really marvellous. I've often wondered why houses were built on land so rich. If that field could be ploughed and harrowed it would make a wonderful cutting garden."

Jane became quietly intent, and Lucy knew she was on the defensive. These two sisters understood each other more by felt undertones than by the actual words they used.

"But what on earth could you do with more flowers than you've got?"

"I could sell them."

"But anyone who wants flowers in Grenville has his own garden."

"I was thinking of selling them in Toronto."

Jane smiled. "Really, Lucy, to hear you talk a person would think we were desperately poor. I know we have to be careful, but after all!"

Lucy heard crickets chirping among the flowers. She saw the white blossoms of the nicotiana closed against the light and drooping on their stems. She felt the pressure of her sister's will like a physical weight against her own. It had always been like this. First her father, and then Jane. They had always had their own idea of her. They had also had their own idea of themselves.

"We've got years to look forward to, Jane. It's quite silly of me to go on growing flowers just as a hobby when I know I can do so much more." She began to speak more quickly. "It wouldn't change anything, you know. I'd start very gradually. But flowers sell for large prices now, and it would be simple to ship them from here to commercial florists in the city. I could get a man to help me with the heavy work. I've really thought it all out."

Jane's fingers continued to drum on the table. "Have you thought out where to get the money?"

"If it was successful it would pay for itself."

Jane smiled again. "Oh, Lucy, as if you knew anything about business! Even Father lost money buying land. And look what happened to Uncle Matt! No, Lucy – really!"

Lucy leaned back in her chair. It was not necessary to mention that the initial outlay for this project would have to be advanced by Jane. They both knew it. It was not necessary to mention that it was impossible for Lucy to obtain another kind of job in Grenville. They both knew that, too.

"You mustn't let yourself worry just because you don't happen to be bringing in any money," Jane said. "You've made this garden very nice. People always admire it when they see it."

Lucy's face looked tranquil, but Jane was aware that she had not yet won a victory.

"You know," she said, "if there was money to be made in a business like that in Grenville, someone else would have thought about it long ago."

Again Lucy remembered the bold, alien self-confidence she had seen in Lassiter's face. A flash of rebellion shot through her.

"We don't have to be so cautious! We really don't. Other people aren't."

Jane smiled, and her voice still sounded quiet and pregnant with common sense.

"But Lucy – we aren't other people, are we? We're just three women. Mr. Eldridge told me the insurance statistics prove that more than eighty per cent of women lose every cent that's left to them within four years. It's seven years since Father passed away and we're still as well off as we were then. That's only because we've been careful."

A cicada screamed. There was a sudden clawing at the screen of the back door and Pan came out, followed immediately by the cat, and finally by Nina. Nina was brushing back her yellow hair with one hand. Her cheeks looked as if she had just rubbed them with a towel. Her lips were less natural in their rosiness. Seeing her, Jane turned with relief to a problem more specific.

"It would be easier for Lucy if you'd be on time now and then."

Nina collapsed into the third deck chair. "Salad again today?"

Jane picked up her napkin. "And another thing. I wish you wouldn't use all that lipstick. It really isn't nice."

"Oh, Jane!"

"Nina, you know I practically never speak about it. But if anyone else had as much on as you have now, people would think she looked cheap. Besides, it stains the glasses and dirties the napkins and makes everything quite disgusting. Lucy has to wash and wash them."

Nina glanced at Lucy's natural lips, only faintly coloured by the noon sun. "Oh, well, the colour does come out, doesn't it?"

Jane picked up her plate and began to eat. After a few bites of her salad she put it down again and spoke in her mild voice. She smiled at Nina as she did so. "Do you remember that girl who was Mr. Eldridge's secretary a few years ago? The first girl in Grenville who painted her nails? I must admit at the time I thought some people made too much of it, but look what happened to her!" Jane glanced toward Lucy, who now became aware that she was being addressed as well as Nina. "A lot of books these days make fun of people like us, but we'll soon see who was right and who was wrong. The world has changed a lot less than some of these clever people think it has. You know, Father never objected to people smoking, but he used to say that his experience in the schools had made him absolutely certain of one thing. The first boy who smoked cigarettes in any class always went to the bad. It was one of those little things you could be absolutely sure of."

Jane began to eat. Nina scrambled out of her chair and served herself with a large wooden spoon and fork. Her easy, rhythmic restlessness was all the more vivid against Jane's preciseness and Lucy's physical calm.

"Cheese again," Nina said. Before Jane could make a remark she went on, "I'm not complaining about it. It's just that I don't like cheese and Lucy knows it."

She hunched forward on the edge of her chair, holding the plate on her knees. Her hair fell forward as she put a forkful of salad into her mouth with no regard for Jane's twinge of discomfort as she did so.

"Umm, this isn't bad!" she said in pleased surprise. "What did you season it with?"

Silence fell as they went on eating; silence the more complete because it was filled with the multitudinous insect noises of a summer noon. A bee circled into the salad bowl, balanced on the edge for a moment, then shot away toward the flowers. Lucy's eye followed its flight, lost it as its colour blended into the bell of an hyperion lily. Her eyes continued to rest on the garden. Now all the thoughtless world was busy fulfilling innumerable life-cycles, most of them with such savage cruelty that Jane would have been appalled if she understood what they meant. Lucy watched the lilies eager toward the sun, the nicotianas standing in the heat like white-faced women with closed eyes, the phlox crowding each other in their struggle to live. It was odd that gardening was supposed to be the gentle occupation. Any garden was an arena of frantic strife. She thought of the armies of ants that carried aphids down to the queen at the roots of the rose bush so that she had to destroy the ants, and then destroy the remaining aphids with nicotine. She herself had poisoned more living organisms than Nero had ever dreamed of.

Her eyes came back to Jane, who now was talking about the public library. Jane was on the library committee and she took her duties seriously. Nothing about Jane seemed more remarkable to Lucy than the way in which she got on with people in the town.

They thought of her as a quiet woman who knew her own mind; a woman of excellent good sense. With strangers Jane was always tactful. She had a real skill in suggesting her wishes to other people so indirectly that they thought them their own.

"I've got to find a way of getting someone to second my motion in the committee," Jane was saying. "Nobody ever seems to want to make the first move. And what can you do with a man like Dr. Grant? He says there's no harm in modern novels. Of course there's no harm for *him*. My point is that they're a waste of money for a library like ours. Nowadays all the decent novels are badly written, and all the well-written ones are indecent."

"Jane," Lucy murmured, "you're being ridiculous!"

Her sister seemed not to hear. It was strange, Lucy thought, it was incredible to remember that Jane was only thirty-seven. She wondered how old her sister felt.

Nina was leaning back in her deck chair with both hands clasped behind her head, looking up at a solitary cloud. It was like a furry white cat, sleeping huge and upside down in a lake of blue. Nina had not appeared to be listening, but in the silence which followed Jane's final remarks she spoke casually. "What was that novel you were reading last week, Lucy? Something by Aldous Huxley. I took a look at it myself, and I must say!"

Lucy leaned back in her chair and her eyes also sought the cloud.

"What must you say, Nina?"

Jane finished her salad and leaned forward to put her plate on the table. "Oh come, Nina! After all, Lucy is practically twenty-eight. *I* don't like the books she reads, but – one book I absolutely insist that we get for the library is that new life of Lord Tweedsmuir. Dr. Grant was telling me about it only last Sunday, and …"

Neither Nina nor Lucy appeared to have any thoughts on John Buchan whose stately and inexorable progress from a Scottish manse to the House of Lords and the Governor-General's mansion in Ottawa seemed to Jane a justification of her own father's entire point of view.

"He proved that a man can be a great writer today without even mentioning sex."

She continued to talk, and further details of Lord Tweedsmuir's greatness took their place in the garden along with the slow hum of the insects, the twitching of the cat's ears, and the noiseless, countless, senseless crawling of microscopic life along the stalks of the plants and the grass.

"Jane?" Nina said after a bit. "You know that blue chiffon dress of Lucy's?"

Jane indicated that she did.

"Well –" Nina hesitated. As Lucy seemed to be paying no attention, she grinned mischievously. "Well, I simply have to have a new dress and I don't want to be spending any more of your money."

Jane interrupted. "Never mind, Nina – we've been through all that before. Your education was taken into account long ago, so please tell me what your point is."

The cumulus cloud was absorbing Lucy's attention. It still looked like a furry white cat asleep in the sky. It hadn't changed at all. Neither had her sisters, and neither had she herself.

"I asked Lucy to let me have it," Nina went on. With sudden impatience she wriggled out of her chair and dropped onto the ground. She picked up a twig and broke off the crooked end of it until she had a sharp probe. Then she began to root into the grass. "After all," she said, "I know it's Lucy's dress, but she hardly ever wears it and we've got to be practical since we have no money. What do *you* think, Jane?"

Nina had to ask twice, for Jane's mind was always slow to move from one channel to another. When she finally understood the import of Nina's question she turned to Lucy and asked what she thought about it.

"Nothing," Lucy said.

"But you must think something. After all, it's your dress."

"That's so," Lucy said. "It's my dress."

There was a pause; a pause suddenly tense. Nina was now on the grass concentrating on forcing the twig straight down into the earth without breaking it.

Jane said, "I don't see why you can't let Nina have it, Lucy. After all, it's the practical thing to do. You won't be using it."

Lucy was quite still in her deck chair. The cloud was still also, and so was the air; so was everything outside herself.

"I wear it at your recitals," she said at last.

She glanced at Jane and turned away, feeling the flush that was beginning to suffuse her cheeks.

Jane said, "But that's utter nonsense! I know it's a pretty dress, but after all – there won't be a recital till next winter. In the meantime, I don't see why Nina can't get some use out of it."

"But I –" Lucy was unable to say anything more.

Jane looked down at her nails. "I don't see how we can afford a new dress for Nina right now," she said finally.

"And of course, we must be practical," Lucy said.

Jane lifted her chin sharply, tried to calculate Lucy's expression, and failed.

"Really, Lucy – I do wish you wouldn't be so difficult. Sometimes I don't understand you at all."

Lucy leaned forward and rose slowly from the deck chair. Without answering, she began to gather up the plates, knives, and glasses, and stack them on the tray.

"Lucy," Jane said, with quiet determination, "please don't be foolish. Hurt feelings are a luxury none of us can afford."

Still Lucy did not answer. She lifted the tray and carried it into the kitchen. A strained silence lingered behind her in the garden. Nina was affecting to concentrate on a colony of ants she had disturbed with her twig. Jane's face glowed slightly in the heat as she sat forward on the edge of her chair, knees pressed together and angled slightly to one side.

"I wish you'd be more considerate of your sister," she said to Nina. Her voice was firm to keep out of it the sadness of her own nature. "I know you've been a great help about the house this summer, but I *was* thinking perhaps you could help Lucy a little more. After all, housework gets awfully monotonous."

"Next summer if I have any luck I'll get a job and be out of here." Nina forgot all about the ants and scrambled to her feet. She went back to her chair again, her young face bright with annoyance. Her voice was petulant, but it was the innocent, unconscious petulance of a very young girl who only half guesses the import of what she says.

"But I don't see why she has to be so selfish. Dresses don't mean a thing to Lucy."

Pan got up and stretched with a yawn, looked around, made a sudden dart at a fly, then trotted slowly over to where Nina was sitting.

Jane suddenly made up her mind. "Go down to Overstreet's this afternoon. They're having a sale. I think we should be able to afford one dress. After all – if a thing is needed, it can hardly be called an extravagance, can it?"

The petulance vanished from Nina's face. She jumped up, her yellow hair flopping and shining in the sun, and to Jane at that moment her happy prettiness was worth the price of any dress in town. She balanced precariously on the arm of Jane's chair.

"You're so nice to me, Jane."

"Don't be silly," Jane said.

"But everyone knows you're wonderful. Everyone in town."

Jane pushed her firmly away. "And whatever you get, be sure it's suitable."

Nina sat on the edge of the table. It began to tip and she scrambled closer to its centre of gravity. Leaning there, her body lithely twisted, she concentrated with sudden eager interest on the grain of the wood.

"Jane," she said in a low voice, "why is Lucy like that?"

From where Nina was sprawling she could not see the look of acute embarrassment which appeared on her sister's face.

"That's a remarkably silly thing to say."

"But why –" Nina began.

"It hasn't been easy for Lucy, if that's what you mean. It's not easy for any girl to be ill in bed for three years in her mid-teens."

"But that was years and years ago. Lucy isn't sick any more. I'm talking about now."

There was a deep silence to which Jane was sensitive and Nina was not. Nina broke it abruptly.

"Do you think Lucy will ever get married?"

"Well …" Jane hesitated and swallowed. Then her voice became briskly matter-of-fact. "Lucy's far more competent than a lot of people imagine. She's a splendid housekeeper. And she has all sorts of ideas, some of them very practical."

Nina, still looking at the grain in the white pine, her falling hair hiding her profile, smiled quietly. "You know she won't, of course. Nobody would ever want to marry Lucy."

Jane rose from her chair and regarded her young sister for a moment, her small mouth very straight. Then she walked into the house.

Insects droned, the cat slept, the heat brooded like something in leash. Pan leaped onto the table and pressed his wet muzzle against Nina's bare forearm. For a moment she fondled him, then pushed him off to the ground.

"Come on, Pan! Let's go swimming!"

Her hair waved up and down as she ran into the house.

THAT evening after supper Lucy went alone into the garden to inspect her flowers before it got too dark to see them. In full sunshine the garden was unchangingly brilliant, but in the morning and evening the flowers were like an assembly of living things, resting in the evening, in the morning like children eager to show how fresh they were after the night and how much they had grown. Now the hyperion lilies had almost closed, but in the gathering darkness the nicotianas had opened and were filling the air with fragrance. A sickle moon was in the sky, half hidden by the upper branches of a maple tree. One pale star was visible beside it.

She bent to smell the white blossoms, saw in the half-light a small patch of crab grass beside them, and stooped to pull it out. When the back door of the Frasers' house opened and closed she stood up, and looking over the hedge she saw Bruce Fraser strolling over the grass with his hands in the pockets of his white duck trousers.

"I came out earlier," he said. "Where were you?"

"Hello, Bruce." Her voice was warm. "Washing dishes, probably."

He passed down the line of the hedge until it yielded to a wooden fence. Then he vaulted over, landing on his toes. Tall, thin, and smiling, he approached Lucy, squeezed her hand, and impulsively put his arm about her shoulders to give her a quick sideways hug. She read no more into the gesture than was intended. He dropped into one of the deck chairs under the apple tree, clasped his hands behind his head, and looked up at the sky. After pulling a few more weeds, she came and sat in the chair nearest him. He sighed luxuriantly, an eager, animal sound that came from his healthy joy in being alive on a fine evening.

"It's good to be back." He was still looking up at the sky. "You know, this town could be made into one of the loveliest places in the world. Pull down the brick buildings on King Street. Rip that damned-fool top off the post office. Build little quays along the lake front and plant them with trees. Recruit a permanent town orchestra. All we'd need would be the money and a new population. Ever thought about it yourself?"

"Often," she said smiling.

"What have you been reading lately?"

"Oh, nothing much. A few novels. I found a wonderful new book on botany, but all it did was show me how little I know."

"I don't believe it. Whenever I think of Grenville and how ignorant it is, I remember you. You know everything."

She laughed. "That's a terrible thing to say about a girl, even if it were true."

"Dear old Grenville! It breeds us modest. No beer, no vice, no nuthin'. You haven't any beer, have you?"

"How I wish we did!"

"In Montreal I floated in it. It was all you could do on hot nights – walk the street, climb the mountain, or drink beer. The taverns reek. You pass their open doors and a wet malty gush of air comes out at you like a cow's breath. I loved them." He twisted his long body sideways and looked at her. "While we're on the subject – have you heard the latest on Wes Muchmore? Remember when he was running for mayor he promised he'd do something for the young men? Well, he's done it. He's had the government liquor commission moved into the back part of town on Dufferin Street, around the corner from the railroad station. Now the boys can get their booze without being seen by their betters as they come and go. But the best part is this. Jonathan Eldridge owns the building where the commission used to be, and he collected a sweet rent on it month by month. Wes told him solemnly he was sure he'd feel better in his mind now that no liquor was being sold on his property. Jonathan, never allowing a drop in his own house, he had no answer for that one. You've got to admit Wes has his points."

Bruce lifted his knees, hooked his heels over the crossbar of the chair, and began to talk about Montreal. History was his special subject, but he had always had an insatiable curiosity to know as much as he could about everything. So he had been attending the Summer School at McGill. Lucy often wondered if Bruce had any clear idea of what he wanted to do with his life. He wasn't making enough money to be really independent and his father was exceedingly ambitious for him. Since graduating from Queen's University four years ago he had been teaching in a private school in Toronto. But he was not a man who fitted easily into the modern scheme of things, which Lucy, with a shrewdness more intuitive than conscious, assumed was better adapted for misfits than for whole men. Apparently Bruce wanted to be a whole man, but during the last four years he had at least discovered something of what he was up against in becoming one. The only jobs available existed for specialists.

He finished talking, and for a time silence settled in the garden. Lucy's hand, dropping over the side of the low chair, touched grass. It was already damp. The August night had come in quickly. The sickle moon had ridden out from behind the trees and now the garden was dark. She knew that Bruce had formed the habit of thinking of her as Nina's older sister, as she always thought of him as the boy next door. Yet he was often present in her mind; rather like an extra dimension, the only person she knew who could occasionally feel about things as she did herself. When she planned new groupings in her garden she wondered if he would notice them. When she read new books, she felt a desire to talk to him about them.

Bruce's voice breaking into the silence, was lower. "I used to think about this garden on hot nights when I was in Montreal. It's funny – when I'm away from Grenville, the chief thing I remember is you working on your flowers here."

Lucy waited quietly.

"These Ontario towns – everyone says they're narrow-minded and dull. I've been known to say the same myself. But when I think of you and what you've done to your place, the description doesn't fit any more."

She had an image of someone cast away on a raft on a quiet sea under the stars; of a ship coming over the horizon and drawing near.

His voice went on. "*Il faut cultiver votre jardin* – people have been praising Voltaire for two centuries for writing that, though neither he nor they ever dreamed of taking his advice. But you've actually done it. You're the only person I know who has. With the world falling to pieces all around you."

His last words made her smile faintly in the darkness; made her like him, too, as some women like a man who is completely removed from a woman's world and can't begin to understand a woman's motives. It was natural for Bruce to link her garden with a political and philosophical idea. Lucy did not expect him to know that the real reason why she spent so many hours over her plants was because she had no children.

Still smiling, she asked, "What makes you think I'm contented, Bruce?"

"Because it's so obvious that you are. Everybody else around here thinks Neville Chamberlain's a great man. They believe it automatically because he's Prime Minister of Great Britain. But you know what's going on as well as I do, and you're still contented. It's wonderful."

"My Uncle Matt wouldn't agree with you. He told me this morning I ought to get out of Grenville."

"What does he know about you?"

The vessel which had neared her solitude was already sailing past. "If you wanted to grow a new flower, Bruce, or a new vegetable – I mean something entirely different, a mutation – where would you choose to live?"

"I don't know! Does it make any difference?"

"It makes quite a lot. Burbank went to California. I don't think I ever realized what a hard country this is until I seriously tried to grow flowers in it."

"You mean, you've really wanted to get away, too?"

"I suppose if I'd wanted to go badly enough I'd have left years ago. One gets used to things. A woman's life in a town like this consists in getting used to many things she knows aren't right."

"I'd hate to see you leave. After all – think how we'd miss the garden."

Her chin lifted as she glanced away from the white blur of his shirt and face and leaned back to look at the moon. Now the passing ship had sailed on to the horizon. Bruce was too young, he was too engrossed in his own problems – in trying to understand the surfaces of so many different things – to be able to feel what lay within her, or even to know it was there. Like most of the men she had met, he looked for nothing in a woman's mind but some reflection of his own. And besides, he was a Grenville boy who wanted to be a success in the world outside. His family background had not been as strict as her own, but he was conscious of the pressure of his father's will driving him ahead, condemning him for being impractical. This, more than anything else, had driven him into revolt against the whole Grenville attitude. Yet he had revolted far less than he imagined. The moment her voice had conveyed the hint of a deep personal emotion he had recoiled from her involuntarily. Generations of Calvinism had made them all afraid of themselves. The great emotions, love and fear and hate and desire, could break like thunderclaps in his mind as in hers, and because of their training they would both try to conceal them with matter-of-fact words or a quick change of subject.

And now she spoke lightly to change the mood. "I was reading a book about an American who'd been in Russia. Apparently the Russians eat a heavy protein diet with hardly any greens. One day on a train to Kiev the American woke up with the insides of his cheeks swollen, craving fruit. He found two honeydew melons in the dining car, sitting in a bowl like decorations. He bought them and ate them, and the swellings subsided within fifteen minutes. He'd never eaten a honeydew before. The Russians told him it was an American fruit and of course they added that one day one of their own scientists would produce something better. It was only then that he realized that Luther Burbank was one of the greatest Americans who ever lived."

There was another silence. Then Bruce said, "I never guessed you took your work that seriously."

"I don't, really. I hardly know anything important about it. But I know I could learn if I had the chance, and sometimes I think it would be wonderful to work for a few years in one of those experimental nurseries in California."

"Then what? Come back and start one here?"

"I don't know. It's just a crazy notion. It's so hard to do the same things here. People wouldn't give you any support if you did."

He took the thought away from her and changed it. "You've got to be fifty years old in Canada before they give you a chance to do anything."

"Is it the same in Montreal?"

"Probably. I don't know. It's all Canada." He was remote from her now, remote even from the garden and the beauty of the night. It was obvious that Montreal had made an impression on him, for apart from Toronto it was the only great city he had ever seen.

"Montreal is tolerant and I found it exciting. Under the surface I have an idea it's beautifully immoral. Anyway, you don't feel as if the whole damned neighbourhood was peeping over your shoulder all the time. You realize Canada is a hell of a lot more than the Province of Ontario. And I liked the French-Canadians. I liked them fine. They may be priest-ridden, but hell, there's only one priest to a village and here we've got about five thousand neighbours to check up on us." He pulled out a packet of cigarettes and lit one. "One night I couldn't sleep. Do nights like that ever get you – when the moon is behind a floor of clouds and everything is pale and hot? I looked out the window and saw some women walking along Sherbrooke Street. So I got up and dressed and began walking myself." His voice rose eagerly. "It's terrific, what you can see in the back streets of that city after dark on a hot night down in the east end. It's not Canada at all down there. I saw the sun rise over the Jacques Cartier Bridge, and there was the city, and the grain elevators catching the first light, and a Cunard liner with a red funnel and white decks and a black hull, and a few seagulls screaming. I was absolutely alone."

Lucy had heard these outbursts of description from Bruce before. Sometimes she wondered if he used them on others, but she rather doubted it. Most people in Grenville would be suspicious of a turn of mind like his.

"Would you like to hear what that night produced?" he said shyly.

"I'd love to."

He quoted a poem he had written. It was conventional, beginning with a general mood like that of Wordsworth's from Westminster Bridge. The middle part contained a passage about sin like a long-eared animal slipping softly around corners under arc lamps while unseen fingers scratched furtively on dark window panes and a steamer's horn throbbed like doom up the narrow trench of deBouillon Street. Then the sun had risen, the river was peaceful, and everything became clean again.

Lucy said with sincerity that she liked it. She wondered if the summer had given him any experience with women, but her instinct told her that the poem itself was proof that it had not.

His mood changed. "Well, it looks as if I'll be going to Europe after all."

"What do you mean? Bruce! You haven't got a scholarship, have you?"

"Don't you read the newspapers?"

Her face fell. Two years ago he had been a candidate for a Rhodes Scholarship and his failure to win it had been a bitter blow to his father.

"I met a Frenchman in Montreal," Bruce said. "He was somebody quite important in the French Government over here on some sort of a mission. He addressed the Summer School one evening, and afterwards we had him upstairs in one of the rooms in the residence. After he'd had something to drink he took his hair down and said war was inevitable because the decent powers had no will left. We're all decadent, he said." Bruce became tense once more. "I think he's crazy. I don't feel decadent. The whole situation seems perfectly clear to me. It's just a matter of organization. For the first time people have reached the point where nobody need be in want any more. Everyone could have good jobs and get married. The battle against nature has been won, but of course the capitalists are all old men and ..."

Lucy listened to a familiar thesis, the litany of the young men of the 1930s, whose political prayer-books were diluted Marx, whose sermons appeared every week in *The New Republic* and *The Nation*, in so many little magazines under so many various suns. Surely, she thought, Bruce knew better than to believe that the battle against nature had been won.

"Well," he ended, "I suppose going over at the government's expense would at least be one way of seeing Oxford and Paris."

She knew then, with a feeling of deep indignation that it had to be so, that his instincts, unlike the top-surface of his mind, were half-welcoming the coming war and were half-grateful for the appalling stupidity of the people who ran the world. It was easier to curse Hitler and Mussolini, whom he hated and had never seen, than to curse his father, whom he knew and loved. She knew the ideology did not lie deep in him. Were it not for the Depression he might not be frustrated at all, for he had always been able to get joy out of being alive whenever the pressure of his father's opinion wasn't forcing him to be a success at he knew not what. And of course Bruce was hungry for women. She knew that his favourite novel was *A Farewell to Arms*. She wondered how often he had pictured himself as Hemingway's hero, lying in bed in an Italian hospital watching the swallows hunting over the roofs, the bottle beside him, waiting for the girl to come, the whole situation four thousand miles away from his father and Grenville. "... but that was in another country. And besides, the wench is dead." The man who used that quotation knew puritans.

A door slammed at the back of the house.

"Lucy – what are you doing out there?"

Nina's voice came through the screen door from the kitchen. It was now full night, but Nina was able to recognize the white patch of shirt and ducks reclining in the deck chair facing her sister. The door opened and her lithe figure, outlined against the kitchen light, nearly tumbled down the steps.

"Why, it's Bruce! When did you get back? How are you?"

He rose and took her outstretched hand with a pleasure neither Lucy nor Nina failed to observe. Nina came close to him: soft, slim, and innocent, holding his hand a moment longer than was necessary, guiding it with a movement apparently absent-minded to her side between them. But there was an edge to her voice as she spoke to her sister.

"You might have told me he was here!"

Bruce picked up the empty chair and turned it around so that Nina could sit beside him.

"Have you forgotten all about me while you were away?" she asked him.

Lucy knew she was not wanted in the garden any more. She had neared his loneliness, knowing it was there, perhaps knowing what caused it, but she had been helpless to touch it. Now she would have to leave him with Nina. After a while he would probably kiss her and Nina's vanity would be flattered. She would make him feel she had granted a great favour and afterwards Bruce would go home and be more restless than ever.

Nina's voice was running on. "We've had all sorts of people here while you were gone. A cousin of Mary Eldridge's and Helen Macdonell's roommate stayed for a week. You don't know what you missed. And of course, Steve Lassiter at the Ceramic. You've heard about him!"

Why did Nina insist on calling Mr. Lassiter by an abbreviation of his Christian name when she had not even met him and would be punctiliously correct if she did? It was one of her mannerisms which grated on Lucy. Away from Jane, Nina worked diligently at imitating the heedless, gossipy girls who had drunk milk shakes in the Manhattan Pharmacy in their high-school days, and now at college probably drank cokes at another soda fountain just like the old one. And yet, perhaps Nina was not imitating the other girls at all. Perhaps that was just what she was like. Why not, if she wanted to be?

Lucy rose quietly and stood for a moment beside her chair, looking up at a sky which had never seemed vaster, more luminous, more mysterious with distance. The moon was about to set. Its lower horn was behind the trees, and in another twenty minutes it would be gone. She began to move slowly toward the kitchen door. Seeing her go, Nina pulled her chair closer to Bruce. But almost at once she twisted her neck around with a movement that made her hair tumble, and while one hand pushed it back into place, she called to her sister.

"Lucy ... I'm sure there's some ginger ale and grape juice in the icebox. Bring some out, will you? Like a dear?"

It was only then that Bruce realized Lucy had left. He turned around.

"Lucy – please don't go!"

Pausing on the top step, she saw the boy and girl like two blurs in the gathered darkness of the garden.

"Bruce's taste runs to beer, not grape juice," she said, and shut the screen door behind her as she went inside.

She walked through the house to the front hall. Through the open door of the living room she could see Jane reading in an armchair, under a shaded light. Jane looked up enquiringly.

"It's such a lovely night," Lucy said, "I think I'll go down to the beach for a while."

Jane's eyes returned to her book. "You won't be late, of course."

LUCY closed the door behind her, went down the path to the side-walk, and walked down to the common. From the belvedere came a faint murmur of voices and a girl's low laugh. She crossed the common, but it was only after she reached the shore that the tremors of anger and humiliation faded away. Far down the beach the keel of a rowboat scraped the sand, and a few minutes later children's voices sounded as they moved up the beach and across the common under the trees. Their high voices were healing in the darkness. She imagined them walking home, growing sleepier with every step, then going upstairs with their hair tousled while they protested to their mothers that their hands and faces were not dirty at all, that they had only been at the lake and how could they get dirty there, and their mothers standing firmly by to make sure they washed before turning in. Finally she imagined the children small in their beds, thumbing their eyes to keep awake long enough to tell about the wonderful day they had passed. Then the eyes closing. The lights going out in the rooms. Their mothers standing quietly in the darkness listening for the deep breathing to begin. Then darkness and the long rest before the sun burst into their rooms in the morning, and their eyes opened in wonder to see it.

The voices faded, leaving Lucy alone. After the moon set there was a great depth of stars. She sat on a log with her hands clasped about her knees. Warm with summer, the trees shrouding the common were still, but the whole night was alive. The deep darkness of an inland night throbbed with thousands of crickets and katydids, the velvet pulse of their noise broken occasionally by a dog's bark, by the muted blasts of motor horns on the main highway, by men's voices abruptly loud as they talked unseen crossing the common. Sitting alone on the beach Lucy was on the edge of a vast continuum of darkness, the darkness of the continental land behind her as she looked out at the residual light gleaming faintly on the surface of the lake. She told herself she was never less solitary than when she was alone.

But she had no wish to be alone, any more than she had a wish to make a frantic, unnatural effort to surround herself with company. It was the life prescribed within the family which had isolated Jane, Nina, and herself. Bruce Fraser knew that. McCunn knew it. Probably a good many people in the town knew it also. But none of them knew it as well as she did herself. None of those who had thought of her father as a cold, harsh man had understood that he had never been cold and that his harshness had mainly been a form of punishment directed against himself.

Lucy remembered his heavy-boned Scottish face as it appeared in his tender moments. These had been more frequent than the neighbours ever guessed. She remembered him sitting in his long chair reading Walter Scott or British history, sometimes demanding silence while he read a passage aloud to the family. She remembered him passing the plate on Sundays in the church, always stiffening slightly as he reached the family pew; and afterwards, at the Sunday-noon dinner of roast beef and browned potatoes, while the family was silent, pointing out to his wife just how bad the sermon had been. She remembered how, when she was very ill, he had come at unexpected times into her room to ask gruffly how she felt, fiddling about to adjust the window in an effort to show his affection while seeming to be doing something practical. The most vivid recollection of all was of the time when she had run a high fever and Dr. Fraser had been coming and going all day. Her father had knelt at her bedside and prayed aloud for half an hour, asking God to forgive him, apparently thinking Lucy was unconscious and unable to hear him.

John Knox Cameron had been no simple religious fanatic, nor in the ordinary sense of the word had he been a harsh or cruel man. He had been an inspector of schools for the county, and in his work he had shown ability and great energy. His knowledge had been considerable, enough to have passed for culture anywhere, but he had never permitted it to give him pleasure. In Grenville he had seemed something of a character because he had always worn old-fashioned stiff white collars that came so high on his neck he could hardly lower his chin. With townspeople he had been formal, distant, and in their eyes forbidding.

Yet whenever he made his rounds of the country schools he had seemed a very different sort of man. He had dressed like a farmer on Sunday, wearing pepper-and-salt suits of rough cloth bought in country stores and the kind of high leather boots lumbermen use. He could talk to farmers about their problems as one man to another, and in the country classrooms he had been famous for a heavy-handed Scottish humor both teachers and children had understood. At least a hundred men and women, plainly dressed, had come in from villages all over the county to attend his funeral.

Lucy remembered her mother saying to her the week after his death, "You know, your father never really loved me. He once wanted to marry another girl, but her parents told your father he ought to have been ashamed of himself wanting to marry a girl like that when he had no money to support her in the style to which she was accustomed. That was a cruel thing to say to him, but the Arkwrights were always hard people and much too big for themselves before *they* lost *their* money. Your father was a loyal man, Lucy. We must always remember that. He was staunch."

And Lucy's mother – what was she? A quiet woman, fiercely protective, yet dominated totally by her husband. Perhaps that was why Jane felt secure in the old house? Perhaps that was also why she found it so necessary to believe she had taken her father's place in it, and to assume, as he had done, that the rest of the world was hostile?

Lucy did not know for sure about Jane. But she did know that this old house, which her father had bought from his wife's uncle, had meant something very special to him. The purchase of the house had been one of the great successes of his life. As a boy he had never known a home of his own. On his death he had been haunted by the fear that he had not been able to leave enough money to keep it up. The house had been a symbol to him, and the symbol had been a fortress.

There were some dusty old pictures in the attic which had told Lucy their own story. There had been a grandfather who drank and had knocked over a lamp which had set fire to his house one freezing night when Lucy's father had been a small boy; that night John Knox Cameron had lost both his parents, and he himself had been rescued by a neighbour. There were pictures of two maiden aunts, raw-boned Scotch women who had brought Lucy's father up and had made his life a Calvinistic horror, forbidding him toys as a child, making him ashamed of his own lustiness when he grew older. There was one picture of John Knox himself, preserved from his college days. It showed a young man with reddish hair and a daring, almost a desperate, cast of features. Lucy knew when she saw that picture that her father's iron self-control had been acquired. It could never have been natural to a man with a face like that.

Lucy rose from the log and looked out at the lake. All the earlier violence of the family had sunk now, like stones beneath the surface. Did it still lie there, heavy like stones? Did the violence of all the men who had broken this hard country lie submerged, too? Ontario had not always lain rigid under this glaze of respectability.

In the semi-darkness of the lake she watched a sailboat drift in to anchorage. It was a large yacht with a diesel auxiliary, probably cruising down from Toronto to the Thousand Islands. She heard the rings clatter as the mainsail fell to the deck. There was a heavy plunge as the anchor was thrown. A few minutes later a series of ripples broke on the sand before her. Then the lake was flat again, and under its stillness, the cold, heavy, invisible stones.

Lucy began to walk slowly along the shore, her hands in the pockets of her dress. She did not pity herself. Understanding had been a purifier. She had learned the beginnings of understanding in her teens, during the years of her illness. Even then she had sensed that for the rest of their lives she and Jane would bear the weight of the merciless religion which her father's aunts had inflicted upon him. It was then that she learned how true it was that the evil men do lives after them.

For the pattern set by her father had remained. The three sisters were held together by the heritage of their father's fierce sense of protection, but they were divided by the cleavages in their parents' minds.

During Lucy's illness, with the life of the whole household revolving around her bed, the growing Nina had felt herself neglected. She had become dependent on Jane whom she half feared, and envious of Lucy with a resentment no less deep because it was unconscious. Worse than anything else was the way both Jane and Nina had accepted the strange picture their father had made of Lucy. Like most sincere Calvinists, he had believed that unless he anticipated the worst in his imagination, the worst was sure to happen in fact. So, just in proportion as he was eager for Lucy to be well, to be a daughter of whom he could be proud, he had convinced himself, as well as her sisters, that she was different from other girls and that no one could expect her to live a completely normal life. He spoke of her constantly as "poor Lucy." By the time she was eighteen, they had all come to take it for granted that she would never marry.

When she had reached the wire fence surrounding the property of the Ceramic Company, Lucy saw the lights on the cement dock that ran out into the water. A small lake-boat was tied up at the dock and a light on its deck blinked on and off as an unseen sailor moved back and forth in front of it in the darkness.

She turned and walked back again. The images of her father's aunts returned, and with them, a rush of indignation and a rise of self-assertive confidence. It was absurd that these two women she had never seen, so ignorant they believed even the misprints in the Bible were sacred, should bind their power into the third generation. Knowledge had power too. She knew what they had done to her father and what her father had done to her. Knowledge was the only power in the world which could undo the chain of evil men left behind them.

Coming back to the log she sat down again. The flat expanse of the lake now glowed with stars. There were muffled sounds from the yacht as the crew talked in the cabin. The riding lights of two vessels neared each other about half a mile from the shore. Turning inland she saw lighted windows glowing here and there through breaks in the trees. Yes, there was knowledge. It exorcised the past from the present. Now this whole night was throbbing with present life, the only thing of meaning and merit; insects sang, unseen crews on the vessels went about their business, in all the nearby houses plain people were living out their time. Knowledge could make them all free. There was also love. A fire of hungry love smouldered hotly in the whole Cameron family and always had. The three sisters were bound warmly to one another; in spite of the confusions and jealousies, their lives were entwined like the shoots of a convolvulus.

The two ships had passed each other and now their lights were drawing apart. A soft undulation in the surface of the lake swelled slowly inward, collapsed with a rushing sound that travelled rapidly away for a hundred yards down the sand, bursting as it went with a continuous rush of soft laughter.

A quick thrill of delight passed through Lucy's body and gave her a prickly feeling at her finger tips and the roots of her hair. She knew what she was, if no one else did. Her lips moved.

When whispering sounds do softly steal
With creeping passion through the heart
And when at every touch we feel
Our senses beat and bear a part;
When threads can make
A heart-string shake ...

One thing had stood by her, and she had learned how to foster it. She had learned how to discover beauty when no one else was near. Through many winters she had memorized the stark outlines of naked trees silhouetted against freezing skies. She had strolled in the autumn through side streets, watching smoke rise from chimneys against pure northern colours, knowing that red-faced housewives were cooking roasts, pumpkin pies, and root vegetables for men coming home from work and boys tired from chores and football. It was the kind of beauty she understood, the kind which exists almost without knowledge of good and evil, probably the only kind possible in a puritan town.

Softened by distance, the bells under the cruet-shaped cupola on the post office struck ten times. Lucy got to her feet, then her silhouette faded from the shore and merged with the deep darkness under the trees as she crossed the common on her way home.

Tomorrow she would cook three meals, dust the rooms, make the beds, buy a few groceries, work in the garden. In the afternoon it would be her turn to serve an hour at the desk of the public library. Tomorrow would be just another summer day.

THE Grenville Public Library occupied one corner of the ground floor of the courthouse, and the ledges of its high dusty windows were only four feet above the sidewalk. It was therefore possible for Lucy, turning her eyes sideways from the desk in an idle moment, to find herself staring directly into the eyes of Stephen Lassiter as he looked in at her from the street. For an instant their eyes met. He smiled at her and she smiled casually back, as she would at someone she had met but did not know well. Then, as rapidly as if she had been stung, she jerked her eyes away.

She remembered that it was only yesterday when she had told Nina she had met Stephen Lassiter, and Nina was in the library now. A flush rose from her throat to her cheeks. Yet because she was free of all nervous gestures, this heightened colour merely accentuated the fine texture of her skin and combined with her wide-set eyes to give her an air of grace she never knew she had. Lassiter saw the change in her face and saw her look away. When Lucy glanced toward the window again, he had disappeared.

She drew a deep breath and slowly let it out. Already her mind had set the scene she imagined would occur if Lassiter entered the library. Already she could see Nina coming forward to be introduced to him; Nina's china-blue eyes, innocently shrewd, darting from Lassiter's face to hers, and then narrowing as she realized that Lucy had never met him at all, and that the trivial lie Lucy had told her proved that her sister was a grotesque sort of woman, the pitiful kind one read about in so many of these library books, who invented romantic incidents which had never happened in order to fill up the blankness of her life. Wildly exaggerating the embarrassment of her position, Lucy was unable for a few moments to think at all.

She got up from the desk and crossed to the magazine table. A blue-suited man with white hair, a red face, and a vast chin oozing out of his collar, was puttering over a pile of *Blackwoods* at one end of it. She straightened a stack of government bulletins which nobody ever read, and returned to her desk with some of her composure recovered. She remembered the night before. The night before, alone on the shore, she had told herself bravely that knowledge had made her free. It was bitter to admit that a woman like herself, devoid of prestige because she had no home or function of her own, could ever allow a trivial situation like this to matter.

"Lucy?"

It was Nina's voice from behind the first stack.

"Yes?"

"You know that book by Aldous Huxley you were reading?"

"Yes."

Nina, still behind the stack and indifferent to the man at the magazine table and the old lady behind the first stack: "What was the name of it? I'd like to read it. After all, you did."

With the instinctive hypocrisy of a shy person defending herself against a possible situation by pretending the situation doesn't exist, Lucy rejected the obvious retort and moved eagerly to comply with Nina's whim. She was about to join her sister behind the stack when the old lady appeared with a battered copy of a novel by Kathleen Norris. Lucy stamped the date in the back of the book, replaced a card in a file, and watched the old lady depart. Then she joined Nina.

"But you can't possibly find it here," she said. "It's among the novels under the letter H." She led her sister to the second stack. "I'm sure it's not out again. It's only a few days since I returned it."

She looked up. Her straining ears had caught footsteps approaching along the corridor. Leaving Nina where she was, she came out into the open, her eyes wary. Her flush had now disappeared. It was momentarily replaced by a dull annoyance at herself for being so vulnerable.

The footsteps passed and the door remained as it was, half ajar. Lucy sat down again and let out a deep breath of relief. Her annoyance faded out and was replaced by a warm wave of affection for the whole world: for Nina, for the white-haired man in the blue suit, even for this dull and dusty library. Apparently Lassiter was not coming in after all and she was safe.

"Lucy?" Nina was still behind the stacks. "Was it *Point Counter Point?*"

"Yes."

"I've got it, then."

Meanwhile the white-haired man in the blue suit had been eyeing Lucy covertly. His wide red face was moist under his white hair as he ambled over to the desk. He moved with a floating movement, waving his hands, and Lucy set herself to receive him, for he was Tom McCarthy, the Grenville poet.

"Ah, Miss Cameron, it was a fine thing I heard you say for Ireland when you were on duty here last week. I've been meaning to tell you. A fine thing, and one that needed to be said, and here of all places."

Lucy had no idea what he was talking about, but it didn't seem to make much difference, for McCarthy was under way.

"When I first set eyes on you, Miss Cameron, I knew you weren't at all like the rest of them here. But I've never said a word." He held one finger to his lips and winked. "And then, last week you said it."

"What did I say?"

"And have you forgotten already? What you said about William Butler Yeats? Now then – there was a poet!"

"Oh!" Lucy said. "I've often wondered if you knew Yeats when you were in Ireland, Mr. McCarthy?"

"Knew him!" McCarthy said, and put a plump hand inside his double-breasted coat. "Man and boy I knew him." The plump hand emerged from the breast pocket holding a crumpled sheet of paper. "And it's only fair to tell you something else, that in Ireland I was considered the better poet of the two."

He began to declaim a poem he had written the night before,

inspired when he had counted seven white hairs resting in the comb after he had finished combing his hair. But a solid-faced woman bounced in, talking as she came, and McCarthy stopped abruptly and stared at her in indignation. Then he put the poem back in his pocket and leaned over Lucy's desk.

"Another time, Miss Cameron? Say the word when. Another time when we're alone?"

Lucy bent her head to the book which the bouncy woman had planked down in front of her, marked it, and laid it aside. When she looked up, the poet and the bouncy woman were staring at each other with mutual distaste.

"And now," McCarthy said, "I must be getting back to my little place. Mrs. Carruthers died last night, as everybody knows." Glaring at the bouncy woman, "It was the heat, but only partly."

He floated out the door on his way to the Olivet Undertaking Parlours. As soon as he was gone, the woman leaned over the desk and nodded to the door.

"What was he saying to you when I came in?" The stage whisper was louder than her natural voice.

"He was telling me he knew William Butler Yeats."

"Oh, he did, did he! Well, I don't know who *that* was, but I know all of Tom McCarthy I ever want to know. Imagine a man like that calling himself a poet! When I die, let me tell you, I'm not going to have his horrible white hands embalming *me*!"

She left without taking out a new book, and then Nina emerged from behind the stacks with *Point Counter Point*. She went to the window and looked out, her shoulders wriggling as she leaned over the sill.

"Do you know what's outside? Steve Lassiter's LaSalle!"

Lucy pretended to concentrate on her book list. Nina left the window and sat on the edge of the desk, one neat thigh showing its contour through the strained cotton of her dress, the book in her free hand dangling at arm's length by her side.

"Lucy?" Her voice was provocative. "Where did you meet him?"

"Meet whom?"

"You know perfectly well who." Nina got up and crossed to the magazine table and began turning over the pages of an *Illustrated London News*.

"What's he like?"

"I don't know. I just met him, that's all."

"Where did you meet him?"

Lucy hesitated. Footsteps were approaching again. But they could hardly be Lassiter's. If he had been intending to come into the library, he would have been here before now. Anyway, he hadn't looked the sort of man who cared about books.

"At the tennis courts," she said.

Nina slid off the table, knocked a magazine on the floor as she did so, picked it up, and then glanced at her wrist watch.

"Bruce should have been here ten minutes ago," she said. "But he's always late for everything. What were you doing at the tennis courts?"

"Watching."

"Lucy, why don't you ever tell a person anything?"

The footsteps drew near and Lucy recognized them as Bruce Fraser's. So did Nina, who opened the door wide and stood there waiting for him to arrive. Bruce entered blinking in the light from the library windows. The corridor from which he had come was a dark place; so dark that people were always falling over the pails and mops the janitor left lying around in it.

Bruce smiled at Lucy. "Is this your day?" Then, moving toward the stacks, "I think I'll see what I can find back here."

Nina tugged him by the arm. "Come on, Bruce – you won't want a book this afternoon when you're in the lake."

He grinned cheerfully. "No, but I'll want one tonight when I'm in bed."

She continued to hold his wrist. He remained stubborn and continued to smile. Finally she went with him behind the stacks, and Lucy's eyes followed them both with affection.

For the next few minutes she was kept busy by a group of women who had come in together to return books and take out a new supply for the weekend. They stayed only a few moments because they all knew what they wanted. They brought new books from the shelves and while Lucy marked their cards they wondered aloud if it would rain for Mrs. Carruthers's funeral. Then they left, and the place was quiet except for the buzz of a bluebottle, the occasional blare of a motor horn in the street, and sporadic conversation between Nina and Bruce behind the stacks.

Lucy had nothing to do for the moment. She relaxed behind her desk and leaned back in her chair just out of reach of the sunbeam which poured like a searchlight through the window. Filled with swirling motes, the sunshine illumined this cave of a room which the local chapter of the Daughters of the Empire had conspired to make as British as *Rule, Britannia!* Directly opposite Lucy's desk was a double portrait of the King and Queen. Beside it was a signed and framed photograph of Stanley Baldwin and his pipe. Over the door hung the royal coat of arms, painted on a wooden shield by a promising art student in the high school; it displayed a sick-looking lion barely able to meet the stare of a unicorn which not only had Byronic eyes, but also a Byronic collar. On the wall behind Lucy was a vast line-engraving entitled *Mrs. Fry Reading to the Prisoners in Newgate Gaol, 1816.* Elsewhere and at random were engravings of Lord Nelson, Queen Victoria opening the Great Exhibition of 1851, the Duke of Wellington, and the Earl of Grenville. Like a bull's eye facing the door was a sign in black and white which said, QUIET, PLEASE!

Once again steps became audible in the corridor, but it was not until they reached the door that Lucy sat forward in her chair into the sunbeam and bent her eyes to the book list. Those steps were so heavy she knew they could only be Lassiter's.

She was aware that he had entered the library. She was conscious of his presence directly in front of her desk. Still she didn't look up.

"Well," Lassiter said, "it seems as if I've found the place I was looking for. This *is* the library, isn't it?"

Lucy had been in profile when he entered the room. The sunshine brought out all the highlights in her dark hair. The flush had returned to her cheeks and her quickened breathing caused a barely perceptible quiver in the soft skin of her lifted throat.

"Yes," she said quietly. "This is the library."

His voice was deep, vibrant, and American. It was quite loud enough for Nina to hear it behind the stacks, and to recognize to whom it belonged. When Lucy looked up she was conscious that Lassiter's eyes were fixed on her, and that he was smiling. His stare was so frankly interested that she could almost feel it touching her skin. She glanced away, astonished and confused. No man had ever looked at her in that way.

"You certainly keep this place well hidden," Lassiter said. He was still directly in front of the desk. "Someone told me it was in the courthouse, but a lot of help that was. Every door in this place looks the same from the outside."

As he continued to talk, Lucy's mind raced. He was so different from what she had remembered or imagined he would be. He tended to separate his words, and he spoke carefully, as though he had learned to play down the effect of ruthlessness suggested by his powerful body.

"So far," he went on, "I've been in two lawyers' offices, the furnace room, and the jail."

Lucy felt herself frozen into the core of the brief silence that followed.

Finally she said, "You're quite free to look around."

"Thanks."

Out of the corner of her eye, Lucy saw Nina sliding out from behind the stacks, an expectant look on her face. It reminded Lucy of a time years ago when she was a child. She was crossing a field on her way home from school with two boys. They knew a grass snake was hidden behind a rock and they prodded with sticks to bring it out, while Lucy stood to one side hoping it would never come. But it did come, and it looked exactly as she had expected it to look, and then the boys had picked it up and thrown it at her.

She caught Lassiter's glance swinging back from the approaching Nina to herself.

"You can take out five books at a time," she said. "Two new ones and three old ones."

Lassiter's deep voice came back at her like a tennis ball bouncing off a wall. "That's pretty generous."

By this time Nina was beside the desk, but Lucy dared not look up at her. Bruce, she supposed, was still behind the stacks. Lucy felt like wringing his neck. Why hadn't he taken Nina swimming long ago?

"Lucy?"

She looked up, and the moment she met her sister's eyes she was sure Nina had found her out. That innocently malicious, half-smiling, half-mocking expression was just beginning to form about her lips. When it did form, when it covered all of Nina's face, Lucy was sure no hole in the world would be too small to hold her. But at the same time she saw something else, and it startled her. Nina's eyes were as bold as Lassiter's own, but bold in the female way of leading a man on while risking nothing. Nina was drinking in every aspect of the American as she affected to pay him no attention whatever. Lucy lowered her eyes to the book list.

"Lucy?" Nina said again.

Then she heard, as if from a long distance, her own voice speaking. "Nina – may I present Stephen Lassiter. Mr. Lassiter, this is my sister, Nina Cameron."

Her eyes dropped, but she saw nothing on her desk except a dancing blur of typescript. She was aware that conventional remarks were being exchanged between Nina and Lassiter, and then, as one second ticked after another, she knew with a wild mixture of relief and astonishment that the situation her imagination had forecast was not going to develop. Bruce came out and Nina introduced him. He and Lassiter shook hands. Lassiter asked if he played tennis and Bruce said he didn't.

Then Lucy glanced up again. Nina's eyes met hers and she caught a look of puzzled respect in them. She saw that Bruce had already disliked Lassiter and that Lassiter had responded with a glance showing total disinterest. Then Bruce and Nina left the library, Nina telling Lassiter she hoped to see him again.

Conscious that her flush had deepened, Lucy was now confronted by one of the boldest grins she had ever in her life seen on a man's face.

"Well!" he said. "What have I been waiting for all the time I've been in this town!"

She opened her mouth to speak, to say something to apologize for her boldness, to make this American realize she was not the kind of girl he thought she was. No words came. She swallowed, and the tip of her tongue moistened her lips. Still she sat calmly.

It was this apparent tranquility which checked the sudden spurt of eager confidence in Lassiter. He failed to understand her flush, or even notice it as such. All he saw was the strange and individual grace which the high colour had imparted to her features.

"I haven't met you before, have I?" His voice was slightly hesitant, his grin had softened to a frank smile. "I've met a lot of people here, but if you'd been one of them I wouldn't have forgotten."

Lucy forced herself to face his eyes. Alone with him in the library now, she became quite cool.

"I watched you playing tennis," she said.

"Oh! Then it *was* you I saw at the courts?"

He took two steps over to the magazine table and perched on the edge of it. The table creaked under his weight.

Looking at her with a mixture of shrewdness and curious amusement, he said, "How did you know my name?"

"This is a pretty small town."

"But you knew my first name, too."

"Perhaps that makes it a smaller town still?"

Lassiter grinned. "You're telling me! You play tennis yourself?"

"Oh no, I'm not good at things like that."

"You probably could be if you tried. But I'm glad you never have. I don't like female athletes."

Her surprising sense of ease with this strange American was almost intoxicating. Still, her face remained serene, her mind active. She was still careful.

"I like watching you play. You seem awfully good." These sentences sounded so flat she groped for something she hoped would sound better. "There was such a difference between you and your opponent. In the way each of you played, I mean."

"So you noticed that?" Lassiter was interested. "That's what makes tennis fascinating. A man's game is a part of his nature, especially in tennis. A man uses what he's got. Now, Carl Bratian – he's the man I was playing with – he's such a little guy he can't hit hard. He built up a game without mistakes, and when he was good he was hard to handle. We were at Princeton together and every now and then Carl would get a good man off his game and cut him down. He took a set off Frank Shields once. He was lucky to do it, of course, and when Shields got going he blew Carl off the court. But that was pretty good, a set off Frank Shields. Right now Carl's washed up. He's been in the advertising business so long he's got no stomach left and that affects his eyes. I'm in rotten shape myself, but I'm in better shape than he is." Lassiter's voice went on, still separating the words. It had that quiet, resonant timbre which makes a good American voice one of the richest in the world. "Carl and I have always been trying to beat each other. We're good friends, but once we get out on the court something happens to us."

Lucy glanced at her wrist watch. "I should tell you," she said, "the library closes in ten minutes. We only stay open till three on Saturday afternoons."

Lassiter gave her another frank look, taking in her features, the line of her throat, her shoulders, and as much of her figure as he could without being rude. He seemed pleased by what he saw, but in such a natural way that Lucy was pleased too.

He got up from the table. "Okay," he said. "I'll look around and see what you've got."

He went behind the first stack and for a moment or two searched half-heartedly. "What happens in this town on Saturday night?" he said.

"Not very much, I'm afraid. There's a movie, of course."

"I know." There was the sound of a book falling to the floor. "I've seen the movie." There was the sound of a book being replaced. "It's a bad one."

A moment later his voice came again. "I'm lost among the *Makers of Canada*. I don't want to be rude about your country, but from the covers on these books it looks to me as if the makers all wore long underwear in the summer. Haven't you got anything new?"

Lucy joined him behind the stack. "What do you want, a novel?"

"That would be better. I like a good mystery. Sometimes I even like a good novel." He followed her to another stack. "I'm the kind of person who always gets lost in a library. In my last year in Princeton I had the key to the stack, but I used to let the desk-girls get the stuff for me."' Reaching the novel shelves, he extracted a book by Scott Fitzgerald which he held up to the light. "*The Great Gatsby*," he said. "Do you like Fitzgerald?"

"Very much."

"He's a Princeton man, too. But I like Hemingway better. Some of his stuff I've read three times."

Lassiter returned the book and looked around again. For a fraction of a second, Lucy met his eyes. They were deep brown, deeper than her own. On the court, squinting into the sun, their colour had been lost and his face had looked boyish and hard by turn. These large eyes of his both deepened and softened his expression, and she glanced away quickly, shaken by the intimacy of his stare.

"These are all the novels we have," she said. "You can help yourself."

She returned to her desk and the moment was broken. Two middle-aged women came in the door, saying loudly how thankful they were it was not quite three o'clock. Lucy sighed with relief. When Lassiter brought two books to be marked, the women were still at the desk, and as they were still talking, he gave them a quick glance and left without comment.

ON Monday morning in Grenville, waking later than usual, Stephen Lassiter lay flat on his back watching the sunshine make patterns on the flowered wallpaper of the best room on the second floor back of the Bessborough Arms. There was a cheap hunting print on the wall opposite the end of the bed; an English hunt, the Belvoir or the Bicester, he had forgotten which. With its rolling fields of intense green, with the sleek-coated horses and hounds, the picture reminded him of his boyhood. He had not belonged to a hunting family; far from it. It was the landscape in the picture which touched him: the gentle, cultivated, well-loved fields, the memory of happy days before he had learned how to worry.

He had wakened last night at four and stayed awake until six. A man could think of a lot in the two hours before dawn.

For three years as a small boy Stephen had lived in a large country house in Dutchess County. There had been lawns about the house and stately old trees, an ancient coach house and a stable with six horses. He and his sister Marcia had been taught to ride by a wizened old man who weighed less than a hundred pounds, a leathery-faced old son-of-a-bitch called Georgie Smith, who had been the greatest chewer and spitter and the dirtiest-mouthed man Stephen had ever met in his life. When Marcia and Stephen used some of the words they had learned from Georgie, their mother never reproved them – Sarah Lassiter thought it wrong to reprove a child for anything – but her husband took them out to the garage and whipped them, making them bend over a sawhorse and laying three strokes onto their backsides with a strip of brake lining so hard that Marcia screamed with rage and bit her father's hand.

To his children, Abel Lassiter had always been unpredictable because he was so busy they saw him only at stray moments, and at these times it was understood that he was irritable because he was tired, and he was tired because he was such an important man. He often informed Marcia and Stephen that their mother spoiled them, and he liked to tell them what his own father would have done to him if he had been as idle as they were. But at other times he seemed proud of them and on birthdays and Christmas he always gave them gifts of money, telling them to buy something they really wanted.

Stephen and his sister had grown up fully conscious of the difference in birth between their parents. Sarah Lassiter came from the Gresham family, old New England stock with ship-owners, mill-masters, clergymen, and finally with intellectuals behind her. She had been a pretty woman, capricious, popular with men, accustomed to a great deal of flattery, and proud of being the rebel in a conventional family. She had many relations who spoke with Harvard accents and had that careful graciousness of manner which makes the American gentry seem the most considerate people in the world. Stephen liked them, and when younger he had been at ease with them, yet he had never been able to take them seriously. The reason for this attitude was his father.

Abel Lassiter had been born on a dirt farm forty miles west of St. Louis, and when he was four years old his whole family had moved into western Kansas and homesteaded in the downland country. Abel's father had been a fierce Baptist and in his Missouri days a deacon in the church. Abel himself never bothered much about churches, but he often told Stephen there was nothing better than a Baptist church for putting an edge on a man. This was a favourite phrase of his; he would never hire a man for anything but a routine job unless he was sure he had an edge. In time, he made it a principle to hire no man with a happy face.

Stephen had never forgotten a book his father had given him once for his birthday. It was called *Great Men of America*, and apart from Thomas Edison, there was not a man in the book who was not an industrialist, a financier, or a railroad king. Their lives had seemed to Stephen depressingly similar. Each had his own variation of the same formula for success. Each had his own variation of the same look in the eyes. "Outside of Morgan," Abel Lassiter told his son, "there was hardly one of them who had it soft the way you do."

Stephen had always felt a little guilty because his boyhood had not been hard enough, and for a time in his youth he tried to make up for it by talking tough and training to be a boxer. In his first contest he beat up his opponent for three rounds but was too clumsy to score a clean knockout and the result was a bloody mess. That was how he discovered how much he hated hurting people.

Once Stephen's father took him into New York early on a Monday morning, and without explanation led him into the stock exchange. Stephen was only twelve at the time, it was a busy morning, and the boy listened in frightened amazement to hard-eyed men shouting at each other about the trading posts. His father tapped him on the shoulder and asked, "Like them?" Stephen shook his head. "Then remember this," his father said. "Any one of those men makes more money on a good day than your mother's brothers make in a year." After this he had taken his son to the ferry and crossed to Jersey City, and they drove in a street car through what seemed miles of slum streets where the people all looked foreign and dirty children brawled at the corners and darted in and out of alleys. Finally they came to the radiator factory controlled by Abel Lassiter, and Stephen observed the deferential way the foreman spoke to his father. It was a hideously ugly place. There was no splendid pageant of blazing molten steel and the machinery was not impressive. The painting of the radiators was done by individual men spraying the liquid aluminum onto the moulds. Through a cobwebbed ground-floor window some of the blighted landscape around the factory was visible with rusted metal lying in disorderly piles among scattered weeds. His father's unblinking grey eyes fixed themselves on his son. "Do you like this place?" Stephen said he hated it. "All right," his father said. "You hate it. Do you like where we live?" Stephen said he loved where they lived. "All right," his father said again. "Do you know why we can afford to live there?" He waited for an answer while Stephen hung his head. "Because two hundred men," his father said in a steady voice, "live and work in this place which you hate. You'd better get to like places like this, son. The places that make the dollars are never pretty."

It was the next year that Abel Lassiter sold his property in Dutchess County and moved into a duplex apartment in New York. "A year or two more in the country and I'd have been putting down roots," he said. "If you want to get ahead, don't buy a house. Your family will get to like it and raise hell when you want to move on." The money from the sale of the property was used as the final extra sum necessary for buying out the rest of the shareholders in the radiator factory, thus giving Abel Lassiter complete ownership.

Those were the years when Stephen went to school in Lawrenceville, while Marcia lived at home and went to a private school in the city and claimed to be much more of a New Yorker than Stephen was. The next move was to Pittsburgh. In Stephen's final year at Princeton his father moved to Cleveland, where he merged his old radiator company with a Cleveland firm which produced bathtubs and another which made toilet bowls and sinks. The result of the merger was the Sani-Quip Corporation, which became one of the largest junior competitors in the plumbing field.

After three years in Cleveland, Abel Lassiter moved to Detroit. He had long been interested in the automobile industry and had already introduced into his Cleveland plant an adaptation of auto-body presses to stamp bathtubs, toilet bowls, and sinks. The ware produced by the new process was of light and inferior quality but could be made at about a third the cost of the older products and therefore could undercut all competition.

Abel Lassiter liked Detroit, considering it the city with the greatest future in America. He had always felt a distrust for New York, mingled with a strong subterranean hostility against it because it was too powerful, too rich, and too enormous to despise. The rawness of Detroit, the acres of ugly houses where the workers lived, gave him an instinctive confidence and assurance that here he would not be likely to meet people like his wife's brothers who would judge a man by values which all his instincts proclaimed ridiculous. Here his bank account and past record could do the talking for him. Yet it was in Detroit that he ruined himself.

In 1928, going against the advice of his banking friends, he mortgaged his future to found an aircraft factory. After the crash a good many businessmen asked each other why he had done it in such a grandiose and almost defiant way, for he had always had the reputation of being a sound man, if not an especially cautious one. They might have looked inside their own minds for the answer, for it is hardly reasonable to believe that any man will do things necessary to make a million or more dollars unless he has some childhood dream to lead him on. In the case of Abel Lassiter the dream was a simple one. Railroads had trailed their names over the prairies where he grew up, and even now their names sounded magical whenever he heard them. His name would flash across the sky. Farm boys in Missouri, Kansas, Nebraska, Minnesota, Idaho, farm boys perhaps all over the world, would look up and point at the shining silver wings of the planes he would build and repeat his name as they recognized the make.

His assembly lines were set up, vast quantities of materials of all kinds were stock-piled, his safe bulged with contracts to firms all over the country when the market broke in 1929. The small bank he controlled in New Jersey was one of the first victims. Then the large banks which were financing the Detroit venture cracked down. Sani-Quip stock cataracted when the rumour went about that Abel Lassiter was no longer sound. He was forced to sell, first his control and then his last remaining stock, in the company that had been his dream. A year later his heart gave out and he died.

It was significant that it never occurred to Stephen that his father was guilty of a flagrant business mistake; that his father's real talent had not been judgment or ability to absorb knowledge but a furious drive forward which in the end he had been unable to control. Because Stephen had always feared his father, he thought of him as infallible, like God. Therefore it was inevitable that he thought of the Depression as a sort of cosmic accident.

In any case, his father's failure had changed his son's life. Stephen left his post graduate studies at MIT to go to Detroit for the funeral, and never returned to Cambridge to take his degree. He looked for a job instead. His mother was protected by her own personal inheritance which guaranteed her six thousand a year. Marcia got married two months after her father's death. Stephen was alone.

Waiting for a job to turn up in a collapsed market, he remembered the hard faces in *Great Men of America*. He realized he would now have to build a career from the ground up among men like these. It was a process he had never counted on. If his father had died with an intact fortune, Stephen's plans would have been certain. He would have sold out his interest in Sani-Quip and put all he had into the aircraft factory. After a time, when the business was firm in his hands, he would have hired the finest technicians available and, working with them, have produced a new plane of his own, and then he would have flown it around the world as Howard Hughes had done.

Instead he had been glad to take a job from one of his father's former underlings in Sani-Quip. He still remembered the glint in Ashweiler's Pennsylvania Dutch eyes the first time he entered his office. Under Ashweiler's scrutiny, he remembered one of his father's sparse sayings: "Everybody is afraid. Find out what he's afraid of and you've got him. Find out what you're afraid of yourself and keep your mouth shut about it. Then you can make your fear work for you. Fear is worth millions, both ways."

What did Stephen fear? It wasn't easy to say without sounding foolish. Certainly not people, or getting hurt. But what was the use of counting the things he didn't fear when he knew perfectly well, deep inside, what he was afraid of? Ever since he could remember he had been haunted by the feeling that he could never measure up to the men his father had tamed and mastered.

A WAGON wheel creaked on the side road leading down to the lake beside the Bessborough Arms. The sound seemed to hang poised in the silence. Then a cicada screamed. Stephen breathed heavily, telling himself it was going to be another hot day.

He loved heat. He loved his present sense of physical well-being. It was at least two months since he had wakened with a hangover. Sunday morning he had spent swimming and lying on the sand, and in the afternoon Carl Bratian, on his way back from Toronto, had stopped and played several more sets of tennis with him. He had taken Carl to the cleaner's this time. Forehand and backhand, he had lammed the ball from corner to corner with almost a perfect length; it had been one of those days when everything came off. After three sets Carl had quit, looking dead.

He was a funny little man, Carl Bratian. He was the son of immigrant parents and he had always worked twice as hard as anyone else, even when playing games. He had an infectious grin and to most people he seemed happy; yet the curious thing about him was that, in spite of this outward appearance, he was the kind of man Abel Lassiter would have hired.

Stephen's eyes closed again. Insects shrilled in the warm sunshine and he felt young again. His breathing slowed to a quiet rhythm. He liked Grenville, but it was a lonely place. At night you looked at the stars over the lake and you thought if you didn't have a woman soon you wouldn't be able to stand it. At night you thought about everything, you asked yourself vague questions, and after a few hours you felt as cheap as a man waiting for the check at the Stork Club with a dollar-fifty in his pocket. He almost fell asleep. He saw an airplane flying over a sea of clouds, then over the turning globe itself. They would do that some day, they would rocket completely clear of the world. A faint snore passed his parted lips.

"I left my shaving lotion in Toronto."

Lassiter opened his eyes and saw in the doorway, above a dressing gown of red silk, the smooth, swarthy face and the big nose of Carl Bratian.

"Look in the bathroom," he said and turned to the wall.

He closed his eyes again and presently heard Bratian's voice coming from a long distance.

"*Spring Time*! What a hell of a name for a shaving lotion!"

Lassiter heard faint slapping sounds as Bratian massaged the lotion into his skin. Carl felt undressed unless he smelled like a man who had just left the barber's chair.

"With this kind of merchandise," Bratian's voice came to him, "the name is everything. It's the principal thing you're selling – the name, the bottle, and the smell. What would a man feel like, going into a drugstore and asking for *Spring Time*? He'd feel like you did the first time you asked for Ramses."

Lassiter heard Bratian emerge and say he would see him for breakfast. Then he rolled over again and daydreamed between boyhood and manhood. Occasionally an idea shot up and nearly wakened him, then died out as the flood of images poured over, drowning it in the sea of himself.

He saw a much younger Stephen Lassiter standing against the wall of his bedroom in the old house. He was home for vacation the year he had made the school football and tennis teams for the first time. His mother had just marked up his increase in height on the wall and noted the date. He felt her fingers lightly exploring his shoulders and biceps and the special tennis muscle that made a knot like iron at the upper end of his forearm just by the elbow. He was grinning down at her. She was small and the prettiest woman in the world. Her body was frail and graceful and she had never weighed more than a hundred and three pounds. He saw the amused pride in her eyes because he, her only son, was growing so big. It was then that an idea had formed: FRAIL WOMEN LIKE POWERFUL MEN. It was true. That was the basis of his mother's fondness for his father which had survived all their quarrels and arguments. He remembered his mother's cool voice saying, "Life might have been easier for me if I'd married somebody of my own sort, but it would have been dull. When the women in a country grow stronger than the men it's a sure sign of decadence. Your father is a very strong man, Stephen, so we can afford to overlook a lot of things about him that otherwise we couldn't. Weak men are like born gentlemen. They can't afford not to be charming." His mother had been a great reader of books and she often said things like that. And she was dead accurate. My God, when you went to New York and Boston these days, the kind of men you saw in the best places! They were getting soft, all right. You saw them in the bars with long-thighed women who could have handled any three of them the same night and cried for more. He knew the look those women had. He'd seen it directed often enough at himself. He would enter a bar or merely walk across the Plaza at five in the afternoon when they were out in the street, and the looks would be exchanged as frankly as in a whorehouse. They wanted a man with a body like his who could really manhandle them, but they wanted money too, and probably they wanted money more than anything else, otherwise they wouldn't bother with some of the oyster-handed men you saw them with. They wanted change and variety, and they needed money to get it. Joyce, for instance. At first, Joyce had never been able to have too much of him. Then suddenly she had become bored, he was not varied enough for her, she said; she criticized the things he liked doing, she let him feel she had no confidence in him. Joyce was a born wanter, and whatever she gave she measured out. You never saw in her eyes the really marvellous look a woman had sometimes, the look his mother used to have, the look a small town girl like that one in the library had, the shy boldness you knew could develop into almost anything if the right man gave it a chance.

Lassiter almost fell asleep again. The sheet down to his waist, he lay over on his back while his chest heaved steadily to his breathing. A cataract of images poured through his mind. He saw men working, wheels turning, tennis balls shooting across nets, he saw a girl's legs and arms unfolding milky-white in slow motion, and then, with exquisite leisure, a bomb looping out from the open bay of an aircraft flying over New York, down into the maze of buildings between the Chrysler and the Empire State, down into a noiseless explosion that blossomed into a full-blown talisman rose.

He sat up, wide awake. He would be late for the office. He felt the familiar prick of urgency along his nerves, the feeling that he was not doing enough, that he was slipping behind. He went into the bathroom and turned on the shower, and his animal vitality returned as the cold jets bristled against his skin. He towelled and shaved and rubbed his face with the lotion Carl Bratian had used ten minutes earlier. He looked critically at the bottle. With its conventional shape and label it looked as old-fashioned as Moxie.

He returned to the bedroom and dressed. Those bottles of shaving lotion were the only things in the world he got more or less free. The little place that made them was the sole survivor of his father's varied enterprises, and now he himself was the sole owner. It netted him about eight hundred dollars a year. The little bald-headed Rahway barber who had founded the business was now its manager and sole operative. Lassiter's father had taken the place over for a bad debt, and it was the final irony of the old man's career that a converted barber shop making shaving lotion was the only one of his enterprises to weather the Depression.

In the dining room he found Bratian smoking a cigarette with a coffee cup in his hand, and Stephen broke into a wide grin. The little man was dressed like a Hollywood version of an English squire. The pebbly brown leather of his imported shoes had a dark, lustreless stain which exactly matched the shade of the Norfolk jacket he had bought, not at Brooks, but at a private tailor's he claimed was more select. His handkerchief was folded into his pocket like part of a design. But he had been unable to resist the temptation of a ring on the fourth finger of his right hand. The ring was large, glowing red, and Bratian claimed it was a genuine ruby.

"This is filthy coffee," he said as Lassiter sat down. "You know, if somebody came up here and went into the hotel business he could make a lot of money. I haven't had any decent food since I crossed the border."

Lassiter smiled at the waitress who stood near the door. She nodded and went into the kitchen, knowing that he ate the same breakfast day after day.

"What they ought to do," Bratian went on, "is take an old-fashioned-looking place and panel it like an English grill-room. There are quite a few old-looking places between here and Kingston. They have real quality. Take a place like that and fix it up with brown walnut panels and heavy-looking silver on the sideboards and a big headwaiter with a black suit and a red face. Give Americans the same kind of food they get at home, but make the surroundings look old and British. These people are stupid. They give Americans the kind of surroundings they find in Napoleon, Ohio, and then they make them eat English food as well."

Lassiter drank his orange juice and grinned. Ever since he had known the little man, Bratian had been telling him people were stupid. Bratian leaned back and looked at the clock over the door. The hands showed five minutes to nine.

"Don't you have to go to work?"

"Most of the real work is done now. I'm boss of my own time anyway. I'm working on my report for Ashweiler now."

Bratian contemplated the ceiling from behind a cloud of cigarette smoke. Lassiter's nostrils twitched as some of the smoke reached them.

"What's that weed you smoke? It stinks."

Bratian produced a gold cigarette case and snapped it open. "There's only one place in New York where you can get these. They're Greek. Look at the quality of the ash they make." He held up the end of his cigarette. "What you smoke is camel dung." He put the case away. "This firm doesn't do any advertising. They're damn fools of course, but they give you the stuff. Don't you know the more a cigarette is advertised the worse it's bound to be?"

"You ought to know."

"Your sister smokes these now. I introduced her to them."

Lassiter had begun to eat his cereal, but now he put down his spoon. "Where have you been seeing Marcia?"

Bratian showed very white teeth in a wide grin. "Everybody sees her."

"I don't."

"So she told me. I like her. I always did. She interests me. She'd been happier if she'd grown up in Europe. She's that type."

Lassiter picked up his spoon, vaguely annoyed at Bratian's air of intimacy.

"She's thinking of going to Sondberg now," Bratian went on. "She told me he's promised to fix her up so she can live in peace with her vices. You know what Marcia's like. She pretends to kid, but underneath she's a pretty serious girl. That's why I get a kick out of her, Steve. Underneath, Marcia always wants to do the right thing."

A tight expression bore down on Lassiter's mouth. "I don't know what's the matter with her. I never did. And who the hell is Sondberg?"

"The psychoanalyst. You mean to say you never heard of him?"

"Why should I have heard of him? What's the matter now? Does Marcia think she's crazy?"

Bratian grinned. "No, she's only uncomfortable. They tell me Sondberg's making a lot of money. He's the one that worked on that Catholic priest a few years ago – you know, that Father Donnelley who got himself analyzed and then told the papers that all religions rested on a guilt-complex."

"Do you take that stuff seriously?"

Bratian grinned.

"How do you always know about people like that?" Lassiter said when he got no answer. Then he finished his cereal in silence and leaned back to wait for the next course. The bacon and eggs came and he began to eat while Bratian watched him. After devouring one egg and four rashers of bacon, he laid down his knife and fork. "Look, Carl – what was behind all those questions you were asking me last night about my business?"

"Haven't you guessed?"

"I'm not a mind reader."

Bratian's face assumed an expression which Lassiter had seen on it many times before, and only lately was beginning to understand. It was an expression so ancestral that it made his English-style clothes look ridiculous. The man who wore such an expression should also be wearing a turban and long silk robes in which the limbs would move suavely. He should be sitting on cushions, not on a hard chair in an Ontario hotel. The expression flashed away, leaving a grin which showed some malice, much cynicism, and even a little affection.

"Eat your breakfast, Steve. If you've got time, we can talk about it afterwards."

"Should I be worrying?"

"Nobody should worry."

"You son of a bitch!" Lassiter said, and began to laugh.

THIS was a morning for remembering. Lassiter's own words had recalled him to another morning fifteen years ago. The place was Princeton. He had just entered the university from Lawrenceville; big, popular, and assuming correctly that the coach had heard all about him. At the first freshman practice Carl Bratian presented himself, and the big nose and swarthy skin under the brown helmet made him the most conspicuous man on the field. Under his pads, the wiry body was like a dwarf's with a humpback. He grinned at everybody, as eager to please as a newsboy at his first basketball practice in the Y.M.C.A., and Lassiter, too young to realize the cruelty of his remark, not really meaning anything by it except that he was surprised at seeing such a man on a Princeton football field, turned to a friend and said carelessly: "Who let that son of a bitch in here?"

Three weeks later he considered Carl his friend. He had tackled him so hard he broke his collarbone and knocked him out, and after the accident had visited him in the infirmary because that seemed the right thing to do. Carl pretended to be indifferent about the injury, but he was pleased to find a man of such importance in his class sitting at his bedside.

"I was stupid," he said. He had a harsh New York accent which he was later to smooth down, but even then his English was precise. If he talked tough, he talked tough like an educated man. "Your tackle is only dangerous because you're heavy and fast. If I'd broken step I'd have faded through you. I made the mistake of trying to go through you on speed."

Bratian said this with a frank grin that Stephen liked. He made no attempt to conceal or minimize his background and by the end of the afternoon Stephen felt he knew all about it.

That night in a friend's room, Stephen became the little man's champion. He claimed that Carl had more on the ball than the whole lot of them put together, and that if he didn't get into a club when his time came up it would be a damned crime. Carl had come up the hard way. He had read all sorts of books most freshmen had never heard of, and if he could get a little more weight on his ribs he'd make a smooth quarterback. He had taught himself to carry a ball by pegging down a straight row of stakes in a vacant lot in New York and spending hours a day, weeks a year, swerving through them and breaking pace as he went. As a result he had ankles like steel. He had learned to play tennis on public courts, but he had learned to play well by getting jobs as ballboy at famous courts where he could study the champions. To earn money he had done the usual variety of things, and in his last high-school year he had made almost enough to stake him through Princeton by driving trucks for a bootlegging syndicate, meeting vessels at obscure points along the Jersey coast, and running the liquor inland. He had been born in Rumania and had come to America at the age of five. His father had been a teacher of literature in the old country until he had been jailed for his politics and barred from teaching on his release. His mother was a Salonika woman, part Greek and part Syrian. In America, Carl's father had been very poor; his English was too weak for a white-collar job. He had supported himself by operating a one-room tailor shop on lower Tenth Avenue, where his wife did most of the work. His name was not Bratian, but Bratianu, and his son had been baptized Carol, not Carl.

Some time during their first winter in Princeton, Stephen made the discovery that Carl despised athletics and naturally wanted to know why he worked so hard at them. Carl had his answer.

"In this country people trust an athlete. Anyone with a face like mine needs all the trust he can get. Years from now when I say I was on the Princeton team in 1925 or 1926 people will relax."

Stephen's friendship was a great help to Bratian at Princeton. Though it failed to get him into a club, it helped make him acquainted with a variety of men who otherwise would never have bothered speaking to him. Soon Bratian had a certain following, and word got around that he was a useful man to know. When the left end of the team thought he had made a professor's daughter pregnant, Bratian knew exactly what to do and told him the name of a druggist who would fill the necessary prescription. A few days later when the football player reported in desperation that he had walked the girl nearly unconscious all the way to Penn's Neck and back in the rain, and still nothing had happened, Carl produced the name of a doctor in New York who would handle the case for three hundred dollars. "He's absolutely the best man. He has every European degree known to medicine and he's making a cool fifty thousand right now. The stockbrokers go to him."

But there were other sides to Bratian. He was one of the few undergraduates in Princeton at that time whom the professors willingly admitted was in search of a liberal education. He majored in history and studied psychology, economics, and a little biology on the side. Though the professors respected his work, none of them liked him, for quite literally he knew too much. He was aware of all the campus intrigues, and though he was always polite, he contrived to give them the feeling that he did not take them seriously.

"That man Bratian," one of them said to a colleague, "studies history as if it were something useful. What does he think he'll do – make money out of it?"

One evening after they had been drinking applejack in Stephen's room, Bratian discovered a loose button on the sleeve of his jacket. He jerked it free and put it into his pocket, and the action seemed to remind him of his parents.

"My father's sitting on the doorstep in Tenth Avenue right now, probably with a bunch of kids around him. He loves everybody. The kids are there and he's telling them stories. They're afraid to go home because their old man is drunk, or their old lady is grinding it out with some bastard who'll give her two bucks toward the rent money, but my old man isn't thinking about any of that. He's just sitting there looking like Toscanini and telling stories to the kids." Bratian knocked a book on the floor with his elbow and didn't bother to pick it up. "Do you know why they all love him, Steve?"

"Why?"

"Because he's gentle. Because they know they can kick him in the teeth and he'll only be sorry for them because they were such bastards they wanted to do it."

Stephen said nothing, embarrassed and awkward. He picked up the book and replaced it on the table.

"And here am I," Bratian said. "Me – that grew up looking at red brick tenements and smelling cooking grease, onions, and the vomit left by drunks on the staircase Saturday nights that nobody cleaned up till Monday morning. And my father was a professor once. He hasn't learned yet he's nothing but a Wop." Bratian laughed softly. "He worries about America. He worries for fear democracy isn't going to turn out quite so wonderful as he thought it would when he was in Rumania. Him – worried about America! Why don't you laugh?"

Stephen did not feel like laughing.

"But my mother," Bratian went on, "doesn't worry about anything so big. She never knew how to read or write till my father taught her. She's not good-looking and never was. But if she'd been the wife of a merchant, that merchant would have made a million dollars. If she'd been a queen down in the Balkans, her country would never have had a revolution. Every night when I'd be studying I'd feel her eyes on me. She'd be sewing. She worked all the time when she was awake, but she always knew whether I was concentrating or not. Sometimes I'd hear her move and look up and find a glass of milk beside me. It was her milk and she needed it badly, for she starved when she was a girl and her lungs were none too good. I'd protest and try to make her drink it herself but she'd look at me like steel and say, 'Do what you're told.' And I'd drink it. It was me she bothered about. She let my brother hang around the poolrooms till he became a two-bit crook, and she knew my sister was being jazzed by half the neighbourhood cats by the time she was fifteen. She let them go strictly to hell their own way because she knew there's nothing you can do with stupid people. But she never took her eyes off me, not once. She never told me not to become like my father. She didn't have to. Don't get me wrong – she didn't despise my father. She loved him. She had a heart ten times the size of her body. But her brain weighed more than even her heart did. She knew my father was a saint and there's nothing anybody can do about a saint. But she knew I wasn't a saint and that I had – in one part of my brain – some of the cogs that made my old man click the way he did. She wasn't going to let my ideas make a monkey out of me."

The two friends continued to drink applejack. Presently Lassiter asked, "Is your mother still in New York?"

"She died two weeks ago," Bratian said.

BUT there was still another side of Bratian that made him incalculable. He was a poet. He loved good music – New Orleans jazz played by coloured men and eighteenth-century classics played by the philharmonic orchestras. One night in June in their last term he and Lassiter were walking back to their rooms from a beer party, their hands in the pockets of their beer suits. It was one of those Princeton nights when the air was hot but still fresh, a spring night of moist, motionless air fragrant with the peach blossoms of nearby farms.

"God!" Bratian murmured. "Oh, God – this is lovely! The most wonderful country in the world." He began to quote poetry, though he knew Lassiter had never willingly listened to a line in his life.

> *"Look, how the floor of heaven*
> *Is thick inlaid with patines of bright gold:*
> *There's not the smallest orb which thou behold'st*
> *But in his motion like an angel sings.*

Poetry, Steve. Do you want me to apologize for it?"

Lassiter, thick-headed with beer but filled with so much vitality he would have climbed one of the elms beside the McCarter Theater if anyone had proposed it to him, began to horse Bratian around, and then announced that he himself had a poem to recite. He began in a loud voice,

> *"It was down in the Lehigh Valley,*
> *Me and my old pal Lou*
> *Were hiking along to a whorehouse*
> *And a Goddamn good one, too ...."*

He went on with the saga through several stanzas before Bratian interrupted him. "Why don't you save that for your first reunion?"

"What's the matter with reunions?"

"Mainly that big, dumb, inhibited bastards like you go to them."

"You son of a bitch," Lassiter said cheerfully. "You crazy little son of a bitch. What do you want now?"

"Have you ever seen the clerks and shop girls on Fifth Avenue looking into the windows at Tiffany's? What do I want? Hell, I grew up on the streets of New York. What do you think I want?"

A month later both of them left Princeton for good. Bratian never returned for a reunion. A week after commencement he went to work in the advertising department of the Sani-Quip Corporation, getting the job after an interview with Stephen's father. Two years later he left Sani-Quip to enter a small advertising agency on Fifty-Fourth Street. Four years after this he switched to a larger agency, taking one profitable account with him. Meanwhile, Lassiter had entered M.I.T. to take the regular course in mechanical engineering and had left without the degree after his father's bankruptcy. The fortunes of Bratian and himself were then almost directly reversed. Lassiter was starting at the bottom in Sani-Quip while Bratian had already established himself and was rising fast.

"THE trouble with Sani-Quip," Bratian said, "is that it's too big. And the trouble with you is that you're not the kind of man who wants to spend the rest of his life making fewer men turn out more bathtubs and toilets."

Through the windows of the dining room in the Bessborough Arms the song of a whitethroat burst with lucid joy. Lassiter wished he were out in the sunshine or even at his desk in the Ceramic Company working in peace on his report to Ashweiler.

"Why did you go in with them anyway?" Bratian asked.

"It was my father's company. It was a job."

"And I suppose you thought Ashweiler and the rest of them would like you on account of your father?"

Lassiter said nothing.

"Do you think I liked you the first time I saw you?"

"I never thought about it at all."

"The first time I saw you I wanted to kick you in the guts. What gives you the idea people like me and Ashweiler take naturally to someone like you?" Bratian grinned. "The funny thing is, most people like you in spite of everything. But not Ashweiler. For twenty years that jug-eared Dutchman worked for your old man. Your old man was harder, tougher, cleverer, and sharper than he was. He used to scare Ashweiler's pants off him. Yes, Mr. Lassiter ... No, Mr. Lassiter ... Just as you say, Mr. Lassiter ... I've heard him do it. And now," Bratian went on, "Ashweiler has you right there in front of his eyes and under his thumb."

Stephen thought a moment. Bratian's old power of fascinating him had returned with a rush. The little man made you feel as if the walls of the room you were sitting in were shifting and had no foundations. He made you feel that if you touched them they would jump away and leave you staring into empty space.

"Ashweiler won't be there much longer," Lassiter said. "When Stewart takes over, things will be different."

Bratian shook his head. "Look Steve – name one big established outfit that isn't filled with men waiting for somebody to die or get out. Then name one that changes its essential nature when somebody does die or get out. Sani-Quip has you taped. You've been with them too long. They won't fire you. They'll let you go on doing the same old stuff till they've sucked you dry."

Lassiter was motionless. His big body seldom gave him away by involuntary movements, but every nerve tightened as Bratian's words sucked him out of this quiet Ontario town into the bleak world of calculation for which, in spite of his father's example, he had never been prepared to take a place.

"A man like you," Bratian said, "ought to be his own boss."

"That's easy to say."

"Or get into some new engineering development on the fringes – something small enough so you can own a piece of the business."

Lassiter laid both hands palms down on the table and leaned forward. "Look here, Carl – what's the idea of making me feel lousy? I haven't done so badly."

"I'm not trying to needle you."

"Then what the hell are you trying to do?"

"I'm suggesting you get out of the Sani-Quip Corporation." He lit another of his Greek cigarettes and eyed the fine white ash critically. "You just don't happen to be a politician. In any big established outfit you've got to be a politician to get to first base. Even at Princeton the professors had to be politicians if they wanted to get beyond the rank of assistant."

Lassiter pushed back his chair and picked up the breakfast check, signed it, and left it there.

"You grew up thinking you'd own millions," Bratian said.

"Okay," Lassiter said, "you've made your point."

They left the restaurant and passed out the narrow hall to the front of the hotel. Near the door a group of American tourists, schoolteachers on holiday, were telling each other how amazing it was to find weather in Canada as hot as it was in Iowa. Lassiter stood on the veranda and looked at the street. The air above the asphalt was shaking with heat and an ice truck in front of the hotel had a puddle of water underneath it.

"This present job of mine," Lassiter said doggedly, "is pretty important. Our stuff will soon be selling all over the world. We've already got branches in Germany."

Bratian strolled out to the curb, then came back with his thumbs in the pockets of his Norfolk jacket.

"Was it your idea, getting over the tariff wall of the British Empire?"

Lassiter made no reply and Bratian changed the subject. "I'll drop you a note when I get back to New York. I've got some ideas."

They went upstairs together and while a porter took Bratian's grain-leather suitcases downstairs, Carl went into Stephen's bathroom and presently came out with the bottle of shaving lotion in his hand.

"You own the place that makes this stuff, don't you?" he said.

"It was all the old man had left. I told you about it."

Bratian unscrewed the top and smelled carefully. Then, with a delicacy that made him look more foreign than ever, he took out his folded handkerchief and sprinkled a few drops on it. He smelled again, his big nose sniffing like a dog's. Then he waved the handkerchief in the air and smelled once more.

"It lingers. At breakfast my face still felt good from it and I could still smell it."

Lassiter was impatient to get away. He was already more than an hour late at the office. "It's only some stuff a Rahway barber mixed up years ago. He's been bottling it ever since. It's nothing but alcohol and a smell."

"That's all it is now." Bratian screwed the top on the bottle and slipped it back into his pocket. "But I like the smell and there's oil in it besides alcohol. It could be called masculine. It could even be called American."

Lassiter broke into a heavy laugh. "You ought to get out of your own business. You guys talk so much balls for a living you believe it yourselves."

Once again the ancestral look appeared on Bratian's face. "How long have you been using this stuff, Steve?"

"I don't know. Years, I guess."

"Okay, that's all I wanted to know."

Five minutes later Stephen saw Bratian off to New York. A mechanic drove a shining black Cadillac roadster from a nearby garage and Carl slipped a dollar into his hand as he took his place behind the wheel. As Lassiter watched the back of the car disappear around the corner he felt empty and alone. Bratian was returning to that fabulous world of New York of which he had once been a part himself. He was going back to the city, where, no matter how many people pretended otherwise, the really successful men chose to live.

WORK made Stephen feel better and by the time the noon whistle blew he was in a much more confident frame of mind. His secretary, who had come up from Cleveland with him, left the office with enough dictation to keep her busy the rest of the afternoon. The first section of his report to Ashweiler was completed, and he was fairly well satisfied with it.

Restlessly, he got to his feet and looked out the window at the lakeboat which lay in the U-shaped dock that belonged to the Ceramic Company. Stevedores were eating out of lunchpails on the fo'c'sle head. It must be as hot as hell out there today on that deck.

As he returned to his desk, he felt a spurt of resentment against Bratian. Until this morning he had been feeling better than he had felt in years. Usually he detested small towns, but he had found Grenville pleasant. Up here he could have an illusion of being his own boss, even though he had come up fully briefed by Ashweiler and was now recommending in his report that Sani-Quip do exactly what it had intended to do anyway.

He shrugged his shoulders. "Well, Lassiter, let's say you've had a nice summer and let it go at that."

Three weeks more and he would be back in Cleveland again, looking at the same faces, going around in the same treadmill. There was not a single person in that whole city he cared if he ever saw again; a few girls, perhaps, but most of them were the kind you spent an evening with and then forgot about until you felt lonely again. He wished he worked in New York instead of Cleveland. In New York the splendour of the city belonged to everyone in it, and made a man feel larger than life. He thought of the sunset light streaming over Columbus Circle and the trees of the park, women passing, softly lit bars mysterious with women; and then taxis crawling down darkened side streets to the theatres. The theatre cabs in New York had always seemed to him to throb with a thousand secrets and expectations. They made him feel lonely as he watched them pass, yet glad of his loneliness because it was so much larger than himself, being his own response to the vibrant life around him.

As he thought about New York, the prospect of still another empty evening lying before him in Grenville became intolerable. The features of the girl he had met in the library fell into place in the front of his mind. A rare girl for a town like this. He remembered the soft curve of her throat as her chin had lifted, the skin white and soft, the shy eagerness in her eyes, and the feeling of surprised pleasure their brief meeting had given him.

He picked up a letter he had received that morning from Ashweiler and left the office with it in his hand. Jim Craig should still be around, for he never went home to lunch until nearly one o'clock. Lassiter entered Craig's office and the secretary showed him through. He handed Ashweiler's letter to Craig, and after they had discussed it for a few minutes he put the question he had come to ask.

Craig answered with demoralizing slowness. "Well, there *is* a family of that name. Three sisters, as a matter of fact."

Lassiter could feel Craig's surprise at his question. He was annoyed to realize that he might be in danger of losing face with the older man. But unless he knew the girl's first name, he didn't see how he could get in touch with her without a great deal of difficulty.

"I suppose it was Nina you met," Craig said thoughtfully. "Yes, it must have been her. They say she's turned into quite a pretty girl."

Lassiter liked Craig well enough, but the manager was fifty-five years old and took his position in Grenville too seriously. He was so careful he even chewed Sen-Sen after taking a drink.

"She's only a kid, Steve," Craig said, and waited.

Lassiter grinned. "I met the kid too. But the one I mean is well past the age of consent."

It took Craig several seconds to get the point of this remark, and when he did get it, he wasn't sure whether it was a joke or not.

"I didn't mean to suggest – well, to suggest that you –"

"I didn't, either," Lassiter said, with another grin.

They both relaxed, and Craig regarded Lassiter with a new interest.

"Well, I wish I could help you out, but the fact is, I'm pretty sure you got the name wrong." He chuckled as if at a private joke. "You know, the idea of a man like you being interested in Jane or Lucy

Cameron –" He chuckled again, a small-town man safe on his own ground. "You should have seen their father. Old John Knox Cameron would have taken the hide off a man who even asked one of his girls to a Sunday School picnic."

"Is the old man still around?"

"No," Craig said, with an amused thoughtfulness which annoyed Lassiter. "No, he's been gathered." After another chuckle he added, "What I'm trying to figure out is who you did meet."

A few minutes later Lassiter left the office in a state of mild frustration which abated as he realized he had at least come close to discovering the girl's name. It was either Jane or Lucy.

When he reached the hotel for lunch he found the hall crowded with local businessmen, and then he remembered he was supposed to be an honoured guest at the Rotary Club that day. He went upstairs to his room and washed. When he came down he heard the buzz of conversation, and listening to some of it he gathered that the news in the papers that morning had been worse than usual, for they were all talking about Hitler. They were so similar in appearance to Rotarians in any old-fashioned town in New England that he was somewhat startled to hear one of them remark to another that in politics the Americans were children and always would be, and that there was no point in anyone expecting Roosevelt to make them internationally responsible overnight.

Lassiter grinned and turned to a man he knew. "I wish you'd hurry up and join the States," he said. "Then maybe a guy like me could know where he stands. Right now I feel as if I were looking at a state of the Union just enough out of focus to make me feel cross-eyed."

THE dark hall of the Cameron house was quiet in the mid-afternoon when Nina came home from her daily swim in the lake. She let the screen door fall closed behind her and called to Lucy. There was no answer. She went through the house to the garden and saw her sister among the phlox.

"For heaven's sake, can't you ever let them alone! You can't do anything with flowers in August except pick them."

"That's exactly what I was going to do."

Nina went down the steps to the garden. "It was wonderful in the water today. You know, Bruce is a marvellous swimmer. Isn't it funny that a man who can swim like that should be such a rotten dancer?" She bent over to sniff the open blossom of a muskmallow. "I love these things. They're as rich as velvet. Bruce is taking me to the dance tonight. I wish he'd let me teach him some steps, or something. It's so dull dancing with a man who just walks around the floor and talks."

Faintly through the warm afternoon air the telephone tinkled.

"I'll get it!" Nina said, and ran back up the steps.

The telephone had been installed in the most public part of the house, in the front hall between the table and the umbrella stand, directly underneath a line-engraving showing the death of Nelson. It was an old-fashioned wall instrument with the mouthpiece on the end of a long arm. Nina unhooked the receiver and stood there, small, neat, snub-nosed, and expectant.

"Hullo!" she said.

A male voice asked if this was Miss Cameron.

"This is Nina Cameron speaking."

"Hullo! Steve Lassiter."

"Yes, I know," Nina said daintily.

A faint chuckle sounded over the wire. "I believe I met you in the library last Saturday?"

"Why yes – yes, you did."

There was a brief pause. "Well, it's another fine day."

Nina's posture relaxed as the pleasure of her anticipation grew. "Yes," she said smiling, "it certainly is."

His voice came through again. "I hope you don't think it's rude of me to call you like this."

"Oh, no. I was ... I hope you're not finding Grenville too dull."

The still air brooded in the hall. Under the sombre line-engraving Nina stood smiling, her neat figure wiggling a little because it could never be still.

"I understand there's a dance at the boat club tonight," Lassiter said. "They've given me a guest membership, you know."

Nina remembered Bruce and frowned. He'd simply have to understand that this was something special.

"Why yes, we always have a dance on Wednesday night in July and August."

There was another pause, and Nina wondered why an American of Lassiter's age from New York – she had always assumed he was from New York – should take so long to get to the point.

"The late afternoon is a bad time to call a girl, isn't it?" Lassiter said thoughtfully. "You might be having tea, or something."

"Oh, no," Nina said quickly. "I was out in the garden with Lucy."

There was another pause.

"I dropped in at the library today, but I didn't find either of you there."

"Jane was there today. She's my other sister."

She heard another chuckle over the wire. "That means Lucy's home now, then?"

"Yes, of course. Lucy's nearly always home."

"Do you mind if I speak to her?"

Nina had been growing increasingly puzzled and now she was too amazed to speak. Then a flush touched her cheeks as the idea struck her that he had been amusing himself at her expense all along.

"She's very busy," she said crisply. "Perhaps I could take a message?"

"Thanks just the same. I don't want to trouble you. I'd like to speak to her personally."

Nina's cheeks were still warm as she went through the house to the garden. "You're wanted on the phone," she called from the back steps.

Lucy took off her garden gloves and dropped them by the basket she had just filled with veronica and white lavender.

"Who is it, do you know?"

Nina gave her a sharp glance as she passed her at the foot of the steps. "I have no doubt he'll tell you himself."

A few minutes later Lucy left the telephone. Without looking over her shoulder to see if Nina was in the hall, she went out the front door and wandered down the road to the common. Mothers were there with their children and bathers were lying on the beach in the late afternoon sun. A radio in a car parked at the end of the road was blaring something about Hitler. In her confusion Lucy felt exposed to them all; her embarrassed excitement had no place to hide. She walked back to the house and through the hall to the kitchen where everything was cool, sunless, and clear. The nickel-plated alarm clock ticked on its shelf above the tins containing sugar, flour, coffee, and tea. The time was five-fifteen.

Forgetting about the flowers she had left in the garden, she struck a match to light the oven, then set a bowl and bread pan on the table, opened the door of the ice-box, and removed eggs, milk, and the minced beef and pork she was going to make into a meat-loaf for supper. From a vegetable pan she took parsley and onions, and assembled her materials together on the table. Then with a quick spontaneous movement she stretched both arms over her head and smiled.

The loaf was mixed and in the pan when she heard the front door slam and Nina's footsteps coming down the hall.

"Here you are! I've been looking all over the place for you."

Lucy pulled open the oven door, looked at the thermometer inside, put the pan on the top shelf, and closed the door again.

"Nina, would you like to set the table? I have some other things to do."

Nina stood watching her with narrowed eyes, her hands on her hips, and all the mysterious antagonism she felt against her sister showing in her face.

"I know perfectly well who it was, you know."

"Nobody said you didn't."

"What did he want *you* for?"

Lucy looked at Nina's face, and wondered why her sister was angry. Expecting mockery, she was astonished to discover this new mood. Then Nina stamped her foot on the floor like a child.

"Can't you ever tell me anything? Why do you have to be so secretive? Living with you, day in and day out, is like is like – How long have you known him, anyway?"

An expression entered Lucy's eyes that Nina had never seen before. "Aren't you making a fool of yourself?" Lucy said.

"A fool of *my*self?"

Still facing her sister, her eyes quietly watching, Lucy said, "You're not a child any more, and it's time you got over these tantrums. It's also time you realized there are moments when I'd prefer you to mind your own business. He asked me to go to the dance tonight."

The clock ticked loudly in the ensuing silence. Nina's mouth was open and her china-blue eyes were staring incredulously. Then anger replaced surprise. Then mockery veiled the anger. Finally an expression almost of alarm covered her whole face and she looked like a little girl who has just been told there is no Santa Claus.

"You said no, of course!"

"I said yes."

Nina walked to the door, but she was unable to make her retreat in good order and turned around.

"Well, I suppose you know what people will say. A girl like you, who never goes anywhere – suddenly appearing at a dance with a man like that! Nobody knows anything about him – I suppose you're aware of that. For all we know he may be married and the father of goodness knows how many children! It stands to reason he is, for he's dreadfully old and – and – Lucy, did you *really* say yes?"

Nina was still in the doorway as Lucy passed her quietly and went into the hall.

"What do you think Jane will say?"

Lucy went upstairs without answering.

But Jane had nothing to say to Lucy that evening. Shortly before six o'clock she telephoned that she was having supper with Dr. and Mrs. Grant at the manse and would go on to choir practice later. So Lucy and Nina passed a strained half-hour eating alone with each other.

After the dishes were cleared, when Lucy went upstairs to dress, she began to feel foolish and panic-stricken. For a moment she would have done almost anything to escape the evening that lay before her and she remembered with an agony of mortification an experience she had once had at college.

In her freshman philosophy class there had been a man called Hardison from Montreal; a rare type for Dufferin College, his face dark with a quality of precocious maturity and weary handsomeness that made him seem to the others like a foreigner. Unlike them, he had plenty of money to spend and drove his own car, and he was understood to have been cashiered from Royal Military College the year previous.

Both Hardison and Lucy sat in the back of the philosophy class, where he passed most of the early lectures with closed eyes. Then Lucy became aware that he often watched her, and she wondered why, though she gave it little attention. After several weeks, when he suddenly invited her to the second formal dance of the year, she was too surprised to refuse and afterwards was too embarrassed to mention his name even to the girls she knew best. Hardison had avoided the college girls all that term, and they believed he sought his pleasures elsewhere.

The memory of the night of the dance had lingered with Lucy through the years like a torment. Hardison had come to the women's residence, suave, poised, and bored among the other students who stared at him surreptitiously and wondered what girl had been bold enough to go out with such a man. When Lucy came downstairs to join him she could smell whiskey on his breath. As they drove to the dance in his car he informed her that she was the only good-looking girl he had seen at Dufferin, offered her a drink from his flask, and showed contempt when she refused. After a few dances he neglected her, went down to the basement of the gymnasium where the dance was being held, and kept coming up with the smell of whiskey still stronger on his breath. When he finally drove her home, his boredom had become so obvious that he hardly bothered to speak to her at all, and in the main street of the town he crashed head-on into a parked truck. Neither of them was hurt, but Hardison's car had to be towed to the garage by a wrecker, a policeman took names, and the dance had been over an hour and a half before Lucy got back to the residence.

It was useless for Lucy, in later years, to tell herself that the matron had been stupid and tactless to use this incident as a means of rubbing a moral lesson into a girl like herself. The humiliation rankled. The whole evening had been so horribly unpleasant that she felt a shudder of shame every time she remembered it.

Now, alone in her room, she felt the recurring shame again. There was not a single party or dance in her life that she could recall with pleasure. She told herself that this evening with Lassiter would be even more unpleasant than the few dances she had gone to years ago, because now it was so long since she had danced with anyone that she was sure she had forgotten how to follow a man's lead. For a moment she thought of going to the telephone to cancel the engagement. Then she realized she had no idea where to find him. There were two hotels in the town and several rooming houses. For all she knew, Lassiter might even be staying with the Craigs.

Hesitating, she caught sight of herself in the mirror over the dressing table, and her face took her by surprise, as people's faces sometimes do when they catch in the mirror the reflection of an expression they had never guessed was there. She realized that the years had not been unkind to her. The expression she saw was a mature one and the agonies of shyness she could still feel were not so visible now. She smiled involuntarily, and as she did so she realized that Lassiter might be neither insincere nor foolish. What she saw in the glass was the reflection of an attractive woman.

Thinking this, she remembered the feline power of Lassiter's movements on the tennis court, and then the frankness of his smile when they had met in the library. She remembered Matt McCunn telling her she ought to escape from Grenville before it was too late. And as she made her decision a quick vibration of life stirred through her body.

She began to dress, decided to wear the blue dinner gown Nina had tried to take away from her, made a few experiments with her hair, and finally brushed it smooth and left it plain. As she manicured her nails she had a moment's fear that her work in the garden had left the skin of her hands too rough for delicacy. But after she had rubbed oil into them, they felt smooth as satin as she touched them to her cheeks.

Through the window came the sound of the town clock striking eight times. Another half-hour remained; another half hour of security. The whole house was still when she opened her door into the hall, and the air in the hall had the warm, delicately musty odour the house always acquired toward the end of a humid summer. A faint splash from the bathroom told her that Nina was lounging in the tub. She went downstairs and out to the kitchen, put away a few pots and pans, picked up a cloth, and went into the living room to dust the tables. There was still twenty minutes left. She sat on the piano stool and began to play quietly to herself. Then, as the movement bore her along, her mounting confidence made the chords fill the house and her fingers struck the keys with hardly a mistake, It was only when she reached the end that she recalled, half ruefully, that what she had played was Jane's favourite composition, the adagio of the *Apassionata*. She thought of Jane and wondered what her elder sister would say in the morning, then forgot all about her when a car door slammed outside and she knew that Lassiter had arrived.

IT WAS only months afterwards that Lucy was able to sort out in her mind the pattern which developed in the hours and days after Lassiter invited her to the dance. Months afterwards she could tell herself what at the time she did not know: that there is nothing unique in the fact that the least probable men and women attach themselves to one another and that time and place are more selective than we ourselves know how to be. People can join as much by random chance as the grains of pollen which meet in the air.

Later on Lucy knew this. Later on she knew also that she had been much less cut off from the world than she had imagined, for Lassiter soon stopped seeming strange to her. Even his maleness became familiar, as though she had always been accustomed to men. By accepting her as a woman he showed her she was like other women after all, and like them desirable. Her world staggered and moved, but she moved with it. After that August night in Grenville, Lucy never felt herself a spectator again.

But at the time, the small things that counted poured by too rapidly for her comprehension. Time had to pass before she could realize that it was this particular look in the eyes, or this touch of the hand, or this tone in a voice used carelessly which changed their personal histories beyond any plans they made or fears they guarded. Time had to pass, too, before she understood how much Lassiter took for granted, how much his natural self-confidence took the place of reflection, his physical strength of calculation. At first she listened for hidden overtones which were not there at all. He was lonely for a woman and he had found her. Then he liked her and then he wanted her; soon he told her he loved her. Lassiter moved toward Lucy with little consciousness of what he was doing. And Lucy, who was accustomed to question herself and reflect about everything, had nothing on which to rely but her own instincts.

The dance that night passed as summer dances usually did in Grenville. Girls and boys in their late teens and a few couples in their early twenties mingled with some visitors from out of town and circled about the floor in the plain, pine-boarded hall of the Grenville Boat Club to the music of the Dixie Moonlanders. The club was not situated on Lake Ontario, but on a small stretch of water two miles inland called Granite Mere. Birch trees stood about its shores and an outcropping of lichen-covered granite formed a small cliff at one end of it. A nine-hole golf course followed the curve

of the lake from the clubhouse, climbed the high ground, and disappeared on the other side.

"I can't get over the feeling that I'm a kid again."

In the half darkness on the gallery Lassiter's teeth showed white
as he smiled. He and Lucy were sitting on the railing overhanging
the water. Farther down the railing Nina and Bruce Fraser stood
apart and apparently they were having an argument. Lucy knew
that Nina was furious with Bruce for having previously argued with
Lassiter on the state of the world, and that Bruce was angry because
the amused tolerance of Lassiter's answers had only served to em-
phasize the difference in age and position between them. But Lucy
herself, now that it was after eleven o'clock, was relaxed and almost
happy. So far, the evening had gone off far better than she had
hoped. Being in this little club was like being in a strange place in
a strange town, for she knew hardly any of the people here. They
were all too young, and she realized with some amazement that
during the years since she had left college a whole new generation
of children had grown into their late teens. Most of them probably
knew who she was, but nothing she would do could possibly be of
interest to them.

Apparently in Lassiter the evening had roused feelings of nos-
talgia. He had been talking about boyhood summer holidays on
Nantucket, about tennis and sailing races, and had made a long
story out of the first night he had got drunk.

Now he said, "I can't get over the idea of being here with all
these kids and liking it. I didn't know it was a high-school dance
I was asking you to. I hope you don't mind. And this band – to
assemble a band as corny as that takes genius. Each instrument gives
out exactly the same kind of corn at exactly the same time."

All evening Lucy had been following remarks like this with a
diligent silence which made Lassiter assume that they shared the
same frame of reference. He went on to talk about Dorsey and
Goodman and Beiderbecke and then came back to the Dixie Moonlanders.

"It reminds me of an outfit called The Hot Sophomores I used
to dance to when I was fourteen. That guy on the traps – my God,
he even keeps the same old red light burning inside his bass drum.
Is his name really Blackman, or did he make it up?"

The lighted windows of the clubhouse made paths on the dark water of the lake, and occasionally a canoe glided into the lights and out into darkness again. A boy of about twenty approached Lassiter and asked for a light. Lassiter handed over a book of matches, and as they exchanged a few words Lucy realized that they knew each other. The boy thanked him, calling him 'sir,' and went away.

Lassiter turned back to her. "One thing the Depression has done – it's given an outfit like the Ceramic better men than it deserves for the kind of jobs it offers. That kid's only a clerk at sixteen a week. He ought to be getting twice that."

The lights in the hall were dimmed until the paths they made on the water faded out. Softly, with all the rubato dreaminess a small-town band can put into a sweet number, the strains of "Chloe" throbbed through the opened doors and windows into the night.

"I can't believe it," Lassiter murmured. "It's a real, old-fashioned moonlight waltz." He reached over and took her hand. "I haven't danced one of these numbers in years. Have you?" He flicked his cigarette into the lake and continued talking as they walked to the floor. "Time was all you needed was a darkened room. Where I've been lately liquor is not only quicker, it's essential."

In the half-darkness Lucy really danced with him for the first time that evening. He was easy to follow. He held her close and firmly, and there was no subtlety in his steps. Now, relaxing and forgetting herself, she allowed her instinctive rhythms to match his, she felt her slim body melting into the direct power of his movements, she turned and swayed with him, and for a few moments it seemed as if the walls which had surrounded her for so long had parted like cobwebs and left her free. Long before tonight, her imagination had been sufficient to let her picture herself in various characters, provided she was alone. But she knew, as she swayed with Lassiter to the beat of Ike Blackman's drums, that from now on she would never seem to others precisely as she had seemed before. She felt his chin pressing her temple, and did not withdraw her head.

Then, as they turned through the glow of light spread by Blackman's bass drum, she saw Nina in the middle of the floor, watching them while she danced slowly with Bruce. Lucy stiffened involuntarily.

"What's the matter?"

Lassiter, head held back, was looking down at her. Then he turned with the music and Nina disappeared behind him. Safe in the half darkness, Lucy looked up and held his eyes, and felt grateful to him. His hand pressed more firmly on the small of her back.

"How did I manage to find you? You're lovely. Look at me more often like that."

The music stopped and she turned in some embarrassment toward the door, guessing that he was a man who found it easy to say such things. Nina was standing in the doorway with Bruce as they passed; her eyes were not so much mocking as amazed. Sentences were exchanged between them. Lucy was aware of Bruce's voice speaking to her.

"May I have the next dance?" And to Lassiter, "Do you mind?"

"Sorry, Bruce," Lassiter grinned. "How about making it the dance after that? I've already booked her for the next one."

Then, his hand on the soft flesh of her inner arm just below the elbow, Lassiter guided her out to the gallery. They sat on the railing again and he lit a cigarette.

"Let's not dance any more. Let's drive."

A small breeze puffed off the lake and Lucy shivered slightly.

"Are you cold?"

"A little. I left my wrap on the chair over there."

"I'll get it."

He came back and put it over her shoulders and stood looking down, large, massive, and confident, one arm propped against a post which ran from the railing to the gallery roof. The music began for the next dance. Nina and Bruce went in to the floor and Lucy's eyes followed them.

"My car has just been tuned up," Lassiter said. "It really moves. How would you like to drive to Toronto and back?"

His boyish eagerness was oddly comforting to her; all evening his naturalness had been increasing her confidence. She held her watch against the light and saw it was half-past eleven.

"Don't tell me it's late," he said. "I can remember when my evenings were just beginning at one in the morning. Lassiter has deteriorated since then, but time was he could take it. Come along, Lucy. This band is too bad to dance to."

She saw the stars glimmering in the lake. "I don't think so."

He was insistent. "That's no reason at all."

For a while he argued the point, but Lucy remained sitting where she was. Finally he said, "Well anyway, let's take a stroll. I'm restless as hell. Normally this would be the time for a drink, but I've been in this country long enough to know you can never get a drink when you want one."

She strolled down the gallery with him and they stood for a few moments on the steps watching a quarter moon setting over the slope of the links. The night was alive with humming insects. A car door slammed and a girl and a boy emerged and came up the steps arm in arm. Lassiter put his arm through hers and they strolled out through the parking space toward the grass. A match flickered in the rear seat of a Chevrolet, a boy's head appeared for an instant in its glow, a girl's hair and forehead, a puffed cigarette, and then darkness. As they moved out onto the putting green he slipped his arm about her waist. She let it rest there for a moment and then drew away.

"We'd better be going back."

He turned toward her. "I wish it were light enough for me to see your face."

"Why?"

"Then I'd know whether you meant what you said." As she said nothing, he continued. "This has been a wonderful evening for me, Lucy. I can't tell you what it's meant. Someone like you is so rare these days I can't quite believe you're real."

Instinctively she rallied to protect herself, not knowing what she was protecting herself against.

"Please don't say foolish things like that when you know they aren't true."

As she moved away from him to the steps she wished her mind could keep up with the mercurial lightness of her feelings. She wished she could give out a sense of smiling with the motions of her body, as Nina did when she was gay.

Lassiter caught up with her and again slipped his arm through hers. "No," he said, "this isn't a line. I don't know how to say it, but tonight – you've made me feel happy tonight, that's all."

"I'm glad."

"An aunt of mine used to say that an air of repose is the mark of a great lady. I used to think it was a comical remark. Now I know it's true."

She had no answer. What his words involved, the mere fact that he had said them, dazed her.

They returned to the hall and she danced with him again. Then Bruce came up to claim a dance and Lassiter sat out with Nina on the balcony rail. Bruce was surprisingly shy with her, and she realized with startling awareness that a man and a woman can never really know each other until they have touched each other's bodies. She could feel the repressed tension in Bruce and knew he wanted to hold her more closely than he was doing.

"You're looking very nice tonight, Lucy."

The odd formality of his remark made her feel older and almost protective and for an instant she wanted to touch his hair out of pure affection and tell him how much she had always liked him. But the music stopped before she could think of anything to say, Blackman struck the cymbal with his stick, and everyone stood at attention wherever they happened to be while the band played "God Save the King." She and Bruce walked together out to the gallery where they found Lassiter leaning against a post smoking a cigarette and looking at the water, while beside him Nina looked restless and discontented.

"Perhaps Nina and Bruce could come in the car with us?" she said.

A shade of displeasure crossed Lassiter's face, but he could find no courteous reason for refusing, and said he'd be glad to have them if they didn't mind being crowded. Nina and Bruce thanked him and went inside to the chair where Nina had left her coat and bag.

As Lassiter slipped the wrap about Lucy's shoulders, he said, "I want to see you again tomorrow night. Please don't say no."

For a moment they were alone on their section of the porch and she met his eyes with undenied intimacy. "I don't know, Stephen. I don't know if I can."

Nina and Bruce returned and Lassiter let them pass ahead down the gallery.

He nodded toward Nina's back and whispered, "Is she the trouble?"

"No."

"I'll call you up tomorrow, anyway. This is one of those things that happens, and we both know it."

But as Lucy drove home with him in the crowded car, all of them silent, she wondered if something really had happened, and if they both did know it. Now that the dance was over, she could think only of the embarrassment she was going to feel when she found herself alone again with Nina and Jane.

Afterwards, in her room in the silent house, she lay awake for a long time. There had been no obvious embarrassment with Nina or Jane and neither had made any comment when the house door had closed and Lassiter had driven away. Trying to put herself in their place, she wondered what comment they could have found to make. But words had never mattered much in this house.

Toward dawn a light breeze sprang off the lake, and Lucy fell into a broken sleep in which Lassiter was present in strange forms and repeatedly woke her up. Then, wide awake, she saw him as she had seen him a few hours ago. She tried to guess what the whole of him meant: how much the tenderness in his brown eyes cancelled the hint of hardness about the mouth, how his mature self-confidence balanced the boyishness which made him seem at times more naive than she had ever felt herself to be. But the calculations all faded out. She remembered the touch of his fingers on the soft flesh of her inner arm and the driving rhythm of his body as he danced. Lucy discovered she was a stranger to herself.

BREAKFAST the next morning was a strained agony for Lucy, for it was one of Jane's talents to create at will an atmosphere in which everyone around her felt guilty. She did this without sulking and without uttering a single direct word of rebuke. Such an atmosphere she built up all through the meal. When Lucy was clearing the table Jane remained behind.

"I must say," Jane said mildly, "I was surprised to find the house empty when I returned from Dr. Grant's. It was a lucky thing I had my own key. I think you might have told me you were going out."

Lucy paused with the tray in her hands. "I'm sorry, Jane. I left you a note. You found it, didn't you?"

"Where did you meet this Mr. Lassiter?" Jane was not smiling, but her voice was pleasant enough.

"I met him in the library." Lucy let the tray down gently on the table. "Mrs. Craig knows him well, you know."

"Was it Mrs. Craig who introduced you to him?"

Lucy's humiliation mounted as she felt herself driven into a downright lie. "Yes."

Jane rose from the table. "I must say it seems very odd for you to go to a dance with a man you've only met once. It's not like you to want to go to a party like that."

Lucy felt herself flushing. "I don't know why."

"Lucy," Jane said pleasantly, "please don't pretend you don't understand what I mean. People know you aren't like ordinary girls and it attracts attention when you behave in an ordinary way. It makes us look cheap. People have always respected the way we live. Father had few friends, but you know he was the most respected man in Grenville." She smiled. "Well, I suppose it doesn't really *matter*. Nina is only a child, and people probably thought you were chaperoning her and Bruce. And of course, it won't happen again."

Lucy left the room, bitter with humiliation. When Lassiter telephoned at twelve-thirty, asking her to go out for the evening, she said she would.

He arrived just before sunset, to find her standing by the perennial border in front of the house. She came quickly over the lawn and slipped into the car before he could get out to open the door. Looking past her toward the house, he saw one of the white curtains in the living room lift slightly at the corner, then fall back into place. Lucy hadn't noticed and he made no mention of it to her, but he thought about it as he sensed her relief when the car left Matilda Lane and reached the highway.

The evening was still bright as they drove out King Street on the Toronto highway. The loafers were out in front of the drugstore and the street had the empty, wistful, waiting aspect of all small-town main streets in a wide country on a summer evening when there is nothing to do but wait for the next day and watch the cars and trucks pass through on their way from one city to the next.

"The other evening I saw a fox," Lassiter said. "It was practically inside the town. I was walking out beyond where the streets end."

"They sometimes come in from the country. I have an uncle who lives on the edge of town. When he kept a cat he used to be afraid of them."

They rounded a hairpin bend that took them between a filling station and the largest oak in the township. There was a legend that a man had been hanged from it a hundred and twenty years ago for stealing a horse. Lassiter began to talk about Bruce and Nina.

"I liked both those kids, though neither of them seemed to know it. I know why I bothered Nina, but I can't figure Fraser out at all. That boy isn't as meek and mild as he looks. Inside, he boils. Maybe with the right training he could be tough. What's the matter with him, anyway? I think he's got ability if he'd use it."

"He has."

"This whole town's got ability. There's a real quality about it. But you all think too small. You could never be dangerous. You see a small town in the United States, in the South or the Middle West I mean, and the people are crude compared to you people here. But they can be dangerous. You can never be sure what they might do."

On the open road he pressed with his foot and the car surged forward at sixty-five miles an hour. For Lassiter, this was a comfortable cruising speed. Lucy sank deep into the seat to prevent the slipstream from whipping her hair. She glanced at the outline of his head, saw the lines strongly marked about his mouth, his lips rather full but firm and solid, and the little furrows of concentration about his eyes as he stared at the road. She wondered what on earth a man like this found in her to make him want to be with her. She realized that if she were a man she would probably resent him as Bruce did. Stephen Lassiter and Bruce Fraser could meet anywhere and know instinctively they were on opposite sides of whatever there was to be on opposite sides of. They were on opposite sides as human beings.

"How did you and Nina manage to grow up in the same family?"

"I've often wondered."

"Is she jealous of you? Maybe not. She's a nice girl. She'll be swell when she gets older. I've always loved little girls like that. They flatter my sense of power."

"Perhaps you flatter theirs?"

"I wonder if that's why pint-sized women have been taking advantage of me ever since I can remember? They think all I've got is size. Hell, this is a lousy road." He slackened his speed, dropped his hand from the wheel, found Lucy's on the seat beside him, and clasped it firmly. "All the same, it must be all right having a sister like Nina. My own sister is a first-class bitch. It must be nice having a family, too. Apart from my sister, all I have now is a lot of stuffy relatives I never see. It gets bleak, living alone."

Lucy breathed deeply, with a quiet sigh in the wind. A weight seemed to slide off her mind. She half-closed her eyes against the sun, for it was poised ahead of them on the end of the road like a soft round ball. Already the fields on their right were losing colour, and on the left the plane of the lake was as pale as the inside of a poplar leaf.

"This is good country," he said.

"It's the only country I know."

"Even the fields look respectable."

"Are we as dull as all that?"

"I wouldn't say you were dull. You're just slow starting." His hand left hers, took his pipe from his pocket, and put it empty between his teeth, the car still running slowly and as quiet as a whisper. "I've always had a feel for country, ever since I was a kid. I think I like country better than people. North of here they tell me it gets wild."

"It's just bush. The bush goes to the tundra and the tundra goes to the Arctic Ocean."

"But it's a safe kind of wildness, isn't it? No lions or tigers. No snakes." He looked sideways at her, caught a brief glimpse of her profile, and was stirred to go on, to dramatize the difference he felt between them. "It makes a difference if a country is safe. Back home – in the South or even in parts of New York and New Jersey – you go bird shooting. There's always the chance of a poisonous snake. It's not a thing you talk about or even think about and you can go all your life and perhaps never see one. But the fear is underneath your mind all the time, and when you go through a swamp in the South or maybe through brambles on shaly ground in the Ramapos you remember it. There's nothing like that here that I know of. Snake-countries are usually cruel countries ..."

"Germany isn't a snake-country."

"You think of too many things at once."

She laughed. "Well, not far from here there's an island with more snakes to the acre than any place in the world."

"Are you kidding?"

"But they're not dangerous."

"Even when they aren't dangerous, I hate them."

He spurted around a truck, the car picking up so fast it seemed to kick Lucy in the back, flashed into the diminishing space between the truck's left fender and an approaching car, then slackened off again.

"I'd like to see this country get stirred up about something to find out what goes on underneath. Because a lot must go on. Jim Craig told me how many of your people were killed in the war. A thing like that means something. Myself, I like a dramatic country, and most of the United States is dramatic. There's something crazy and dangerous about it, but it makes you feel alive. You can get into the deadest town – so long as it's west of the Appalachians or south of the Mason-Dixon – and you can imagine anything happening in it. My father came from a tank town in the plains, but he saw his own father help string up a rustler. Up here I bet you never had any rustlers to string up. Down in the South you can go along a little dirt road and there's nothing to see in the day time. But at night you go along it. You can pretty easily imagine a lynching party, if you're in the right district of the right state. And you ought to see the Middle West in a fall thunderstorm. No wonder the small-town people in the Middle West have that strained look about their eyes. People here haven't got it. But you're not soft, either. I've found out you don't dent easily. You're just different – as if you'd never got started, somehow. You don't make the money you should because you don't think big enough. You're too content to take what people give you. You're too polite." He stopped abruptly. "And Lassiter seems to be talking a hell of a lot."

She protested that he was not; and then she was reminded of Bruce Fraser, who also talked a lot, and she wondered if there was some quality in herself which made both these men want to shock a response out of her.

"I never thought about Canada before I came up here," Lassiter said. "And when I did come, I found all of you looking down on Americans."

"We don't."

"The hell you don't!"

"Well, perhaps its an old habit we got into."

"Is it because you're British and the British look down on everybody?"

"They look down on us, too."

"I'll bet they do."

She marvelled at the silence of his car. It whispered along a road that was too narrow and pock-marked from thousands of patches where winter frosts had heaved the concrete. Lassiter drove by the feel of the machine as if he were a part of it. They idled through a small main street and when they came out on the other side it was so dark he turned on the lights.

"Does Nina think Bruce Fraser is in love with her?"

"I don't think so."

"She'd better not, because he isn't. He likes you better."

She smiled to herself, amazed at the thrill of joy these surprising words, one after the other, awoke in her.

"You don't know any of us very well, do you?"

"Well enough to know that," he said. "I can't get him off my mind. He's a well-educated boy. Why the hell doesn't he get out of a town like Grenville?"

"He only lives here in the summers."

"What does he do in the winters?"

She told him.

"Yes," Lassiter said, "I might have known."

Lucy bridled at his dismissal of Bruce. "Why shouldn't he be a schoolmaster if he wants to be?"

"No reason why he shouldn't, except that you know damn well he doesn't want to be."

His casual hardness made Lucy draw away from him. Then, with amazement, she realized the underlying import of what he had been saying. Apparently he exempted her entirely from the shy hesitancy he saw in Bruce Fraser. What did he think she was?

"It's not his fault," she said. "Things haven't been too easy for him. But you're right about the school-teaching. He doesn't really like it. I wish he had a chance to travel. Living the way he does, he hasn't been able to measure himself against anyone, and he can't find out whether he's good or not. I suppose that's the trouble with most people in small places."

"He ought to bat around. My family – my mother's side of it – tried to make me settle down. I wouldn't let them."

He told her a story of which he was obviously very proud. There had been a kid living on the outskirts of Trenton when he had been at school at Lawrenceville, and the kid had been tough. His name was Joe Boyce. Lassiter had got into a fight with him once, and this had been the beginning of a friendship. Boyce had found an old Mack truck in a junkyard and Lassiter had bought the remains for thirty dollars. Then Boyce had worked on it for two months, and in the time he could get away from Lawrenceville, Lassiter had come over to his backyard to help him. When the truck was able to march, they began hauling a few small payloads for farmers into the Trenton and Princeton markets, and then they decided to set out across country to San Francisco, with the general idea of making the trip pay for itself by picking up any loads they could find along the way. One Saturday afternoon Lassiter had walked out of Lawrenceville with his bag in hand on the pretext of going home for the weekend. He didn't get back to Lawrenceville until three months later.

"We were laying plans for the big trucking service that was going to make our fortunes. We didn't do so badly, either. We got to Stockton, Kansas, before the old truck fell apart. But before it did, we saw a lot of country. In a November freeze we broke down in the Pennsylvania mountains and it was so cold that when the sweat came through our jerseys it froze our backs to the road while we were working under the car."

As he went on talking about Joe Boyce, Lucy noticed that he seemed a much younger man than he had half an hour ago; and somehow less genuine, for he was not really admiring Boyce so much as he was admiring himself for once having been intimate with a man like that.

"You ought to see Joe now. He owns and operates one of the biggest trucking services in the United States. You should see the trailers rolling out of his main depot in Chicago. And Joe sits up there in his office with diamond rings on his fingers that he doesn't even stop to take off if he has to step out to slug a guy. He's still got a picture of the two of us standing beside the wreck of that old Mack truck in Stockton. And I'm telling you, he's a hell of a lot more real than an uncle of mine who reads all the time and tells people the engineers are destroying the world, when he doesn't know enough engineering himself to take the front wheel off a bicycle."

It was twilight and then it was dark. For about half an hour they drove without saying much, while a half-moon slowly dominated the sky. Far on the left its beams quivered on the lake, making the surrounding darkness a mauve colour. But on the highway the headlights of the cars flickered thickly all the way to Toronto. The headlights kept coming at them. The lights would grow hard against their eyeballs; then for a second their car would be in a blaze of rushing brightness; then the light would flash behind and the pupils of their eyes would slowly expand again.

"What have you been thinking about?" he said.

"That's a wide question to have to answer."

"I've been talking too much, and you've been saying nothing. I always talk too much to girls I like." He put his arm about her shoulder and drew her against his side. She stiffened involuntarily against him.

"What's the matter?"

"Nothing."

He took his arm away and pushed the accelerator down to the floor. "I'm restless. Do you like speed?"

"Perhaps, I don't know."

"Then let's see what we can do."

He pushed the LaSalle up to eighty-eight and the trees swirled by. Leaning back out of the slipstream that snatched at her hair, Lucy saw the galaxy stationary in a vast, waving splash across the sky. Lassiter slowed for an abrupt turn and did not try to build up the speed again.

"You'd like flying," he said. And a moment later, "I've always wanted to build airplanes. It must be good fun to do what you want."

"Don't you like what you're doing now?"

"It's a hell of a business. Bathtubs and toilet bowls – can you see any startling changes in a business like that?"

She had nothing to say.

"Meanwhile other people are just beginning to scratch the surface of speed. Pretty soon they'll be going as fast as sound. That will be the next frontier. When you reach the speed of sound, vibrations develop that tear you apart unless you shoot through that danger area fast enough. But they'll do it. Meanwhile, I'm a plumber."

"Why does speed mean so much to you?"

He made no answer directly and for several minutes he made no answer at all. They entered the small town of Marlborough, passed through the pool of light thrown over the road by the Shell station on the outside corner, then through the main street with its dark shop fronts and past the local movie and the lighted drugstore with the kids and loafers standing outside and the radio blasting through the screen door.

"The women in my family – on my mother's side – want to turn the whole United States into one goddam big museum. Their brows are so high I don't know where they leave room for the hair. They fill their houses with old colonial chairs that break when you lean back on them. I have one aunt who talks about *Mister* Emerson and *Mister* Thoreau as if they were still alive, but if she'd met Wilbur and Orville Wright when she was at college she wouldn't have noticed anything but a couple of bicycle mechanics from Ohio. My father hated the guts of that whole family. He wasn't their kind and they let him know it. When he finally lost his money in the crash, my mother's family were so glad to see him fall it made you sick to hear them talk. All they'd ever done with their money was to sit on it like incubating hens, but my father took chances. He knew what counted. That's why I got into engineering, even though I do have a friend who tells me I'm a sucker to stay with it."

He pushed his foot down to the floor and the car leaped. The wind drummed past, and soon the needle stood at eighty again. Occasionally as the car swung to a curve the wind smashed in and struck Lucy's face a solid blow. For a few seconds she was frightened. The rough defiance in his voice made her wonder what was the matter with him, if he was safe to be with in a car or anywhere else. Then she saw his hands clutching the wheel and knew he was at least safe in a car. There they were on the wheel, dimly visible in the light of the dash, strong enough to break her wrists. But they were also carefully groomed, and she remembered how he had touched her at the dance, delicately, as though his finger tips felt that her flesh was precious. Then he slowly raised his foot from the accelerator and let the car run down until all the wind-noise ceased and the needle of the speedometer fell back to fifteen. He turned off the highway onto a rutted dirt track which ran beside a row of willows through oatfields to the lake. At the end of the road he stopped in an open space where the grass was dusted with blown sand from the beach.

For a moment the headlights flared out into the moon-path on the water, then he snapped them off and cut the engine and sat hunched behind the wheel staring ahead.

Presently he turned to her. "If I weren't alone so much I probably wouldn't talk so much."

His arm went about her shoulder and drew her close. She lowered her chin and felt the roughness of his tweed jacket against her face.

"You do like me, don't you?"

"Yes, but –"

His arm tightened around her, and through the cloth of his jacket she felt his heavy muscles mass and shift. She was acutely conscious of her own fragility and inexperience.

"The first time I saw you in the library –" he began.

Then he tried to kiss her and she resisted, holding her face down against his shoulder.

"Don't do that, Lucy."

She did not move.

"For people like us, the way things are now, moments like this are all that's left."

"Stephen," she said.

"What?"

"You don't know anything about me. I don't know anything about you."

"More than you think."

His hand came up against her chin, trying to lift it so that her lips would be below his. She resisted the movement, but something uncontrollable made her lower her lips and brush them against the back of his hand, and when he felt them touch his skin he murmured in her ear and pressed her more closely.

"Don't do this to yourself, Lucy. No one with lips and eyes like yours should ..."

"No," she said. "Please, I've got to tell you something."

He relaxed the pressure of his hand on her shoulder. "Go ahead."

"You've been imagining things about me that aren't true." She took a deep breath and her voice was calm. "Whatever you thought you saw in my face that day in the library simply wasn't there. I was embarrassed to death, that was all. You see, I'd told my sister I'd met you, when I hadn't. It was a perfectly silly thing to say, but when women live alone with each other they always say foolish things and make mountains out of mole-hills. I was so – so embarrassed when I realized Nina would find out I didn't know you that I spoke to you as if we had already met."

"And from that you think I formed the wrong idea of you! What a darling you are." He chuckled. "So Grenville really is as strict as it looks on the outside!"

"Oh, it's not Grenville. It's just – you see, Nina really did want to meet you."

"Nina would want to meet any new man in town. Don't worry about that young sister of yours. She's going to do all right for herself, even though she'll never get all she wants – you know it as well as I do – because she'll never give enough to get it."

Not until Lucy drew away did Lassiter realize that he had probably broken another code of manners in Grenville by talking so candidly to a girl about her sister.

"Lucy," he said. "I may sound crude to you, but I'm honest. I've grown up in a society that says what it thinks. When I said that about your sister I wasn't thinking of her as a member of your family but as someone who has hurt you again and again. I don't know why but I do know how. Someone has got to say these things to you. I'd only be thinking about you if I said another thing I believe – that Nina is the last girl, as a type, that a wise man would choose to go to bed with."

Lucy was utterly still at his side.

"Do you see how I'm only trying to help you by saying that?"

"No."

"Well, give me your hand again and let me explain." Her hand was still in his. "If a man doesn't admit to himself that it would be a pleasure to go to bed with a girl it means one thing. It means he doesn't respect her as a woman. It doesn't mean he's going to do it. It means that other things being equal it would be a pleasure. That's always been a fact and today it's more true than it ever was. Look at the way most people live today. Most of them never see anything but paved streets and brick walls and ashcans along the curbs. They don't have trees and flowers around them the way you have here. I've met people to whom a spruce tree is something you buy on Third Avenue at Christmas. But there's one thing they have got. They've got pictures of beautiful women to look at on every billboard. For ten cents they can buy a magazine full of naked girls with beautiful bodies. That's why sex is the city man's poetry." He grinned at himself in the dark. "Maybe I'd better pipe down or somebody'll think I'm taking myself seriously."

Her hand was warm in his, but she still sat motionless beside him.

Presently he went on, speaking more slowly. "Canadians are still pretty religious, aren't they?"

"I don't know. All of Canada isn't like Grenville."

"Well, so far as I can see it's dying out back home. The same principle works there that works in industry. If a technique stops paying off, it's scrapped." After a long silence he said, "You and I aren't so different from each other, you know. You're honest and so am I. And I like you very much."

Again he put his arm around her, and though she did not draw back this time, she gave him no co-operation.

"I'm not used to men, Stephen," she said finally.

Now that she had said it, she felt as empty as a spilled pail. She stared out at the lake. There it was, this flat expanse extending out of sight in the darkness down to the United States. She felt his hand tighten over hers.

"No, Lucy – I don't believe you are!"

She could feel the flicker of curiosity pass along his muscles, through his fingers into her hand as he held it, and surprisingly a small anger hardened within her. The powerful intuition developed by solitary women who live observing others, protecting themselves against others, resigned to being spectators, informed Lucy as clearly as if she were looking at words printed on paper that her inexperience was like a veil making Lassiter think her more interesting and more desirable than she could ever be to any man. He put his arms about her with eager power.

She heard her own voice say, "Please don't try to teach me anything."

He paused, hunched massively beside her, and slowly his head went back. Then he laughed.

"You certainly know how to let a man have it." He laughed again. "And was I wide open for that one!"

"It's just that I don't think I'm –"

"Lucy, honestly – I may be crude but I'm not a bastard."

"I know."

"You're lovely," he said softly. "You're a lovely girl. You're marvellous."

She drew away from him. "You know perfectly well I'm quite plain."

He saw her face white in the moon, clean cut and averted, its lines sharpened by all absence of colour, and he realized that without the softening effect of her changing expressions the bone-structure made her face look dominant and almost statue-like. With a certain sense of shame he understood how he had underrated this woman. Even though he had sincerely liked her, he had still assumed she was more or less like all small-town girls. One way or the other, they always guarded their vanity against the city man's assumption that they knew nothing of the world.

She turned and faced him. "I know that tonight is just another evening for you. That's all it should be, for you have your work and you don't live in a place like Grenville. But for me it's so unusual that even though I know it doesn't mean anything I'll never be able to forget it. And that makes – well, it makes the situation between us unequal."

"I told you last night you made me feel happy. I told you it was a feeling I hadn't had much of lately. Does that make it unequal?"

She breathed deeply and looked away. "I don't know. I'm too confused to know, I suppose."

"Are you sorry you came out with me?"

The trace of a smile flickered about her eyes. "No."

He relaxed and took out his pipe. Slowly he stuffed it with tobacco and lit it.

"What have you been doing all these years in Grenville?"

"So little I'd be ashamed to mention it."

"Go ahead."

"Well, both my parents are dead and ..."

"Mine are too. Yes, and you live with Jane and Nina. Jane I've seen and Nina I've met. Tell me some more."

"I read books. I keep the house."

"You must have friends?"

"In a town like this everyone knows everybody, but that's not the same as having friends. I've had friends, of course. But my two best friends aren't here any more. I never see them. One is married and lives in Victoria. The other works in Toronto." She smiled. "I hardly need add they were both girls."

He regarded her quietly. "And you've been to college. Nina told me that when I was talking to her on the porch of the club. As a matter of fact, she said you'd been quite brilliant at college."

"Did she?" Lucy smiled again. "I have a large garden, too."

"Which you like better than keeping house?"

"Yes."

"May I see it? Say tomorrow afternoon – after work?"

Lucy stiffened involuntarily, wondering what to tell him. Then she wondered if she would have to tell him anything. For a moment, frightened of the newness she had discovered in herself, she was sure she would never dare to see him again. Then she knew the thought was foolish. She would see him again, if he came to her.

She looked at the clock on the dashboard, bending forward to see the position of the hands.

"We'd better go back now," she said.

"Why? It's still early."

"My sisters will be waiting. Jane worries a lot." She looked at him and he held her eyes. "Please forgive me if I've seemed stiff and stupid tonight. An evening like this is new to me."

The tobacco glowed rhythmically as he puffed his pipe.

"Is your family queer?" He turned a key in a lock. "Excuse me for putting it like that, but most families these days are queer. I know families in New York that are all in the hands of psychiatrists. But yours must be a different kind of queerness. For a girl who looks like you, to be what you say you are – it isn't normal."

She laughed then, and felt the relief of it. "My father *was* queer, but it was such a Scotch kind of queerness we never noticed it till after he was dead. Jane doesn't realize it even now."

She spoke a little more about herself while he listened. Then he talked about his work for a time, and told her how much he disliked Cleveland, and speaking like this, alone with each other on the lake shore, now that he no longer pretended anything and she no longer tried to protect herself, they drew together naturally and inevitably as they opened doors and showed a little of the loneliness inside.

Finally he pressed on the starter and looked at the clock. "We'd better not let Jane worry any more. It might be tough for you."

He drove back at a steady speed, and they were quiet with each other in this newly found intimacy. Before they were half way back to Grenville, Lucy felt drowsy with relief from the strain she had been carrying the past few days. For now it had lifted from her, leaving her resigned to the position in which she had placed herself. Whether that position was serious or would last only for the evening she did not know, and for the moment could not care. She felt her shoulder meeting his, utterly relaxed, and he made no attempt to caress her or to put his arm about her.

Once he said, "I've always wanted women, but most of them have only made me more lonely. You don't."

They reached Grenville just before midnight and he drove down the little street to her house.

"May I see your garden tomorrow?"

"Call me about noon and I'll tell you then."

He opened the door on his side of the car and she said, "Please don't get out."

So he leaned across and opened the door on her side of the car. She returned the pressure of his hand, he saw in the semi-darkness the trace of a smile about her eyes, and then she was gone. He sat watching the door of the house open, her dress cross it like a rustling shadow, and then, with a slow swing and in complete silence, the door closed. He waited in the car. The hall light went off. The light that had been shining in one of the upstairs bedrooms went off just as the one in the room beside it flashed on. He waited to see if she would come to the window, but she did not come and when that light also went off he let in the clutch and backed silently up to the King's Highway.

THE next morning when Lucy came down to breakfast she found Jane's place vacant. Her used plate and the empty coffee cup beside it showed that she had made her own breakfast and finished it early. Lucy and Nina ate alone and few words passed between them, though each was well aware of the tension within the house.

"Jane must have gone out for a walk," Nina said. She added: "It was terrible last night. She didn't go to bed till after midnight."

Lucy said nothing. She cleared the table and washed the dishes. While she was bending over the sink she heard the tinkle of the first piano lesson. Apparently Jane had returned, for Bobby Harmon was again fumbling his way through "Sunday Morning at Gilion." Jane would never let her pupils advance beyond a piece until they could play it at least once without making a mistake. The music lessons continued all morning while Lucy did her housework. She went out to the garden but found little to occupy her there. She returned to the house and listened while Jane's prize pupil, a sixteen-year-old girl, played the whole of the "Sonata Pathetique" without making a single error. When the girl had finished, she heard Jane's voice speaking to her in the impersonal accent she always used with her pupils.

"The tone in your slow movement isn't quite full enough. Listen."

Then Lucy heard Jane begin to play it herself and once again she marvelled at her elder sister. One would expect her to be at her best with a Bach fugue, but it was only in these slow movements of Beethoven, where religion mingled with a deeply sublimated sexuality, that Jane really found herself in music.

"There!" Jane's voice said. "A little more weight in the bass. But you made no mistakes, and after all, that's the main thing."

Then the living-room door opened and the girl left. As soon as the outer door of the house had closed, Lucy went into the living room. Jane was arranging sheet music on the top of the piano.

"I'm sorry I didn't tell you I was going out last night," Lucy said. "I know I should have done so. I was afraid we'd both be embarrassed."

In the ensuing silence the whole room seemed to Lucy to be pulled tight around her. The trace of a flush appeared on her sister's cheekbones and it was obvious that Jane was taken by surprise.

"It has become quite clear," Jane said without looking at her, "that you don't care either for my opinions or my feelings. In that case, I suppose what you do is your own affair. You're certainly not a child any more."

"Oh, Jane – please don't say things like that to me!"

"Can you suggest anything else for me to say?"

Lucy said quietly: "You look as if I'd done something abnormal and dreadful."

Jane continued to arrange her music.

"Why can't we talk naturally to each other?" Lucy said. "*Naturally* – the way other people do! We're both grown up. We're sisters."

Jane's face was completely calm. "I don't know what you mean."

Lucy breathed deeply and looked away. She moved across the room past Jane and sat in a chair near the window.

"You have your work," she said softly. "You have the responsibility of the house. I have nothing. Nothing but my garden. Have you no idea how much I've longed to live naturally – the way the rest of the world does? We're no different from other people, Jane. We're human."

Jane turned toward her. Her neat figure stood there easily, her hands hanging down in front of her, the small fingers lightly interlaced. The force of her silent will was terrible for Lucy.

"Stephen Lassiter would like to meet you," Lucy said, but the words lost themselves in Jane's icy silence. "He's already met Nina. I think it would be nice if we could ask him to the house."

"Do you? Do you *really*?"

Jane turned and picked up another sheaf of music which she tamped into a neat pile. Then she crossed the room and sat down facing Lucy, but in such a way that the light from the window was in Lucy's eyes while her own were in the shadow.

"I stayed awake most of last night," she said calmly, "and I'm not quite myself this morning. Perhaps if my head were a little clearer I'd be able to understand why a girl like you – Lucy, my own sister –" for a second an almost primitive passion quivered under Jane's soft voice "– could allow a man like this Mr. Lassiter to make use of her as if she were a common waitress."

"You're absurd!" Lucy whispered. "You don't know what you're saying."

Jane's voice remained soft and gentle. "I believe I do. *You* think because we live quietly and decently here, I'm ignorant of the world. I know very well what goes on. I've seen this Mr. Lassiter. He didn't look to me like a man who would respect a nice girl. He didn't look a man who would even *like* a nice girl. Do you expect me to believe that an American of his type would go driving at night with a plain, inexperienced girl like you just for the pleasure of her conversation? Haven't you ever heard of the clever, rich man from the city who comes to a little town and is bored? Hasn't it occurred to you that every decent person in Grenville has been watching this Mr. Lassiter and wondering just which girl would be fool enough to provide him with the amusement he wants?"

Pressing her palms together, Lucy asked herself why she was sitting here listening to such things when she could walk out of the room any moment she chose. Was it only because she was economically dependent? She knew it was more than this. The quivering of her nerves told her it was much more. Jane's words, like fingers, were twisting around her roots. Jane could do this to her because they had always been so near, because they had always loved each other. Lucy could walk out of the room, but she could not walk out of the situation.

"Jane," she said, "he's not like that. He's – he's very nice."

The older woman looked at her with steady eyes. "I'm not a fool and I'm not unobservant. A man like that is quite obvious to anyone who knows anything. If you don't know already, you'll soon find out that the only thing he could possibly want from you is something unpleasant. In any case, he'll leave Grenville in another week or two, and then where will you be?"

Jane got up and crossed to the piano. She swung the cover down over the keys and pushed the stool in close.

"I meant to tell you that from now on Bobby Harmon will be coming at nine every day. His mother says if he doesn't come first thing in the morning he won't come at all. He's such a dull pupil. His hands are always dirty and I get tired of sending him upstairs to wash. A long time from now these children will be grateful for what they're taught, but that isn't now."

Jane seemed so calm and matter-of-fact that it was almost impossible for Lucy to believe her change of subject was merely a technique to consolidate her victory. If it was a technique, it was certainly not a conscious one.

"Jane," she said, "we can't leave things like this."

"Why not? There's nothing more to say."

Lucy watched her sister intently. "Haven't you ever wanted a man to like you?"

A slow colour began to rise in her sister's cheeks. In all her life, Lucy had never seen an embarrassment more terrible. For several minutes Jane's lips did not move. Her self-control kept her from making a single betraying motion. Lucy's mind, leaping frantically to save itself from the pressure of her sister's will, suddenly recorded the fact that Jane was neither distorted nor queer. Everyone else in Grenville made terms with the code by which they lived without even guessing how illogical they were. Privately, they were kindly people who led sensible lives. But Jane, privately, was like their collective conscience. She was the only one of them who followed, in thought and in life, all the principles of the religion and morality which the entire Protestant part of the country professed to honour. The great crimes had no reality for her whatever. She had never in her life seen an act of deliberate wickedness. It was quite natural for her to believe that sex was the dirtiest thing in the world, and near to the root of all evil.

"I think you've said enough!" The contemptuous anger in Jane's voice made Lucy flinch.

No one had ever asked Jane a question such as Lucy's. No man had ever indicated so much as a passing interest in her. Jane's face showed that she had taken Lucy's question as a deliberate suggestion that she harboured unclean thoughts. In the silence the clock ticking in the hall was loud.

"Very well, Jane. But I've asked Stephen Lassiter here for tea this afternoon."

Jane left the room.

It was minutes after she had gone before Lucy's tears came. Then they streamed down her cheeks. She wiped her eyes and got up to look for something to do. She went out to the kitchen and found a duster, returned, and began cleaning the window sill. When she stopped moving her hand back and forth and raised her head, she saw clouds like a solid roof between the earth and sky. Then a few glaucous patches appeared, paling and darkening and paling as the sun tried to fight its way down. She stood looking out with the duster clenched in a ball in her hand and her hand against the glass. She stiffened but did not stir when she felt an arm slip about her waist.

"Don't cry, Lucy. I can't stand to see you crying."

Nina's childish face looked on the verge of tears itself.

"I heard it! Jane was terrible to you. Why is she like that? When I want to get married will she be like that to me, too?"

Lucy put her arms about Nina and each sister felt the other's cheek wet against her own. They were crying now because they were surprised at each other, and because they knew that the house would never be quite the same again after this, and perhaps because each was sorry for the years when they had kept so many feelings frozen and concealed which might have served to make both of them warm.

"Don't think badly of Jane," Lucy said. "She can't help the way she is. She won't be the same to you. It isn't that she disapproves of marriage. It – it's something else."

Nina drew away and regarded her sister as though she had never seen her before. "You've looked so nice the last few days."

Lucy passed her hands over her face and began to smooth her hair. She found herself weak and on the verge of shrill laughter. "Aren't we three fools!" She looked at Nina, smiling. "It's getting late. Would you like to help me pick some lettuce and carrots for the salad?"

Nina brushed her hands across her forehead and went ahead of her down the hall to the back of the house. She turned at the door with her face alive and smiling, her eyes still a little red from her tears but her whole body seeming to ripple with the joy of being alive.

"I'm going to ask Mr. Lassiter to have tea in the garden this afternoon," Lucy said. "For some reason he wants to see it, though I'm sure he won't be able to tell one flower from another. Will you and Bruce come along, too?"

Nina shook her head vigorously. "No, that would spoil it."

"But I wish you would!"

"No – I'm not really that mean." Nina laughed and opened the door. "To think you were on my side all along!"

FOR two hours Lucy and Stephen were alone in the garden, for Nina was somewhere on the beach and Jane had gone out. Stephen had nearly finished his report to Cleveland and felt very good about it.

"You know, it's a wonderful thing what words on paper do to you. I hadn't thought I'd done very much up here, but when I got down on paper all the stuff I've accomplished, it looked like a hell of a lot. Maybe that's why Carl Bratian thinks he's one of the biggest shots in the U.S.A. Every time he turns out an ad for a refrigerator all in colour with the baloney printed like poetry underneath – he probably thinks he's invented the goddam thing. Today I feel as if I'd rebuilt the whole Ceramic Company."

Lassiter knew nothing about flowers, as Lucy had guessed, but it made no difference in his pleasure at being in the garden. He walked around the beds while she named the flowers for him. Then he sprawled in a deck chair and ate cucumber sandwiches and drank two cups of tea. He asked her no questions about herself and seemed unconscious of the strain she had been under. He told her about the place in Dutchess County where he had lived as a small boy, but when she asked him questions about the gardens on the place, he could recall nothing about them.

"The thing I remember best was the gym I fixed up for myself in the garage. It was an old coach barn, and upstairs I had a punching bag and rings and a rowing machine." He grinned at her affectionately. "What muscles I've got I didn't get for free." He flexed his arm, and she saw the coat sleeve pack tight with the swell of biceps and deltoids. "A woman's got more than one advantage over a man. If she's born with a figure, all she's got to do is lay off chocolates to keep it. But if I got soft, this arm would be nothing but a lot of fat."

While they were eating, a chipmunk appeared on the lawn and circled around them with quick darts. Lassiter looked at the animal and remarked that all chipmunks seemed to be on the verge of a nervous breakdown. She took a few shelled nuts from the pocket of her dress and laid them on the palm of her hand, then held the hand some twenty inches from the ground and waited. The chipmunk jumped up in a quick, sure leap and crouched on her palm, stuffed the nuts into his craw with both paws, jumped down and up again to see if there were more, then darted off across the lawn and disappeared among the flowers of the perennial border. Lassiter was as pleased as a child with the chipmunk's performance, and then he wanted to know how such an animal stayed alive near a house with a cat.

"Taffy's too old to do anything but sleep," she said. "Anyway, the chipmunk doesn't live in the garden. He lives in the field behind it. He hasn't much sense of self-preservation. I suppose that's why he's easy to tame."

Lassiter laid down his cup. "You know, this is the first tea I've drunk in five years?" He gave her a meditative glance. "I feel good today. I feel relaxed. The only times I've been able to relax since I left college have been when I wasn't quite drunk and wasn't quite sober. It takes a lot of experience to be able to get that way, and to stay that way so the cylinder doesn't begin to roll. I said that to the hotel manager's wife the other day – about the drinking, I mean. She shook her head and gave me one of those looks the women around here specialize in. Then she said, 'You Americans must be very unhappy people.' I thought it would be a shame to spoil her idea of us, so I said, 'Madam, you've missed the point.

Americans aren't interested in being happy. They're interested in having a good time.'"

To Lucy it was a delicious feeling to know that he liked sitting quietly with her in her garden. His eyes showed that he was enjoying the concealed excitement and sense of life he had aroused in her, and Lucy's happiness was not spoiled by the realization that he had always found it easy to make women like him. She was not even disturbed when she realized that he was fundamentally a sensual man, for he was not calculating, like the Europeans she had read about in books. He seemed to assume that he shared this quality in himself with every normal man in the world, and she wondered if his assumption that his desires would be taken for granted was partly the basis of his attractiveness to women.

By six o'clock the shadows were long in the garden, the sun was half-hidden by trees, in the pale Ontario sky above them a gull slowly circled, and as coolness grew, the nicotianas began to open. Lucy found herself talking about her flowers again, trying to explain why something which was quite unprofitable and such hard work meant so much to her.

"You know, a garden measures out all the good times of the year. I've arranged it as nearly as I can so that the colour-masses balance and complement each other. Spring is the best time, naturally. First the cool colours – the crocuses and hyacinths and lilies-of-the-valley. Then the daffodils and tulips, and just before the tulips fade, the whole garden bursts out like a full orchestra." She looked at him smiling, and without shyness she added, "You've missed a lot in your life, haven't you?"

"I've missed at least half a dozen years out of it on account of the Depression. I'd like flowers if I had time or a place for them, but flowers in themselves – well, they don't lead to much, do they?"

"What would you want them to lead to?"

"Money, for one thing."

"And if you got money, where would that lead to?"

"There'd be time to figure that out when I had it. To all sorts of things. I guess it's been bred into me to think that way. I don't give a damn about money for its own sake, with me it would be something to work with. I know I'm not a creative engineer, but I've got ideas. With money, I could hire technicians to try them out. My father made quite a few millions and making them was a game to him, but he always figured that when he had made a big enough pile he'd found a trust of some sort. He'd be ashamed of me if he could know how little I've done so far."

"But your father lost his money?"

"Yes, but he'd proved he could make it. He'd lived a full life. He'd shown what he could do." He saw her smiling. "What are you thinking about?"

"After what you've just said it would sound rather foolish."

"What is it?"

"Well, to me just being – just existing – would be a full life, if –"

"If what?"

"If I felt I were making the most of all that lay around me. If I felt I were doing things I really liked. If I felt free to be myself as natural as one of those flowers. Stephen – doesn't it seem pointless to use up all the best years of your life just making money like your father did, so that when you're an old man you can build a memorial with it?" She smiled again. "My uncle, Matt McCunn, says the only time money is important is when you haven't got any."

He looked at her curiously. "He worked at the Ceramic, didn't he?"

"Yes."

"I was sorry I had to let him go."

"He doesn't mind. He's really a very happy man."

Crickets and katydids enhanced the long silence which followed. He watched her as she lay back in the chair, and realized that her attraction for him was unique. Usually he was drawn to boldness in a woman, or the piquant suggestions her figure evoked in his mind. The feelings aroused in him by Lucy were subtler and almost mysterious, they warmed him inside. As he wondered what expression her face would hold if he ever made love to her, he realized that he had no idea what it would be. She was not conventionally beautiful; probably she was not beautiful at all. He tried without success to find a phrase to describe her. She was virginal, yet often she seemed more mature and knowledgeable than most of the women he knew. She seemed very sure of her ideas, without trying to force them on anyone else, the way his sister Marcia did. Probably she had what one of his uncles would call a philosophy.

Lassiter got up and crossed to her, and standing behind her, laid his fingers on her dark hair. He liked the texture of it, but wished she would fix it less plainly. A hairdresser in New York would be able to transform a girl like this in a single session.

"How did you learn so much, living here?"

She looked back and up at him, her forehead wrinkling, her lips breaking into a smile. "Me? I haven't learned anything much. Only a little about myself. In Grenville there's at least plenty of time to think."

"I heard someone say once that if you knew yourself you knew everything. Or was it Socrates who said it? I don't know. Anyway, Socrates didn't know calculus." He grinned down at her. "I'm one up on him there. I used to be good at it."

He looked up at the sky. The moon was clearly visible, pale as a white flower in the faded blue of the sky. He moved around to the front of the chair and held out his hand.

"Let's get out of here before your sisters come back. Let's drive to Toronto and see what kind of a dinner Ontario's big town can give us?"

She thought of Jane as he pulled her to her feet, and supposed there would be still another scene in the morning if she went with him. Then she felt his arm about her waist, his body as strong and solid as a wall, and again she felt the excitement of knowing a man really wanted her company.

"I'll have to change."

She left him in the garden and went into the house. When she returned she was wearing a natural linen suit and brown accessories.

"It suits you," he said. "You're so cool and lovely it makes me feel good just to look at you."

OVER the weekend the weather broke and a heavy gale rode inland off the lake. The Cameron house was so dark that lights had to be turned on during the day and a wind that had started far down the Mississippi Valley and then had been pushed eastward by a cold front moving from Hudson Bay tore over the rolling Ontario land. On Saturday afternoon Lassiter called Lucy to say that the power system at the plant had failed and that he would be working late that night and would have to work all day Sunday to complete his report to Ashweiler and he wished he could see her but he couldn't.

Tired from three late nights in succession, and from the strain of resisting the sense of guilt which Jane's close-lipped and forbidding silence spread through the house, Lucy rested and tried to interest herself in a novel. That night she went to bed early and fell asleep with the house trembling in the wind and the thunder of rapid waves hitting the beach in her ears.

On Sunday morning the whole country looked wet and flat. A few lonely cars swished over the King's Highway and the pavement was black in the rain. The wind had ceased, but the rain still fell, and just before eleven o'clock the sidewalks of King Street were filled with people walking under umbrellas to the churches.

There was tension in St. David's that morning, and Lucy noticed that a good many of the middle-aged men were wearing service buttons from the war. Most of the veterans had discarded the habit of wearing them years ago, but now they had taken them out of drawers, polished them, and quietly fitted them into their lapels. She found herself counting their young sons who sat in the pews beside them, the ones in their middle teens who were still at school. Remembering Lassiter's tanned face, she noticed how the English and Scottish ruddiness predominated in the complexions of all these Grenville men. She found herself comparing the younger ones with their fathers. The fathers' faces looked heavier in expression than their sons' ever would. Not sad, but ponderously confident, more rugged and less sensitive, and the difference was not entirely caused by the difference in age. These youngsters were a new breed for Canada. Their features showed less stubbornness and perhaps less durability, but more refinement and more imagination. Across the aisle and several pews ahead she saw Bruce Fraser. He was one of the few men present who was in his early twenties, but there was no doubt that he was far closer to the sons than to the fathers. A world in which he would feel at home would be a very different place from the world John Knox Cameron and Jane had made for her.

Dr. Grant rose in the pulpit. He had been a chaplain in France and he was still close to the returned men. His powerful hands gripped the lectern, his short grey hair bristled, and his large nose seemed to grow larger still.

"Pour out thy fury upon the heathen that know thee not, and upon the families that call not on thy name: for they have eaten up Jacob, and devoured him, and consumed him, and have made his habitation desolate."

He preached for half an hour to these innocent people about the evil that was inherent in mankind. He was sick with anxiety about Hitler, and it was clear to him that Hitler would never have been allowed to reach power if the world had shared his own Presbyterian conception of wickedness. "They thought they could abolish evil by appointing committees of experts to deal with it."

After the service the three sisters went home to the usual Sunday dinner of roast beef and browned potatoes and a trifle for dessert. All the time they had been listening to Dr. Grant the roast had been cooking in a slow oven. During dinner the rain stopped and a changed wind sprang off the lake. About three o'clock Bruce came over and they all sat down to listen to a summer concert on the radio, but just when the last noisy surge of a Wagnerian overture was finished and Mozart's flutes began to sing into the room, they had to turn off the radio to receive callers.

Bruce went home and Jane poured tea for two elderly women and one white-haired man who stayed till half-past five. By that time the sky had lightened, the clouds broke open, and the sun drove to the west in a blaze of ruddy gold. Robins appeared on the soaked grass of the lawn. They made quick running steps and froze with heads cocked to listen for worms, their beaks darted and then they shot forward over the grass again. The garden beds were spangled with white, lavender, and pink petals beaten from the phlox by the rain and the wind.

No one in the Cameron house mentioned Lassiter's name throughout the day, though all three sisters, each in her own fashion, was acutely conscious of his presence among them.

WHEN Lassiter called for Lucy late Monday afternoon she knew that the easy atmosphere of their last meeting was not going to be repeated. There was a tight look about his mouth and he seemed irritable.

"I've had another letter from Cleveland," he said when they were out on the road. "You pour yourself into a job like I've been doing and it just looks like routine for them. I don't know. You never can be sure what Sani-Quip will do because it hasn't got any feelings. When they want to be, they can be very tactful. Last year when they took over the Ceramic, the big shots that came up here were so tactful that Jim Craig still thinks they're swell. It's part of the system. If they fire Jim they'll give him a pension because Canadian good will is worth the price." He shrugged his shoulders. "My good will doesn't matter a damn and they know it. I'm just another engineer."

After that he drove for miles in silence and some of his tension spread to Lucy. She felt helpless to say anything to make him feel better, for she knew nothing about his work. Just after sunset they slowed down as they entered a town grim and angular with brick houses. The town hall was red and there was a red factory with windows dark and some of them broken. Men and women with grey faces were crowded around the door of a movie house when they parked the car and got out. A middle-aged man with two front teeth missing asked Lassiter for ten cents for a cup of coffee and Lassiter gave him half a dollar. Then they looked through the fly-blown windows of a place called the Maple Leaf Cafe and Lassiter swore.

"What's the matter with this country? Doesn't anyone but Greeks and Chinamen run restaurants in Ontario? Do you want to go on to the next town?"

"I doubt if it will be any better. We might as well have supper here. Let's try the one across the street."

They edged into a booth in a place called the Radio Cafe and ate leathery steaks in a smell of stale cooking grease, tobacco smoke, and the sourness of spilled milk which had accumulated spill by spill over the months and had never been adequately cleaned from the flooring. On and off, a juke box blared so loud they found it hard to talk.

"I hate textile towns," he said.

She laid down her knife and fork with the steak only half-eaten.

"All the same," he said, "this town here counts for more than Grenville. It's got four times as much industry. Do you know what that means?"

"I'm not sure that I do."

"It means for one thing that nice places aren't important any more."

She wondered what lay behind the odd defiance in his manner tonight, but did not try to say anything.

"Outside of New York, what places are important on this continent? Pittsburgh, Chicago, Detroit, Youngstown, even a place like Ponca City in Oklahoma. That's the kind of town that counts. Newark is a dump but it counts. And I'm not talking about the best sections in those places, either. I'm talking about the worst." He looked up at her. "Your world is dead, Lucy. Do you know it?"

His strangeness startled her. "What is my world?"

"I was thinking of you in the garden. It shows in your face, what you feel about that garden. You're beautiful in a way hardly any women are any more. The women you see in New York crossing the Plaza at five o'clock are supposed to be the most wonderful in the world, but they don't look like you. They never remind anybody of a garden. You see them there, they're polished and their clothes cost a fortune, but – but what do they mean? Of course, they're the product of a system, and Carl Bratian says the final product of any system is never any good for anything. Yet every woman in the United States who has to work for a living, every ordinary housewife in the sticks – no matter how plain she is, she's aware of those women in New York."

Lucy wondered whether he was talking against her or against a preconceived idea in his own mind. Her intuition told her he was not talking against her, and presently his eyes softened as he turned away.

"You're lovely," he murmured. "No, I'd never want to change you."

She looked directly at him. "I don't think anyone could."

"Then my being around here hasn't made any trouble for you?"

"Not much."

"Wasn't it simpler before?"

"Only on the surface."

He pushed aside a plate containing soggy apple pie and lit a cigarette.

"It's a funny thing," he said. "Back home a lot of people think I'm soft. I don't mean physically – they never thought I was soft when I played football. I mean people like Ashweiler and Carl Bratian. They think I let it matter too much if I like somebody. But up here I've had the feeling that Jim Craig and a lot of others think I'm hard." Seeing her smile, he added almost indignantly. "Are you laughing at me?"

"No."

"Then what are you doing?"

"Using my imagination, I suppose."

"Yes," he said softly, giving her a sudden intent look. "Yes, you're always using it." He continued to look at her steadily. "Does it matter to you that I've known rather a lot of women?"

"Should it matter?"

"What would your sisters feel about it? Would they think I was immoral if they knew?"

She broke into a laugh which disconcerted him. "They both know anyway."

On the drive back, the moon rode with them. It was almost full now and it whitened the fields. The Ontario lake shore, so gentle, so immature, as if the people who lived here were afraid of losing the austere and bitter innocence of youth, and so kept themselves more plain than was necessary by building their homes with harsh and angular lines, red brick or wood painted in drab colours, was now so transfigured by the moonlight that one's imagination could discover in it almost any shape of beauty found existing within one's self. The car whispered along quietly and once Lucy had the sensation of being at rest while the landscape shifted and flowed past. She pictured the waterway stretching from here back eastward along the trail of the *voyageurs* to the point where Lake Ontario ends and the St. Lawrence begins, through the flat land of Dundas County where lighted ships in the canals seem like long, low houses moving across the darkness of the fields, through the blaze of light at Montreal and thence down the avenue of the river past the intimate lights of parish after parish, past Quebec and the Ile d'Orléans till the river widens into the solitudes of salt water and no lights remain, and the air is cold and surges smash and drag in the darkness along the empty cliffs of the Gaspé and Labrador.

His voice broke the reverie. "If you left here, would you miss it?"

"Yes, of course."

"Would you mind leaving?"

"I don't know. It would depend."

His right hand closed over hers. A mist had risen and it lay on the water like a range of broken hills facing the undulating land, gleaming in the moonlight.

"Are you getting cold?"

"A little."

"It seems to get cold about a month earlier here than at home. You notice it at night."

He stopped the car and snapped the top into place, then drove on more slowly. By the time they reached Grenville swathes of mist had drifted inland, up Matilda Lane as far as the King's Highway, and the trees loomed through it without shadows while the pale light rode above them. The LaSalle glided to a stop.

"Every light in your house is out." His lips were almost at her ear. "Maybe your elder sister has got used to me at last."

"Have you known all along how Jane feels?"

"I guessed some of it from your face when you mentioned her. Then Jim Craig helped. He says she's pretty strict."

Lucy shivered slightly.

"Cold?"

"Not very."

The muted sigh of a truck passing on the main highway puffed down the street and it was followed by the forlorn wail of a whistle as a freight train approached a level crossing. The town clock, very faint, struck the half-hour.

"Lucy?"

His voice was low. His hand gripped hers and she felt it quiver. Her free hand opened the door, she released herself and slipped out. Then he joined her under the trees.

They walked slowly down the end of the street toward the commons. A light burned in the Frasers' house and she knew it was in Bruce's room and that he was probably reading in bed. With the grass of the common soft under her feet she felt the mist enfolding them, felt it cold and wet against her face, and then they stood on the shore staring into nothing. Under the mist a wave turned over and broke with a gasp.

His hand found the soft warmth under her arm, and slowly turning, she lifted her face. As the whole length of her body felt his strength against her, his thighs and chest flexing hard as he strained her close, he kissed her so hard her lips felt bruised. Then he bent and picked her up as if she were a child.

He stood there on the sand in the darkness holding her, his cheek rough against hers, and it was several minutes before he became aware of her lack of response. He set her down and she stood beside him looking out into the dark mist, hearing the occasional wash of a wave, feeling his hand about her waist so tight she had to strain

to breathe against it. For several minutes Lucy felt cold and empty
and more alone than she could ever remember feeling in her life. A
man she liked better than anyone she had ever known had touched
and caressed her, and the strangeness of it had daunted her.

His hand moved to her shoulder and she felt his fingers stroking
her hair and cheek.

"If I'd never touched another woman – would you like me better?"

Her heart stirred at the wistfulness in his voice. He seemed so
strangely and surprisingly immature. With a sense almost of physical
pain, she felt the hard core of resistance created by her whole life
begin to melt. In this sightless mist there were no shapes or straight
lines or even movement or sound. She took the fingers of his hand
from her hair and pressed them to her cheek. He made no attempt
to kiss her again. He simply stood there with her head against his
shoulder and his fingers in hers against her cheek.

"How did you happen?" she said simply. "What made you think
you'd like someone like me?"

"I don't know. At least, not to put it into words."

"Was it only because you've been alone here?"

"At first, yes. At first I thought you'd be different. You'd be something new." He stopped. "But that didn't last very long."

She made no move and for many minutes they were silent.

Lucy's mind became cool as it informed her she was at a crisis
of her life. It informed her that she had no experience, she had
nothing to go by but intuition. But she knew that she understood
at least one part of him; she understood his loneliness. Almost, she
understood that his boyish sensuality was perhaps the best part of
him because it was his own blind way of trying to discover himself.
The world his conscious mind admired seemed both senseless and
harsh to her. He valued none of the things she loved best. He had
none of Bruce Fraser's desire to make the world a better place.
Almost, his conscious attitude seemed to state without words, "I
didn't make the rules. And I know, as in your heart you know, that
there's nothing to be done about them."

When he spoke his voice was quietly intense, as if he were talking
to himself. "Wanting a woman isn't the same as loving her. The way
I've lived, it's been simpler to want things. You see what you want
and you try to get it. Generally you have to pay for it." His voice

grew heavy with emotion. "But loving isn't wanting, Lucy. I wish it were. Then maybe I could understand it. Last night, alone in that goddam hotel room, I got scared."

She heard his words with wonder. She knew then that he was more lonely than she herself had ever been. She could sense that his eyes were straining through the darkness toward her.

"For hours last night I lay awake listening to that town clock beating itself up and all I could see was your face. Not your body, but your face. I remembered the way you'd looked at trees and flowers as if nobody had ever seen them before. Nobody has looked at me the way you do since I was a kid."

A series of small waves broke with a slow rhythm on the sand, and they took a few steps backward to avoid the upward wash. Her mind leaping for an instant out of the intensity of the second, she wondered where the waves had come from.

"There must be a freighter out there in the fog," she murmured.

He paid no attention to her remark. He probably did not even hear it.

"Last night I was thinking about myself. I've taken a wrong steer some place. I don't know what it is. I thought I was getting ahead with Sani-Quip. Now Carl's made me see I haven't a chance with them. I don't know what's the matter. That crowd in Cleveland ..."

He stopped, and for a long time the only sound was the whisper of water drops falling from leaves as they congealed into globules, and the globules slid off the slope of the leaves in the dark.

"Then I came up here. I'd never lived in a place like this before. It seemed like – well, like the United States might have been forty or fifty years ago. Maybe like parts of the South are now where things haven't really begun to move. Then I began to wonder what the hell had happened to all of us – my family, I mean. My mother had everything she wanted, but before she died she didn't even have a real home. Her relatives were just so many names in an address book. My sister is as clever as hell, she knows all the answers, but Jesus – she's made a mess out of her life. She's not thirty yet and she's gone through two husbands already. And yet we had everything. We ought to have been the happiest people in the world." A silence. "Then I met you. You've never been anywhere, but you make me feel ignorant. You seem to understand things I don't know anything about." He stopped, and then he went on with a surge of emotion.

"I never wanted to fall in love with anyone like you, Lucy, but I have."

Her face lifted and her sigh lost itself in the mist. He kissed her very gently. His hands caressed her breasts, and her head dropped back. As she felt his strength urgent against her body, her mind lurched and swayed, and a quiver of ecstasy flashed along her nerves. Out of the darkness the ecstasy grew and became visible, a jet of unbelievable flame flaring out of primeval darkness.

"Lucy!" He was holding her up, and she realized she had gone limp in his arms. "Are you all right?"

She tried to see his face in the darkness. She slipped into his arms and for a long time her lips were hungry under his. Then abruptly she broke free as implanted fears surged up and made her ashamed. Even as her mind told her there was nothing to be ashamed of, she felt drained and helpless. In clinging to him as she had done, in yielding to his hands on her breasts, she had revealed the heat of her own desire, and so had surrendered to him forever the gift of her invulnerability.

"I'm in love with you, Lucy."

The words hit her mind like the clang of a bell.

"There's never been anything like this for me before. Say something, Lucy, for God's sake!"

She could not answer him. She heard his voice begging, begging for what she did not know, in her dazed confusion his voice became like a choir: "I love you, Lucy. I can do anything now. I can trample down everything that's kept me back. It's been inside me, that's where the trouble was. I love you, Lucy." She turned from him and moved inland. In this haunted, luminous mist the trees were strange. They were cool and ghostly like fungoid outgrowths of the darkness itself, like the colourless, scentless, noiseless landscape of a dark dream through which once she had wandered lost and alien, and then had awakened in the familiar room, her body floating weightless on the bed while her reason recorded the fact that she had returned from a journey through herself and had found a mysterious peace in that foreign place. But now she was alone in the empty room of the night, alone with her ignorance and guilt and pity that things must always be as they are.

He was still beside her, holding her wrists. "I love you, Lucy. This is real, you know."

Her lips opened but nothing came from them. Her mind said, What is love, What is love? And then crazily, she heard Jane's voice. God is love, Lucy. Lonely God.

Her eyes groped through the dark for his massive presence beside her. That was all he was in this mist, a present mass. She had forgotten even what he looked like. He seized her almost roughly, as though his muscular strength could break down all obstacles in her, his hands caressed her body with fierce boldness, his lips passed over her eyes and cheeks until she was physically exhausted.

Then abruptly he broke away. "I've been alone too long. I'm sorry."

A startled night-bird screamed in the darkness over the lake. She stood there silent and invisible beside him under the trees.

"There's something I want to tell you," he said. "But I'd rather let it go until some other time. It's not important. It hasn't anything to do with you and me." She was silent, so he said, "We'd better go back. Tomorrow – if you will – we'll sit quietly and talk."

Her eyes blurred with tears and she laid the back of his hand against her cheek. It was so large her face felt frail against it.

Then she turned toward home and he walked quietly beside her as they passed up the common through the trees to the road. He kissed her lightly as she opened the door of the house, then turned without a word and went back to his car.

THE next morning Lucy was wakened by the sound of Jane giving a piano lesson. She heard a spatter of rain against the window and closed her eyes. Fifteen minutes later she opened them with a start and saw by the clock on her dresser that it was five minutes past ten. She remembered she had forgotten to set the alarm the night before, and wondered if Jane had been cross about having to get the breakfast herself. Slipping out of bed, she put on a dressing gown, stretched, and went to the window. Her eyes were heavy with sleep as she looked out at the rain. She remembered having heard the first drops just before falling asleep at four in the morning.

Her lips were tender, and she started impulsively to the mirror to see if his kisses had bruised them, thinking from the way they felt that they must be tell-tale to everyone. All she saw in the mirror was a sleepy face. It was only then that she noticed the bowl of flowers on her desk. Five roses, with a few raindrops still clinging to their petals.

When she entered the hall she heard Nina moving in her own bedroom and Lucy went to her door impulsively.

"Oh, Nina, thank you for cutting the roses."

"It seemed a shame to leave them out in the rain. And don't worry about breakfast. I got it for Jane."

"Thank you," Lucy said. There was more than gratitude in her voice.

At half-past eleven Lassiter telephoned. "Look," he said without preliminaries, "this is the devil. I've to go back to Cleveland right away."

She was ashamed to be trembling all over at the thought of his leaving her alone again.

"For good?" she managed to say.

"God, no! Only for a week. Maybe I'll even be back before that. Working for Sani-Quip is like being in the army. You're never sure what's cooking." His voice sounded almost gaily casual as he added, "Going to miss me?"

Lucy glanced down the hall. Nina was upstairs and Jane was giving a lesson to an exceptionally bad pupil who was making one mistake after another in a complicated series of scales.

"Yes. How soon are you leaving?"

No sound came from the other end of the wire. Then she realized he had put his hand over the mouthpiece to speak to somebody in the office. His voice came again.

"Wait a minute." She could hear him talking impatiently to someone at the other end, then he returned to her. "These bastards say I've got to leave right now. They're driving me to Toronto to catch a plane and they're in a hurry. I hate to go like this!"

"It's all right, Stephen."

"I'll be back soon. Only a week at the most, darling. Think about me while I'm gone or I won't be able to stand it."

She murmured something and the wire went dead, leaving her staring up at *The Death of Nelson*. Rain drummed on the clapboards and the entire house brooded in dark shadows and grey light as she went down the hall to resume the mechanical routine of her housework.

At noon a pupil left and Jane turned on the radio for news. Nina came downstairs and all three listened to the exquisite voice of the BBC announcer who had been carrying the world crisis for over a month into every little town along the Canadian railroad tracks. Today the announcer told the world that this year's conference of the Nazi Party at Nuremberg was going to be the most dramatic ever held, that the *Diplomatische Korrespondenz* had produced another threatening editorial, and that Mr. Chamberlain had no comment to make.

"I can't understand," Jane interrupted, "why England goes on pampering those people."

ON THURSDAY evening of that week Lassiter telephoned from Cleveland. When Lucy came downstairs in answer to Nina's summons, she was aware of a muted sense of excitement in the house. It was her first long-distance call. He began by telling her he would be back the following Tuesday. For several minutes he kept up a half-kidding conversation, and she answered in such a low voice he thought the connection was bad. It never occurred to him that her sisters, one in the living room and the other just out of sight at the top of the stairs, were listening to every word she said.

Finally he burst out, "God damn this phone! It's bad enough being more than five hundred miles away from you without – can't you hear me yet?"

"Yes," she said. "You could easily be right here."

"Well, I can hardly hear a word you say. Lucy – I'm as lonely as hell. But I've found out something important. You and I are made for each other. We've got to get –"

Jane came out of the living room and Lucy shifted to one side in hasty embarrassment as she passed down the narrow hall. The receiver twisted against her ear and his next words were blurred. Jane passed on up the stairs.

"... and remember it till I get back."

"I'm afraid I didn't hear," she said. "Not all of it."

"God damn this phone, it's got me licked! I'll be back on Tuesday. In the meantime, remember I love you. Did you hear that?"

"Yes."

Then he hung up and she went into the living room. Her embarrassment gave way to wonder as she realized the full import of what he had said.

She switched on the light over the piano, sat down, and tried to compose her nerves by playing the music which was open on the rest. It was the "Waldstein Sonata" and the allegro movement was much too difficult for her fingers. Then Nina burst into the room.

"Oh, for heaven's sake, Lucy – stop that! It sounds terrible."

"I'm sorry." She turned from the piano.

Nina's impish face appeared in the light. "How does it feel? Long-distance calls and everything! He didn't call just to hear the sound of your voice, did he?"

"Long-distance calls don't mean anything to Americans."

"From the expression on your face they mean something to you. You look like the cat –" She lowered her voice to a whisper. "You should have seen Jane."

"I did."

Lucy got up and turned her back, her old habit of defence against Nina reasserting itself. She picked up a book and went upstairs to her room.

But that night when she lay in bed unable to sleep, her mind was filled with a sort of wild radiance. She whispered to herself in the empty room, "How could a thing like this happen to me! How could a man like Stephen fall in love with someone like me!" Then she remembered the feeling of his lips on hers. She remembered the enormous strength of his body as he had held her. She recalled how people in Grenville had looked up to him as a man with authority who knew his job. She knew nothing of his work, but it was good to know he was respected for it. She felt strangely proud of him. And then she recalled the wistfulness in his voice as he had spoken to her that night on the beach in the darkness. He was not miraculous. He was not someone out of a fairy tale coming to rescue her from frustration. He had known many other women and yet he had singled her out from them all. She closed her eyes and listened to the stirring of a faint wind in the trees. She tried to imagine herself with children, living with freedom in her own house. She felt an overpowering gratitude to this man who had been the first to recognize her as a woman. Again she recalled the feeling of his lips on her own, and her body moved in bed as she turned on her side, her fingers against her cheeks. He needed her and she loved him. Whatever he wanted she would do.

For the remainder of that week she felt utterly alone, but not solitary. She was unable to imagine what the next months would bring. She merely waited out the days until his return with a confidence she had never known. Several women she met in the town commented on how well she was looking, and Jane, sensing in her sister an invulnerability and a dignity she had never remarked before, was puzzled and disturbed.

This mood of wonder, doubt, and excitement lasted until Sunday.

They were in church again, and the sunshine of a fine day poured in through the gothic windows. Even more of the older men were wearing their service buttons; but today, in this lovely end-of-the-summer warmth, there was no tension in the church. They sang "The Lord Is My Shepherd" to "Wiltshire" and followed it up with "Fight the Good Fight" and "The Church's One Foundation." The anthem was "Lift Up Your Heads," and when Jane's choir broke into it the faces of the singers shone with their pleasure in the music. Watching them, seeing the sunshine pouring into the church on bald heads and white hair, on young children with their parents, Lucy thought what a laundered, soap-and-water appearance the people all had this morning, and the other side of the Presbyterian faith, the great and noble side enunciated in the response to the first proposition of the Catechism, struck Lucy with a force she had never felt in a church before – *Man's chief end is to glorify God and enjoy Him forever!* Her father, she thought smiling, might have wanted to believe that, but he had never felt it safe to take a chance on it.

When the service was over Lucy and Nina waited on the lawn for Jane to join them from the choir entrance. Family friends stopped to speak, and the usual fragments of conversation drifted about: "I thought the choir was simply marvellous this morning. Miss Cameron's really wonderful with them, don't you think ... If only Dr. Grant wasn't so depressed about Hitler ... But he's *so* right about committees ... look at Mrs. Edgerton's work to get a committee together to get rid of that pool room! She's losing her mind and the place is still open for business ... The Baptists must have had a long sermon today ... Poor things, Dr. Puddington is such a trial to them ..."

The doors of the neighbouring church opened and let a flood of Baptists into the street. Jane appeared from the side entrance, came out along the path, and joined Lucy and Nina. Out of the press of Baptists heading west, Mrs. Craig, the wife of the manager of the Ceramic Company, detached herself and approached them. They all agreed it was a fine day.

Looking at the sisters with a smile both kindly and meaningful, Mrs. Craig said, "I've been wanting to tell you. I thought it was so nice for Mr. Lassiter to be able to meet you all when he was here. Jim and I liked him so much, and we used to wonder what he'd do for company in Grenville. A man like that is used to so much excitement and activity. I'm sure you were a godsend to him."

Before Jane could speak, Nina cut in. "He was probably good for us, too," she said.

Mrs. Craig nodded to a passing acquaintance. "I hope he'll be able to bring his wife back with him," she said. "I'd like to meet her. From a picture I saw of her in the society page of *The New York Times* she must be an exceptionally striking-looking woman."

A lifetime habit of control kept Lucy's face expressionless. Out of the corner of her eye she saw that Nina had given a quick start and had flushed. The silence which followed Mrs. Craig's remark lasted no more than two seconds, but to Lucy it seemed eternal.

Jane broke it. She smiled easily, and her voice was quietly matter-of-fact. "We only just met him, you know, and he barely mentioned his wife. One day he was in the library when I was on duty and he asked me a lot of questions about the books we had. Later on he came to tea in the garden." She paused to speak to a friend, then continued, "His wife must be famous to be in the *Times*. Is she an actress?"

"No, I don't think she's *that* famous." Mrs. Craig's eyes passed quickly from Jane to Lucy, and Lucy knew that the next remark was intended for her. She also knew that the older woman was being kind. Mrs. Craig liked to talk and Jane thought her a fool, but she was one of the most tolerant people in Grenville. "He stayed with us the first two weeks he was here, you know." She smiled and nodded to another friend. "He used to get the Sunday papers from

New York and he gave them to me when he was finished. I was quite excited when I saw a picture on the society page with the name underneath – Mrs. Stephen Lassiter. I asked him if she was a relation. I thought of course he knew it was there. Then he looked at the paper and said, 'So she's in the paper again, is she?' Then he grinned – you know that funny kind of grin so many Americans seem to have, as if they were making fun of you and themselves at the same time. 'Meet my wife, Mrs. Craig,' he said to me. Then he handed the paper back and asked me what I thought of her. I was so taken aback I hadn't the slightest idea what to say, it seemed such a funny question to be asked."

Nina turned to go, but Jane remained where she was, speaking quite calmly. Lucy was motionless. Her face had become pale, and she knew it.

"Of course," Jane said, "we're so quiet I'm sure we bored Mr. Lassiter almost to death, but on the other hand, I must say he didn't have much to talk about that interested me." She nodded to another acquaintance and turned toward the sidewalk. "Are you going our way? I'd meant to ask someone what Mr. Orme finally chose for his anthem in your church this morning. He told me Friday he wanted "God Is a Spirit," but he thought his sopranos were too loud for it. I know *mine* are."

"YOU'VE made me lie," Jane said when they had reached their own living room.

Lucy looked at her dumbly and shook her head. Nina went out into the hall and they heard a sudden burst of sobbing. Without raising her voice, Jane turned her head to the open door.

"Nina, stop being hysterical." Then, turning back to Lucy with her high cheekbones flushed, she said, "I never thought we'd have to be ashamed."

Lucy lifted her chin and her voice was steady though her hands trembled. "No one has to be ashamed. There was nothing done to be ashamed of. All he said was that he loves me, and I still believe him."

"You pitiful fool!"

Nina burst into the room and flung herself at Jane. "Don't you say things to Lucy like that! Can't you see – can't you ever see anything, Jane? She's in love with him and it's beautiful and you're killing her, talking like that."

Jane's hands traced the beginning of a caressing motion over Nina's tousled hair, but she suppressed the gesture and forced her young sister away. Nina stood back, looking at her with an expression of bewildered and angry fear under her tousled yellow hair.

"Can't you ever think of how people feel? What will happen to me when I fall in love if you're going to think I'm terrible too?"

Jane's steady gaze reduced Nina to silence. Then she said quietly, "I'm old enough to be your mother, Nina. In a few years you'll understand what that means. Now please go out and lay the table for dinner. I want to talk to Lucy and I want to talk to her alone."

Nina stared back, but only for a moment. Then she dropped her eyes and did what she was told.

Jane turned calmly to Lucy. "I never thought I'd have to tell a lie to anybody, much less to a person like Mrs. Craig. The Craigs have never had anything but money and they haven't had that for long. They'd be very pleased to be able to look down on people like us." She created a long, deliberate pause. "I suppose you're aware that she knew I was telling a lie?"

Lucy looked into her sister's eyes. They were large, black as buttons, and they gleamed with intensity.

"I don't care," she said. "You had no reason to tell her anything, except for the sake of your pride. If you wanted to tell her something, why didn't you tell her the truth? Or what you thought was the truth?"

Jane looked at her steadily. "Father loved you more than he did any of us, and yet he never quite trusted you. He was always afraid you'd be too soft."

Lucy turned her back on her sister and looked up to the mantelpiece. Her father's picture stared back at her.

"What are you trying to do, Jane? Drive me out of the house?"

She turned and saw Jane make a small motion with her hand.

"Don't be silly and don't make a scene," Jane said. "Neither you nor Nina can earn your own living. You seem to forget we're poor and that none of us is clever. If we lose our self-respect and common sense, we're completely ruined. We've never been able to afford luxuries, and these – these emotional upsets are the worst luxuries of all."

Lucy felt as if her whole body were surging away from Jane. Actually she moved quietly, with her usual slow constrained motion, across the room to the window. Clear and radiantly blue, the lake reflected the sky.

"I'm sick of hypocrisy," she said. "I'm sick of living with fear. Fear of what?" Her voice almost broke. "Fear of nothing but what people like Father put into our minds when we were helpless children. I'm not ashamed. I'm not ashamed I fell in love even if Stephen is married. I don't mind Mrs. Craig knowing the truth."

"*Knowing* the truth!" Jane's lips became a thin line, and her voice quivered with the passion of her bitter knowledge. "Have you become soft-headed as well as soft-hearted? What does knowing the truth matter? Anyone who stops to think – even for a few minutes – knows the truth about most people. What matters is *talking* about it. When people talk about it, it becomes different. It becomes horrible."

Lucy turned quickly. "Jane – that's mad!"

"Is it?" Jane said grimly. "Is it? Let me tell you something. Elizabeth Craig may have thought I was lying to her this morning. But she only *thinks* I was because I kept up appearances. As long as she's not absolutely sure, she's not going to talk about you. That's the kind of a woman she happens to be, and you can count yourself lucky."

The expression on Jane's face was one Lucy had never seen before. It was completely unmasked. It was the expression of a woman infinitely shrewd.

"I don't care," Lucy said desperately. "It's degrading to live in hiding like this. People here aren't cruel. People in Grenville are kind if you give them a chance."

"People here," said Jane softly, "are like people anywhere else. They don't really like women like us. They don't like men like Father. There's nothing to be done about it and it doesn't matter. For they always respect us."

"Respect us? For what we do? Or for what we don't do?"

"For what we are! And you can be very sure they'll be merciless if we ever give them a chance to say we aren't what we seem to be. It's too late, Lucy. It's too late for you to be another kind of woman even if you want to be."

Lucy put both hands over her face. In a whisper she repeated, "I'm not ashamed. I won't let you make me ashamed."

For several seconds Jane regarded her. "You will always have to live here," she said. "I see nothing else for it because these days a woman has to be very highly trained to become anything but a shopgirl or a kind of servant." She paused, calmly waiting. Then, her voice still quiet, she continued. "If everyone in town went about telling everyone else that you'd been keeping company with a married man – you, a girl they've had the impertinence to pity because you've been quiet and cultured and decent – if they said you'd been committing adultery with this sordid American – and you may be quite sure that's exactly what they *would* say if the talk started – if you knew, every time you passed people on the street, what they'd say the moment you were out of earshot, and if each time you remembered you'd have to go on living with such talk for years until you were an old woman – do you think you'd be able to tell me *then* you weren't ashamed?"

There was a long silence. Lucy's knees grew weak and she shook her head slowly. "No," she said in a whisper. "No."

Jane drew in her breath. "Now run along, and let's have our dinner in peace."

THAT night Lucy slept only a few hours. She woke in the morning to a cool fresh day, made breakfast, and went out to the garden. It was no comfort to her, for the whole enclosure ached with the recollection of her own happiness. She saw the deck chair in which Stephen had sat and talked. Its canvas seat was limp and shabby and ruffled in the light breeze.

She left the garden and returned to the house and tried to get through with her usual work. Bobby Harmon was bungling his first piano lesson as usual. He jangled, stopped while Jane lectured him, then blundered on again. She left the house and walked into town, hoping to meet the postman on the way. She knew there would be no letter from Stephen, for he was not the kind who would write letters even if he had something to say; if he wanted to talk to her he would telephone. She did not see the postman, but by the time she had reached the highway she had almost persuaded herself there would be a letter from him in the morning mail; there would surely be something to explain what he had done. A man like Stephen, she told herself, was far too frank and direct to tell her he loved her, practically to ask her to marry him, if all the time he was already married himself.

She met the postman on her return and he handed her only one envelope, which was not from Stephen. It was addressed to the Misses Cameron in Mrs. Craig's neat, correct and commonplace handwriting, and it contained a brief note and a clipping from a newspaper. Lucy crumpled the note and dropped it into her pocket, took a quick glance at the picture and slipped it into her shopping bag. Then, as she looked up, she saw Matt McCunn waiting for her at the corner. He was as neat as ever, this morning wearing a blue polka-dot tie, his trousers threadbare at the cuffs but freshly pressed, his face genial and almost dapper.

When she reached him she made no attempt to return his smile. "I thought you'd gone up north for the winter?" she said.

McCunn grinned. "Well, everything was against it from the beginning. I got no further north than Sudbury, where I met some old hards I used to know and won a hundred and fifty dollars in a three-day poker game. Then I started listening to the radio and what was the use? You can't stand it alone in the bush when things are getting ready to snap. Don't you know there's going to be a war?"

"Is there?" she said.

She started to walk back the way she had come. He had been the first man in Grenville to enlist in 1914 and he was probably intending to be the first to try to enlist when the new war began. She walked quickly back to Matilda Lane. Only when she was completely alone, walking down to the lake under the trees, did she take the clipping from her basket and examine it.

The picture showed the world's idea of a beautiful woman. Her blonde hair was tailored, her face narrow with arched cheekbones and eyebrows. Her nose was as delicately haughty as an Egyptian's. She was the kind of woman who wore clothes such as Lucy had never seen except in the pages of a magazine. She was the kind who was at home in any drawing room in any city of the world. Her manners were cool, considered, and flawless. If she and Lucy were ever to meet face to face, she was the kind of woman to whom a girl like Lucy would exist merely as something which for the moment interrupted her line of vision, or imposed on her code of manners an obligation to be distantly polite. She was a woman who knew her price and had always known it, who quietly took it for granted there would never be a lack of men like Stephen Lassiter willing to pay it. The caption under the picture told nothing further about her.

It stated merely that she was chairman of a committee of a Junior League charity ball.

Lucy looked at the picture until she had memorized it. Then she continued her walk home and entered the house, and when Nina spoke to her, trying to be kind but unable to keep out of her voice some traces of her old habit of depreciation, she had nothing to say. She felt completely stunned. An hour ago, in spite of the evidence Mrs. Craig had given her, in spite of the lingering horror of her scene with Jane, she had been sustained by the inner conviction that Stephen Lassiter was in love with her. Now, having seen the picture of his wife, she was sure he was not. No man married to such a woman could feel anything but a passing affection for someone like herself; or, being lonely and bored, could do more than want her casually as men apparently always wanted women, as casually as they wanted food, contriving to press each incident for what it was worth in order to squeeze the last drop of pleasure from it. She closed her eyes. The worst thing of all was the fact that when he had made love to her he had been sincere. Her senses told her that. Therefore sincerity was something which could be casual too. She knew that if he appeared and touched her again she would be helpless against him. In bewilderment she realized that once again Jane was right. If you let your defences down, everything flowed over you.

Then her brain clogged and froze. It refused to work any more. The image of Stephen Lassiter's wife floated across her eyes once more and her lips set for a moment, then grew soft. The image faded out and she went upstairs to lie down and try to rest. But she was unable to sleep that morning nor again that night. She was stunned, her nerves remained on edge even while her mind refused to function, and the next day she was so silent and abstracted that Jane began to worry about her.

EARLY on Tuesday afternoon Lassiter telephoned to say he was back in Grenville and would be calling to see her within the half-hour. The sound of his voice made her tremble and he had to repeat himself before she replied.

"I can't see you."

"Why not? Anything the matter?"

"No. But I can't see you, Stephen."

His voice sounded disappointed, but it remained fairly casual. "What about tonight then, after supper? My job here is finished. I didn't come back to the factory, I came back to see you. You tell me when ..."

"Not at all, I'm afraid."

"What?" His tone quickly changed. "Look, Lucy, has anything –"

She hung up before he could finish and looked down the empty hall. Then, realizing that he would probably come over directly, she left the house and walked down to the common, across and up the next street to the highway. She had no errands, but she could go to the library for a while. There are always errands to invent in a small town.

When she was two hundred yards eastward on the main road she saw the LaSalle approaching and knew that he had recognized her. She saw him pulling over to the wrong side of the road, and as she reached the corner of Minto Street she turned quickly to the right to avoid having to meet him in the view of a pair of elderly women she had seen approaching. Minto Street was empty. The car entered it and stopped beside her, and she saw his puzzled face leaning toward her.

"What's this all about?"

It seemed foolish to continue walking, so she waited for him to get out of the car and join her. As she saw his large, lithe body sloping around the end of the car and coming near, every nerve tightened as she tried to keep the returning fondness from infecting her. She began to walk back toward the main road, for Minto Street ended at the beach on the town side of the common, and at this hour there were many people at the water's edge. He fell into step beside her, looked at her curiously, and said nothing. They walked past the head of Matilda Lane, past the filling station and the giant oak tree, and soon were on the country road on the edge of town with a farm on one side and a fallow field on the other rolling down to the lake.

"What's the matter, Lucy? Why can't you see me any more?"

She felt the colour mount to her face. It hurt to ask the question she had to ask now. It sounded vulgar and theatrical.

"You're married, Stephen. Aren't you?"

He stopped and looked at her. "So that's what it's all about!" he said quietly.

She began to walk again. Walking, looking straight ahead, she could break the spell of his fascination.

"Mrs. Craig told me on Sunday." Suddenly the statement of bare facts was comforting. Facts had a sort of life of their own, unaffected by emotion. Her voice was level as she continued. "She showed me a picture of your wife that was in the *Times*. She's very beautiful."

Lassiter hunched his shoulders and kicked a pebble out of his way. It shot in a low arc twenty feet up the road, then bounded off at an angle into the grass. They stood aside as a truck passed, and again stood aside as a pair of cars followed it.

"Let's get off this road," he said. He turned toward the lower field. "God damn it – ever since we've met we've been running away from some place or other to be alone. It's no good."

A wire fence blocked entrance to the field and there was no gate. He leaned against a fence post and took out a package of cigarettes, offered them to her automatically, took one himself when he remembered she did not smoke, lit it, and flicked the match across the shallow ditch onto the pavement.

"I should have told you," he said. "I was going to tell you today."

She looked away across the fields.

"Joyce is getting a divorce now," he said. "She left New York for Reno last week. I talked to her from Cleveland before she left. I think she wants to marry somebody else, but I'm not sure. Maybe she only wants to get rid of me. She never told me anything I wanted to know." He stared into her face, but she frustrated him by continuing to avert her eyes. "Joyce and I have been washed up nearly two years."

She was quivering like an animal in the cold when she put her hand on the top wire strand of the fence. It seemed a terrible place to have to talk to him, to settle this affair standing by the highway on the edge of a field.

"It has nothing to do with you and me," he said.

His blindness to her state of mind shook her. She covered her face with her hands, then was ashamed for revealing such weakness and emotion to a man she was trying to think of as a stranger.

"Why couldn't you have told me? Why didn't you tell me long ago?"

"Well" – he tried to grin, but without success – "suppose I had?

Joyce hadn't made up her mind what she was going to do then. How would you have felt?"

"At least I'd have known."

She realized that in his eyes the fact that his wife was getting a divorce cleared up everything. Within a few weeks he would be free, like an apartment vacated on the first of the month, ready for the new tenant to move in. He was not trying to excuse himself. He felt there was nothing to excuse.

She turned and forced herself to concentrate on his expression, like a student looking at a page in the text book during the last minute before an examination begins and all books are closed. For a moment she felt cool and untouchable, and this gave her an access of strength. She saw him now as a person who had been so spoiled by someone in his childhood that it was practically impossible for him to imagine that he could ever commit a serious wrong, or ever do anything that others would not be glad to forgive providing the forgiving put him in good humour again. And yet, he was not that simple. Somebody else had always resented him. Of course, she thought; that someone had been his father. She remembered his saying that his father had been a rugged, self-made man, while his mother had been gently reared. How much of what he now was could be traced back to his boyhood? He had no deep need for male friendship, just as he must always have been sure of himself with women. He was sure even now, and his confidence wounded her pride. He had invaded her solitude and taught her finally that she was passionate, probably more passionate than the average woman, until she was ashamed of how vulnerable he had made her.

He took a step toward her, and she was afraid that if he touched her she would be helpless. She put up a hand as if to ward him off.

"Lucy, my dear, don't you realize that where I come from divorce is a pretty common occurrence? Everybody makes mistakes. Don't you think you might try to see my side of it?"

She clung to the top wire of the fence.

"Do you think," he said, "that it's been any fun finding out that the woman you married doesn't like you any more? You were quite right about Joyce. She is beautiful. But I didn't enjoy her beauty half as much as she did herself, and no man ever will." He paused as if waiting for her to respond to the tone of his voice. "You're intelligent, Lucy. Particularly about people. Well, you saw Joyce's picture. Do you think she's generous? Do you think she's warm?"

Lucy looked down over the field to the lake. Near the shore some boys were swimming and trying to duck each other. Otherwise the lake was empty.

"Lucy, will you marry me? Because I love you so much."

"Don't!" she said. "Please don't say any more."

"I've said it to very few in my life, you know. I'm not a complicated man, and maybe I'm not very bright. I make mistakes. Only you're not one of them. You're different from anyone I've ever known. You're simple and decent and lovely. Joyce will get a divorce in a few weeks more and after that I'll be quite free to get married again. But it's got to be you."

Her mind asked itself why she could not simply say yes and drown her whole background in her longing for him. Her brain had years ago rejected most of the values by which Jane lived. But apparently the brain was not a very important part of the human organism. She could not say yes to him now. The attitude of many years was too heavy, making her feel deep in her core that marriage between someone like herself and a divorced man like Stephen Lassiter was so unthinkable it was taboo. Where could the marriage occur? Here in Grenville, where everyone would say that Lucy Cameron had broken up a marriage and had hardly waited a day after a Reno decree before taking the other woman's place? And then, seeing how confident he was in spite of the pleading note in his voice, her pride was wounded again.

"No," she said quietly, "I can't." She turned to leave him. But, curious to know one more thing, she paused and asked, "Have you any children, Stephen?"

An angry flush touched his cheekbones. "What do you think? I'm no angel, but I'm not a heel, either. If I had children, they would matter to me and I'd have told you long ago."

Their eyes met and for a second a flood of sympathy passed between them. In alarm she turned and began to walk away from him. He came forward, lithe and instinctive as an animal, and took her in his arms. A truck swished by and he paid no attention, but swung her around and kissed her fiercely on the lips. She struggled, helpless against his strength, loving the sense of his physical power. He kissed her again, then released her and looked at her with the flash of a boyish smile.

"Don't touch me!" she whispered. "Don't ever touch me again!"

She turned and walked quickly back along the road, and he remained behind, motionless with astonishment. He watched her figure receding, thinking how small and graceful she was and how strange, and asked himself in angry bewilderment why in hell everything that mattered in his life always went wrong.

When Lucy got home she met Jane in the hall, and for a moment the sisters' eyes met. It was evident that Jane had guessed who had made the telephone call an hour ago.

"He's not really married," Lucy said in a flat voice she could hardly recognize as her own. "His wife is in Reno, getting a divorce." Jane's eyes opened wide with alarm. "I had nothing to do with it. It was going to happen anyway." She began walking up the stairs, adding as she went, "He's leaving Grenville tomorrow. I won't be seeing him again."

But when she reached her room the finality of her last words hit against her mind and tears began to stream down her cheeks. In tormented confusion she asked herself why she had sent him away, why at the crisis she had been unable to discard the superstitious sense of taboo under which she had been reared? Was it pride or fear or merely lack of imagination, the inability to conceive of anything real outside a town where people never divorced, where passion was either orderly and blessed by clergy, or else concealed and crushed out of existence?

She went to the bathroom and bathed her eyes, and a few minutes later she heard the front door open and close. Jane had left for her afternoon walk. She went downstairs and stretched out in the long chair before the fireplace, her mind stunned, her senses in turmoil. The phone rang four times and she made no move to answer it. Fifteen minutes later the doorbell rang and she remained where she was, sitting in the long chair in the living room. Then there was silence for several minutes in which she heard footsteps on the gravel as somebody walked through the narrow lane on the left side of the house to the garden. Deliberately she turned her face away from the window and looked up at the twin photographs of her father and mother on the mantel.

AUGUST slipped into September. Shortly after Labour Day, Bruce Fraser went back to his school in Toronto. The nights grew colder and the first signs of red appeared on the maples. Grenville seemed empty after the handful of summer people returned to Toronto and the hotels received fewer tourists. The Ceramic Company was now working more or less on the schedules Lassiter had laid out for it, but the talk spread around the town that after his departure another expert, a man higher up in the Sani-Quip Company, had come to check his work. There was a wide-spread belief that Lassiter's recommendations had been more favourable to old Grenville employees than the parent company desired.

During that September in Canada, as everywhere else in the western world, people shared the same agony of fear and shame when Hitler revealed that he was at last in a position to disgrace the entire human race. When Chamberlain went to Munich something happened in Canada which few people understood at the time. Outside of Quebec, they had been taught from childhood to believe that their principal glory as a people rested on the fact that they were part of the British Empire. But along with this sense of continuance from the Old Country, which Americans had largely lost through the revolution, they had for years accepted British foreign policy like a handed-down suit of clothes. Now a psychological break occurred. Inarticulate people began to realize that Canada, in fact, was standing more and more alone, and they had a feeling a little like the mingled sadness and tenderness which comes over a growing man the first time he fully understands that his father is no wiser or more infallible than he is himself. But overshadowing all sentiment, as everywhere else, was the fear of the war. Unlike the Americans, they knew they would be in it from the beginning, and it gave them a feeling of being trapped.

For Lucy, that month of September was a time when news broadcasts formed a rising crescendo to her own unhappiness. Jane turned on the radio at least five times a day to listen, and produced argument after argument to convince herself that instead of being scared to death, Chamberlain was following a policy so profound nobody could understand it. In her preoccupation with the world crisis, Jane almost succeeded in forgetting Stephen Lassiter. One evening the telephone rang when Lucy was out of the house and

Jane told the long distance operator to inform the party in Cleveland that Lucy Cameron was no longer in Grenville. But Jane never told Lucy about this call.

Chrysanthemums and Michaelmas daisies gave a final show of colour in the garden. Apples were picked from their one tree, they preserved peaches and pears and made crab-apple jelly, and put up the last of the beans and tomatoes. This was the only kind of housework that Jane enjoyed. She liked seeing the rows of jelly jars gleaming as she thought how much they would all enjoy them in the winter months. The whole town began to tidy up against the winter, and on the day Chamberlain flew to Munich, the Grenville streets were blue with the smoke of burning leaves. Lucy began to prepare her cold frames for the winter; she spent hours in the garden with a chart of the plants, making notes for transplantings in the spring.

Chamberlain flew back to Croydon bringing peace in his time, and the newscasters reporting his return brought to Grenville a cessation from anxiety. At least there would be no fighting in 1938. Nina left for her third year at Queen's and Lucy and Jane were alone in the house.

EARLY in October Grenville felt its first frost. Waking shortly after dawn, Lucy got up and walked about her room. She saw the first rays of the sun striking red through the trees and colouring the wisps of hoarfrost on the grass of the common. It was the beginning of the season all Canadians love best, and for a short while, in the clarity of the air at sunrise, Lucy felt some of the weight of her depression lift. She went back to bed and fell asleep. When she got up for breakfast at eight o'clock the last of the hoarfrost had melted and she knew it would be a fairly warm day.

About mid-morning she walked northward out of the town. She left the houses behind her and then left the inland road and walked up through a footpath in a cropped field until she came in sight of the cottage where Matt McCunn lived. Here the land rose to a height of about two hundred feet, the fields bosoming upward in softly contoured slopes. It was not a range of hills, but an isolated eminence on a gently rolling plain, and it seemed higher than it really was because of the flatness of the surrounding country.

McCunn came out on the veranda as she approached and waved to her, then disappeared inside the cottage. By the time Lucy reached the steps he was out again with a glass in either hand. One contained whiskey and the other water. He handed her the water, saying he didn't like to drink alone.

"Well," he said offering her the lone rocker on the porch, "so the war didn't start after all! Never mind. It will in the spring. And that bloody fool Chamberlain has added two years onto the duration."

She sat down on the top step and felt the warmth of the sun on her shoulders. Her fingers touched the battleship gray paint of the steps and it felt suave.

McCunn was in his shirt sleeves but he looked tidy and well groomed. Lucy wondered whether or not Jane would revise her opinion of him if she ever came out here to see how he lived. McCunn's cottage was not very comfortable, but he kept it scrupulously clean and neat.

Her dark hair gleamed in the light as her eyes searched the fields rolling down to the lakeshore plain. From here Grenville looked like a cluster of trees with four steeples and the cupola of the post office resting among their tops and shining in the sun. Beyond the town, the lake shimmered deep blue under a cloudless sky.

"Well, Lucy," said McCunn.

She looked up at him, her forehead wrinkled slightly, but she managed to smile. "Well, Uncle Matt."

McCunn sipped his whiskey and looked at her gently. "Why don't you get in bed with the big bastard?" he said quietly.

She flushed. "You certainly manage to reduce everything to bare essentials."

"Why not? Isn't it what you wanted me to say – only maybe in politer words? Your expression showed it the minute I saw you."

"You manage to read faces easily."

McCunn grinned and crossed his legs. "Any woman's, Lucy. It's my talent. That's why they unfrocked me. I made them too uncomfortable."

The familiar pattern was repeating itself. McCunn's genius for irrelevancy, for building up a fantasy world resting on a limited amount of acute observation, was beginning to develop.

"Did they really unfrock you?" she said drily. "I never quite believed that story, you know. I think you just retired."

He grinned. Knees spread, head on one side, he set his glass on the floor. His face, incongruous under the noble dignity of his white hair, looked innocent and rather childlike.

"You're not happy here, are you, Lucy?"

"For the first time I'm willing to admit I'm not."

A tender expression followed the grin on his face. "You know something? In spite of it all, I love Grenville. I always did and I always will."

"You seldom talk as if you did."

"Whom the Lord loveth, he chasteneth."

She laughed quietly.

"No," said McCunn. "Don't laugh. The people here are bright and clean, they've got the whole future before them and they've got savour. They're warm, Lucy. That's the funny thing about them – under the surface they're warm. I don't mean the ones like Jonathan Eldridge. But our Highland people – I learned this in the ministry – they really want to do the will of God. But the information they got on that subject all came from John Calvin, and all he told them was what not to do. Now me, I always thought John Calvin was a son of a bitch, and that's the main reason why they unfrocked me."

She looked at him without comment.

McCunn chuckled. "But they're a lusty lot here. In spite of everything they're lusty. You'd be surprised, if you knew them as well as I do. Don't judge them by Jane and your father. Those two just happen to be the incarnate images of the kind of morality the rest of them pretend to believe in but really don't. A lot goes on here, and a lot more people get tousled than you think. The fact is, the town has always thought Jane and your father a mighty peculiar pair." He gave her a sideways look, took another pull at the whiskey, and laid the glass down again. "I used to watch the people from the pulpit in the old days," he said with another grin. "The young girls with their plump arms and shining morning faces, the young men with necks and shoulders like prime young bulls looking up the earnest way they do as if they wanted me to know how eager they were to do the right thing. It was a touching sight to see. But then I'd look at their parents. And I'd see your father in his old pew on the middle aisle, waiting to hear me say something he could disapprove of. And then I'd get sore. So one day I told the congregation right out what was the trouble with the whole lot of them."

Again McCunn stopped to pick up his glass. He took a long pull and half emptied it, then wiped his lips with a handkerchief and laid it down again. His eyes began to twinkle as he looked over the slope of the fields to the church steeples rising above the trees of the town.

"That morning I told them something no preacher ever dared say from a pulpit in the whole of Canada. I told them the Province of Ontario was so innocent the only sin they could understand was the sin of fornication. I said they put so much stress on it, the worst kind of crook could cheat them and exploit them, and they'd never be quite sure he was a crook so long as what they called his morals looked okay. Why right here in this town, I said, there's one of the biggest skinflints and widow-cheaters that ever lived. But so long as he keeps out of the lawcourts he's going to get by, for he don't drink, he don't play cards, and he'd be scared to look at a woman sideways so long as anyone from his home town was within fifty miles to tell someone else he did it." McCunn stopped and eyed her again, very pleased with himself. "Of course, I was talking about Jonathan Eldridge, and they all knew it. But I didn't stop there. From now on, I said, when I preach about sin – and I'm going to do it aplenty – I want it clearly understood I'm thinking about what the old ones do in their business hours, and not what the young ones do in the hammocks behind the ivy. Little children, I said, looking at a young couple in the second pew, love one another."

McCunn stopped, shook his head and rubbed his hand over his face as Lucy's level eyes watched him.

"Do you expect me to believe you preached a sermon like that?" she said.

"As sure as my name means a son of a bitch – and in Gaelic that's what it does mean, with a root right back to Sanskrit, that's what I preached. You asked me why they unfrocked me. I've told you. Of course, they brought up some more reasons besides. They also said I was divisive." There was a long silence. "Now, did what I say make sense, or didn't it?"

Again she laughed quietly. Uncle Matt really was preposterous enough to have preached a sermon like that in a Presbyterian church.

"Lucy," he said, "everybody thinks I'm a fool. Well, what is a fool? Generally it's a man who isn't shrewd. I admit I'm not shrewd.

But there are times when being shrewd doesn't get you anywhere, and you're at one of those times now. The whole world is, for that matter. You want to do something perfectly natural. Why don't you do it? You don't because of how your father and Jane brought you up. Those two were shrewd. And what did it get them?" His voice suddenly became angry. "God help a people if they think sex is the only important sin there is, for the day will come when they find out they've been lied to and cheated, and then they'll cut loose and make a mockery of sex and go straight to hell the way the Romans did. Don't forget, Lucy – the old Romans were puritans too!"

The snake and the dancing girl twitched rhythmically on Mc-Cunn's forearms as he gestured.

"I don't know," Lucy said, looking away from him. "Stephen and I are too different. He – he seems to take a divorce completely for granted – like buying a new car or renting a new house."

"That may be true. But that's not the reason why you're afraid to marry him."

There was a whistle as a train approached the level crossing at the eastern end of Grenville. They could see it winding in over the green plain, then disappearing into the town like a long, calm snake entering cover.

"It seems unnatural." She looked up at him, and again her forehead wrinkled. "Unnatural for me, I mean. Our backgrounds are too different. I've never been any place and he's a wanderer. The only thing we have in common is that we're neither of us happy."

He drained the last drops out of his glass, looked at the light coming through it, and laid it down again.

"I don't like to see you pitying yourself," he said.

"Am I doing that?"

"You soon will be, at this rate. What do you mean – you feel unnatural? You never felt as unnatural as I did once, and I got over it. By God, you never felt in your life the way I felt in 1917 when I was wounded."

She showed her surprise. "I never knew you were wounded. People always said it was a miracle you came through the war untouched."

"Miracle, hell!" McCunn was indignant. "A man can have his head blown off and they put his name on a monument. He can have his leg shot away and he comes home a hero. But he can lose his most priceless possession for King and Country and he's not supposed to mention it to a soul. Miracle, hell! Even if he talks about it to the boys in the back room, what do they do? They laugh." He gave her a curious, appraising glance and rose from his chair. "I'm going to tell you something I never told anybody unless the circumstances were such that I bloody well had to account for myself. On November thirtieth, in front of Poperinghe, just toward the shag end of Passchendaele, I had my left testicle shot off."

She flushed and turned away.

"You talk about feeling unnatural!" McCunn continued. "You never had a thing like that happen to you. I just looked up at the ceiling of the base hospital and let the tears stream down my cheeks, and I'm telling you, if I'd had a gun handy, I'd have blown my brains out. But the doctor pulled me around. He did a beautiful job and he saved the other one, and when he let me loose he told me to keep my chin up and take it easy. Did I take it easy? I did not. I got out of the army and for three years I lived like a tramp. I went out to India and the China Seas and I've been as far south as Valparaiso. But all the time I wanted to get back here, and finally I did. It wasn't easy then. The women expected everything to go on as if a quarter of the young men of the town weren't dead bones in France and Flanders. But I stuck it because I love this town and I wanted to improve it, even though they laughed at me and told each other I was no good. For a while I made one woman happy, and I only had half of what any police-court bum thinks he's got a right to take for granted. I'm proud of that, Lucy, I don't mind telling you, and if there wasn't something missing inside my brain – something I've never quite figured out – I think I'd have done quite a lot with my life. But you're better than I ever was. You've got a fine mind and up till now you've had plenty of courage. I don't want to see you waste yourself."

Again the snake and the dancing girl twitched on McCunn's forearms. He got up and sat on the step beside her and laid a hand on her shoulder.

"I know," he said quietly. "Every time I get talking I can't stop. I know. Now you listen to me and I'll try to make some sense. There's something about yourself you've never grasped. The whole set-up here has made it impossible for you to get it."

"What do you mean?"

"You're an exceptional person. You can't be ordinary." He waved aside an interruption and continued. "Your trouble has been that you've always tried to be like everyone else. You've tried to be ordinary. Listen, Lucy." He paused. "Rule-books only work for commonplace people. The one thing I hate about the point of view of this province is that it glorifies the commonplace at the expense of the exceptional. Look, Lucy." She had never heard his voice more earnest. "I know it would be easier if Steve Lassiter was the kind of man people here approve of. It would be fine if he'd never been married. It would be perfect if he came to you fresh, and you knew exactly what he was like and what you could expect. Ordinary people have to be sure about things like that, and they have to go by a book of rules to make them feel sure, for they can't think for themselves. But it's the nature of exceptional people to change and develop. Ten years from now you won't be the same person you are today. Exceptional people need changing conditions around them if they're to grow. And you – you've reached the point where you've got to take chances. You've got to give that man a try even if you don't completely trust him. You've got to marry him, divorce or no divorce. Otherwise you may as well resign yourself to drying up. For one thing I can tell you – the only kind of man who'll ever want to marry someone like you is an exceptional man. That's a fact, and not all the conforming you try to do will ever change it."

After a while Lucy left him. She walked down the slope of the field with a rising wind blowing her dark hair, and she felt better than she had felt in weeks.

A FEW days later the first of the autumn storms struck the town and Lucy woke feeling the house quivering. She looked from her window to see the treetops writhing in the rain as a cold, wet wind drove off the lake with the power of a whole gale. The storm built itself up to hurricane force, and by mid-afternoon the earth, sky, and lake were confounded into a weltering turmoil of dark leaden grey with the frantic brilliance of autumn leaves swirling through the air. The lake boiled up on the beaches and long sluices of water came in over the sand to flood the common. By late afternoon the band-shell and the belvedere were islands, and the trees seemed to be growing in the lake itself.

The house was in semi-darkness that afternoon. Jane's pupils had not come and Jane herself was working on a report for the library committee in front of the fire. The fire baffled from the wind in the chimney and occasionally puffed small clouds of smoke into the room.

Lucy sat down with an unopened book in her hand. McCunn's words were still fresh in her mind and she saw herself sitting in this same chair forty years hence. She saw herself growing queer and silent, like old Mrs. Mcdougall who had lost her husband thirty years ago after a few months of marriage, had lived with her only sister for twenty-five years, and now lived alone.

"A storm like this reminds me of when I was a little girl," Jane said. "You were too young to remember when we first moved into this house. I used to be frightened then, but Father always said it was nonsense and he made me so ashamed of myself I stopped thinking about what was going on outside."

The lights went out and the room was so dark the sisters could barely see each other's features across the hearth.

"I wonder how long it will take them to fix the line?" Jane said.

Lucy got up and lit a pair of candles in brass candlesticks on the mantel. The soft yellow light gleamed on the glass-covered photographs of her father and mother. Her father was seated before a shelf of books. His face looked gruffly kind, but he seemed doubtful if the photographer knew his business, and certain that somebody would say he was vain for having his picture taken at all. Lucy's mother looked out from the twin frame beside him with an unobtrusive smile. Suddenly Lucy realized that her mother's face, when young, must have been lovely. Even in this picture, taken when she was fifty, it was a delicate oval, softly curved.

"You look as though you'd never seen those pictures before," Jane said.

"I was only thinking what strangers they were to each other all their lives."

Jane looked at her sharply. "That's a peculiar thing to say."

"Did you ever really know Mother?"

Jane's lips were pressed closely together. She looked back at the papers in her hand and when she answered her voice suggested she was putting facts before a committee.

"Father and Mother understood each other very well. Things were different in their day and much harder than they are now. You forget what a struggle they had to make both ends meet. In her own way, Mother was a very happy woman. It meant a great deal to her when she and Father were able to buy back this house where she was born. They both understood that the only way honest people can make money is to save it. She and Father never disagreed about anything important."

Lucy said nothing and the darkness continued to brood in the room.

"You know," Jane said, "I don't mind a storm like this at all now. It makes me feel so safe when I'm inside. Do you remember our old Sunday evenings after tea when Father rested before church? It was cozy then."

The house trembled quietly and steadily in the wind as Jane continued to talk.

"Remember how I used to play the psalm tunes for him? 'Martyrdom,' and 'Balerma' and 'Dundee' – he never seemed to like any of the others. Oh yes – he liked 'O God, Our Help in Ages Past' if I played it to 'Irish.' It's such a warlike tune and he always thought about the Roman Catholics when he sang it. People never seemed to realize what a warm-hearted man Father was. And he was happy, too – in his own way."

Lucy half closed her eyes. Again she saw herself sitting in this room, year after year trying to communicate with her sister.

"You really believe Father was happy?" she said.

"Of course he was."

"Why can't you ever face the truth? He was afraid to be happy for fear somebody would notice his happiness and take it away from him."

"That's not true," Jane said mildly. "But it would be a fairly sensible point of view if it were. Whenever people are obviously happy something always comes along to spoil it for them. Anyway, there are other things much more important. Nowadays everybody seems to be talking about the *right* to be happy and it's such a lot of nonsense. It should be obvious to anyone that they're far less happy now than in the old days when they just tried to be decent."

Lucy got up from the chair and went to the bookshelves. A complete set of Sir Walter Scott, her father's favourite author, stood behind the glass. She crossed the room to the window and parted the curtains. A wet maple leaf, red blending into pale yellow, was plastered against the pane. Behind her Jane's quiet voice was still going on.

"You know, Father wasn't at all like the Methodists. Cheerfulness comes much too easily to *them*. Poor Father – at the time of the Church Union fight he used to warn people of so many things about the Methodists that were completely true, and it never did any good. I think he used to complain sometimes about the world in general just so he wouldn't have to complain about himself."

Lucy closed the bottom part of the old-fashioned shutters and continued to look over them at the storm.

"Why don't you write a book, Lucy?" Jane said. "I've been wondering if something like that wouldn't help you to pass the time."

Lucy turned with her hand on the shutter. "A book? About what?"

"Well, about the Loyalists, for instance. You could write about our ancestor who was a judge in Massachusetts before they burned his house down and nearly murdered him. The Americans admire themselves so much, it would be a good thing if somebody reminded them about the other side of their picture. They've become intolerably conceited and it would do them good if someone took them down a peg or two."

Lucy was no longer listening to Jane. She continued to look over the closed bottom shutter at the storm. A lot of leaves were down. Water was sluicing in the gutters. A boy was coming up from the common with his jacket in both hands, wringing the water out of it. The rain had licked his hair flat on his forehead and his shirt clung to him like wet skin. As he trudged past the house, Lucy could see the water bubbling out of the seams of his shoes.

"Bobby Harmon looks half drowned," she said.

She went upstairs to her room, aimless, with nothing to do. She sat in a chair by the window and watched the storm for a while, then closed her eyes and let a stream of images pour through her mind. She felt an ache of loneliness as distorted images of Stephen Lassiter began to cross her vision in sequence. She saw him on the tennis court, the great muscles of his thighs and calves flexing and relaxing as he stroked the ball. She saw him grinning down at her on the porch at the club dance. She felt his fingers touching the soft flesh of her inner arm. And she wondered where he was now, and what he was doing, and if he was thinking of her. And then the thought came to her: what if she never saw him for years, and then, some day when she was white-haired and used up, they were to meet somewhere quite suddenly and look at each other, and nothing would have the slightest reality but the fact that thousands of days and nights had passed with nothing to show for them but the slow stain of unused time.

ON THE Friday of the second weekend in October Lucy added some extra touches to the dinner. It was the weekend of Canadian Thanksgiving, and Nina was expected home that night. But the train from Kingston arrived and left and Nina was not on it. Neither Jane nor Lucy worried, for the holiday was short and Nina had been away from home for only a little while. At eight o'clock Bruce Fraser came over, but when Lucy told him Nina was still in Kingston he stayed only a few minutes and then went home again. He was rather pleased with himself because a Toronto friend had lent him his old Ford for the weekend.

That night the air was still and there was a sharp frost. In dozens of Grenville homes men oiled their guns and got out their high boots and windbreakers for a weekend of bird-shooting. In the morning they found a hunter's world. The sun came up like a red ball over fields crisp and clean with hoarfrost, and an exhalation of mist rose from the lake and shimmered in the rising light.

After breakfast Lucy made out a grocery list, saw Jane leave the house on her way to pick up an order of sheet music from New York at the post office, and then was about to leave the house herself when the telephone rang.

"Yes," she said into the mouthpiece. And once again, "Yes."

"I've left Sani-Quip," she heard Stephen saying, as though he had been discussing the matter with her yesterday and thought she might like to know the outcome. "I'm going to work with Carl Bratian in New York. There are a lot of new developments and nothing has completely jelled yet." His voice went on and she knew he was trying to be impersonal in order to hold her there listening until she could become accustomed to the sound of his voice. "Anyway, I'm going back to New York. I'm glad to be getting out of Cleveland. Lucy, how are you?"

"I'm fine," she said softly.

"Lucy –" There was a brief pause. "I've called you because – Look, I've been talking to Nina."

"*Nina!*"

He laughed. "Only by long distance. I remembered where her college was and I called her there a few days ago. She told me a lot of what's been going on between you and Jane. It sounded pretty bad and I'm sorry if it was my fault. I didn't know it would be like that for you."

"It's all right, Stephen."

She looked up at *The Death of Nelson.* Incongruously, after the countless times she had looked at that picture, this was the first time she realized what a horrifying scene it portrayed.

"Is it really?" Lassiter said. "Nina told me to try calling you about eleven o'clock some morning because Jane would either be out of the house or busy at that time."

Again he paused. When Lucy made no reply, he said, "I've missed you. All sorts of things have been happening down here, and still – have you missed me, too?"

"Terribly."

"Do you know you're going to marry me?" he said.

She seemed to be seeing his face directly in front of her. It was strong and self-confident as his shoulders thrust toward her.

"Yes," she said. In the total silence which followed the word she laughed softly into the phone.

"Jesus Christ!" he said softly. "Just like that!" Then his voice came through solidly. "I won't try to say now how I feel. Just listen carefully and I'll tell you what you've got to do. The divorce is settled and everything's in the clear. I found that out definitely last night. Now look, Lucy – there's not to be any more waiting around. You're to meet me in Montreal on Monday morning."

She took a quick breath. "But Stephen, I haven't –"

"Never mind," he interrupted. "I've figured everything out. I'm flying up to Montreal and I'll meet you in the Windsor Hotel on Monday morning. We'll fly back to New York, leaving before noon. We'll probably have to be married somewhere out of town, because there's a three-day waiting period here, but don't worry, I'll arrange everything. Don't waste time about clothes or anything like that. Just bring yourself and bring a birth certificate to show the immigration people who you are. I'll look after the rest."

She tried desperately to think. "But today is Saturday and –"

"I know about your Thanksgiving holiday. It makes no differ-ence. The trains run. Catch the train from Toronto when it goes through Grenville on Sunday. I've already made a reservation for you at the Windsor Hotel in Montreal. It's only a block from the Windsor Station. The holiday should help you. You can pretend you're visiting Nina in Kingston if you have to."

She was still trying to think. "Is that why Nina didn't come home?"

"That's why. Nina's been swell in this."

It was impossible to think. He seemed to be standing there right in front of her, and for the first time in her life she knew the delightful experience of having a man take all the details out of her hands and tell her what to do. Not even her father had ever done that.

"I'm going ahead," he said quietly, "on the assumption that you'll be in Montreal on Monday. The time has come for a big dive into cold water. Once that's over, everything will be wonderful. I've told my sister about you and she thinks it's grand. Incidentally that's the most sensible remark I've ever heard Marcia make." Another pause. "Lucy, dear, will you marry me now?"

She heard Jane's feet on the porch outside. "All right," she said quickly. "I'll be there."

His voice remained calm and solid. "That's wonderful. I know you will. One more thing – I know what a tough thing this is for you to have to do. But don't worry about it. Just keep busy till you get away."

Jane's hand was turning the knob, but the parcel she was carrying fell to the floor and she stooped to pick it up.

His voice came over the wire, softer but strong with emotion. "Since I left Grenville I've only felt half alive. I love you and I want you – both together. That's straight and hard, and it's the truth."

"Yes," she said, "I know."

She hung up as the door swung open and Jane entered the hall. Then she turned and went through the house to the garden, thinking she might avoid Jane by working there, thinking she might quiet the wildness in her nerves. The garden looked a ruin today, for yesterday she had cut down all the long stalks of the perennials and the debris lay thick on the beds and spilled over onto the edges of the lawn. Hours of work would be required to prepare the garden for the winter. The manure had to be laid on, the debris had to be carted to the compost heap, several dozen transplantings had to be made among the daisies and especially among the lilies which had massed so tightly they threatened to take over whole sections of the beds.

She picked up a rake and began to pull some of the debris clear of the beds into a pile on the grass. Then she dropped the rake and looked helplessly about her. The garden no longer mattered. After Monday it would not even be hers and all the work she had put into it would go to waste in the future. Inside a few years, weeds and the stronger plants would run wild all over the beds and Jane would never care, for flowers meant nothing to her. Then in sudden alarm Lucy remembered that it was already eleven o'clock; the bank would close within an hour.

She hurried into the house, spoke briefly to Jane, and left for King Street. In the bank she wrote out a check for two hundred dollars and cashed it. The money was handed through the wicket in crisp ten dollar bills, and they made a bulge when she folded them into her purse. As nearly as she could recollect, she still had about twenty dollars left in her account. It would at least serve to keep the account open.

As she left the bank, the thought that money had become so vitally important began to frighten her. She knew the value of a few dollars, but she had no idea of the value of money itself. Jane had her earnings and a backlog of ten thousand dollars in four-per-cent government bonds, all her father had been able to leave her. That capital of ten thousand had never been broken, but they had always spent the interest on it together. Every month since she could remember Jane had worked on a careful budget which they never exceeded. Now the time had come when Lucy would be entirely dependent on somebody of whose attitude toward money she knew nothing. The last fiction of her independence was going.

But she kept busy. She went into the best shop in King Street and spent an hour examining dresses and lingerie. They had little variety in Overstreet's, and she knew Stephen would insist on her buying new clothes in New York, but she would be ashamed to go to him with the few old clothes she had in the cupboard at home. She selected two dresses of plain material with a fairly good line. They did little for her, but she hoped they would be in good taste anywhere. There were no satin dressing gowns, and she had to be content with a lightweight blue flannel one. She looked at only one nightgown, a flesh-coloured filmy thing like a stylized version of a Greek *chiton*. It was expensive and rather an amazing article to find in a place like Overstreet's. The sales girl was a stranger to Lucy, but she looked envious when Lucy decided to buy it. She paid the girl and asked to have the parcels wrapped and put aside to be called for later in the day. In the shoe store and millinery shop she went through the same procedure, and by the time she was finished she had only sixty-seven dollars left of her original two hundred. She still needed a new coat and at least one good piece of luggage. She decided she could afford only the suitcase, and after buying it she had thirty-two dollars and a few cents left. By this time she was sure all the merchants in Grenville were telling each other that Lucy Cameron was acting very queer.

It was nearly one o'clock before she started home again. On the way she bought groceries for the weekend, as she had meant to do before the phone rang in the hall. Now her mind was working fast. On her way down Matilda Lane she saw Bruce wiping the dust off his friend's Ford in front of the Fraser house. She laid her basket of groceries on her own front step and joined him.

"Bruce, how long will you have the car?"

He looked up from the right front wheel and smiled at her. He was wearing a tweed jacket over grey flannel trousers.

"Till I go back to Toronto. Some time Monday afternoon."

"Are you busy tomorrow?"

"I've got nothing to do at all tomorrow." He recognized her quiet intensity, and his perception was comforting to her. Bruce had always sensed her moods.

"Is anything the matter?" he said.

She glanced over her shoulder before replying. "I'm leaving Grenville, Bruce. I desperately need your help."

The duster dropped from his hand as he stood up. Once before she had seen him look at her like this. It had been the night of the dance when he had observed her with Lassiter and for the first time had found her attractive. Now he looked at her with deep fondness, quiet wonder, and great respect. He had understood.

"Yes," she said, "I'm getting married."

He reached forward impulsively and took both her hands in his.

"I'm so glad, Lucy. I'll miss you terribly, but I'm still glad." He continued to hold her hands and then suddenly he let her go. "What do you want me to do?"

"Could you drive me to the Montreal train tomorrow morning?"

"I'll drive you all the way to Montreal if you like."

"No, just to the train. There's a question of luggage. I'll have two bags. Jane will be practising at the church after supper tonight. Would you mind putting my bags in the trunk of your car then?"

"You mean, you're not telling Jane?"

"No."

"You ought to, Lucy."

"When Jane comes back from church tomorrow she'll find a letter from me on the hall table. It's the only way, Bruce. Afterwards, when I'm married, perhaps she'll accept the situation. I don't know, I can't think that far ahead. Jane is very lonely, and lonely people are usually very soft or very hard. Jane is harder than you'll ever guess."

He looked at her without speaking, and the fondness they felt for each other was recognized between them.

"I wasn't thinking of Jane," he said, "I was thinking of you. I'd hate to see you do anything you'll be sorry for afterwards."

In a flash she saw Bruce as he would be fifteen or twenty years from now: dignified, competent, and at the same time somewhat illusive, as imaginative people always are who finally come to trust completely in themselves.

"Sometimes you can't avoid doing things you'll be sorry for," she said.

He put his hands in his pockets. "Let's take a walk," he said.

They began to stroll down the road toward the common. She moved with him, her hands in the pockets of her skirt, and at the edge of the grass they stood side by side and looked out over the lake.

"Why do you have to go away like this?" he said. "You should be getting married in your own house with your friends around you. It's not natural to run away. It's not like you."

"Stephen was divorced only a few days ago."

"Oh."

The familiar lake shone in the sun, the air shone above it, blue the colour of infinity above and below.

"Have you any idea what kind of life you're heading for in the States?"

"No."

"I wish you wouldn't do it," he murmured between closed teeth.

"What kind of life do you think I've had here?"

For a moment neither of them spoke. Then he turned and they both began moving slowly back to the road.

"Has Jane driven you to it?"

"I don't know, Bruce. Perhaps she has. Perhaps many things. I don't know."

"I mean –" He forced the words out almost against his will – "Are you in love with him or are you marrying him just to get away from your sister?"

"I'm in love with him."

Bruce stood still and she forced herself to meet his eyes. She had never liked him more than she liked him at this moment.

"It's not a thing I should try to explain. But he's the only person in the world who ever took it for granted that it was natural for me to fall in love like anyone else."

Bruce looked away. "I know what you mean," he said. "But why do so many of us have to go away before we can do what we want? We all protect ourselves too much. Look at you, Lucy – your family has always tried to protect you from everything – from depending on others, from having people talk about you, even from being noticed. And look what it's led to. Now you're running away into a kind of life that's the direct opposite of everything you've ever known."

She wondered why Bruce's nature forced him to philosophize at such a moment. A form of protection, she supposed. He always tended to cloak his emotions under general ideas.

"I hope you'll be happy, Lucy."

"You don't like Stephen, do you, Bruce?"

"I don't even know him. No, I don't like him. But if he makes you happy, I'll say it's the best thing he's ever done in his life. What I like least is the way he's making you run away from here to join him in a strange city. Why doesn't he come here and walk into your house and talk to Jane straight?"

She shook her head. "Stephen is doing this the only way it can be done. You don't know Jane. You don't know me, either. If Stephen came here –" She turned from him and began to move up the walk to her own front door. "I prefer it this way." A softer expression touched her face. "Will you speak to Jane after I leave?"

"If you want me to."

"Tell her I'll always be thinking of her. Tell her I'll always be grateful for so many things she did. Tell her I'll want to come back and see her if she'll let me. And one other thing. You still have your old camera, haven't you?"

"Yes."

"Take a snap of her in the garden some time and send it to me. You know, Jane has never had her picture taken once in her life."

As they reached the Cameron front door he kissed her with a quick, fierce longing, then turned without a word and walked back to his own house. Lucy went inside and carried the groceries to the kitchen. She remembered the garden, and decided that if she worked for three hours this afternoon she could at least clear away the debris and scatter the bone meal over the beds. The lilies would have to be left to multiply and choke the more sensitive plants, but at least when she went away the garden would look cared-for and trim.

THE plane lifted from St. Hubert and circled, the field dropped below them, the land spreading flat as a saucer southward toward the United States, north to the St. Lawrence. Montreal slid into view in brilliantly clear sunshine, grain elevators and docks, church steeples and domes, factory chimneys and streets, thousands of acres of masonry crowded about the whaleback of Mount Royal. The plane headed south as the city and river dropped behind. It gained altitude, it kicked upward under their seats and dropped them as they hit the first bumps over the Green Mountains in Vermont.

Lucy looked at Lassiter's profile beside her. He was smiling, confident, and happy, his hand holding hers. Some of his confidence infected her, and she pressed his hand and looked up at him and smiled too. Nothing was pleasing him more than the speed with which he was effecting the transformation in her life. He leaned sideways in his seat and kissed her ear, and an elderly American businessman in the seat opposite gave them a friendly grin.

The plane roared south, the sun glinting on its wings, the roar of its engines loud in her ears, killing memory like an anaesthetic. Occasionally she looked out the window and saw the vast shadows of wandering cumulus clouds shifting slowly in the mountains. She saw lakes and a road and tiny moving dots on the road, and her stomach heaved for a moment as they dropped down to Burlington. They took off again and continued. After a while the Hudson was below them, and then New York rose in confusion over the earth-curve and they began the final descent. They crossed the river, there was a brief swirling vista of a sea, of giant buildings, docks, ships, chimneys, factories, canals, and more cities looming under a thin haze of smoke, and then they settled over the Newark airport and taxied to a stop. They transferred immediately to a small plane and flew to an airfield on the outskirts of Wilmington. There a taxicab was wait-ing to drive them to Elkton, Maryland, where they were married.

Lucy's ears were still deaf from the roaring motor of the little plane which flew them back to Newark when Carl Bratian joined them as they walked off the field. She recognized him at once, the man who had been playing tennis with Stephen that first day she had seen them both in Grenville.

His eyes ran over her in quick appraisal. He saw a slim girl so unobtrusively dressed that he decided her principal motive in buying clothes was to look as little different from other women as she could. The light top-coat she wore made it impossible for him to estimate her figure. She met the glance of his quick, penetrating eyes, and his wide mouth broke into a frank smile under his big nose. Then he went around to the back of the car while the luggage was being stowed in the trunk of his Cadillac. After tipping the porter, he followed Lassiter to the front and got in behind the wheel.

"Ever come into New York from Jersey before?" he asked her.

She told him it was the first time she had ever been in the United States.

"Well," he said, "prepare yourself."

They drove off the airport and joined the flood of traffic curv-ing up to the skyway and then moved with the stream over the marshes, factories, and garbage heaps in toward Manhattan. It was a moment Lassiter had been waiting for ever since leaving Montreal.

"Look at it!" he said, indicating the skyline across the river. "What I'd give to be seeing that for the first time!"

But to Lucy the whole Jersey side of the river seemed like a re-volving nightmare as they followed the curve of the skyway. She smiled, unable to speak. Cars and trucks in double lines poured in and out of New York, the traffic of a dozen King's Highways driving with direct, imperious, and almost brutal force, driving over a fantastic ribbon of concrete that led past the belching lips of factory chimneys, over canals, actual cities large enough to house the populace of a small nation.

Lassiter touched her elbow and pointed. "Look!"

For one second in the far distance she saw uptown New York emerging like a desert mirage through the smoke, the smoke tinged with gold, holding the group of skyscrapers immobile and unreal, dwarfing them as each of them dwarfed the other, yet combining to create a unity more magically and incredibly beautiful than she had guessed any city could ever be.

Lassiter was saying, "Let's take a bus up Fifth and ride on the top. We'll have time before it gets dark. We should be able to reach the Pierre before sunset."

Bratian dropped his hand on Lucy's knee as if he had known her all his life, and she knew the gesture was more friendly than intimate.

"For God's sake," he said across her to Lassiter, "stop trying to knock her out!" And to Lucy, "That's a nice-looking town you came from, though I wouldn't want to have to sell advertising in it."

The ordered chaos of the skyway increased as cars kept pouring up the ramps from Newark. Suddenly she was looking at the cliff of tenements that rise like a ragged Chinese Wall over the butt of Jersey City.

"You'd better keep your eyes shut here," Bratian said. "That's always a good thing to do around Jersey City."

When finally they entered the tunnel Lucy did close her eyes, and the hum of the enclosed traffic added its volume to the roar of aircraft motors that still beat in her brain.

THE hum was still in her head at three in the morning as she crouched alone at the window of a room in the Pierre and looked down at Fifth Avenue twenty floors below. Her knees were on the carpet, her forearms rested on the sill, her hair was loose over her shoulders as she knelt there looking out at the city. Behind her in the dark room Lassiter lay asleep on the bed.

Lucy lifted her arms and drew the dressing gown closer about her body, then her forearms returned to the window sill and she remained motionless. Her head and shoulders made a small, solitary outline in the frame of the window against the glow of the sky over New York.

As far as her eyes could see, the traffic lights on the avenue were red. They changed. And as far as her eyes could see they were green. A vagrant taxi whispered down the avenue below her window and turned east into Fifty-ninth Street. Two other taxis were passing slowly along Central Park South. A solitary man was leaning against a tree on the opposite side of the avenue, so motionless he seemed like a part of the tree. And the lights kept changing: green and red, green and red, and in spite of the silence of the room and the apparent silence about the hotel, there was a humming sound every-where, not like the beat of a heart but like the multitudinous life-force of millions of insects throbbing in the darkness of a summer night. Yet different even from this, for there was no variation in the hum, no rise and fall or cadence, but only this unbroken monotone as steady as eternity. The towers were silent and majestic. Only their upper parts were visible above the massive darkness at the base and the paler darkness holding the stars. She wondered why so many of them still had lights burning. Across the park, in one of a pair of dark towers, she saw a light break out in a single room, a solitary cell near the top of the tower, it winked off and came on again immediately, and it remained, flickering the size of a star across the park into her eyes. For half an hour she knelt there motionless until her legs began to grow cold. Then she got up and felt the stiffness behind her knees and realized how tired she was. Her hands passed slowly and wonderingly over her breasts and loins and her memory of everything older than twenty-four hours was as vacant as an empty room. No solitude she had ever known had been like this. Her mind was bursting with strange new images, but she could think of nothing. For a moment she tried to pray, but could find no words, for even God seemed irrelevant in this region of random lights en-cased in thousands of cells of invisible ferro-concrete between the earth and the sky.

Moving carefully so as not to make a sound, she crossed the carpeted floor to the bed. It was too dark in the room to see anything but vague shapes: three chairs, a writing desk, a dresser, and the double bed. There was still a brightness behind her eyes. It was the image she had seen earlier that evening when Bratian had left them after cocktails and they had stepped out on the pavement in front of the Pierre to confront one of the most immense spectacles in the world: the mighty rampart of checkered light leaping out of the purple darkness of the sky above Central Park South, the moving blaze of taxi headlights, and then, as they strolled hand in hand an unknown distance down the avenue, many blocks farther down the island yet so brilliant it seemed imminent above her, the icy stalag-mite of the Empire State.

Stephen was a dim bulk as he lay on his back, the covers down to his waist, his powerful torso naked. She lay down beside him. The exposed skin of his chest and shoulders was cold, but under the sheets his thighs were warm. She lay there wide awake, while his chest rose and fell as he breathed in his sleep. For many minutes she did not stir.

She was remembering a winter day in her childhood in Ontario years ago. Her father as a special treat had promised to hire a horse and sleigh and take Jane and herself for a drive one Saturday after-noon. They had looked forward to the drive all week. But when the afternoon came the sun went under the clouds and the frost cracked down, a raw wind blew out of the northeast, the maples were stark against the deadness of the snow, and she had shivered with cold. Her ears had frozen to numbness but she had been ashamed to mention it because the sleigh-drive was a treat and her father would have been disappointed if she had not enjoyed it. Afterwards in the warmth of the house her thawing ears had burned so hotly she had been conscious of nothing else for hours.

Her heart felt that way now. Her whole body and mind felt that way. All her life she had been wrapped up like a child against the winter, only her ears hearing rumours of the lives of other people, her eyes trying to content themselves with the austere and distant beauty of bare trees and hill-lines silhouetted against winter skies. Now her whole soul seemed to be unfreezing. She was like other women after all. She would have children as other women did. Tears started to her eyes and she had to repress a longing to throw her arms about the strange man beside her and bring him back to her out of his sleep.

The weight of her head against his shoulder finally woke Stephen. He stirred and she heard him murmur her name; then he surged up, a shadowy mass against the pale frame of the window, his arms came about her again, and with a slow and formidable tenderness he held her close. Out of the darkness she heard her own voice call-ing his name.

TWO

⌒⌒⌒

LIKE SO MANY CANADIANS BEFORE him, Bruce Fraser came down
to the United States in 1940 on the defensive, subconsciously determined not to be lured into discontent with his own country. After
stepping off the Montreal train into Grand Central at seven-thirty
in the morning he began to walk around the city. His first impression
led to astonishment when he discovered that New York, in addition
to being stupendous, was also friendly.

It was late afternoon by the time he found the upper reaches of
the Fifth Avenue shopping district. Sometime during the day the old
inherited attitude had disappeared. As. he walked north with alert
steps he was pleased when people noticed his new Airforce uniform
with the Canada shoulder-flashes. The light in Fifth Avenue was
faintly golden. New York was at its best; it was beginning to reveal
the pastel quality of a fine autumn evening.

He paused in front of Van Cleef and Arpels to look at unset rubies
which lay on a bed of satin in a box window, a great single jewel
surrounded by a garland of lesser ones, lying only a few inches from
his eyes. It was like observing a queen naked, near and naked to tempt

her subjects, surrounded by her women and guarded by an invisible wall. Bruce wondered how much they cost. Then the puritan side of his nature was assuaged by the consideration that these imperious stones, valuable enough to support a family in comfort for years, would probably be bought by a newly rich merchant who feared inflation, to be hidden in a bank vault or hung about the sinewy neck of a faded wife.

He smiled to himself and continued his walk. A faint odour blended of numerous perfumes clung to the humid air, and once again he became conscious of many women. As he walked north the avenue opened up before him, running into the Plaza with buses and taxis and cars and people. The hard faces, the indifferent faces, the happy faces, the beautiful women, the spoiled women, the women looking forward to being loved, the women no man would ever love again – he saw them all with a clarity that generally needs fatigue or drink or even drugs to make it sharp, he saw moving in front of him a tall lithe girl with tawny hair, slim hips, wide shoulders, and beautiful rhythmic legs, he reminded himself that he had never in his life talked to a girl who looked and carried herself like that, and wondered what kind of life had bred such an Athenian self-confidence, and how a man like himself would seem to such a girl if he could ever meet her.

This was a new kind of perspective for Bruce. He had always taken it for granted that most people his own age would find him interesting, and he had always felt a mild superiority to Americans in general, without knowing anything about them except what he read in the newspapers and magazines.

This section of New York continued to take him aback. He had expected no such grace or dignity in an American city, for until today the only other one he had seen was Detroit. So far as he could tell, nearly every important building on Fifth Avenue except the churches and hotels existed solely for business purposes, and it was almost a shock to see such grace of design in buildings used for earning a living. The astonishing thought occurred to him that there must be people here who considered that business itself was beautiful.

It was now a quarter to five. Lucy had asked him to come to their apartment at six to be in time for cocktails before dinner. He still had more than an hour to kill.

As he turned east into Fifty-ninth Street the feeling of vitality continued to bear him along. All day he had been feeding on the power and self-confidence of New York, lapping up all of it he could absorb. From a stationery shop came the good smell of clean stacked paper and fresh cards. He paused to examine the bright jackets of new novels in a bookstore window. A refrain sang through his mind in time to the drive of the traffic: "They'll never beat us, we'll knock hell out of the sons of bitches, they'll never beat us." It was the first time in six months that he had felt this way about the war. It was peculiar to come down to New York, which was supposed to be in a neutral country, and have the city make him feel like this.

The traffic was thick when he reached the darker, more serious air of Madison. He went into a flower shop where the chrysanthemums looked so fresh and fluffy he would have ordered a couple of dozen of them if he could have afforded it, but the export of Canadian currency was so closely controlled just then that he had to be satisfied with half a dozen. The clerk promised to send them out at once.

When he left the flower shop the air seemed much darker. The sunshine was still bright on the tops of the buildings on the eastern side of the street, but on the pavement there were no shadows. More people: a woman in a black dress with a lifted face, tightly squeezed hips and a high bosom, a string of graduated pearls around her neck, and perfectly slimmed legs; their eyes met for an instant, he felt the impact of a cosmic disillusionment, and then she was past. Two laughing girls. A white-haired gentleman with a black homburg and an erect back. A Mediterranean type gesturing happily to his wife. A woman in a mink coat coming out of a Gristede's with two bags of groceries in her arms.

Suddenly Bruce felt very tired. He had absorbed all of New York his senses could take for a while. North of Fifty-ninth Street he turned into a restaurant with a bar at the front, sat down in a dark corner, and ordered a rye and soda.

The drink warmed, softened, and loosened him. He glanced at a solitary girl near him who was sitting with a drink in front of her, apparently unconscious. The barman was talking to the proprietor about horses. Bruce leaned back with his eyes half closed and whole sequences of New York scenery began to jump through his head.

He wondered how much of the city he had really seen that day. He smelled again the pickles, spices, and fresh fruit which had delighted his nostrils that morning on Third Avenue. He smelled subways. He remembered the curious procession of shipping clerks pushing racks of women's dresses somewhere on Seventh. Popcorn and peanuts – where had he smelled them? He remembered the sharp bite of salt air when he walked up from the subway in Bowling Green just before noon, and the old lady on the Fifth Avenue bus, the one who had got on just above Washington Square, who had bent toward him across the aisle to say, "I just want you to know I feel grateful."

God, it was a friendly city! It had lifted him up and let the weight of the past six months slide right off the edge of his mind.

"Down on leave?"

He opened his eyes and saw that the little table next to his own had been occupied by an American lieutenant about his own age. Bruce had not seen many uniforms in New York today.

"Yes."

They began to talk. The American said he had been in the army seven months, since before the draft started. The politicians, they should take them out and line them up, there wasn't any equipment in the whole goddam country. What New York needed was a stick of bombs right across the length of Times Square, a whole line of them pounding right across from the Times Building to the Wrigley sign, and then maybe the country would wake up. On second thoughts probably not even that would be enough. Right now the country was sleep-walking. Did Bruce think he was fooling? Right now a Panzer Division could land at Provincetown and feed itself on filling stations from there to California and have a swell party all the way so long as it kept out of Texas. Yes, he came from Texas. Bruce ought to go down there some time. It made no sense to try to judge the United States by New York. That was what foreigners did all the time and they made their mistake right there at the beginning. What were the chances of getting some action if he went up to Canada? He was sick of the infantry and wanted to get into the Army Air Corps, but what the hell could you do in that outfit when the politicians were fighting about contracts and there weren't any planes? The bastards had him in the infantry. What was it like up in Canada, Canada was at war wasn't it, what was it like up there?

Bruce wondered if he could even tell him what it was like if he tried. Sometimes the whole metabolism of a country changes, but the change is internal and hardly anyone is aware of it until long afterwards. On the surface there was so little difference that everybody felt guilty because the country was doing so little. There was no equipment. The army was drilling with wooden rifles because most of the real ones had been sent to England after Dunkirk. Seventy-ship convoys were leaving Halifax escorted by four destroyers, and sometimes, if there were reports that the *Scharnhorst* or a pocket-battleship was out, the old *Revenge*, the Jutland veteran, lumbered along in support with fifteen-inch guns that shook the guts out of her every time she fired them.

"You boys certainly shellacked the bastards over London yesterday," the Texan said.

"It'll be all right if they can keep it up."

"Why can't they keep it up? Aren't they knocking hell out of them? What do you fly yourself – fighters or bombers?"

"So far nothing but an Anson training crate."

"When you get over what'll they put you into?"

"Bombers, probably."

"If I get into the Air Corps I want a pursuit ship."

Looking at him, Bruce guessed he would certainly get one. He was the type. He had the jutting jaw, sandy hair, and the loose, bold cockiness that went with the natural fighter pilot. Besides, he seemed the kind of man to whom a certain amount of fighting is absolutely necessary to mental health.

"George," the Texan drawled to the barman, "let's have two more of the same."

The drinks came and they continued to talk shop. It seemed a natural thing to do. And yet, only a year ago, nothing had been more unnatural for Bruce than to talk shop about the war. He had entered the Airforce in angry resignation, telling himself bitterly that everything had happened just as he had foreseen, that the old men had got him just as they had got everyone else. Those were the days when men who had been on relief for years joined the army to get a job. They were the days when the recruiting sergeants often sent men home if their shoes looked too worn to survive the first fortnight's drilling, before proper army boots came through in the issue. They

were the days when businessmen congratulated themselves on
Hitler's pact with Russia, telling each other in their clubs that now
they knew where they stood.

Those days seemed to belong to another century now. You wrote
your own life off and achieved a certain freedom as a result. You
were a man apart, one of the first who would get it. The others would
get it too, but they still deluded themselves that they would slip by
without death noticing them. Now only the form of death remained
fearful. Death itself had become a sort of goal for everybody. Bruce
didn't exactly put it this way to himself, but it was roughly how
he felt about it.

He pushed the table forward and got up, telling the Texan how
glad he was to have met him but that he had a six o'clock date and
would have to be on his way. The Texan insisted on appropriating
the bill. They argued about it, but the lieutenant was firm, and Bruce
finally thanked him, shook hands, and left.

When he reached the pavement the traffic was a throbbing mass
waiting for the lights to change. He walked north two blocks and
got into a bus. It was jam-packed and when it started it gave such
a jerk a heavy man was thrown against him. He struggled clear and
found a little blonde girl pressed against his side, too short to hold
onto a strap. She had wistful friendly eyes and a soft dimpled chin.
They smiled at each other without speaking and it was a pleasure
to brace her against the sudden lurches. When he got off the bus at
Seventy-second Street he felt a sharp sense of loss, knowing he would
never see her again.

Then he began to think of Lucy and the prospect of finding someone familiar in this city. But his ideas were jumping around, and by
the time he reached the foyer of her apartment building he began
to wonder if it had been such a good notion to let her know he was
coming down to New York to spend his leave. He wanted very much
to see her, he had thought of her often during the past two years,
and the last time he had been home in Grenville the little lane where
they had lived all their lives had seemed empty without her. But he
knew from experience how disappointing old friends can seem in
new surroundings. You remembered only the part of them that was
valuable to you, and when you met them again this old familiar part
no longer counted for much in their eyes and you both had to go
through the fiction of pretending it did.

THOUGH the Lassiters' apartment was not large – Lucy called to him from the kitchen as the maid took his cap and coat – it seemed fabulously luxurious to Bruce. Gold damask drapes caught the lights and contrasted with bluish-grey walls and dark broadloom carpet. The functional furniture was upholstered in ocean blue, some chairs were striped with gold and others were plain blue. Three bowls of yellow calendulas stood on glass-topped tables. The hearth was smooth and black, and a square, unframed mirror rose to the ceiling above it. There was precision in the beauty of the room, as well as in the way the mirror doubled its apparent size.

Lucy came in from the kitchen bearing his white chrysanthemums in a tall glass vase, smiled at him, and made a helpless gesture with her shoulders as he moved forward to shake hands. She set the vase on a coffee table and turned to greet him, and he saw that on the surface at least she was no longer shy.

"What an amazing room!" he said. "How on earth did you do it?"

She moved toward a chair at one end of the fireplace and indicated that he was to sit on the small sofa opposite. Instead he stood in front of the hearth looking down at her, repeating how good it was to see her again while all the time his surprise was making him feel unnatural and his elbow kept reaching for a mantelpiece that wasn't there.

"This place is wonderful, but how do you ever relax in it?"

She laughed, and he noticed a new gaiety in her voice. "We've lived in it for over a year but it still seems an absurd room for someone like me to have. Marcia – Stephen's sister – told me I'd be a fool if I tried to put anything in a Seventy-second Street apartment that would remind me of home, and at the time I was glad enough to take her advice. Stephen let me do whatever I liked, but I think he's regretted it since. I have, too. This isn't a room for a man to have to live in."

He looked down at her and tried to think of something to say. In the old days her hair had been unnecessarily, even aggressively plain. Now it was cut and softly curled, it was dark and lustrous, and in the shaded light it brought out the deep brown of her eyes and the warmth of her lips. She was wearing a dinner dress of lime-green silk held at the waist by a wide belt of gold kid. It moulded the lines of a figure he realized for the first time was charming. The maid came to the entrance of the living room to ask a question and Lucy rose to join her in the kitchen. When she moved there was the slightest sound of silk; she was so attractive and supple that he wondered what had been the matter with him in Grenville that he had never seen the possibility of Lucy Cameron turning into a woman as maturely lovely as this.

He prowled restlessly around the room and soon discovered many indications of a male personality. He flipped open a silver cigarette box, held a cigarette between thumb and forefinger while he closed the box, and examined the inscription on the cover. It was a trophy won by Lassiter in 1927 for men's singles in a closed tournament at a Long Island club. There was an extremely awkward silver bowl with heavy knobby handles which he supposed was another trophy. On a small side table was a Dunhill pipe, and on the wall opposite was an old portrait, with cracked canvas, of a truculent man with bushy eyebrows.

Lucy came back while he was looking at the picture. "One of Stephen's ancestors on his mother's side," she said. "He was a brother of one of the men who signed the Declaration of Independence. Can't you just feel him disapproving of us?" She slipped her arm through his. "Do sit down! You must have been walking all day long. When I first came to New York I was tired for months."

He sat down on the sofa and watched her as her eyes went to the white wing on his uniform curling upward out of the N which indicated his navigator's status.

"God, you're lovely!" he said. "Forgive me for being blunt but I can't help it. Are you as happy as you look?"

"I think so."

"No reservations?"

"I stopped making reservations the day I left home."

He smiled. "I stopped making them the day I enlisted."

The maid entered bearing a tray containing a decanter of rye whiskey, one of Italian vermouth, glasses, a thermos bowl full of ice cubes, a pitcher, a small bowl of cherries, and a spoon. She set the tray on the table and left without a sound. Lucy rose and Bruce joined her at the table, and as she picked up the decanter of rye she gave him a rueful smile.

"Does it seem ages ago since the night when you came home from Montreal and I couldn't even give you a glass of beer?"

"Eons ago."

She measured vermouth into the pitcher while Bruce picked up the cherries and dropped one into the bottom of each glass.

"An American chap in the squadron told me to be sure to drink at least a dozen manhattans a day while I was in New York. He says this is the only place in the world where they're any good."

"That's what Carl Bratian says, too."

"Bratian?"

"Stephen's boss in the agency. He's the main reason why we're living in New York. He's an old classmate of Stephen's and he persuaded him to drop his engineering work and go into advertising. You'll be meeting him tonight."

"Will I like him?"

"You might. You've always liked clever people."

She stirred the mixture slowly until it became a murky amber under the light. She told him that their friends were mostly people like themselves, hardly any of them native New Yorkers, some they had met at parties, others business acquaintances. Stephen made a point of avoiding his relatives.

"Do you miss your garden?" he asked.

She picked up her glass and went back to the sofa. "Terribly." And at once she changed the subject. "You'll be meeting Stephen's sister tonight, Marcia Stapleton. She's a grand person." Lucy turned her head as she heard a noise in the hall, but it was only the maid getting something out of a closet. "Stephen should be home by now. He promised to be early, but he can never really plan his time. Something always seems to be turning up."

Bruce was still too restless to sit still. Glass in hand, he walked across the room. The gold damask drapes covered the windows, but he slipped his hand into the place where they met together and drew them slightly apart. The alcohol he had drunk earlier was quick in his veins, he was physically tired, and his mind was racing. New York was a vast explosion of light against the gathering darkness. In the middle distance was a splash of red from a neon sign, and as he watched the spectacle he felt a hot stab of desire. He turned from the window and let the gold damask fall into place.

"It's incredible!"

"What is?"

"New York. It's even bigger than the war." He went back to the sofa, sat down, and looked at his black service shoes. Lucy was watching him calmly, perhaps finding him as changed as he was finding her. "How old is John now?" he said.

"Almost a year."

"May I see him?"

"Of course you may. I try not to show him off if I can help it, but I'm really terribly proud of him. Molly's feeding him now. Wait till Stephen comes home and then we'll all go in to see him."

Bruce sipped his drink and smoked, but his nerves remained tense.

"Tell me about Grenville," Lucy said quietly.

"I probably don't know any more than you hear yourself."

"Nina only writes occasionally, and she never says much in letters."

"Doesn't Jane write to you?"

"I've had one letter from her – last Christmas."

"Oh."

"How is she, Bruce?"

He smiled. "She's rugged. But I don't know, really. I've hardly been home myself. When I heard about John I thought it would make a lot of difference to Jane. Hasn't it?"

Lucy shook her head. "I've begged her again and again to come down for a holiday. It's no use."

"Well," he said, "Jane may stay the same but Grenville's changing. There's a new Airforce camp being built four miles out. Beyond your Uncle Matt's place." Some of the lightness left his voice. "I don't know how you've felt down here, but it's been an awful year in Canada. Everybody's worried sick about the war and feeling guilty because there's so little they can do."

"It came just as you prophesied, didn't it?"

"The war?" He shrugged his shoulders. "I used to think I was pretty clever, didn't I? It's a lot different from what I expected it would be."

A key scraped in the lock of the outer door and Lassiter entered the hall. Lucy rose and went out to him, they exchanged a few words, and then he came into the living room to welcome Bruce.

"Swell seeing you." They shook hands and he waved toward the room. "Don't let the stage set fool you. Lucy's the same girl she always was, only better. I've been trying for months to show her the town but she won't budge. You're a fine excuse for a party and we're going to have one – I hope." His eye shot to the cocktails. "I need one of those. Mind if I have a quick one before I change?"

Lucy's hand was in one of his. "Was it a bad day?"

"Ashweiler's been in town since seven-thirty. That ought to answer your question."

He downed a cocktail and refilled his glass. Then he lit a cigarette and sat down, crossing his legs, big and solid in his chair. He puffed quickly and set his cigarette on the edge of an ashtray and then took a quieter sip of his drink.

"Carl handed Ashweiler over to Stan Pratt for the night," he said to Lucy. "That means the Diamond Horseshoe, wouldn't you think?" He covered his mouth to hide a yawn. "A year ago Stan was just another Yale boy coming to town with an idea! Tonight he's arrived – he's got Ashweiler."

Lucy went out to the kitchen and Lassiter grinned as he saw Bruce's eyes follow her.

"She looks wonderful," Bruce said.

"Doesn't she? Ashweiler used to be my boss," Lassiter went on. "I was reporting to him when I did that job in Grenville. Now I handle his company's account in the agency. It's a hell of an account – the only thing good about it is the advertising appropriations it carries. Everybody uses plumbing in America. What I'm really after is Harper Aircraft. The public doesn't know a damn thing about planes, it only thinks it does. I want a chance to do the telling. As a matter of fact, an aircraft account would be a national service at a time like this. Do you see any Harpers up in Canada?"

"A friend of mine crashed one in Lake Saint-Louis last week."

"Then it's a fact they're bad at the take-off?"

"They have that reputation."

"Did your friend get out in time?"

Bruce shook his head.

"Sorry." Lassiter looked at the amber liquid in his glass. "Myron Harper's a genius, but he slipped up on that model. Wait till you see their new stuff. I've looked at the models and they're just going into production. He's calling it the Privateer – the best medium bomber yet."

"We could use them."

Bruce tried without success to keep a spark of resentment out of his voice, for lately the papers had been full of stories about American planes coming up to Canada in quantity and the public believed they were true.

Lassiter glanced enviously at the wing on Bruce's chest and shot quick and informed questions about training methods in the R.A.F. What kind of training aircraft were they using in Canada or was it a secret? The current American theory about fighter planes, a special plane for four different levels of altitude, was absolutely no good in practice. He had it on authority that the army had always been against it, but of course it looked good on paper and made a fine story in public-relations handouts. There was going to be an awful payoff if they ever tried to use that kind of an idea in combat. The trouble down here was that Americans knew they could knock hell out of Hitler if once they started and that was the very thing which made them put off starting. He wished he'd finished his course at M.I.T. He had always wanted to work with planes and now an aircraft engineer could name his own terms anywhere. What kind of a plane was Bruce flying himself? Bruce told him, adding that he had seen only one Hurricane and had yet to see a Spitfire.

"And probably no real bombers at all?" Lassiter said. "But it's going to be a bombers' war, from what I hear. You know what I did yesterday? I paid a visit to your consulate to ask questions about enlistment in the R.C.A.F."

Lucy had returned to the room; she was at Lassiter's back and Bruce realized that he didn't know she was there. Her face had frozen at her husband's words.

"When he found out I was thirty-five plus he shook his head and thanked me. Of course I probably couldn't have got away from the job anyway, but a man gets restless. A hell of a thing to be told, that you're too old for the Air Corps." Lucy moved across the room and he said, "I'm not old, am I, Lucy?"

She told him he was the same as always, and he drained his glass and put his arm about her waist. They smiled at each other and his hand slipped caressingly over the curve of her hips. Bruce felt himself excluded completely and finally. He had never seen a woman regard a man as Lucy did Lassiter at that moment. It was not the look of a woman who loves a man blindly, but of one who has come to love him as much for his weaknesses as for his strength, who has found something precious in him that nobody else knows. With a touch of malice, Bruce told himself that Lassiter seemed to others a good deal older than he seemed to himself. There were streaks of grey in his tawny hair, he had grown heavier, and lines were about his eyes. Bruce was measuring him against the men he had left behind in the squadron, and he knew this was unfair, for they were in training and there was the unnamable quality of dedication about them all. It was too easy for a soldier, and especially for an airman, to take advantage of his status. Bruce decided that although he didn't like Lassiter he wished he were able to like him better, for the man was sincerely fond of Lucy. In those stupid, naive days before the war, when Bruce himself had felt mildly sorry for her, it had been Steve Lassiter who had recognized what she really was.

Lassiter was looking at his watch. "It's about right, now," he said. "Come on." He nodded to Bruce with a quick grin. "Come and see what Lucy's done since you saw her last."

Bruce followed them into a room in the rear of the apartment. The maid had just deposited a fat baby behind the bars of a white-painted crib. He looked at his father and mother and then at the face of the stranger. When he looked back at his father he laughed. Lucy and Stephen began to talk to him as parents do to an infant too young to talk back, and Bruce fumbled without much success for words of his own. He had never known what to say when confronted with a baby as young as this one, but he admitted aloud that the child had charm.

AFTER Stephen had changed, they left the apartment, took a taxi down Madison, turned east into a street in the Fifties, and got out at a restaurant which called itself the Jardin de Cluny. Inside, Bruce looked around and wondered where the flowers were kept. It was a long narrow room with leather seats running the length of the walls and a small bar in front. The ceiling was only six inches above the crown of his head. The air was blue and the back part of the room was so dimly lit one received an impression of many people eating in a smoky cave. Over the bar the lights shone on the glistening forehead of a barman who looked like Napoleon and on the diffuse faces of hungry people drinking cocktails while they waited to eat. All the stools at the bar were occupied and half a dozen men and women were standing behind the stools with glasses in their hands. More drinkers sat at small tables set near the wall opposite the bar.

A French woman with skin like a dried larigan, wearing heavy keys at her waist, watched over the entrance to the inner room.

A tall girl detached herself from the crowd at the bar. She had long black hair like a cavalier's mane reaching to her shoulders, a dominant nose, full lips, and large black eyes. She came away from the bar with a langorous movement, but when she spoke her voice throbbed with vitality.

"Why did you pick this place?" she said to Lassiter. "Don't you see enough of it every day at noon?"

"Best food in New York," Lassiter said. "Best drinks, too."

"The best what?" She slipped an arm around Lucy's waist and her voice was warm. "Hello, darling, you look lovely. Steve didn't give me a chance to suggest some place else. He left the message when I was out. Is this Bruce?"

Lucy laid a hand on Bruce's forearm. "Stephen's sister, Marcia Stapleton."

"Hello!" Marcia said with a rising inflection. She looked him frankly in the eyes. "Isn't Lucy a darling?"

In some bewilderment Bruce murmured agreement.

"Let's have a drink," Marcia said. "What have you been drinking, rye?"

She went to a corner of the bar where she leaned past a man with hooded eyes and ordered four rye sours. As she stepped back, the man stared at her as if she were something on sale in a store.

"Damn it," her brother said in irritation, "why can't you let me do the ordering?"

"You can pay for them, darling."

Marcia turned back to Bruce, but at that moment a group of four left one of the tables and Lassiter, followed by Lucy and Bruce, took their places.

"This place isn't corrupt, you know," Marcia said to Bruce as she joined them. "It's merely unpleasant." The man with the hooded eyes was still staring at her, and Marcia, meeting his stare, continued without dropping her voice by so much as a decibel. "This is a place where you meet people who are trying to turn themselves into a hick's idea of what a New Yorker is like. Corrupt places have a savour of their own, but this bistro is merely corrupting. There's a difference, don't you think?"

"I'm afraid I don't see it."

"But in this case there really is a difference," Marcia insisted, apparently forgetting the man with the hooded eyes. "This is where Steve and his friends from that lovely business of his meet over lunch with their clients in order to corrupt America. The tables are always full when they arrive, so there's nothing to do but wait and drink, and by the time they get something to eat their clients are half drunk, particularly if they come from out of town and like having smart New Yorkers treat them like kings. That's when Carl does his business with them. He never drinks at lunch himself. He tells them he has ulcers which of course he hasn't at all, and they believe it because it's part of their picture that all ad-men should have them. Carl is *so* clever! Steve and I had a grandfather who always did his business after lunch, but he was very religious and believed God was on his side whenever he put something over on a drunk. He owned a woollen mill."

"Marcia," Lassiter said, "Bruce is down here on leave and up till now he's been having a good time." He got up from the table, inserted his shoulders between a pair of drinkers at the bar, and spoke to the Napoleonic bartender. "Did Mr. Bratian say he'd be late, Jean?"

The barman, with both hands on a shaker, paused just long enough to say no.

"I don't think Carl had to see anyone tonight." Lassiter's voice sounded worried as he came back to the bar. "He may have forgotten, though."

"When did he ever forget anything?" Marcia said.

The barman was holding up a tray with four drinks so that they were visible over the heads of the people at the bar. Lassiter rose again, and Bruce watched in fascination while he manipulated the tray. He withdrew it between the left elbow of a tall man and the right breast of a short woman, handed one glass to Lucy and another to Marcia, and set the tray on the table. Bruce took his glass and turned toward Lucy, but her eyes were on her husband. Lassiter was flushed and tense, though his big body was immobile as he sat with the drink in his hand. Then Bruce realized that Marcia was talking to him and turned to listen to her.

Suddenly everyone in the room seemed to be in disguise, Marcia especially. Her voice and manner reminded him of somebody he had seen and he guessed it must have been a movie actress, though which one he couldn't remember. And yet he was sure she was not innately theatrical. She was like a person doing what had always been expected of her without exactly knowing why. She had a superb figure, her dinner dress was black velvet, and it made the most of her. She wore platinum jewellery and a white ermine jacket. Now she slipped the jacket off and held it out to Bruce.

"Take it from me, will you, like an angel? It's so hot in this place."

Bruce took the jacket and put it on the bench beside him. When he turned back to the table, Marcia was looking at the men standing at the bar. Her lips were parted and she seemed childlike and rather forlorn. Bruce sipped his drink and his mind began to race. He was exhilarated by the rapidity with which it moved today; normally he was slow to estimate people, but today he was surprising himself. His eyes met Lucy's across the the table and he felt a warm glow from their mutual consciousness of one another, from their surprised pleasure at finding each other changed and yet permanently themselves. He turned to Marcia again, and as her gaze came back he decided she was probably more sensual than passionate; he was not very sure what the distinction meant, but he was pleased to be able to make it. Then Lassiter's chin rose, and turning to follow his eyes, Bruce saw a little man with sallow cheeks and a big nose coming in the door. A moment later he was introduced to Carl Bratian, and in the quick flash of those gypsy eyes he felt an appraisal of himself far more thorough than his own appraisal of Marcia. Bratian was wearing a dinner jacket under a closely fitting topcoat and he carried suede gloves in his left hand.

He shook hands with Bruce and apologized to them all for being late. He sat down between Lucy and her husband and began to talk across her.

"He came after you left," Bratian said.

"Well?"

"He's still making up his mind."

Lassiter frowned and said something Bruce couldn't hear. Again he saw Lucy's eyes intent on her husband's face.

"Quit worrying, Steve," Bratian said in a harsh, precise voice. "Everything's going to be okay. Relax. So what if he hasn't made up his mind yet? He will. You made a good impression on him last week." He turned to the others. "Let's get out of here. This place is like an annex to my office." His eyes ran quickly over the flank and shoulders of a girl seated at the bar and then he turned to Lucy. "I've booked a table at the Marguery. Specially for you."

The cool night air made Bruce giddy and then it cleared his head. He found himself in the back seat of a cab next to Lucy, Lassiter on his other side, and Marcia and Bratian perched on the drop-seats. His hand closed over Lucy's and she answered the pressure gently, as if to let him know she was there and was thinking of him. In the half darkness he saw her profile as she leaned forward to speak to Marcia, but for most of the ride to the Marguery she was just a presence beside him. His head was clear when he stepped out on the pavement of Park Avenue while the commissionaire held open the taxi door, he saw the traffic disappearing into the wall of Grand Central Station, and looking up, he saw the tower above the station bursting with lights. When he entered the Marguery the silence was so dignified he could almost hear it reproving him. An elderly gentleman with a face like a British Prime Minister of good vintage was speaking to the headwaiter by the door of the restaurant. Bratian went to look for a telephone and Bruce was conscious of Lucy by his side, while Marcia and Lassiter were several paces away.

"Have you really enjoyed your day?"

Their eyes met, each of them a little shy of the other.

"Wonderfully."

Marcia seemed to be arguing with her brother.

"Poor Marcia!" Lucy said. "She's separated from her husband again and she and Stephen always seem to get into an argument. They both worry about each other when they're apart, but the minute they get together they begin to argue. I'd hoped you'd like her, because I like her so very much."

"I do," Bruce heard himself saying. "I do."

But he was not looking at Marcia as he said this. He was looking into Lucy's eyes, and suddenly his heart felt so full that tears started and he had to blink them back. For months he had been hardening himself against feeling anything. It had seemed the only way he could face what lay ahead; to make himself mindless, factual, to think of women as pin-up girls, to turn his flair for poetry into composing bawdy limericks, to do anything for a laugh. Now in this quick exchange of glances between Lucy and himself the attitude melted away.

It was not a look of understanding which passed between them. It was not even a look of recognition, the kind exchanged by husband and wife who have experienced every shade of each other's moods. Rather it was a look of startled awareness, a sudden involuntary touching by each of the mystery at the core of the other. It was as if their hidden spirits, issuing for an instant into the light, had brushed in passing. His imagination leaped wildly. He lacked the experience to know that such a meeting is more poignant and more dangerously disturbing, perhaps even keener and more profound, than mature love can ever be, for mature love is a matter of endurance, a matter of wisdom and care. He felt new, naked, reckless, and powerful. His hands quivered as he clasped them behind his back.

The next thing he knew, Lassiter was speaking to him. "What must you be thinking of us? You come down here on leave from the war and we go on talking business, talking as if what we were doing mattered a damn –" His big hand closed affectionately on Bruce's arm, just over the elbow. "I'd give everything I've got to be with you, boy! It won't be long, don't worry, before this whole country is lined up where it belongs."

Bratian reappeared and began to talk to the headwaiter. Marcia joined Lucy and Bruce, and the next thing Bruce knew they were walking over a soundless carpet to their table.

For the next half-hour, while they sat at a large table and a pair of grave men served them, Bruce was incapable of hearing anything anyone said. Cocktails were ordered and he drank another manhattan. Sole was served after the soup, a slim, finely drawn sole with the tang of the ocean still perceptible in its meat. A pale German wine appeared with the fish and he drank two glasses of it. When he realized he could not taste the superb wild duck Lassiter had ordered, he had enough sense to let the burgundy rest in his glass, lifting it occasionally to the light and pretending to sip it, looking into its glowing heart and remembering the rubies he had seen that same afternoon on Fifth Avenue. All the time his eyes kept straying toward Lucy on the opposite side of the table, longing for a trace of recognition in her glance. At the same time, as Lassiter talked to him eager for him to feel at home and enjoy himself, Bruce found himself drawn to him too, told himself he had misjudged Lassiter, and cursed himself for being such a fool as practically to have fallen in love with his host's wife.

Marcia was speaking to him. "How long are you down for?"

"Three days."

"Would you like to see me tomorrow?"

"I'd like to very much."

Her head inclined toward his. "You lived next door to Lucy for years, didn't you?" she said in a low voice.

"Practically all my life."

She knows, Bruce thought. I don't care if she does know.

"Lucy's in love with Steve. But really in love. The way people used to be. It's incredible, isn't it?"

He had no idea what to say and wondered if he was drunk. All sense of time had disappeared and the people around him seemed to be floating. He took a package of cigarettes from his pocket and offered one to Marcia. She picked up the package with curiosity and the yellow cardboard gleamed in the light.

"Black Cat – what a name for cigarettes! I think it's rather sweet. What are they – Canadian?"

Before Bruce could answer, Bratian extended a long silver case which he snapped open. "Try one of these. They're Greek. There's only one place in New York where you can get them."

"Carl knows the one place in New York where you can get anything," Marcia said.

Bruce took the flat, slender cigarette and lit it. His palate was now so dulled from drink and excitement he could have been smoking shag without knowing the difference.

"Tell me something, Fraser," Bratian was eyeing the end of his cigarette, "up in Canada have you been surprised at the way the British have held out?"

"Not since the first of July."

Bratian smiled. "Why are they so good now when five months ago they didn't know what they were doing? That's the most important question raised by the whole war."

"That means Carl thinks he knows the answer," Marcia said.

Again Bratian smiled. "It happens that I do know the answer. Churchill. People in the mass are like animals. I don't care who they are, that's what they're like." His oval eyes held Bruce. "Why does every animal in a herd suddenly lift its head and start running in the same direction? Because a single animal – at a precise moment – has translated what the others feel into a specific action. The real leader of any people has got to be a medium. Are you interested in history?"

"Before the war I thought it was my subject."

Bratian tapped the white ash of his cigarette. "Some day I'd like to write a book on the philosophy of history. I have an idea an advertising man might have something important to say on that subject. After all – what is our job? We're mediums. What we feel today, the masses will want tomorrow."

Bruce wondered what the man was driving at. Was he testing him out? Lucy, on the far side of the table, sat calmly without a word, and for the first time in months the war seemed far away to Bruce, a trivial episode, a saga he had read about years ago in his study at Queen's.

TUGBOAT whistles blowing in the East River woke Bruce at seven-thirty the next morning. He opened his eyes and a soreness at the back of the neck and a dryness in his throat informed him he had a mild hangover. The whistles continued to blow intermittently. In the near distance a riveting machine was racketing like a Vickers firing bursts on a beaten zone. The drum beat of New York going to work pulsed in a steady undertone through the open window and after a few minutes he realized he would not regain his sleep that morning even if he stayed in bed until noon. He threw off the covers, got up, and stretched, and his eyes squinted against the sunlight pouring into the room. Then he got rid of his hangover by standing for nearly a quarter of an hour under the shower. He shaved and came back to the room with a towel around his waist and stood in bare feet looking out the window. His room was on the east side of a hotel in Tudor City – he had been given the address by an American friend in the squadron before coming down – and he could look across the river to Long Island City. A new destroyer was moving up the channel toward the Queensborough Bridge with her guns wrapped in canvas jackets.

It was while Bruce was dressing that the sensation of warm and excited fullness, still lingering from his meeting with Lucy the previous night, changed to one of aching surprise at himself and astonishment that such an emotion could have struck him so quickly and left him with the feeling that he had been ham-strung. He glared at himself in the mirror as he fixed his tie and pulled his face into a stern frown. A few minutes ago he had been planning to telephone Lucy the moment he finished breakfast. His imagination had been completely uncontrolled. He was in love with her. He had discovered the only woman he could ever love. Her eyes had revealed that she had discovered him also. He brushed his hair slowly. Her eyes – how did he know what lay behind them?

Then the thought occurred to him that he had done something wrong. If Lucy had been deeply stirred by him, he was culpable. Somehow he had always felt that if men and women got snarled up in each other's lives, it was the fault of the man.

After breakfast he left the hotel and began to walk. It was another hazy, golden day, and the people on East Forty-second Street moved without hurry. Bruce began to look into their faces as though they could somehow tell him more than he already knew about himself. His eye fell on an itinerant shoe-shiner. The man was squatting on the pavement beside his footrest and a box of polishes and old rags, his shoulders hunched over, his back against the front of a cigar store, his eyes closed against the sun, head dropping so far sideways his left ear almost touched his shoulder. The sun gleamed on a flat forehead, and a ring of worn black hair circled a bald skull the colour of ivory.

Looking at the man led Bruce to look at his own shoes. They were scuffed and dusty, so he stopped in the middle of the sidewalk. It seemed a strange, public way to improve his appearance, but apparently it was a custom in New York, so he moved over to the footrest and put his right foot on it. The man came to life, looked up and smiled, and then crouched on both knees like a slave before his master.

While he worked, Bruce stood there near the corner of Forty-second Street and Third Avenue, one hand on his hip, the other at his side clasping his leather gloves. He listened to the enlargement of noise as elevated trains roared by overhead and receded again, to the clanging of streetcars and the honk of horns, and he felt completely alone. His thoughts began to march with a cautious inner honesty.

He informed himself that he had been a fool not to have seen Lucy with different eyes all the years she had lived in Grenville. It was almost shameful to have come to New York and here see her with her husband and child before discovering that she was a beautiful woman. Two years ago, as he now knew only too well, he had been nothing but an inhibited Ontario boy. In the last twelve months, with his life committed, with the lonely tensions crawling through the night when he had forcibly to grip himself and explore his mind as if to prove in advance that he could control his fear when the time came, he felt he had grown many years older. He told himself coldly that if the feeling which had emerged between himself and Lucy last night were allowed to grow and spread, it would take over his whole life. It would unman him if Lucy did not respond to it, and it would ruin Lucy if she did.

He tried to straighten his shoulders and found it difficult to do so with one foot raised on the cleaning-rest. He pressed his lips together and his face twitched as once more the profile of Lucy, transfigured by his imagination into a vision sad, fragile, and mysterious, floated across his mind. But was she really beautiful? He had never thought so before yesterday. A woman like Marcia Stapleton would be called beautiful by almost anyone. Nina was certainly prettier than Lucy. Among all the individual girls to be seen in the crowds of New York, a stranger passing Lucy on Fifth Avenue would hardly notice her at all. Yet the question as to whether she was beautiful or not made no difference today whatever. For him she had a quality far greater than any objective beauty of figure or features. She had the power of making him think of beautiful things, of lifting his imagination. Through her he longed to discover everything yet to be learned, and his intuition told him that a search of Lucy would be endless. The thought brought a feeling of joyous power throbbing through him.

The man at his feet tapped his shoe and Bruce changed one foot for the other on the rest. Could any man, he wondered, feel as he was feeling about any woman? Perhaps falling in love was never more than what one did to one's own imagination, letting it play upon a woman's image like a pianist before a piano.

Bruce stood there with one foot raised, testing this new idea for a moment, and then with a ruthlessness toward himself which was typical, which in fact was a product of his whole life-training, his will-power took control and crushed the colour and the wildly trembling excitement into the hinterland of his mind. Lucy was married. Therefore it was impossible to fall in love with her. Therefore he did not love her. Therefore he must think of something else.

A girl in a light wool dress walked past and his eyes followed her. She was everything Lucy was not. She had the face and shoulders of a Slavonic peasant, large breasts which quivered to every step; her hips, heavy and suggestive, rose and fell under her tight skirt. But his eyes continued to follow her until she turned the corner.

That's why men go to whores, he thought. Whores are safe. They never touch the imagination. They make a man feel worse, rather than better. They always disappoint him and so they don't necessarily cause him to disappoint himself.

He laughed, and the Italian's forehead wrinkled as he looked up. In Grenville, Bruce thought, you believed you were in love with a woman if you had a means of supporting her and wished to marry her. Otherwise you were merely infatuated and the feeling was not serious. It was not a thought which the Italian would have considered cause for laughter.

He had finished with his brushes and now set about giving a final polish to the second shoe with a blackened cloth. Once or twice he looked up at the man above him, the yellowish whites of his eyes showing, but he had no way of guessing what lay in Bruce's mind. Perhaps he wondered if this tense young foreigner would some day drop bombs on the helpless little town in southern Italy which he had left years ago to follow a dream of making a great success in America. Perhaps he thought only of the difference which stood between them, the one blue-eyed, keen and erect, quick and dangerous, the kind of man invariably chosen to drop bombs; the other on his knees, loose and shapeless, yet slow and softly durable, with inarticulate, useless but ultimate knowledge in his eyes.

As the toe of Bruce's service shoe took on its final polish, Bruce began deliberately to cauterize his mind of the soft persuasion of beauty and mystery with which he had wakened that morning. He was making himself bare, bleak, and self-reliant again. In line with his entire life-training, he encouraged himself to expect little and to be thankful for what he had, yet to feel guilty for not being able to do more. He also encouraged himself to beware of happiness unless it were the kind he could pick up and lay down at will. He would not, he told himself, make any attempt to see Lucy again.

The Italian had finished his shoes and now was sitting back on his haunches with the dirty rag in his hand. Bruce reached into his pocket, took out a quarter and gave it to the man, who smiled, touched his forehead, and put the coin in his own dirty pocket. Then Bruce turned on his heel and began to walk rapidly toward Fifth Avenue because it was the direction in which he had started. On the corner of Fifth he was stopped by traffic lights. The open door of a bus was in front of him so he got in and climbed to the upper deck, where he sat staring at the neck of the man in the seat in front. At Eighty-second Street a number of people got off the bus in front of the Metropolitan Museum, so Bruce followed them. And there he spent nearly two hours roaming through the galleries, identifying originals whose copies he had seen in many books. The American Wing held little interest for him, so he walked down the stone stairway and for nearly half an hour he looked at the statue of the Etruscan spearman. In his present mood he seemed to feel things which even two days ago he believed he would have missed: the merciless truth in that merciless figure, its functional, necessary, and dutiful ferocity. He left it reluctantly and went in search of a telephone booth.

There was a long delay before Marcia Stapleton's voice came onto the phone, following two suave female voices who announced themselves and then switched him to other extensions. Marcia informed him that she was delighted to hear from him and the eagerness of her personality seemed to be in the booth with him.

When he walked out into the sunshine he felt once again as he had felt twenty-four hours ago, adventurous and brimming with vitality. She had agreed to let him take her to dinner that evening.

IT WAS another evening with a flaming sunset over the Hudson followed by darkness and the same flowering of electric lights all over the city. Bruce met Stephen's sister in her apartment in Sutton Place, a very different kind of apartment from Lucy's. It was old-fashioned and prim, as if a prized New England interior had been transported to New York and installed within view of the East River. Electric lights had been covered by frosted glass originally designed for oil lamps. The chairs were antique, brittle, and unsafe for anyone heavier than a small child. Over the mantel hung a line-engraving of New Bedford harbour, a period piece in which a flotilla of brigs and three-masters with yards backed lay at anchor among waves that resembled a mass of twisted black wires. On the other walls were three paintings with highly lacquered and cracked canvases of black-suited men displaying grim red faces and bitter turned-down mouths, apparently representing the heads of a family in the first three generations of its wealth. The family resemblance was strong in all three, though the first wore a round collar and was certainly a clergyman and the second wore a stock and was probably a merchant.

Bruce had always felt an insatiable curiosity about the insides of other people's houses, so now he prowled around the room while he waited for Marcia to change for the evening. He discovered a pair of small photographs on the mantel and decided they must be Marcia's parents. Her mother's features were delicate, she wore her hair in bangs, and it was evident that she had been both a charming and beautiful woman. Her husband's square jaws and hard eyes made no impression whatever on Bruce; the type was unfamiliar to him.

As Marcia came in from the bedroom wearing a rich blue velvet dinner dress with a gold belt and gold jewellery, Bruce turned away from the pictures, his expression showing startled approval. She came across the room and stood before him, smiling like a friendly child.

"Kiss me!" she said.

He put his arms about her obediently, but when he felt her body quiver and her lips open beneath his, he thought Good God, what have I here?

She stepped back, drew a deep breath, and then she smiled again. "You're awfully nice! And don't look so surprised. I've been in the office all day doing something completely useless. I wanted to kiss you the first time I saw you last night. You liked me, too ... before you started looking at Lucy." She glanced around the room. "Damn! I've forgotten the drinks. Wait a minute."

She went into the kitchen and came back with two glasses, one in either hand, containing rye, ice, and water. She handed Bruce one glass, set the other on a table, then laid her fingers, cold and slightly damp, against her forehead.

"Do you know what I do for a living?" she said.

"No."

"I'm in the research department of *LIFE*. Somebody over there discovered what this place is like ..." One hand swept in an arc to indicate the room ... "So for three weeks I've been getting up material on old New England interiors. They may do a piece based on my findings sometime. And they may not."

"It sounds like interesting work."

She studied him a moment before she answered. "I'm one of the very most obscure individuals in the whole enormous staff of that magazine. Fortunately, I still get a pittance from my last husband to keep me in hair-ribbons." She sat down in a fragile chair beside a Duncan Phyfe table, picked up her glass and drank a third of its contents, and seeing his eyes travelling over the room again, she twinkled with amusement. "This room's not genuine. It's just a family museum. After Father died, Mother collected all this stuff from her family's old homestead in Massachusetts. This was her apartment before she died. Making it look like this was her way of trying to forget her life with Father, I suspect. Or maybe she was simply trying to escape back to her childhood. Ever since I've lived here I've found my ancestors rather embarrassing."

Bruce got up and crossed the room to stand, glass in hand, in front of the oldest painting. Authentic puritan eyes, framed by an authentic puritan face in which the bone structure seemed to be straining at the skin, stared bleakly back at him. All his life he had seen faces like that in Grenville and it had never occurred to him to consider them distinguished.

"Everything Mother ever did was terrifyingly symbolic," Marcia said. "When she married Father there was a wild fluttering in the dovecotes. Some of the relatives said he was impossible and one or two of them said he'd graft new energy onto the family tree. Father was crude, but considering Steve and me, I guess his energy was no more use to the Massachusetts blood of Mother's family than a truck running downhill with no brakes. All he gave Steve was a compulsion to pretend he's a lot cruder than he really is."

Bruce looked down at her and gave her a puzzled smile. "Do you always add up scores like that?"

"Don't take me seriously. Nobody else does. Relax and drink your drink peacefully."

He returned to his chair and wondered if he looked as tense as he felt.

"Did Lucy tell you about my two failures in marriage?" Marcia said.

"Only that you were separated."

"That's all she would say. Lucy's so tactful. Or rather, she's just plain damned nice." She got up and went into the kitchen and came back with a bowl of ice. She dropped a piece in Bruce's glass and one in her own. "I hate divorce," she said. "I really do. I haven't divorced Arnold – my third husband – but I suppose I'll have to. Men are so chivalrous these days. They commit adultery and then allow the wife they don't want any more to go out to Reno by herself and announce to the whole world that she can't hold her husband."

She went into the kitchen again and returned with a half-empty bottle of rye. She poured some in his glass, poured some in her own, and then stood over him, looking at a white scar which ran behind the knuckles of his left hand.

"Don't try to make something symbolic out of that," he said. "It came from a scythe when I was working on a farm the summer I was sixteen. All it means is that a farmer threw a scythe on top of a load of hay and it slid down the other side of the wagon and hit me."

She continued to stand in front of him with a mocking, childish smile on her lips. He got to his feet, took the bottle and her glass, and set them down, and then put his arms about her and kissed her again. Her fingers teased his hair.

"You're so defiantly healthy minded!" she said when he finally released her.

"Oh, to hell with you!" He kissed her again. Then he went to the kitchen himself to search for water and a pitcher to carry it in. By eight o'clock she had finished three more drinks and Bruce was hungry, but Marcia was in no hurry to leave.

"Tell me something," she said, showing no evidence of having been drinking anything stronger than lemonade. "Why did Lucy marry Steve?"

"She was in love with him, I should imagine. And she was very lonely."

"What's the matter with the men in Canada?"

He avoided her questioning eyes and fumbled for cigarettes. "In 1938, there wasn't a man Lucy's age with a decent job in the town where we lived. Not an unmarried one, anyhow."

"Did that include you?"

Instead of answering her question, he said, "Lucy's changed since she married your brother, you know. If she went home now people would hardly recognize her."

"Nonsense. She hasn't changed at all. Underneath she's always been exactly what she is now."

When Bruce made no reply, she added, "Lucy's too good for Steve, you know."

He found her eyes and held them. "I wouldn't know about that. Everyone liked Steve in Grenville."

"That's why he was sent up there."

Bruce eyed her with curiosity. "Why do you dislike him?"

"I don't. As a matter of fact, I'm sorry for him. After all, I knew his parents." She looked down at her empty glass and decided it was time for them to go out and eat.

But later on, in a restaurant of her selection with a ceiling quite as low as the one she had objected to the night before, Marcia began to talk of Lucy again.

"Sometimes when I'm horribly down, I think about her and I feel better just to know she's alive. And I'm not even envious. Women like Lucy don't usually like me, but she's never held me off. I don't know why. But I also don't have any idea what she thinks about us all. She seems to have emerged from an earlier segment of time."

Bruce looked down at his plate and impaled a piece of marinated herring on his fork. He heard French spoken at a table on his right and an unfamiliar language at the table ahead of them. The man with the unknown tongue was bald-headed and he wore his napkin tucked into one side of his collar; the young woman who faced him had black eyes which darted from a mid-European mask and she gestured with suave hands which made arabesques over her food.

Marcia followed his glance. "I met him once when he first arrived, but he wouldn't remember. All he remembers is how much he hates being here. She smuggled her diamonds out in jars of cold cream and they've been living on the proceeds ever since. New York's become queer since history moved in on us."

Bruce finished the herring and stole another glance at the unhappy couple. He heard Marcia speaking softly.

"I wish you weren't in the Airforce," she said.

"Why?" He turned his glance back to her.

"Because I like you."

He smiled grimly. "Maybe you'd have liked me better two years ago. I was a pacifist then."

"Why did you change?"

"This is the season of the universal payoff. The era of good intentions is over."

She thought about what he had said, and when she answered her voice was wistful. "I call us the well-meaning generation. We threw away the wisdom of the ages because we quite correctly despised our parents. In our own way we were so terribly moral. We slept with each other whenever we felt like it because we thought it was hypocritical not to follow our natural instincts. We believed that wars were made by munitions-makers and old men who should have been dead, and so we let this one become possible because we weren't going to let ourselves be fooled a second time. We thought science had arrived to take the place of religion, and we believed the only thing needed to make us good was a good economic system. Because our parents were wrong about nearly everything, we took it for granted we were automatically right whenever we disagreed with them. If Jesus Christ appeared today, we'd send him to a psychoanalyst to get rid of his maladjustments."

Only a little of what Marcia said touched an emotional chord in Bruce, for he had met nobody in Canada who thought as she did, nor did her words agree with most American opinions he had seen in print. She stirred his senses every time he looked at her, but his soul felt empty and his mind confused.

As though to regain the attention she sensed she had lost, Marcia's voice began to rise, and the couple at the next table concentrated on their plates with the abstracted attention people always give to their food when they are straining their ears to listen to somebody else's conversation.

"Steve's custom-made," she was saying, "and yet I know a gross exactly like him. They all went to Yale or Princeton and they all graduated into the big time in New York and they all had tough, silent fathers who were successful in the neolithic age and they can't realize that the future belongs to smooth little swine like Carl Bratian who can size them up and undress their minds for them. They ..."

"Does it?" Bruce interrupted.

"Does it what?"

"Does the future necessarily belong to men like Bratian? I don't think so."

Marcia made a gesture of despair. "And I was doing so well! I was being terribly serious."

"You certainly were."

"But I do know what I'm talking about. Men like Steve use women to prove something to themselves. They think the only thing women want of a man is for him to be super-colossal in bed. My first husband believed that, and since he wasn't very strong he had an inferiority complex and ended by hating me. Steve isn't that bad, of course. At least he's strong."

Bruce said nothing more until he had finished his steak. He wished Marcia would stop talking about her brother, for he knew that Lucy was in love with Steve, and he knew that his sudden new feeling for Lucy had been aroused by the emanations of her love for another man, and. from this he tried to reason that love was infectious, like a disease, and that it was probably a mistake to pin it directly on a single person when you caught it.

While they drank their coffee he asked Marcia if she would like a brandy, but she shook her head impatiently.

"Let's get out of here," she said when she had snapped her compact shut and dropped it into her purse. "There's a new place I want to see. I've been thinking about it ever since you called me."

Soon they were in the full course of one of those evenings cut from a pattern set in the last war, developed in the long armistice, and celebrated in a thousand novels until it had become as formal as a ritual. Drinks in clouded bistros, growing intimacy, mutual discovery of each other's inevitable loneliness, taxies in the night, a few dances, more drinks, a conversation on the curb in front of a night-club in the Village with a drunk who claimed that Mike McTigue would have been the daisy of them all if his hands hadn't been so brittle, another smoke-filled joint, and a piano player whose eyes were bright with marijuana as he rolled out the barrelhouse.

Some time after two in the morning, riding back uptown in a cab with his arm about Marcia's shoulder and her hair in his eyes and the perfume she used wild in his nostrils, Bruce remembered the war. It was easy then to face the fact that he was sure he would be dead before long. Would it be quick, a stitch of bullets across his chest, blacking him out as the hot, antiseptic metal snapped his spine? Or would he be trapped in his plane, and slide down the sky in a long, slow-seeming arc, beautiful to the onlookers as he burned alive?

"Your jaw's too tight, darling. Relax."

"Is it?"

"Don't think so hard. Nothing in the world's worth the effort of thinking about it."

"We've got to knock hell out of them."

"You're too serious."

"Why not? It's your war, too."

"It's not my war. I live in the United States."

"You're a North American and so am I. You've got to knock bloody hell out of them, too. We're not washed up on this continent. Not yet."

Silence. The taxi lurched as it turned off Madison and headed east.

"Do you love me?"

His jaw tightened again. The taxi passed Park, ran rapidly between silent buildings, and crossed Lexington.

"It's such a little thing to say," she murmured. "Please say it to me."

Silence again as they passed under the Elevated at Third, Bruce feeling the tension rise within him, thinking of more things than he could understand if he had a whole year to consider them. Alone with Marcia, longing for her not because she was Marcia but because she was all women, in love with Lucy whom he had never taken seriously when he might have loved her, in New York, in a war, sitting close to Marcia who used perfume behind her ears and made him feel grateful because she liked him so much.

"Right now is all the time there ever is," she said.

He thought of Grenville and the long, cautious nights where desire is an ache under the moon, and marriage an endurance, and the future the sole reason for the present.

The tires bumbled on the paving blocks of First Avenue. As they passed through the yellow splash of a street light Marcia's face became visible.

"Darling," she whispered. "Please stop thinking. You must. At least for tonight."

He crushed her in his arms, but the cab lurched and threw them apart. He caught a blurred vision of the cage-like girders of a section of the Queensborough Bridge.

Less than half an hour later, watched in the dim light by still another of Marcia's New England ancestors, Bruce Fraser came to the end of a trail he had been following since adolescence; and in the conflicting tensions of the moment he was not sure whether he had crossed the frontier of a deeper mystery or merely entered the first of a long series of empty rooms.

For his remaining day in New York he made no attempt to see either Lucy or Marcia again. Shy with himself and deeply disturbed, he spent his last American money on two bouquets, wrote a brief note to accompany each, and ordered one sent to Lucy and the other to Marcia.

When he found a seat in the day coach for the bumpy night ride back to Montreal he was hungry, after a supper limited necessarily to a single hamburger and a cup of coffee. He was too tired to sort out his feelings and his eyes closed before the train left the station.

The hard, green-plush seats of the old coach were filled that night with exhausted Canadian soldiers and airmen, as broke as himself, all returning from leave in New York. They were all too tired to talk, too tired even to look at one another. All military glamour was gone when they took off their tunics and sprawled on the seats in their wrinkled khaki or sky-blue shirts with the braces pulling their trousers halfway up their backs.

As the train stirred and began to rumble along the tunnel under Park Avenue, Bruce's lips moved in a trace of a smile in answer to a rueful gleam of self-knowledge. A month from now this holiday would seem like a mirage in a desert. When poetical moods came upon him he would think of Lucy's face; with reawakened desire, Marcia would surge back imperiously; his imagination would distill them into beings who never existed. By that time he would again be the man he had been trained by his background to become, strong in the knowledge that whatever he most wanted he would probably never have and would certainly never enjoy.

THREE

FOR FIVE YEARS FOLLOWING the Autumn of 1940, Bruce Fraser
saw neither Lucy nor Marcia nor any of the people he had known
in Grenville or New York. In the spring of 1942, navigating a Wellington bomber on his twenty-third mission, he was shot down over
Mannheim. The pilot, a boy who had once operated a hot-dog stand
in the Toronto ball park, with one hand blown off and his body
creeping in flames, held up the nose of the craft long enough to let
the rest of the crew escape.

Bruce was blown away from the city and came down in fairly
open country to the south of Ludwigshafen. One side of his face
was injured, one eye blinded, and his left shoulder shattered, and
he remembered almost nothing until he was discovered the next
day by a French prisoner-of-war on his way to work in the fields.
The man concealed him until night and then arranged for another
Frenchman to have him smuggled across the German border in a
freight car. Three days after the raid a doctor in a small town in
the Franche-Compté operated on his left eye and removed it. The
shrapnel had crushed some nerves in his left shoulder and for many

days he was in great pain, lying alone in the attic of a house he had never seen. The doctor visited him often and finally contrived to get him into a hospital for another operation. Afterwards he conveyed Bruce to a private home in the country near Besançon where a French family, at the risk of their own lives, nursed him back to health. By August he was well enough to travel, though there would always be a scar crossing his left cheek from the temple to the chin, he would never be able to lift his left elbow above shoulder height, and he would one day have to exchange the glass eye with which the doctor had fitted him for a plastic one.

By slow stages he managed to reach Perpignan, and five weeks after crossing the Spanish frontier he was back in England. From there he was sent home to Canada, ordered to appear before a medical board, and released from the Airforce.

In the winter of 1943, Bruce returned to England as a minor correspondent for the Canadian Press. At first he was given routine office work in London. He asked to be sent with the army on the Sicilian invasion, but he was turned down, and finally late in January in 1944 he was ordered to a night-bomber station in Yorkshire to do a series of impressions of an airfield in operation. It was a job he could have done in the London office from memory, but he was bored with London and glad of an excuse to get out of it for a week.

It was a cold night when he reported at the station and the northern edge in the air reminded him of Canada. He watched the planes get away, made a few notes for local colour, and then the long wait began. It was the first time he had ever been forced to stay on duty at the base to sweat out these hours of the night, and an overpowering loneliness began to grow out of his sense of being utterly useless. It was less than a year since he had been flying over Germany himself, but already those days seemed to belong to another era, almost to another war. He felt superannuated from life.

He found a corner of the lounge where he would not be disturbed, opened his notebook, and on the coarse grey paper covered with green lines he began to write a letter. He gave it no heading and no salutation, but he knew he was talking to Lucy.

Perhaps if I see a little more of the war I'll learn finally why things have to be as they are, he wrote. Tonight I feel either

too old or too young for the world I'm living in and I don't
know which it is. A few hours ago I was talking to a Pole with
that look so many escaped Europeans have – their eyes remind you of statues in the British Museum – as if they had
seen the beginning and the end and had nothing more to learn.
Thank God the English haven't got that look – not yet anyway. But the war has taught me one important fact – the world
is filled with men of good will. Even that Pole is a man of
good will. It comes out in some people as intense loyalty –
even the Nazis are loyal to Hitler. And in that case loyalty
seems to be no more than a trap. Why? Because it is fixed on
a system instead of on people? I seem to be haunted by the
fact that at a time when more of us have good will in our
hearts than ever before, the organized doing of evil has become our chief industry.

There's been too much feeling for us in too little time. Too
many ideas to understand without enough information. For
instance, everyone of my old crew is gone, all but me. Why
should I still be alive?

Tonight I'm supposed to be writing about an airbase, but
I won't be able to do it – not honestly, at any rate. So for a
little while I'm going to write to you, instead. After that I'll
set down the routine and meaningless facts. Of course, the
whole organization of an air base has a sort of superhuman
grandeur about it. It seems to make us all, for a short while,
larger than life, but there is the evil of it. During the Depression I was nothing. As navigator of a Wellington I was part
of a certain greatness. I love planes even while I hate the idea
of them. A year ago I even loved the moment when the bombs
dropped. Had I been on the ground when our own bombs fell
I'd have hated myself for what I'd done. And now I feel old
and out of it and at the same time glad I didn't fall apart when
the pressure was on me. Do you understand what I mean,
Lucy, when I say that it's horrifying, sometimes, to feel safe
again?

I've stopped writing poetry. You'll probably be glad to hear
it, considering what my old poetry was like. It makes me wonder if the war has killed all natural beauty for me. Today as
I came up here there was a bright morning sun – a wonder-

ful light over everything – but I hated it because it reminded me of the same kind of sun that was shining the morning a friend of mine was killed on his first operational flight when an Me-110 dived at him out of such a sun. He should have known better, of course, but he was a kid – he couldn't have been old enough to get into the Airforce legitimately.

Do you think the war may have killed all my sense of feeling? I begin to suspect it has, you know. I watched the planes go out tonight and all I could think about them was that they were a great machine and I hoped the human elements in them wouldn't make any bad mistakes. What I mean to say is this, I don't think I got that way from callousness but from a surfeit of feeling. Battles of all kinds are a colossal sensuality. You can't think, except to do your job almost mechanically, but the moment the height of the danger passes you feel with an incredible intensity. That's when you discover your buried self. You get so close to the buried *you* – that part of us that the mind of Ontario tries to censor out of existence – that sometimes you become afraid of yourself. But it doesn't last long because after a space your feelings seem to dry up and you begin to talk and think like staff officers and air marshals and when that happens you know that the war – so far as you're concerned – ought to be over.

I hope you don't mind what I've said about Ontario. Something quite wonderful has happened to Canada in this war and I don't mean to belittle it. Over here in the Canadian Army and the R.C.A.F. you can almost see and hear Canada growing up. We were sent over so early, you know, to train here instead of at home, particularly the men in the army, and that meant that for three years we were dreadfully isolated. All we had were letters that didn't tell us very much because they come from people who don't express themselves any too freely, and a few baseball bats and worn-out footballs and hometown newspapers weeks old. The British were in their own country, the Americans who finally arrived three years after the war began came as lords of the earth, but we were just Canadians in everyone's eyes. Nobody knew what we really were, or cared much. So we had to think more about ourselves and our country for ourselves. Nobody else had ever set much value on her and we tried to figure out why. So we discovered her for ourselves – in the things men say to each other after lights-out, in the subtle differences between ourselves and the Americans whom we had always assumed were about the same as ourselves. We liked the Americans and we got on with them, but they weren't the same. Particularly they weren't the same when we felt deeply about things, for in those moments we found we no longer talked precisely their language.

Dear Lucy, I was thinking about you when I began this letter, but I've forgotten how to talk easily of the things most human beings find to say to each other. I would like to be able to ask the questions that would lead you to answer – to tell me about yourself and your husband and Marcia Stapleton and your son, whatever you like that would give me a glimpse of your life. But I've forgotten how to word such questions. Still, I believe your intuitions are quite good enough to understand a good many things I can't say – why I'm writing you tonight, for instance, what I'm thinking when I think about you now, what I thought all through that night I spent with you in New York, though hardly any words passed between us the entire evening. The feeling I had then is still there, though I'm no longer fool enough to let it take me at the back of the knees the way it did once.

Forgive me if I've said too much. It's four in the morning and no man is safe with himself at such an hour, particularly at a bomber station in Yorkshire waiting for the planes to come back and remembering so much more than he can understand.

Bruce tore the pages he had covered with pencilled lines from the notebook and folded them to fit a crumpled envelope he found in his pocket. He wrote Lucy's married name on the envelope, tried to remember her New York address, failed, and returned the envelope to his pocket, the letter sealed within it. It was several days later before he found it there, for the letter went out of his mind as soon as the bombers began to return that morning. When he did look at it again he turned it over in his hand, opened it, and read it through for the first time. It was the kind of letter, he decided, that a man writes only for himself and should never mail. So he tore it into scraps, promising himself that he would try to remember to send Lucy a card one day soon.

A month after D-Day Bruce was allowed to follow the army into France, and after the breakthrough at Caen he went on through Belgium into Holland and finally into Germany. As he was never given a by-line his name was unknown in Canada, but for a few months millions of people read the reports he wrote. Most of them were small items picked up from individual soldiers or companies, from stretcher-bearers and overworked orderlies at dressing stations, stories personal enough to have human interest and impersonal enough to pass the censor. Toward the end of the war in Europe his mother and father, listening to the radio one night in Grenville, heard his voice in a transcribed news report from Holland after the capture of Bergen-op-Zoom.

AFTER taking her degree from Queen's University, Nina Cameron got a job in Toronto as secretary to a prominent lawyer and she lived in the city for nearly two years, sharing an apartment with two other girls she had known in college. It turned out to be less fun than she had always thought such a life would be. She spent the Christmas of 1940 in New York with Lucy and Stephen and she was bewildered by the apparent change in her sister. She returned to Toronto with an odd sensation that she was alone in the world and with a suspicion that somewhere along the line she had missed a cue.

When the Wrens were organized Nina left her job in the law office and enlisted, convinced that the Wrens were the most select and desirable of the women's services. Dressed in a flat sailor's hat, navy suit, black stockings, and well-shined black oxfords, she saw herself at the elbow of handsome officers heavy with gold braid and a natural shyness, men to whom her charm and gaiety would be unexpected comforts. But after months of hard training, she was stationed for nearly a year in a small town on the lower St. Lawrence, doing routine work in signals and feeling herself totally cut off from everything she wanted. Though she encountered a certain amount of gold braid, all of it was wavy and none of it was exciting.

So Nina went back to Grenville whenever she had a long enough leave. There was an Airforce training camp only four miles away from the town and the older merchants were doing well. On Saturday nights King Street was filled with airmen trying to raise hell without much help from anyone but Nick Petropolis, for most of the girls who lived there had followed the native young men into one of the services. But Nina stayed close to the house with Jane whenever she was home. There was no one on King Street any more whom she knew well enough to speak to.

Late in 1943, she was transferred to Halifax, where she worked as secretary to an elderly desk-commander in the Dockyard who had won his medals in the old war and treated her with a distant and fatherly consideration. She was still discontented because it seemed to her that by now she should have been at least engaged and in Halifax it was impossible to meet the kind of boy she understood, as she might have done in Montreal or Toronto.

Halifax during those last years of the war was bursting at the seams, mostly with young men who wished to God they were somewhere else. Crews coming in from the convoys had no place to relax and get a drink or a change of feeling except in a hired room or in somebody's house, and by this time there were no rooms for hire and fewer invitations to homes because there were almost as many servicemen in the town as citizens. There were no taverns in Halifax because the Calvinists who dominated the place thought it more moral for a man to buy a bottle of whiskey at the government commission and drink it in secret in a boarding-house room or behind a tree in the park than to sit at a table or stand at a bar and drink it comfortably in public. Halifax was a fairly tough town, but its toughness was so old-fashioned it was almost Victorian and the inlanders who comprised most of the corvette crews that came and went with convoys were unable to understand it. They failed to realize that Halifax was so accustomed to wars of all kinds that she was making the mistake of trying to take this one in her stride, never guessing how the boys felt about the place until the day the war ended, when the sailors joined forces with the slum population and tore the town apart.

The sense of savagery and desperation under the surface of the town during the last years of the war often frightened Nina, but she began to feel better when she met three boys in succession who showed interest in her, all veteran airmen.

The first took her to several dances before she discovered that he had a wife in Vancouver. The second, stationed in Canada on coastal command after a tour over Europe, took her out five times before she saw him in the Nova Scotian with the middle-aged wife of a colonel of ordnance then posted in England. The Wren who was with her at the time, a sharp-eyed French-Canadian girl, indicated the older woman with a lift of her eyebrows and murmured, "*Comme le Belt Line Tram, eh? Tout le monde peut monter.*"

Nina flushed and decided never to go out with him again. If that was the kind of man he was, what would people think when they saw her with him?

Her third boy came from Peterborough, a town which she thought must be enough like Grenville to be practically the same except that it was larger. He had been at Queen's a year ahead of her and he had already won a D.F.C. She felt very proud when they danced at the Lord Nelson and she could introduce him to friends, or when they sat under the trees at the Waegwoltic where people could see them together.

One afternoon, at an hour when he knew she would be free, he turned up with a borrowed car and they drove out of town over a rocky road to Terence Bay on the seaward side of the Halifax peninsula. For nearly five hours they were alone under an enormous blue sky. They listened to the sea sucking at the rocks and insects murmuring in the blueberry bushes that grew in crevices of the dusty grey granite. They lay on their backs watching gulls wheel in the sky. And the air was astringently clean, yet aromatic, for the northwest wind blowing over them had sifted through thousands of firs and spruce on its passage across Nova Scotia to the sea.

He pulled a bottle of Scotch out of a pocket, offered her a drink, and when she refused, took a drink himself. After that he took another drink every half hour. "The ship came in this morning," he explained. "So it's my last three days. They've not told us yet, but we know it's the one we're going on."

As the whiskey worked in him he told her things about himself he would not have said normally, for he was a tense, proud boy. He was afraid of going back. He had never admitted his fear to anyone else, but he had to tell her because he had to know now whether or not she understood how he felt. He asked her if she knew what the initials L.M.F. meant. "Lack of moral fibre," he said. "That's what they put on your record if you welsh on your target too often."

"But they've never put that on your record!" Nina protested. "You've won the D.F.C."

He looked at her strangely. "So I have," he said. "And that's supposed to fix everything forever, isn't it?"

He made Nina uncomfortable so she tried to change the subject by asking him what he planned to do when the war was over, though she already knew that he intended to study law and she thought it would be fine to be the wife of a lawyer with a practice in Toronto, a man who would be a replica of the lawyer she had worked for there, a man with a Buick, a blue Homburg hat, three children, and a summer cottage in the Muskoka. But her airman just smiled to himself.

That evening in Halifax, eating at Norman's with the usual crowd standing in front of the doors waiting for a table, the boy asked Nina to spend the night with him. The hunger in his eyes frightened her and she flushed and refused stiffly, not even offering as an excuse the fact that she would hardly be able to get away from her quarters for a whole night. He took a long look at her face, seeing the blue eyes and the yellow hair falling in curls under her Wren's cap, and the faint trace of two lines which had begun to show on either side of her mouth. Then he got up from the table without a word, paid the bill, and Nina followed him across the room. As she walked out through the crowd of servicemen at the door she hated them all. They seemed to be jeering at her with their eyes. No matter how nice they might seem on the surface, they all held together whenever one of them tried to get a girl to step out of line. She had never felt so vulnerable in her life.

Without a word the boy drove her back to Stadacona. When he left her at the door he said, "I wonder if you'd been in England for the past few years if even then you'd know there was a war on."

She never saw him again and he never wrote to her, though she half expected he would. Four months later she learned that he had been killed in an accident over his home field in Yorkshire.

The next time Nina was posted for leave she wrote to Lucy, suggesting that she would like to visit New York again. Lucy answered by return mail.

I'd love to have you because it's so long since I've seen anyone from home but you wouldn't like it here right now, Nina.

We're in too much confusion. Stephen has so much work to do he's hardly ever home and I have no servants and John and Sally are pretty demanding. You know we've moved out from New York to Princeton, but you probably don't realize that Princeton is hardly any larger than Grenville, and what you need, probably, is fun in a gayer place right now.

Nina felt that Lucy's answer meant more than it said. She was disappointed, so she went home to Grenville, and it was on this trip that she realized for the first time that Jane was showing her age. Her sister's movements had become stiffer and the lines were hardening and deepening in her face. She seemed to belong to a different level of existence from the one Nina had come to accept as her own. Jane didn't seem to matter much to anyone any more, and for the first time Nina felt superior to her.

Even the old house seemed to have grown smaller. The garden, which Nina had never given much thought when Lucy was at home, made her feel sad, for Jane had hired a man to dig up at least half of the beds and plant them with vegetables, and only the hardiest of the perennials struggled for survival in the other beds among the rank weeds that had flourished in the rich soil. But Jane was proud of her Victory Garden; it gave her much satisfaction to see something useful coming out of their own ground, and she pickled tomatoes and cucumbers and gave away quantities of beans and carrots and lettuce to the neighbours, and people continued to say how wonderful it was that a solitary woman managed to get so many things done. Jane had as many music pupils as ever. She worked at the Red Cross, organized rummage sales at the church, still sat on the library committee, and was now convenor of a town improvement society formed by a group of women for the purpose of obliterating the pool room which Nick Petropolis had expanded into a thriving business for the purpose of selling airmen drinks after hours.

One rainy evening as Nina sat with Jane in the dark living room where the furniture seemed more dusty and dilapidated than it ever had before, she fingered the pages of the book on her lap and wondered if there was any place in the world where she could feel that she belonged. She watched Jane counting the stitches on her knitting needles, and suddenly she said, "Why doesn't Lucy ever come home? She's been away more than six years and she's never been back here once."

Jane continued to count stitches and when she reached the end of the row she said, "Because I've never invited her."

"But why not?"

Jane turned the row and started to knit again, and to Nina, sitting on a hassock in front of the empty hearth with her yellow hair loose over her forehead, the pause seemed eternal.

"Lucy made a deliberate choice," Jane said finally. "She left us as casually as a servant girl who gets into trouble. After twenty-eight years of living in this house, she went away without even saying good-bye to me."

Nina was unable to realize that Jane's bitterness came from her terrible loneliness and from her pride in never revealing it. She opened her book again, deciding that Jane was so old-fashioned she was incomprehensible.

That night when she went to bed in the familiar room in which she had slept as a child, the feeling came over Nina that she had been cheated. After all these years – after college, and her training in the Wrens, and her life in Halifax – she was still a small-town girl who had not managed to get a husband. And she couldn't understand why. She had always been told she was a pretty girl, and boys in school and college had always liked her. If she couldn't get a man, how was it that someone like Lucy had succeeded?

The small lines which had begun to form around her mouth tightened in the dark. She was sure she was prettier than Lucy had ever been, her figure was better, and her hair – she reached out to feel it with her hands – was really lovely. She wondered how Stephen Lassiter had ever come to pick out Lucy, of all the girls he had met in Grenville. And then she wondered what she herself would have said or done had Stephen shown any interest in her that summer he had come to Grenville. She would probably have refused him. He reminded her a little of the first airman she had met in Halifax. Well, at least she had never made herself look cheap.

At breakfast the next morning, while Jane was pouring the coffee and talking about the war, Nina decided she couldn't endure even three more days of Grenville. The old house was nothing more than a lair where Jane lurked and grew old.

MATT McCUNN told the crews of the various ships on which he served that if he had received a stripe for every time he was torpedoed he would have been a vice-admiral by the end of 1942. As it was, he never rose higher in the merchant service than quartermaster; he was considered too old to be worth training into an officer. But even if McCunn had been younger he would probably have stayed where he was, for his heart was in every fo'c'sle and privates' mess in the world. So long as there were people anywhere who rejected the idea of success, he was with them.

He was first torpedoed off Newfoundland in the fall of 1940 on a former Greek vessel which had been put on the fringe of the convoy because she would have been the smallest loss if she was hit. McCunn was glad to see the ship go, for she was the worst he had ever sailed on, so badly balanced that the best quartermaster in the world couldn't keep her wake from looking like a corkscrew. McCunn walked off her and onto the deck of a destroyer without even wetting his feet, and he was in Halifax four days later. Another ship went down under him the next April, in the night; and during the twenty minutes he spent in the water he nearly froze to death. His worst season was the winter of 1942, when he was torpedoed five times, three times on a single convoy.

After that voyage McCunn spent several months in a boarding house in Liverpool, but he got restless again and went up to Scotland, and in Leith signed on a vessel for the Mediterranean. He knew as well as anyone that Malta convoys were the worst in the war, but by this time he was beginning to feel himself indestructible and he was interested in warmer water than the north Atlantic. He made Malta on one convoy in which his ship and three others were the only merchantmen out of twenty-four to get through. He saw a bomb hit the *Formidable* and a second later the whole carrier flash into a moving sheet of flame, then sail on, and an hour later receive planes back on her deck. That, he said to himself, is what comes of having men on the bridges with straight stripes on their sleeves.

Later he watched a large bomb curve down for the *Rodney* and disappear just under her forefoot, then the sea jerk as though somebody had kicked it underneath, rise in a mushroom of water a hundred and fifty feet high, and the *Rodney* walk through it and come out with her decks streaming and all her guns firing, lashing out with all nine sixteen-inchers on her long foredeck at a formation of torpedo planes. McCunn had never seen a sixteen-inch gun fired before, much less at an airplane, and he thought with exhilaration that if they were using H.E. in shells that size against aircraft this must be the hottest convoy action of the whole war, and by God, here he was in the middle of it! Looking around at one after the other of the merchant ships in his convoy being hit as he leaned on the rail, he found himself admiring the feathery wakes made by torpedoes in the blue Mediterranean, the wild flaming arcs of struck planes, the big Royal Navy ships handing it back, and he couldn't help comparing this scene favourably with the Atlantic where he had never seen a better ship than the *Revenge* and attacks were always made at night with corvettes and destroyers exploding millions of dead fish to the surface for every submarine they touched. The Mediterranean seemed a very good sea for a war. McCunn found himself enjoying the sheen of sunlight on the white plumes of bombed-up water, almost hoping that a twisting, turning Heinkel would get through so there would be another bomb-burst and another plume of water glistening in the sun against an azure sea.

That night when his ship docked in Malta and the let-down set in and a crowd of half-starving Maltese worked frantically to get the cargo out of her before the dive-bombers returned in the morning, McCunn wondered if he might just possibly be going crazy. It was a bad sign when a man enjoyed the sight of a torpedo coming at him. A friend of his in the old war had become the same way he was now, so shell-happy he had thought himself immortal until he stopped taking cover, and the same shell-burst which had relieved McCunn of one of his most prized possessions had killed the man because he had made no attempt to get out of the way.

On his return to Gibraltar, McCunn managed to get himself transferred to a vessel bound for Alex around the Cape. The long voyage made in complete safety rested him and gave him a hankering for the shore. He had been in the war for more than three years without seeing a single German, with the exception of a corpse which a wavy-navy lieutenant-commander in charge of a corvette had hoped would be accepted as evidence for a sinking, and that had been two years ago in Greenock where the body had arrived preserved in ice. So in Alexandria he got himself transferred again, this time illegally, to a special unit of Americans who had volunteered to convey supplies to the partisans in Yugoslavia. The Americans called him Pop and the officer in charge had no idea what to do with him when he discovered, after the unit was under way, that McCunn was not the interpreter he had been given to understand he was and could speak no word of any language but his own.

McCunn stayed with them, however, and when they landed at night in a cove not far from Dubrovnik and went inland with a group of Dalmatian shepherds guarding a straggly caravan of donkeys and mules, he was glad to leave the sea behind. For the first time he felt close to the war and close to the Germans he had fought in the last one, and he could climb as well as any of the younger men. But he had to be silent on this strange march, and so he began to think of Grenville, and thinking of Grenville to be a little homesick, almost for the first time in his life.

EARLY in 1941, Marcia Stapleton went out to Nevada to obtain her third divorce. On her return she continued working for the magazine and continued to work competently, she saw her old friends and her energy was enough to carry her through evening after evening she later wished she had never spent. She took up her psychoanalysis where she had dropped it, but nothing much came of it and after a while it simply petered out and left her drained.

The analyst may have come to the conclusion that she was a difficult case, but he at least managed to leave with her a strong sense of guilt and a feeling of remorse for having had three husbands without conceiving a single child. Two months after Pearl Harbor she gave up her job and enrolled as a nurse's aid, and for the required length of time she worked in Bellevue, cleaning up after the regular nurses, handling bedpans, and frequently working past the point of exhaustion. She watched human beings die. She saw men lie in the wards with their faces exposed to everyone's eyes after receiving death sentences from doctors. She learned that most men at such moments grieve less for themselves than for their failure to provide for the families they are leaving behind. So New York, which hitherto she had seen only from the upper surface, began to appear like a gigantic aquarium teeming with ancient and invisible life: raw, terrible, humorous, brave, and infinitely various. Her own problems faded into nothing, and she wondered if this was how women of society had felt centuries before when they took vows and entered religious orders.

Marcia began to realize that some of the regular nurses and even a few of the doctors considered her useful. It was the first time people she respected had ever thought such a thing about her. Patients found ways of showing they liked her. A boy of six patted her hand and said she was like his mother. Poor women told her in foreign accents about their husbands and children. A little tailor, tremendously proud of his honesty and his skill at his trade, explained that he would never have been so successful if it were not for his wife. "My memory is bad, but Mrs. Shapiro is vondervoll. She knows every pair of pants in the neighbourhood, so for vat do I need a secretary?"

Later in the war, after she had taken several specialized courses, Marcia was admitted to work in a military hospital. One night when she was off duty and ready to go to bed an orderly told her that an airman, so horribly burned that after nine months and many grafts he was still swathed in bandages, wanted to see her. "He's on his way out," the orderly said as she stood with him in the elevator. "He wants to see you before the priest gets here."

But the priest had already arrived when Marcia reached the bed and he was administering the last rites. After the boy was blessed, Marcia took his hand which was motionless and still covered with bandages. The boy could not talk and he seemed to be unconscious, though his eyes were open. Somehow he reminded her of Bruce Fraser, and she sat for several hours by the bedside with the priest, thinking of Bruce and wondering if she would ever see him again and whether or not he would like her better if he knew her now. "I spoiled everything by going to bed with him when he didn't love me," she thought.

The airman died in the early morning and a little later Marcia was standing with the priest on the steps of the hospital, glad of the fresh air, glad of the sight of city roofs beginning to emerge out of the mists of the night, but with sorrow inside her mind.

"Last week," she said, "that boy was glad to be alive, and tonight he was just as glad to die. It's horrible."

"Horrible?" he said. "You're mistaken."

For the first time she noticed the priest as a man. She saw that he was not much older than herself, that he had intense black eyes, black hair, and rugged physical strength. She wondered why such a man, so full of vitality that if he had been in lay clothes any normal woman would have been instantly aware of him, had chosen to become a priest. She had never known any priests or for that matter many Roman Catholics; they had always seemed to exist apart and she had thought them primitive and backward, opposed to everything the well-meaning generation had stood for. Now, looking at this man, she recalled a remark she had made to Bruce Fraser about herself and the kind of people she had known. "We've all gone straight to hell trying to do the right thing."

The priest, apparently believing she was still thinking of the boy who had just died, said quietly, "It's not unnatural for a man to be glad to be alive and to be glad to die a week later. Sometimes people have to find themselves in hell before they can see there's a way out of it."

Marcia started. "Yes," she answered. "Yes, I suppose so."

CARL BRATIAN, who claimed to be free of illusion in most matters, had no difficulty in persuading himself that he had none whatever about the war. The fact that it was taking place at all merely reinforced his conviction that in the twentieth century the human race was completely helpless, and he watched with cynical satisfaction an acquaintance who had worked diligently for World Peaceways, Inc. rushing off to Washington to make sure of a job for himself in OWI. "If you can make them believe they're fighting for a better world," Bratian said, "you can make them believe anything."

In January of 1942, Bratian pulled out of the agency in which he had been a junior partner and founded a new one of his own, taking with him three account-executives, including Stephen Lassiter. Stephen was of use to him because only shortly before he had landed the Harper Aircraft account, had turned Ashweiler's plumbing account over to a junior, and had made so marked an initial success with Harper's that he was able to take the account with him into Bratian's firm.

The contracts which Carl drew up with his new associates made it impossible for any of them, if they chose to leave him, to take their accounts with them. In return for this lack of freedom each man was guaranteed a larger share of the profits.

In a profession which had become one of the notably unhappy ones of this world, and which seemed to become more unhappy the more intelligent it became, Carl Bratian really enjoyed his work. He had an authentic money-hunger; he had, in addition to a natural flair for getting inside the minds of other people, the one faculty without which no man is ever supremely successful: the ability to get along with only half the normal amount of sleep. He was always awake by six in the morning and he did his heaviest work after midnight.

During his boyhood on lower Tenth Avenue, Bratian had lived in a place where the noises seldom ceased from dusk to dawn. It still seemed a luxury to him to be alone at two in the morning in a clean, sound-proof office, knowing he was the only man working with his brain in that dark shaft of a building, feeling good, feeling a wonderful sense of private power whenever the conviction came over him that he, alone of all the men he knew, completely understood the time in which he lived. The money-hunger might be in him, but something else was there too, something which was a legacy of his father's ideologies. It was essential for him to believe that he, Carl Bratian, really knew what he was doing; that he, Carl Bratian, was superior to the others who were merely smart. He could save his energy while the rest of them worried, and it made him feel good to think how much they did worry. He was living in an age of anxiety, but the anxiety did not touch him. Other men worried over their wives and children, over their jobs, over money whether they had it or not, over the gnawing self-hatred some of them felt because they did work they despised but wanted the money it brought, over the women they wanted to sleep with, had slept with, wanted to get rid of, over the mere fact of being alive. From the whole spectacle of his time he derived a satisfaction that was almost savage. "Do you want a symbol of it?" he asked. "I'll give you one. A Hollywood actor – making three thousand a week – joining the Communist Party because he thinks he's prostituting himself."

More often than not in the summer Bratian worked until dawn and left the office with his brain racing so fast he felt he understood everything that was or had been or ever would be. At such moments, seeing the buildings hazed by the early morning mist, his nostrils scenting in the haze the premonitions of coming heat, New York seemed to belong to him as surely as the whole world belongs to a boy walking silently along a country lane to a trout stream while the first light is fingering the sky. Where were they now, the kids who had pushed him around twenty-five years ago? He knew where

one of them was – Tony Fasanella, with a flattened nose and permanent welts over his eyes, dead broke when he wasn't selling pop or
programs at Jamaica, breaking into a laugh whenever anyone spoke
to him. And Carl remembered his mother: "So if he does kick you?
You run away. You don't let him get his hands near your brain!"

Members of Bratian's firm asked themselves how his brain really
did work. Which came first with him, the hen or the egg? Were his
methods the result of his theories, or were his theories simply a part
of his general attitude of making himself out to be so much more
intelligent than the rest of the trade?

Outwardly his methods were orthodox enough. His establish-
ment had the usual false front of culture–tooled leather chairs,
crowded bookcases, walnut desks, an array of charts and graphs
and etchings on the walls, and a lithograph of Abraham Lincoln in
his pre-whisker days in the outer office. Bratian might trust his flair,
but he never overlooked a chance of checking up on it and he went
in heavily for research and reader-acceptance tests. Although he was
entirely unimpressed by the few surviving megalomaniacs from the
neolithic days of advertising who still flew by the seat of their pants,
he had no scruples about borrowing even some of their corniest
tricks. In the conference room, on the wall behind the chair in which
he sat, hung a framed slogan: IF ANY IDEA IS TOO BIG FOR YOU,
YOU'RE TOO SMALL FOR THIS AGENCY.

It was Bratian's pride to believe that he had a special insight into
the workings of history; like the Communists, he thought he could
use it as a direction-finder. He claimed that America was developing
into a modern Roman Empire, and to make his point visually clear,
he kept at hand a book of photographs of Roman portrait busts by
which he tried to prove that the faces of famous Romans before
Julius Caesar resembled Americans like Daniel Webster, Henry Clay,
and William H. Seward. He would then flip the pages over to
Romans who had flourished at the time of Claudius and Nero and
compare them favourably with famous businessmen of the Babbitt
era. First a republic, then a military republic with generals making
the policy, then – Bratian would grin and shrug his shoulders.

"What we deal with," he said, "are the psychological by-
products of that set-up. Let's say our business is to be vulgar – but
brilliantly vulgar. The bigger the country gets, the less sure of himself every individual in it is going to become. All right. Go hard for

nationalism. Go hard for sex. Go hard for efficiency. Make every grass-root in Kansas think it's getting a raw deal if it can't pass for an orchid. Keep on telling them they deserve the best because they're Americans and that the American way of life is the best because it's the most efficient. But don't forget this – the only thing all of them are interested in is sex. Think about it. Dream about it and you can't lose."

But in the account for Harper Aircraft, Bratian allowed Stephen Lassiter a free hand. There was no need to remind Stephen that efficiency bred power on the American plan; he believed it completely. When display ads for Harper Aircraft went to press they showed sleek, beautiful planes flying over cities, seas, and plains, they showed intense designers poring over drafting boards and grim engineers doing a man's job in organizing assembly lines nearly half a mile long. After the United States entered the war, multiple colours were called upon to show battle scenes in which a Harper plane scored an American victory. In 1943, Stephen had his greatest success with an original idea – a comic strip magazine called *The Privateer* in honour of the famous Harper medium-bomber. It was the kind of magazine designed for boys with an eye to their fathers' interests, and in it was recorded every notable war achievement performed by a Privateer, including the names of the heroes who had manned it. Within a year the magazine was being read by millions.

One of Bratian's best accounts was a company which produced men's cosmetics, the same company he had once hoped to control himself before Stephen Lassiter sold the patent rights of the after-shaving lotion inherited from the estate of his father to Mark Wisden, the banker. Wisden kept it as a one-man business but gave the advertising account to Bratian and left it with him.

Carl Bratian had always loved barber shops; he convinced Wisden that a men's cosmetic company was bound to succeed because the barber shop was a symbol of luxury to a large proportion of American males. Such a business would put a fine choice of barber's lotions within the range of every man's purse any day of the year, and it would provide wives with convenient gifts for their husbands. Bratian also believed that social evolution was on his side in advertising the cosmetics. He was sure there was such a desire for sexual sophistication throughout the country that smells had become a profitable commodity for men as well as women.

When the campaign was launched it was jeered at from coast to coast, but the jeers helped sell the product. In display ads soldiers, filthy from slit-trenches and insect-eaten in jungles, were shown as yearning for the after-shave lotion with the lingering smell, for the talcum powder that matched their complexions, for the scented shaving soap in the imitation walnut bowl, for the copper-coloured oil which matched a suntan when it was rubbed into the skin.

Wisden, who had once had a classical education, announced that he was calling the products Centurion, and he suggested a display showing a naked Roman soldier, identified by his breastplate, shield, greaves, and gladius spread beside him on a curule chair, lying beside a swimming pool being massaged by a slave. But Bratian persuaded him to change his mind. The firm was called Green Ranger. The Roman soldier was used as an inset, with the figure of Major Robert Rogers, dressed in Lincoln green standing beside him, and the legend read, "What do you mean, it's Roman? It's *American*!" A green-clad ranger adorned all the jars and containers of the product.

In the last years of the war Bratian's business rose in volume like a tidal wave, and its success was accompanied by strange manifestations of guilt-neurosis on the part of some of his subordinates. The account executive for a perfume company, who in 1933 had been an instructor of English at Cornell making fourteen hundred a year, began to write articles for rough-paper magazines in praise of Soviet Russia. The head of the art department wrote a monograph on Titian, aiming to prove that if Titian were alive today he would have worked for an advertising agency. Bratian regarded these excursions with amusement, and when he found that another of his best men who had once been a divinity student was drinking too much, he guided him gently toward Alcoholics Anonymous.

Bratian's reaction to his own success took the form of a new interest in politics. He gave large parties for certain senators and committee members in Washington, and he laughed at clients who complained that the government was ruining business. To Bratian, government *was* business, a peculiarly modern form of it, and he believed that the bigger it grew, the greater would become the demand for a man like himself.

As he made more money and as the atmosphere of New York became more markedly international, Bratian began seriously to collect famous names. He made it a point to meet distinguished re-

fugees who were experts on this and that, and he liked entertaining
them in his newly acquired nine-room apartment which overlooked
the East River. His living room contained a Rouault and a minor
Picasso, and on either side of a mammoth fireplace shelves of rare
books reached to the ceiling. There, with conversation buzzing
around him, with the clever men telling each other what Churchill
said to Roosevelt over the scotch in the White House, what the deal
was going to be in India or China, talking over the affairs of the
world in the same spirit of reality adopted by actuaries of an insurance company in discussing the lives of their clients, with the
women among them clever and stupid, lush and icy slim, all selected
by their men for some peculiar value of which they themselves were
consciously aware – standing there by the window in his living room
looking down over the river and the hospitals on Welfare Island and
beyond to the factories and massed dwellings of Long Island City,
Bratian sometimes laughed silently as he reflected what a joke it was
that nobody except himself seemed to know in his bones that life
was completely without meaning, that it was merely a fact and should
be treated as such, that the only difference between success and
failure was whether you satisfied a longing you had acquired in
childhood – or you didn't satisfy it.

ONLY in a certain sense did Stephen and Lucy rise with Bratian, for
in so far as they could they tried to keep his business outside their
personal lives. In the early years of their marriage his cynicism never
touched Lucy directly, for Stephen refused to think of himself solely
as an advertising man. In working for Bratian he believed he was
on his way to something better.

"The only way for a man to protect himself against this lousy
business I'm in," he said frankly, "is to admit it's lousy. I was in a
lousy business before but I didn't have the guts to tell myself the
truth about it. This time it's different."

As the months and years went by and Lucy expressed no opinion
about his work, Stephen would return to his favourite subject. "Don't
worry about some of the bastards you meet in the office. They're better than you'd think. Some of them tried to be poets and novelists,
some of them tried to be professors, and now they're all trying to
get used to the idea of living with themselves. I was trained to deal
with facts and machines and in a way I'm still doing it. There's not

another agency man in the city with enough engineering background to handle this job for Harper without making Harper sick
every time he has to talk to him. If it weren't for the Depression I
might have been one of Harper's top designers now. This is the next
best thing. Without money behind you, Lucy, you've got to take the
third-rate job some second-rate son of a bitch offers and be glad to
have it. Once we've got enough put away in the sock I'm going to
quit Carl and go back to M.I.T. for a year. I know exactly what I've
got to learn and it's not too late to learn it. After Dad died I lost
confidence, and God knows being married to Joyce didn't help. It's
different now. With you, and a little money behind us, the sky's the
limit."

Such speeches usually ended when Stephen crossed the room and
took Lucy in his arms, regardless of what she was doing at the time.
As she felt the strength of his arms she thanked God for her incredible fortune in being married to a man who had learned to look
facts in the eye, a man who could confront the kind of niggling
anxieties that beset people in Grenville by throwing his head back
and laughing. In spite of her desire to be loyal to the only two men
she had known previous to her marriage, she found it difficult not
to compare them with Stephen to her husband's advantage. Her
father had been obsessed by religion, and Bruce, it seemed to her,
by ideas; on both was the weight of an apparent necessity for cor-
relating all knowledge into a pattern. But Stephen felt only the flat,
factual sureness of an engineer. His only test of an idea was whether
or not it would work. And with this factuality went a boyish enthusiasm when he was away from the office which more than offset
his imperviousness to the kind of music she liked or the poetry she
read or the flowers she wished she could grow in New York.

Lucy loved her husband's maleness. Every aspect of it she not
only accepted but consciously enjoyed, even to the way he left his
clothes strewn over beds and chairs, spilled ashes on the rugs and
insisted it was good for them, called his friends on the telephone at
any hour of the night and wise-cracked like an adolescent, insisted
on her enjoying Princeton football games when she was half frozen
and didn't know the rules. He made her a full part of this overhang
of college life he had resumed on returning to the east from Cleveland, and it gave her a fine feeling to see that his old college friends
remembered him, were still fond of him, and – perhaps because there

was not a single man of abstract ideas among them – shared his pleasure in the fact that he was getting on.

For nearly a year their only friends in the city were men Stephen had known in Princeton who came in groups to drink beer and whiskey and talk about themselves while Lucy sat quietly and listened, filled with a sense of wonder at being a woman surrounded by men. But their circle of acquaintances soon widened; an industrial designer and his wife whom they met at a large cocktail party sensed common tastes or interests and invited them to dinner; at the dinner they met an architect and his wife, and a doctor and his wife who was a child psychiatrist, all friends of friends who had time in so large a city to reach out with warmth toward a strange Canadian wife. Their spirit was new to Lucy. She never felt she knew any of them deeply; she never felt that it mattered much that she should. They were mostly like Stephen himself, living in the present, forgetful of the past, taking their chances with the future. It wasn't that they were more generous than Canadians at heart; the difference depended, she knew, on the fact that Canada was a harder country than the United States, chances were fewer, and people had to be more cautious. It was easy to forget about caution in New York.

And yet Lucy's old habit of reflection never left her. She discovered as she met more and more people in New York that she was almost too observant, too acutely aware of individual personalities, and she learned to conceal her opinions from Stephen, whose likes or dislikes were immediate and unqualified, because he became disturbed if she mistrusted a man he had put down as a swell guy. Gradually she managed to make their entertainment more selective, to invite only those people to a single small dinner party who were most likely to enjoy each others' company. Stephen had no sense of the human ingredients which go to make up good entertainment; if left to his own devices he was content to ask half a dozen men to dinner, together with their wives, who had nothing more in common than the fact that they all happened to be living in New York. But he enjoyed the parties Lucy gave and he was pleased when Bratian told him she was the best natural hostess he had ever met.

Years after she felt herself fairly well established, with a real identity in this new world, Lucy maintained her sense of wonder and gratitude for her position as Stephen's wife. She loved the sense of his physical strength standing between herself and the new, strange ways of a vast and indifferent city. Along with his physical strength went a physical candour which rapidly effaced the last traces of puritan shame she had brought with her when she married him. Stephen had a natural sexual gusto and he took an unquenchably boyish pleasure in the fact that she not only appreciated it but learned to respond to it with an eagerness as frank as his own. When they were at parties together, often the length of a room apart, she would discover his eyes following her, so that she knew she was never alone in the midst of strangers. She would meet his look with a private smile and pass the rest of the evening warmed by a secret glow of anticipation, knowing that he, too, was waiting for the moment when they would be alone again.

Stephen was enormously proud of his son. After John was born he began to act the role of the conscientious father with a diligence which Bratian said was corny. He enrolled John at Lawrenceville when he was two weeks old; he arrived home with presents every Saturday afternoon; he talked of the advantages of having a large family. Even before Sally was born his interests began to widen. Theatres, night clubs, and the ballet gave place to weekend drives in the country. After they felt they could manage a competent nurse as well as a maid, Lucy went with him on occasional business trips.

In spite of all she had read about the United States, Lucy made discoveries that amazed her, aspects of the country which surprised Stephen as well when she talked about them, since without meaning to she saw a different side of the many facades he had always taken for granted. Some of the people she met from old eastern families seemed to her more like the English than were any Canadians she knew. She quickly discovered that the famous American eagerness for money was nothing but a by-product of the American generosity. Above all she loved the openness of Americans, their quick way of saying what they thought whether it sounded rude or not, as they made no attempt to hide themselves from their neighbours. Her strangest discovery of all was this: while as individuals most Americans she met seemed younger than Canadians in the way their minds worked, less reflective and quicker to be satisfied with an easy answer, their society as a whole seemed older in every way, more advanced in time.

But the real adventure of Lucy's marriage was not what she saw and did and learned; it lay in the mere fact of living day after day with a man who loved her, and in seeing the world day after day through a man's eyes.

The money continued to come in, not big money as Stephen's father would have understood it, but not money his father would have despised, either. The plans they made took more definite shape. Stephen wanted a hundred thousand dollars in gilt-edged securities; then he would leave Bratian and go back to engineering. He wanted four children if they could be divided among sons and daughters, and a place in the country near New York. To be a part of such plans, even though she knew that at his present rate of spending it would be years before Stephen accumulated so much in the bank, seemed to Lucy more important than their realization could ever be. Making plans meant that Stephen was giving her room in which to grow, that their life together had a definite aim, so that even though they were living in an ultra-modern apartment in a strange city, she had a home of her own at last.

Ten days after Pearl Harbor Stephen tried to enlist in the Army Air Corps, taking it for granted that he would be accepted, in spite of his age, because he already knew how to fly. He was turned down when the doctors discovered that he had a tendency toward high blood pressure. The same thing happened a month later when he tried to enlist in the Marines. It was a defect which would have gone unnoticed for years if he had stayed away from recruiting stations, but the knowledge that he had a physical defect of any kind was a violent shock. The shock worked itself out in a sense of humiliation over being ruled out of the only important enterprise in the world while men he had always considered his inferiors were swarming into it.

In the early spring of 1942 he approached the president of Harper Aircraft whom he admired more than any man he had ever known. He asked to be given any job in the Maryland plant that would directly help the war. Myron Harper refused to consider the request. "You're doing a swell job of public relations right where you are," he said. "Stay with it. That's exactly where I need you. And don't try to get away from me because I'll make it tough for you if you do. I've got enough pull in Washington to nail you right where I want you."

So Stephen stayed with Bratian's agency and worked harder than ever on the job of keeping the name of Harper planes in the public mind. But he was growing too old to take frustration in the same manner he had learned to accept it in the Depression.

The months and the years passed. His big body made him conspicuous in any crowd and he had the feeling that people were criticizing him behind his back for not being in uniform. His restlessness frequently made him irritable. He fell into the habit of drinking two cocktails before lunch and three before dinner. Sometimes he picked up service men in the city, took them into bars, and gave them drinks; often he would go into a bar, see a group of boys in uniform at the other end of the room, slip the barman twenty dollars, and tell him to give the boys drinks as long as the credit lasted. Too often he lay awake in bed thinking about the war, seeing with self-accusing eyes the long layers of protection between himself and the enemy – the workers in war plants, the sailors on transports, the Negroes unloading *matériel* at the docks in Africa and Italy, divisional headquarters, the brigade, supplies rolling up the roads behind the fronts, aircraft covering them, artillery flashing from gun pits, and finally half a dozen lonely bastards crawling forward on their bellies into the mortar fire. On the nights when he did sleep he dreamed about it, seeing himself a hero in one of those outer layers, imagining new and impossible technical inventions for doing the enemy some incalculable damage that would end the war overnight.

In the life of every man there is at least one group of words, one phrase or sentence spoken carelessly by a friend or a stranger, which lingers like a barb and hurts whenever it stabs its way to the front of his mind. To Stephen, the words had been spoken by Myron Harper the day he asked for a war job in his plant. "You're better at agency work than you'll ever be at engineering." Because of his admiration for Harper and his inability to get into uniform it didn't occur to Stephen to question the validity of the words. They meant that he was a natural public relations man, a bluffer, a user of coked-up phrases to make a public of demi-morons conscious that men of genius were worth the taxes that kept them in business! They meant that in his fortieth year he had discovered his true level.

During the month before Sally was born Stephen's restlessness increased so markedly that Lucy became acutely worried about him. Night after night he got out of bed and roamed about the apartment, and while she was in the hospital he spent most of his visiting hours talking about how much they needed a real home, some ground under their feet, something more permanent than a city apartment. Before she was ready to leave the hospital and go home, he had bought a house in Princeton.

After that his exuberance seemed to return. They disposed of the apartment overnight and sold most of their modern furniture to the new tenants. His mother's fine old furniture, and the contents of her trunks, which had been in storage for years, were moved into the new house and Stephen worked furiously to get the place settled in a single weekend. Lucy was as delighted as he was because Stephen seemed to be himself again. He told his friends how wonderful it was going to be to sleep in fresh air for a change, to grow vegetables, to catch up on his reading on the trains to and from the city. And most of his friends agreed because they were now living in Princeton, too.

The following summer was nearly over before Stephen discovered that a man should never go back to the place where he was young in the expectation of rediscovering his youth. He remembered Princeton as a place teeming with life and excitement. He found it a quiet, mannerly town with no niche for outsiders who had little part in its inner life. Once he had been recognized as a big man on the campus. Now he was just another of the three hundred-odd commuters who lived on the fringes of Princeton society. He liked it best on Saturday nights and weekends when he could get together with old classmates who also commuted to New York. But on weekdays the long train trip in and out of town tired him. He had fallen into the habit of stopping at a Madison Avenue bar with men from the office when they left at six o'clock, but the habit had to be broken when he moved to Princeton for fear of missing the last train that would get him home in time for dinner. Finally there were many nights when his work piled so high that he couldn't get home at all. That winter he found a room in an uptown hotel near Madison Avenue, where he kept enough of his clothes to last him from one weekend to the next.

And Lucy found herself virtually alone again. She was busier than ever with the children, for her nurse had enlisted in the Spars and her maid had refused to leave New York, but she no longer had the sense of belonging to the life of a man, of being an integral part of his maleness, of understanding what was happening in the world as she saw it through his eyes. The war was everywhere, yet she was totally secluded from it. Stephen was no longer there to tell her of his problems in the office and find his way through them simply by listening to his own voice as he talked. On the weekends when he did come home he was too tired and too depressed to do more than sleep and play with the children.

Imperceptibly, Lucy's old Grenville habit of quiet and watching reserve began to ebb back, so gradually they both seemed unaware of the change.

FOUR

ON A FRIDAY AFTERNOON IN MID-APRIL in 1945, Carl Bratian and Stephen drove out to Princeton in Bratian's convertible. When they came out of the tunnel onto the skyway the whole countryside smoked and throbbed like a single gigantic factory extending on all sides as far as the eye could see, spiked by thousands of belching chimneys, threaded by oily black canals, hideous as a battlefield, indifferent as a locomotive plunging over a cliff, the most important piece of land in the world.

They passed Newark Airport and Lassiter looked out over the flat pan of it to a Liberator taxing along a runway, turning slowly like a dinosaur and finally coming to rest with its props fanning. The Cadillac raced smoothly on through the jungle of barbecues, diners, gas stations, taverns, billboards, crossings, and traffic lights that fringed US1, past the raw edges of Rahway, Metuchen, and New Brunswick and finally into the rolling open country that Lassiter loved. The heavy tires screamed on the concrete as Bratian cruised at sixty miles an hour, mopping up the trucks and old cars rolling along on worn rubber and recaps. Along one section of the road they overtook a convoy of army trucks moving at a steady pace with even distances between each of them. Soldiers stood in the backs of the trucks with their heads turned from the wind. Bratian pulled into an open lane and swept past the whole convoy in a further burst of speed, while Lassiter stared straight ahead and huddled his big body a few inches lower behind the glass. Being in a car like Bratian's in times like these made him self-conscious, particularly in the presence of soldiers.

They turned off at the Princeton Circle; the tower of the Graduate School rose over the trees and Lassiter relaxed. The rich, familiar feelings returned. To him, Princeton was the one priceless jewel in an otherwise loathsome state, whether it was approached through the New Jersey marshland of factories or through the desert of Philadelphia and Trenton.

As they crossed the bridge over Lake Carnegie he watched eight men lifting a racing shell out of the water onto the dock while the cox stood by giving his orders. The surface of the lake was dark near the banks and the thin threads of water streaming off the tilted keel made widening circles that fanned out of the shadows into the light. The crew got the shell over their heads and walked it into the boathouse and Lassiter eyed them enviously.

"There's your new American type," he said. "Everyone of them tall with wide shoulders and long legs. I wonder if they're as strong as they look."

"They don't have to be," Bratian said.

"Remember Bill Sayre? He played next to me in the line. I was talking to him the other day in the club and he says these long-waisted kids haven't got much stamina. And that was one thing Bill always had."

"Why not? He had to have something."

The air was clear and cool, and the tree branches, dusted with opening buds, were delicate against a saffron sky. Grey clouds towered over the fields to the south; it was turning into the kind of evening that always bred mists in Princeton. They passed Palmer Stadium on the right and skirted the end of the campus on the left, then turned into Nassau Street. It was blue with naval uniforms and Renwick's looked crowded. Bratian slowed down for a woman who was pushing a baby carriage. They passed Jack Honore's barber shop and when Stephen saw Jack in the doorway wearing his fawn alpaca jacket he waved.

"How about a quick one at the Nass?" he said.

"I want to see Lucy's garden before it gets dark."

"What the hell do you care about gardens?"

"Not a damn thing, but it flatters her and she can use more than she's been getting lately. Women are like the lower classes: if you flatter them enough you can get away with murder. Something for you to remember, Steve."

"You're a crazy bastard. If you think you've got Lucy figured out you've got another guess coming."

Bratian's quick sidewise glance was lost on him, for Stephen had recognized another friend standing on the corner near the memorial and was shouting something unintelligible to him. The man waved and called back.

"Who was that?" Bratian said.

"Joe Hickman. You remember him. He used to drive a hack. He's still around."

Bratian laughed silently. "God, they're all still here!" He passed the memorial and idled out of town at thirty miles an hour along the Trenton pike. "You've been living here two years now. When are you going to move on again?"

"Why should I move on? This is the best town in the whole damn country."

"You could sell your house for twice what you paid for it."

Stephen leaned back and looked at the great trees lining the road. At the end of a sudden vista of lawn between shrubs he saw a bed of blue scillas and a burst of forsythia in bloom.

"It's the earliest spring I can remember," he said. A second later he added, "I bet it looks good to the boys in Germany."

"Twenty years from now they'll be talking about the war the way you talk about Princeton at reunions."

"Maybe. And what if they do?"

Bratian changed the subject in his quick, sharp voice. "Tell me something – has Lucy made any friends out here?"

"Of course. She makes friends wherever she is."

"Real ones or Saturday night ones?"

Stephen let the question go. He knew that Bratian found Lucy of more than passing interest, even that he was attracted to her sexually, but he was shrewd enough to guess that the basis of the interest lay in the fact that she was one of the few individuals Bratian saw repeatedly whom he couldn't fathom.

"She's too intelligent for the sort of people she meets here," Bratian said. "Old classmates – they must be tough to take more than once."

"Oh, can it," Stephen said, his voice on the defensive. And he knew that Bratian observed it. The little bastard noticed everything. He'd always been an outsider at Princeton and he'd never been able to understand what a place like Princeton meant to a man who had once been a real part of it. At least their friends here were real people, even if most of them were old classmates who had lost their great expectations in the Depression, made money in the war boom, and moved their families out to decent surroundings.

"The funny thing about Lucy," Bratian went on, "is that she's the sort of woman an ordinary man never notices while a first-class man always does. I told her that years ago. She's the sort of woman who ought to be at the top. She's deep."

Bratian was right, Stephen thought. Lucy was deep. But beyond that, what did Carl know about her? What did any man know about women unless he'd been married to at least one of them? He thought of Joyce and for a moment he remembered how attractive and desirable she had once seemed. The last time he'd heard of her she was married to a man in California and she still had no children. Yet Joyce, now a stranger, owned a small part of him still. Women did that to a man when he lived with them. They entered his mind and it was no longer entirely his. Nobody had ever done that to Carl. Let him live with an intelligent woman day after day and no matter how nice she was, no matter how generous she was or how eager she was in bed, he'd soon discover there wasn't a corner of his mind he could call his own.

Lassiter frowned, hunched lower in his seat, and said, "Some day I'd like to see a woman give you the business."

Bratian grinned as he turned off the main pike into the side road leading to Stephen's house. "No woman gives any man the business if he knows what he wants from her."

The car dipped into a pothole and lifted voluptuously out of it.

The unpaved road had once been a farmer's track and it was little more than that now. Only two houses had been built on it, separated and concealed from each other by a hundred yards of trees and shrubs. It ended in Stephen's garage on the far side of his house. Beyond that was open country, an historic country dotted here and there with metal plaques which had been erected by patriotic societies.

The Lassiters' house was made of grey fieldstone with white clapboards encasing the upper storey. It had been built in 1928 by a New Yorker who had lost his money the following year, and since then it had changed ownership three times. It still looked so new it was impossible to imagine that it would ever look old. The flowering shrubs in the front had been there when they bought the house, but the perennial borders in the back had been laid out by Lucy and Stephen.

They drove up before the house and turned into the narrow drive that led to the garage. Beyond the garage a sizable patch of ground had just been harrowed for vegetables and the moist earth glowed in the slanting sunlight. Beyond the patch the land sloped abruptly down a bank to a stream so shallow that its bed was usually dry by the first of August. On the other side of the stream a field fanned out, part of a farm owned by a man named Sam Hunter who had been born on the place, a fact which made him oddly authentic in a town like Princeton, where antiquity was so prized that most of the famous buildings in Oxford and Cambridge had been studiously copied in the college architecture, and the old Nassau Inn had been replaced by a new Nassau Tavern carefully built to look more typically mid-eighteenth century than the original structure had ever looked.

"You'll have to leave the car here," Stephen said as Bratian idled the motor. "The station wagon's inside the garage."

Lucy came out the side door wearing a grey flannel skirt and a blue cardigan sweater. She smiled and waved and Stephen jumped out of the car and swung her off her feet as he kissed her. Bratian watched them with an inscrutable expression drawn over his face. When Lucy was on her feet again he reached behind the front seat of the car, pulled out a long box, and handed it to her.

"You promised you'd stop doing this," she said as she took the box.

"They're only store roses. I want to see your daffodils."

"Oh, let's go inside. I've been out all afternoon. How are you, Stephen? Has it been a bad week?"

A small boy wearing a pair of overalls came from behind the garage, stopped to look at them for a moment, then ran to his father. Stephen picked him up under the arms and lifted him high while John squealed with excitement and kicked his legs. The moment he was put down he begged to be lifted again.

"Mummy and I went to the Junction last night, Daddy." John's voice was breathless as he spoke in starts. "You said you were coming. Why didn't you?"

Bratian slipped his arm through Lucy's. "Some day John will make a first-class examining lawyer."

At the same moment Stephen answered his son, "You'd better ask Carl. He knows everything."

John stood looking up at Bratian. "Why didn't Daddy come home last night, sir?"

"Oh, he had work to do in town. He was making lots of money yesterday."

Bratian was never at home with children or even vaguely interested in them and John had long ago sensed it. He was aloof with this man who called himself his Uncle Carl, though his feeling had nothing to do with the formality of his language; Lucy had taught him to call all older men "sir." John had coarse blond hair like his father's and he was so strongly built that he looked at least two years older than his actual age, but otherwise he was predominantly Lucy's son. His eyes were wide and brown, his features slim and finely cut, and he had much of Lucy's reserve of manner. He never gave much response to heartiness in his elders and Stephen sometimes had the uncomfortable feeling that his son saw through him and made allowances for his behaviour; yet Stephen was proud of the boy and there was no doubt of John's affection for his father.

They went into the house, Lucy and Carl leading the way, John following, and Stephen bringing up the rear with Bratian's bag. Carl complimented Lucy on the spring flowers from her garden he saw on a table in the hall and stood in the living-room doorway, looking it over with his usual appraising air as if he were calculating not so much what it had cost as the effect it would have on various kinds of people who might see it.

"New slipcovers?" he said.

Lucy smiled wryly; she could change half the details in the house without Stephen noticing, but Bratian observed everything. "They're made from some curtains I had in town. If they look new it's because they've just come from the cleaners."

"Once you get inside this place it's got distinction. You've managed to disinfect it from the suburbs." He turned back to the hall while Stephen went upstairs with his bag. "Come into town one day next week. I want to do my drawing room over again and I'd like your advice. It's got no more distinction than a Calvert whiskey ad."

"Why bother?" she said. "You did your whole apartment over last autumn and you'll do it again six months from now."

Bratian gave her an intimate smile. "It's nice to see you again."

Lucy laughed.

"I mean it." He moved nearer but made no attempt to touch her. "You're the only reason I come out here. You know that, don't you?"

Stephen came downstairs and Lucy sent John up to wash and change his clothes. Bratian decided he would do the same and on his way upstairs turned to announce that he would be down shortly to inspect the garden.

When they were alone together Stephen put his arm about Lucy's waist, his hand found the curve of her hip, and he turned her slowly until her face was under his. He kissed her, found her lips warm but passive, and kissed her again, holding her with sudden fierceness as if trying to prove something to himself. Her eyes half closed, slowly her fingers began to tense into his shoulders as her body yielded against his, but his quick lift of relief disappeared when she broke from him and turned away.

"I'm awfully sorry about last night," he said.

"Never mind. It's all right."

"Honestly," he said, watching her closely, trying to read her mind. "I had to work last night. It was one of those god-awful days. On Wednesday I shoved everything aside when Myron Harper phoned he'd be in town and then when he didn't show up it was time out and I had to work overtime to catch up. When you called Wednesday I thought I could make it. I'm sorry I forgot to phone yesterday to tell you I'd changed my mind. It was one of those things. I did mean to." He went into the dining room and opened a cupboard, there was the clink of a bottle against a glass, a short pause, and then he came back into the hall. "I only remembered when I was in bed last night that I'd forgotten to tell Miss O'Neill to call you."

Lucy was busy putting toys into a cupboard underneath the stairs. "Never mind, Stephen. You don't have to explain every detail to me, you know."

"I'm not trying to explain." His voice was growing irritable. He felt in his pockets for cigarettes, found only an empty package, went into the living room and took one from a silver box and lit it. By the time it was burning and the smoke had reached his lungs the intimacy between them was fractured and a state almost of formality had taken its place.

"How's Sally?" he said. "I haven't seen her anywhere."

"She's gone to a birthday party. Shirley's getting her now."

"Shirley?" His eyebrows raised with the question. "Oh, yes – the latest. How's she working out?"

"Not too bad. I'm glad to have anyone at all. She comes in every day after school, and she seems willing to do anything I ask. What's more, she's quite agreeable to giving me all day Saturday – so far."

He turned and started upstairs, turned again and went back to the dining room where he poured himself another drink. He came out to the hall with the glass of neat rye in his hand. Lucy was no longer there.

"Lucy!" he called. "I'm going to take a bath before dinner. I'm tired as hell."

She answered from the kitchen. "Will you be ready for dinner by seven-thirty?"

He went upstairs holding the glass in his hand and emptied it in the process of taking off his clothes. Then he went into the bathroom off their bedroom and stretched out in a tubful of water so hot it turned his skin pink. The lines relaxed about his eyes and the whiskey sent warm waves of comfort along his nerves. A great and omnipresent weight seemed to lift a little, lift but hang over him as if at any moment it would snap back again like the lid of a mummy case. The bathroom was at the back of the house, the window was open a few inches to let out steam, and through the blur of his thoughts he heard Bratian talking to Lucy in the garden. Some day, he thought, that little bastard is going to wear down, too.

AT FOUR in the morning the house was still. In the guest room Bratian opened the window to let out his cigarette smoke and then he dropped a trayful of butts into the darkness. He got into bed, turned out the light, and in five minutes he was sound asleep. His lithe little body was relaxed as his soul greyed off into innocence. The file of papers on which he had been working lay in a neat pile on the bedside table, unruffled by the faint breath of air which seeped into the room.

Faintly into all the windows came the sound of a train whistle as a long freight carrying field guns from Pittsburgh to Hoboken neared Princeton Junction. All the loneliness of America was in its call.

The noise of the distant rolling cars rumbled heavily across Lucy's consciousness and she stirred and woke. Then in the following silence she heard a murmur from Stephen's bed and her eyes opened in the darkness. He was groaning in his sleep. She listened in intent agony to the sounds, thought he was repeating a name, but could not recognize it. She lay there almost willing herself into his half-sleeping mind, trying to discover what troubled it. She remembered reading, years ago in Grenville, that the night can be a bad time for solitary people. Was there any loneliness in the world comparable to the kind that can exist between two who love one another?

Stephen's murmurs died out but Lucy remained awake with the whole night around her. In New York they had shared the same bed until Stephen's increasing restlessness, his tendency to wake and require a cigarette to relax him for sleep again, had sent him out to buy twin beds. She wished there were only one bed in the room now so she might touch him, even wake him out of his dream, and lie close in his arms. She thought how strange and ironical it was that someone like herself should have been able to reach Stephen more easily through her body than through her mind. He was afraid of her mind; she felt it between them like a barrier, but there had been moments when she knew her physical response had given him a kind of glory. Wishing first not to disappoint him, then longing to make him happy, then loving him sufficiently to obliterate herself and all her background, she had learned to respect his capacity for losing himself in physical love, as she had learned to do the same.

And now she was conscious of this growing barrier between them, aware of vague resentments in the deep of his nature; now there were moments like this when each was isolated in the same room, their separate lives lying apart.

He murmured again and made a sobbing sound.

"Stephen," she cried softly. "Stephen, wake up!"

She heard him surge in the darkness. "What is it?"

"Darling – you were having a nightmare."

His voice blew her miles away as he answered, "Oh, for Christ's sake, let me sleep!"

Silence again and a great weight of darkness, and presently a resumption of his heavy breathing. But Lucy lay awake wondering what to do, feeling the load of his inner unhappiness and disappointment in himself and in her as she asked herself how she had failed him.

The long minutes ticked off, heard but unseen in the clock that lay on the table between them, while all of America seemed to be closing in around her, thousands of cold eyes watching a stranger in the dark.

WHEN Lucy got up at seven-thirty Stephen was motionless on his back and she let him sleep. She bathed and dressed, heard the children in the nursery, went in and greeted them, helped Sally with her clothes, and then went downstairs to begin a series of breakfasts. John came down and laid the table, arranging the silverware precisely. When he finished he went out to the kitchen to help his mother; it was his job to put the bread in the toaster after she had sliced it and told him when to begin. Sally came down and tried to help John, and by the time the coffee had bubbled into the top of the Silex a discreet odour of Green Ranger shaving lotion announced the presence of Bratian on the ground floor. He came in wearing a tweed jacket, brown whipcord slacks, suede shoes, a dark blue woollen shirt, and a flaring silk tie splashed with orange.

"I've had four hours' sleep and I've done an hour's work already this morning. How's Steve?"

"He's still asleep. He was awfully tired last night."

"What's he got to be tired about? The only way a man gets tired is worrying." He gave her a sharp look. "You're as handsome as ever. What's he worried about?"

Lucy made no answer as she turned out the gas under a frying pan and filled a platter with scrambled eggs. John followed her into the dining room holding a plate of toast in both hands, walking carefully with his eye on the toast, and finally sliding the plate onto the table and then looking up to make sure his mother had noticed that he had done it without disturbing any of the knives and forks or spilling any of the slices on the cloth. Lucy served Bratian, John, and Sally, but took only toast and coffee for herself.

"What's the matter?" Bratian said. "Don't you like your own cooking?"

"Not much this morning."

"You worried too?"

"I never eat much for breakfast."

"Foolish of you. It's the best meal of the day."

She forced herself to listen while he excluded the children by talking politics throughout the meal. Occasionally Sally paused with her spoon halfway to her mouth and stared at him, but Bratian no more noticed the children than he noticed the furniture, and it occurred to Lucy that he had become less sensitive to atmosphere than he once had been. For years she had tried to keep him from realizing that John resented him the way a family dog resents an interloper.

"When the war's over," Carl was saying, "I'm going down to Washington, just about the time all the boys down there now get tired and start for home." He pushed his coffee cup aside and produced a cigar which dwarfed his face when he lit it. "The old stock in the State Department did all right so long as they made the rules and kept their eye on the ball, but they're slipping fast. How much public opinion do they control now? Public opinion grows out of taste, and who gives them their taste? Hollywood and the networks. I give them some of it myself." He flipped his orange tie outside his jacket. "Where did this fashion come from? Savile Row? They used to sell ties with patterns like this in pushcarts on the streets where I grew up."

Lucy got up from the table. "Will you excuse me, Carl? There are so many things to do around the house in the morning."

"Where's that farm girl you had helping last time I was here?"

"She's working in Trenton. I have another one but I don't know where she is this morning."

He glanced at the children as though he wished they were somewhere else and John stared back. Then he slid off his chair, excused himself, and went to the kitchen and Sally followed him. Lucy watched them go with a faint smile playing at the corners of her mouth. As Bratian got up from the table she left the room and started upstairs, hoping he had not seen the smile, for had he guessed her thoughts he would not have been flattered. In spite of the fact that he was Stephen's employer and one of his oldest friends, she found him a pitiless bore. Since her marriage she had met many men in New York and Princeton whom she liked, some who let her know they were attracted to her physically and some who did not. Bratian seemed to her obtrusively sexless.

She reached the upstairs hall and paused outside the closed door of their large bedroom, listening for sounds, but there were none. Stephen had slept like this weekend after weekend with a fatigue she knew was unnatural. If only they could be alone together for two or three consecutive days perhaps she could discover what it was that was exhausting him, but it had been months since they had talked about anything that mattered.

Going into Bratian's room she opened another window to let out the stale smell and began putting the room in order. The papers on which he had been working before breakfast were spread on the desk and one of them blew onto the floor with a gust of spring air. She picked it up and replaced it, noticing that it was some kind of financial report. A contemptuous anger for his whole business struck through her as she recalled the fantastic private office where he presided in his agency on Madison Avenue. In Bratian's phrase, even his tooled leather chairs were designed to flatter the backsides of prospective customers. She remembered the graphs and charts on the walls, all so impressive to owl-faced practical men who had to be shown. She remembered the windows of the conference room so carefully planned to frame a view of the R.C.A. Building – another study in flattery. She remembered the puffy look about the eyes of the account executives, the hopped-up enthusiasms and periodic frenzies that swept the place whenever one of them thought he had a new idea, the false optimism of those who believed their own build-up and the equally false cynicism of those who didn't. It was a business, she thought, that could have been devised only by men; the women who worked in it had always seemed to her – no matter what records some of them set in hopping from bed to bed – as basically passionless as Bratian.

She went back to the hall; still no sound from their room. She thought of dishes in the kitchen, grocery orders to be given, laundry to sort, lunch to be started. But she had no intention of going downstairs and talking to Bratian before Stephen got up. Nothing had become more unpleasant to her lately than the subtle way in which Carl contrived to let her know that he, too, was observing Stephen closely, that he, too, was aware that her husband was deteriorating. Her mind had framed the phrase involuntarily; her whole body winced as she shuddered to realize that she could have thought such a thing.

She heard Sally call from the landing and presently saw her face emerge as she came up the stairs, right foot first on each step. There was a smudge of dirt on the child's face and Lucy led her into the nursery bathroom to wash it off.

"Daddy's still asleep," she said as she brushed the golden curls. "He's tired this morning and we must be careful not to wake him up. So run downstairs and play quietly with John and when Daddy gets up we'll all have fun together."

Sally went off toward the stairs and Lucy watched the small fat legs disappear down the first step. Then the pudgy face turned about and smiled for no reason except that she was contented. As Lucy turned back to clean up the nursery she felt a surge of warmth run through her veins. Sally was Stephen's favourite, perhaps because she was more tranquil than John, perhaps because she was more helpless, perhaps because she was a girl who had been named for his mother.

She began to look over the children's summer clothes, and as she closed one drawer in the chest where they were kept and opened another she heard the back door slam and knew that John was on his way over to Sam Hunter's farm. Sam was a wonderful neighbour. Only three mornings ago she had been wakened by strange sounds outside her window and there was Sam with his horse, harrowing her vegetable garden. His own son was in Germany and he always liked to have John around the farm, watching him at work through the seasons, learning to milk his two cows, discussing matters of great import between men.

Then she heard sounds from the bedroom across the hall. When she opened the door she found Stephen sitting on the side of his bed rubbing his forehead.

"Poor darling," she said. "You breathed so hard all night and talked so much in your sleep you can't have rested at all."

"What did I talk about?"

She smiled at him, knowing a smile was necessary at that moment. "I listened carefully, but I couldn't catch a word."

"Sorry I woke you."

She stood beside him and put her hand behind his head, gently stroking the back of his neck.

"I suppose you think I've got a hangover," he said with sudden sharpness.

She took her hand away and walked across the room to the window. Red peony shoots were standing six inches high among the daffodils and narcissus. This was the season she had always loved best in Grenville, the time when the daffodils made splashes of gold among brown shrubs at a moment when winter seemed endless, when she mixed bordeaux in the greenhouse and found plants she had forgotten over the winter coming through the dark ground, when her garden had seemed the most important thing in the world. But peonies were peonies everywhere, even if her sense of their importance had altered, and the ones down below would have to be sprayed at once if she expected a full blooming in early June. She wished again that Carl would stay in New York for a weekend now and then and leave her alone with Stephen. If Carl weren't here Stephen might help her all morning in the garden, and it was always easier to talk to him while they were doing some kind of work together.

Behind her Stephen said, "Is Carl up yet? I suppose he is."

"We've all had breakfast."

She came back to the bed and sat down beside him, longing to slip in beside him and feel his arms about her. There, at least, he could be sure he was stronger than she was. There, holding her close, he could forget how observant she was, could stop wondering how much she guessed, how much she knew, how much she thought, how much she feared, how much she worried about him.

"Don't get up if you'd rather not," she said. "I'll bring you some orange juice or a glass of milk, and you can sleep till afternoon if you like. This is your day."

In the ensuing silence she could feel the strain in him, and she knew his mind was trying to ward her off. Why, she asked herself. Why must he? His face looked so naked and hungry when he first woke up, not buoyant the way she liked to remember it, but tortured by conflicting emotions, all of them strong.

"How's Sally?" he asked.

"She's fine. She seems to have survived her first party beautifully. She's playing downstairs, waiting for you to get up."

He rubbed both hands over the blond stubble on his face, and with a pang Lucy wondered how often he woke up alone in the city feeling as he did now. He had not been drunk last night. He was drinking far too much, but he was never drunk. It was something else that had grown slowly and at first imperceptibly like a wall between them. Why won't he let me try to help him, she thought. No matter what it is, why won't he let me talk to him?

"It makes no sense, the way I feel this morning," he said. "It wasn't so late when we got to bed."

She avoided his eyes, knowing he wished to avoid hers. Sure now that he was awake for the day, and that as soon as he began to move around she would be unable to talk to him about anything, she said, "Last Tuesday evening – no, it was Wednesday – a man called to see you. Drove out in a car. He said you'd know who he was. His name was Carson."

"Carson?" Stephen frowned, then gave a sudden start. "S.H. Carson?"

"I think so. Yes, that was it."

"Well, for God's sake!" His voice had come alive. "He's the man I was named after!"

"So he told me."

"I told you myself. When we were first married."

She smiled. "Not me. But he's a good man to have been named for."

Stephen rubbed his face again. "I'd forgotten his existence. If I'd been told he was dead ten years I wouldn't have been surprised. Mother used to think he was wonderful. He was her second cousin and according to Marcia she was in love with him once. What was he doing here?"

"Consulting someone at the Flexner, he said. He got our address from alumni files at the university and he seemed surprised to find us right here in Princeton."

Stephen pulled himself up from the bed. "He used to be a civil engineer, but he was a crazy duck and for years he wouldn't work in the United States. The last time I heard he was in China. Dad never thought much of him. What's he doing now – raising money for Chiang Kai-shek?"

"He's connected with the Shasta Dam. He was terribly sorry to miss you. I'm sorry, too, because I liked him a lot." She paused and waited for him to turn around. When he did she looked into his eyes and said, "He wants you to work with him, Stephen."

"What do you mean, work with him?"

"He's got a job for you on the Shasta Dam."

"In *California*?" He made a wry face. "That's the other end of nowhere. What kind of a job?"

Again she sensed his defensiveness; this time it moved over her like a wave of cold air. "He left some papers for you to look at," she said. "They'll explain everything, he says. I didn't mention it last night with Carl around, for obvious reasons."

Lassiter sat down on the bed again. His hair was tousled and his pajamas rumpled, but his face was alert.

"Funny," he said. "Somebody still remembers I'm an engineer." Then more sharply, "Does he know what I'm doing now?"

"I told him."

"What did he say?"

What Carson had said had been precisely what she knew Stephen himself had thought many times: an engineer's business is making things, not writing words about others who do.

She looked at her husband. "He has a job he thinks you can do better than anybody else he knows at the moment. I don't understand what it is, but the papers will probably give you some idea."

"Do you realize," Stephen said defiantly, "that I haven't done any real engineering for years? Do you realize it's highly specialized work?"

"Of course. But Mr. Carson said he wanted you for something to do with personnel management."

"Like my job with Ashweiler?" He laughed shortly.

"No. It would require a trained engineer who could also handle men."

"Do you think I could do it?"

"Of course. But it's not for me to decide what kind of work you do, Stephen."

"Since when?"

She held one hand tightly in the other. "Since always. I've never pretended to know anything about your business."

"I suppose he wanted to know why I wasn't in the army, too."

"He didn't mention it." She smiled and touched his hand. "You agreed to stop brooding about that long ago."

The silence between them enlarged rapidly and she got up from the bed, picked up a sweater she saw lying on a chair, and put it in one of the drawers of his chest.

"Would you mind telling me something?" he said. "For just how long have you been ashamed of the work I'm doing?"

He was watching her closely now, watching her as if she were a stranger, but her old Grenville habit of masking her face had returned and he could read nothing from her expression. She closed the drawer with her knee and said quietly as she turned around, "I liked Mr. Carson very much and I know you'd like him, too. He's everything that Carl isn't. If you worked with a man like that everything in the world would seem different to you."

"Different from what?"

"Oh, darling – don't pretend you don't know what I mean!"

But her eyes moved away as she saw the defiance in his. Long ago she had learned what most women never know, that when men say they want their wives to understand them they seldom mean it. What Stephen wanted was to be taken for granted by his wife, not understood. She sat on the window ledge, wondering what to do or say next, and her whole soul longed to cry out, "Stephen, I don't care what you do so long as you're happy. If you're satisfied with yourself, we'll all be happy."

What she did say was, "You've always been generous to me. I never forget that for a minute. So please be generous enough to admit to yourself that I'm not criticizing you. I never talk about Carl. I don't want to now."

"If a man wants to eat," he said, "he's got to compromise."

She made a quick gesture with her hand. "Stephen, you aren't cynical by nature and you can't make yourself cynical by habit and get away with it. There's death in a man like Carl. Ultimately he kills whatever he touches. And the worst thing about him is that he knows exactly what he's doing."

"What do you expect me to do – reform his character?" His hostility was growing. "For God's sake, what kind of a world do you think we live in? When I first met you I told you I didn't make the rules. That was one thing I learned early. People like you and me don't ever make the rules. We learn them. And while we're talking about it – why don't you try to remember that the work I'm doing doesn't happen to be the same stinking stuff the rest of them do? There's a considerable difference between handling an account for the best medium bomber in the United States Army Air Forces and dreaming up seduction scenes for underwear or men's cosmetics."

He reached for the bedside table, pulled open a drawer, took out a package of cigarettes, and lit one. She felt the weight of his irritation with her and her impulse was to leave the room, but she knew if she did she would not be with him, either in body or spirit, for at least another week. He would take his bath, eat his breakfast, and spend the rest of the weekend with Carl and his Princeton friends.

"Stephen," she said quietly, "this isn't a thing to quarrel about. I won't let you misunderstand me deliberately and make a quarrel out of nothing. Apparently I'm very bad when it comes to using words."

"I've always thought you were pretty good with them."

She let the remark pass. "Your work – your personal work – has always been your own business. You know I've never criticized it and you know that's not what I'm talking about now. It's something else and I'm not sure how to say it. You're with Carl five days a week and you're down here only for two. Surely you don't have to bring him here so often. I can't help wondering sometimes if you do it simply because you don't want to be alone with me."

She saw a flash of warmth and tenderness cross his face. He sat looking down at his hands and the smoke of the cigarette trailed up between them.

"Our life together," she said, "is the only thing that's ever mattered to me. I feel now as though I never lived at all before you came to Grenville and took me away. But sometimes now I feel quite helpless. Perhaps I'm not hard enough. Perhaps I'm not gay enough, and you do deserve someone who knows how to have fun in your own way. But I think it's more than that. You're not happy, Stephen." She watched him get up and move across the floor. He pulled a clean shirt out of the chest and looked for a tie in the closet to match it. "I wish you didn't have to work with people you don't respect," she went on, "trying to convince yourself that you don't make the rules, thinking about money far more than you have to. But maybe I don't understand because I'm a Canadian. I hope that's all it is. And I wish you wouldn't shut me out."

His expression was softening and she could almost feel the workings of his conscience. When he hurt her, he hurt himself at the same time. It was one of the things she dreaded most of all, for it made her too much of a burden to him.

He swung around and put his arms about her. "You're a funny girl sometimes," he said. He placed a finger under her chin and lifted it until their eyes met. "I think you're just being a Cameron today – a little crazy because you're more than a little Scotch, and still very much a Calvinist."

She mustered up a smile. "Probably."

"The Scotch are a wonderful people, but they certainly make things tough for themselves." He put both hands on either side of her head and her hair was pressed flat against her temples as he looked down at her. "What you need is a change. You spend too much time out here with nobody but the kids to talk to. As soon as the gas ration's lifted we'll get the hell out of here and go across the continent again."

She wondered as she smiled back at him if they ever would. Stephen began to hunt in the drawers again for socks and shorts and her mind went back to the first time they had crossed the continent before the war. That was when she had fallen completely in love with him; it was the time when she had really come to know him, when she had discovered that New York was almost as foreign to him as it was to herself. The farther west they went, the better he liked the country. In Stockton, Kansas, he had hunted for the old junkyard where he and Joe Boyce had sold the remnants of their first truck after they had run away from school. Miles west of Stockton he had stopped the car on a rise of ground and pointed to a distant water tower stark in the afternoon sun and without speaking had handed her the field-glasses he had bought especially for the trip. Looking at the tower through the prisms she had deciphered the words *Lassiter City*.

"Where my grandad settled."

The name sounded queer to her, but she was pleased because he was pleased. "You never told me, Stephen!"

When they reached the place it was a ghost town of empty shacks with brown dust driven against bleached wooden walls. A few rusted ploughs lay half submerged in patches of nettle and tumbleweed behind broken fences, and grasshoppers puffed as high as their shoulders when they stepped out of the car beside the road. There was a filling station with a single pump served by a lone survivor who looked as if the years of blowing dust had eroded him; the dust was pitted into his skin and it had browned out the blue of his overalls. "Everything's bin agin us out here, Mister. Ain't bin gittin' any rain in years. Folks moved out quite a time back. Went West, most of 'em. Guess some went East, too. But it used to be mighty purty once, standin' on this hill and lookin'."

After the tank was filled Stephen had hunted for the graveyard, found it near a bleached and cracked wooden church, and Lucy had jumped back as a copper-coloured bull snake crawled away from a headstone. "Thomas Lassiter – the Founder of This Town. Born 1827 – Died 1899." The snake slithered out of sight, the tumbleweed rattled in the wind, the grasshoppers rose in clouds as they walked away, and their nostrils smarted with the fine, drifting dust. The place had moved Lucy far more than it moved Stephen. She learned then a little of what it meant to be an American with a press of lonely, hopeful men behind you, still carrying within yourself something of the belief which had brought Thomas Lassiter here from Missouri, and his father to Missouri from Ohio, and behind him the long line of lean men threading west out of New England, no poetry in them, no music, but the necessity of believing that westward things were better, over every mountain a valley richer than the last, carrying wherever they went the qualities that made them unlike any other people who had ever lived, the great refusal to be satisfied, to rest and sit down, the unwillingness to be content which was as hard as a rock in the soul. First the Lord had hounded them, and when the Lord grew remote, they had hounded themselves.

"The old boy should have known he couldn't count on water in a place like this. It isn't a plain, it's a plateau," Stephen said.

She asked if he remembered his grandfather.

"Never saw him. And Dad never talked about him much, though I think that was Mother's fault. Let's get out of here."

The grasshoppers fretted her legs as she went with him to the car, and she knew the lonely sighing of the tumbleweed had entered her ears to stay.

Four days later they were in a different land, in Boulder City, and Stephen was explaining eagerly the whole system of the dam. She had forgotten its details long ago, but she would never forget the white miracle of that upward-sweeping concrete with Lake Meade resting behind the bastion like a shining blue eye in those terrible mountains scorched by the sun to the colour of slag heaps. "When we came out here," the man who was showing them around had said, "nothing could live on them, not even cactus. We've come quite a way." And he motioned toward the cool, shaded streets of Boulder City, the white houses framed by oleanders, the green lawns and children playing on wide porches, with the pride of an American who can think of no greater achievement than making something work where nothing worked before.

Now, thinking of the dam and remembering Stephen Holt Carson, a vision came to Lucy that she knew was sentimental and perhaps impossible, yet it was the kind of vision Stephen himself might have encouraged a few years ago before New York had filtered his enthusiasms: a garden of fruit and flowers belonging to Stephen and herself in a land which once had been a desert but now was the richest growing country on earth, watered by a great and distant dam which Stephen himself, even in the smallest possible way, had helped to build.

He dropped his pajamas and she watched his arm muscles mass as he flexed them to get the blood stirring. She saw him look at his reflection in the mirror on the bathroom door with boyish pride, for his chest and shoulder muscles had retained their solid outlines even if his stomach had not. His expression changed as his eyes dropped lower and his hands gripped the superfluous flesh at his waist.

"God damn it, that looks like hell," he said.

"As if it mattered! I never notice it."

"Well, my tailor does."

She wanted to lay her hand on the offending flesh and feel its warmth.

"Maybe if I got back to tennis," he said, "I could get some of it off. The trouble is, I'd feel a heel playing tennis in wartime."

She slipped her arms about him and laid a cheek against his naked shoulder, but with a barely perceptible movement he shrugged her off. He had done the same thing a hundred times in the past year, never positively, never rudely or even consciously, but she had gradually come to take it for granted that his physical desires had cooled. This morning, in a flash of intuition, she realized they had not. He was still looking at himself in the glass. He was the man he had always been; one who loved his own body because he saw it reflected in a woman's eyes.

Lucy was startled by her own white face in the mirror as she turned away abruptly. With perfect certainty she realized that the vague suspicion which had haunted her for months was based on fact. The woman in whose eyes Stephen was seeking his own re-flection was no longer his wife.

"Where are those papers Carson left?" he was saying.

"In the right hand top drawer of my desk."

"I'll have a look at them tomorrow. As a matter of fact, I'd like to see that dam. It's quite a project. I don't suppose Carson men-tioned what they'd pay."

Looking out the window, aloof and numb inside, Lucy said, "Six thousand to begin with."

She heard his laughter. "Did you tell him what I'm making now?"

"He didn't ask."

"Well, for God's sake be practical. How could we go on living the way we do on six thousand a year?"

"We couldn't."

He began to shave and after a moment he said, "You're funny this morning. You think too much, you know."

She heard the water run in the bathroom and then she felt his arms come about her shoulders and his hands cup her breasts. For an instant she leaned her head back against his chest and guarded a thought she knew was true: this present gesture of his, outwardly false, was inwardly honest. Oh, Stephen, she thought, when will you ever make peace with yourself? The world is full of men who have to do work unworthy of them, full of men haunted by injustices they have suffered in childhood, so full of boy-men like you. Why hide from the fact of yourself by looking for confidence in the flattery of women who wouldn't dream of flattering you if they really cared? You can take every woman you meet, one by one, and all they'll do is multiply the mirrors, multiply the reflections, and change nothing.

THE rest of that morning seemed to Lucy to climb upward in a long, jangling ascent. Half an hour later, while she sat at the breakfast table with Stephen, and Sally prattled to him about her own imaginary world, Bratian came in from the garage and sat down at the table. Stephen sent Sally off to play and Bratian asked for another cup of coffee. Lucy went out to the kitchen to pour him a fresh cup and when she returned with it Bratian was talking.

"... she's as thin as a tulip stem, with a pure Greek nose and lips like a white nigger's. A woman born with looks like that could end up only one way. Maybe that's why she's crazy. But she's a hero as well. She won the George Cross in the Blitz in 1940."

"Why doesn't she go to Hollywood?" Stephen said.

"She can't act and she's smart enough to know it."

Lucy picked up some plates, stacked them, carried them out, and returned to finish clearing the table. Bratian looked up at her and grinned. "Sit down, Lucy. You'll be interested. We're talking about Lady Pamela Grantchester. Steve hasn't met her yet, but she's going to work for us and I'm using her on the Adams bed account."

Lucy went out to the kitchen again and stayed there. Through the open door Carl's voice drifted, explaining that for five thousand dollars Lady Pamela was willing to sit on the edge of the bed in a housecoat with a phone in her hand, but for ten thousand she would lie on it in her negligee with her legs in an appropriately informative position. Lucy only half listened. What was reality? Was it what you could become a part of, or what you looked at from the outside? Was it what you knew you were, or what grew over you like a fungus? At the moment she seemed a part of nothing. At the moment she felt nothing but a sort of frozen pain.

She heard the rasp of Stephen's chair as he thrust it back from the table and his voice raised in anger. "For God's sake, shut up! What are you trying to do, make Lucy think I use whores in my work the way you do?"

"You would if they paid off for you." Then Bratian's laugh. "Take it easy, Steve. You'll get an ulcer."

She heard Stephen in the front hall and the sound of the door opening and closing. Then she heard the station wagon backing out of the garage and knew she would not see Stephen again until lunch or later. He had gone in to Nassau Street to look for friends.

THEY were in the garden, Lucy in her work gloves spraying bordeaux mixture on the new peony shoots, Bratian following her along the bed.

"You're uncommonly silent this morning," he said.

She laid the sprayer on the grass, took off her gloves, and faced him. "All right, let's talk," she replied.

He looked at her enquiringly, his oval eyes widening, the smoke spiralling up from his fine-ashed cigarette. She moved toward Sally's swing that hung from an old oak at the back of the garden.

"You can sit on John's wagon," she said as she balanced herself on the board that separated the ropes.

Again his eyes widened and again he said nothing. She waited until he had spread a handkerchief on the wagon and then placed himself carefully on the white square.

"Do you know why Stephen is so unhappy?" she said.

"Is he?"

The sun was warm on their faces; it was like a June day in Grenville.

"Carl, in your own way you've several times paid me the compliment of believing I'm not quite as stupid as you think most people are." She paused and then she went on. "I love Stephen. If he's happy, our whole family is happy. Perhaps I shouldn't have let myself become so dependent on him, but I have." She gave a quick look around. The garden was empty and there was no sound but the breeze. "If he goes on much longer the way he's going now he'll have a breakdown. And then he'll be of no use to you at all. You know that as well as I do."

Bratian was still calculating some aspect of her as she looked calmly back at him.

"All right, Carl," she said. "If you don't want to talk to me that's your own affair. In that case I'll have to ask you to leave quietly before Stephen comes back. I can't have the two of you against me in my own house."

For the first time since she had known him Bratian looked surprised. "Okay," he said. "What do you want to know?"

"For the past six months I've been seeing Stephen an average of twice a week. I'm not complaining about it. I'm even selfishly glad he's not in the Pacific." She paused. "You'll know exactly what I mean when I ask you this – is it really necessary for him to work every night in the week?"

Bratian's face still told her nothing. "These are the years, Lucy. If a man doesn't pick his lettuce now, he'll not have another chance after the men in uniform get home."

Lucy seemed not to have heard him. She continued almost as though she were talking to herself. "You and I both know that Stephen is a man who could never bear to be alone. Is it just that he's got into the habit of spending evenings with other men like himself – who also can't bear to be alone? Drinking too much and feeling they can't spend a good evening unless they have women around? Is it just –" She stopped abruptly and turned away. "Or is Stephen in love with somebody else and afraid to tell me so?"

Bratian got to his feet and shook the dust from his handkerchief. "Any woman who starts checking up on a man who works nights is asking for trouble, Lucy."

The ropes crossed overhead as she turned to face him, then fell apart again. "When I married Stephen," she said, "I didn't expect him to be faithful to me physically. He's not the kind of man who could be – forever." She saw his long lashes flicker slightly, but she could not tell whether he was suppressing a smile or a look of surprise. "I told myself it wouldn't matter so long as I didn't know about it. Things like – like that aren't easy for Stephen. He's – well, in a way he's still very young."

"He's been voting for nineteen years," Bratian said.

She watched his face, saw that he was against her, saw that he was finding her situation with Stephen amusing, finding it just another proof of his theory that no matter how hard people try to live a normal life they were sure to end up like this. She left the swing and put on her garden gloves, picked up the sprayer and began to work on the peonies once more. Patches of virulent blue splashed onto the shoots and the dark earth around them and for several minutes there was no sound but the hiss of the mixture shooting out of the sprayer. Finally her contempt became intolerable to him. He snapped away his cigarette and lit another.

"Don't want to talk any more?" he said.

"No."

"You've still got a lot to say."

She made no answer and her silence exasperated him. "Listen, Lucy – what do you expect these days? You're still new down here. It's a bigger place than Grenville, Ontario. What's happening to Steve is what goes on all the time in New York. Steve was trained to feel like a heel if he didn't make money and he was trained to feel like a heel if he made it the way everyone else makes it. So he's right in there between two sides of himself and he can't make up his mind to choose one or the other. If it makes it any easier for you to understand, call it the American disease."

She stopped spraying and measured out her words one by one. "Carl – what makes you so stupid?"

He stared at her and a slow flush mounted to his forehead.

"Do you really believe that what you just said means anything? Has your brain become as superficial as one of your own ads? Do you imagine you can explain away a man as complicated as Stephen Lassiter in a few cheap generalities you picked up from a book you read somewhere?"

His lips puckered and he made a whistling sound. "For Christ's sake!" he said. "All right, you asked for it. You said you wanted to know." He waited a timed second. "Steve's got another woman. There's always one available and he's found his."

His eyes seemed to fix on her face as if they were claws, but if he expected her to show pain, shock, or fear he was disappointed. He got nothing at all. She picked up the sprayer and went back to work on the peony bed.

He watched her a moment and then he said, "All right, you win, Lucy. No wonder Steve feels he's licked."

She continued to spray until she reached the end of the border. When she straightened her back and turned to meet his eyes, raw sexual desire was all she could see in his face. So they stood for several frozen seconds. And then he laughed.

"Get wise to yourself," he said. "You and I are the same kind. They think they can push us around, but you and I know we can do what we like with them. You don't belong in a hideaway like Princeton. You belong on top." He made no move to draw closer to her. "You're the same kind my mother was. Only you're a lady and you use correct English and you don't have to start with two strikes against you."

The sprayer was dripping thick blue liquid as she stared at him. When he smiled again and threw away his cigarette she said, "Please, Carl!"

"Okay." The desire disappeared from his face as though he had drawn a mask over it.

"I'm sorry," she said. "Forget it. I've still got a lot to do out here this morning and I'll do a better job if I'm alone."

He pulled out his handkerchief and sat down on the wagon again. "But you wanted to know something, didn't you?"

"I only wanted –" Her voice shook a little. "Suddenly it's become horrid and embarrassing. I thought I could –" She turned away from him. "Carl, just tell me this, please. Do I know her?"

"I don't think so."

"How old is she?"

"Early twenties, but she seems older. And don't ask me what she's like. She's one of those girls that come to New York. You meet them all over the place and for a little while everyone thinks they're pretty good. I don't know much about her. Maybe her old man was a doctor or a lawyer or maybe he sold dry goods in Napoleon, Ohio. Whatever he did for a living, she's got enough background not to have to bother about it. Her name's Gail Beaumont."

"Is she married?" There was something irrevocable in knowing a name.

"Maybe she has been, but I doubt it. Right now she's on her own. She works for CBS and she got the job all by herself, so I understand." Sarcasm had found its way into his voice. He was very much himself again. "She writes programs about democracy. I heard one and I forget whether it was about Abe Lincoln or Thomas Jefferson, but it was a pretty slick job technically. Lousing up Lincoln and Jefferson is a new racket this year. There's not much money in it but it's got prestige."

Lucy waited while he talked and she said nothing when he

finished. As he continued to look at her the quality of his voice changed.

"Don't ask me what she's like because the only thing I know about her is that she's a smooth number and can look after herself. She may be sweet and lovely in bed or she may be a combination of Van de Velde and *The New Republic*. I wouldn't know."

Lucy was suddenly afraid she was going to cry. To do so would be an unbearable humiliation in front of Carl.

"I'm throwing a party next week," he said. "Cocktails on Thursday in my apartment. You've been to hundreds of them and this is just another. Why don't you come in for it? Everybody will be there."

"No," she said quickly. "I couldn't."

"Think it over. You ought to see for yourself. Hell, she isn't Madame du Barry. She's just another girl who came to New York."

She tried to keep herself from saying it, but her lips moved automatically. "If he just goes to bed with her I don't care, but – do you think he's in love with her?"

"How do I know? They're always in love with somebody." His eyes became as cruel as a cat's. "Love, for Christ's sake! The opium of the people and Hollywood knows all about it. A jerk has no brains so give him love and it doesn't matter. A guy takes a look in the glass and maybe for once in his life he gets the right idea about himself. So he falls in love and he thinks he doesn't stink any more. Do you find people like my mother around these days? Do you find her any place that counts?" He got to his feet again, his wiry shoulders tense under his neat tweed jacket. "Right up to the end she let my old man go on thinking he was a big shot who could save humanity if humanity would only listen to him. Old Jan Bratianu who used to give the neighbourhood kids ice cream on hot nights while my mother was wearing out her eyes sewing indoors. There was an Irish priest who knew my old man was a socialist but he used to say that God was in him just the same, and the old man swallowed it whole! Once –" Carl's voice dropped so low she could hardly hear him. "Once in Rumania – I don't remember but my brother told me – once in Bucharest the dope got himself locked up for passing out revolutionary leaflets and my mother worked as a whore to keep us fed and have a couple of rooms waiting for him when they let him out. And she wasn't soft, either. She was as hard as a rock. Those are facts, God damn it, and I'm not making them up. Is that love or do you want a new name for it?"

Lucy wondered as she listened if he was telling her anything new about himself or if she had always known it: the lonely, undersized foreign boy transferring to the New World the hatreds of the old. Then she thought of Stephen again and knew just how frightened she really was.

BRATIAN'S cocktail party on the following Thursday was neither better nor worse than other such parties Lucy remembered at his place. The people he asked to his place were either successful or intellectual, sometimes they were celebrated, and seldom were they common in the ordinary sense of the word; yet the atmosphere of the ensemble was always oddly promiscuous. This afternoon Lucy arrived late and when the junior of Carl's two Filipino servants showed her into the living room the noise of seventy people yelling at each other hit her ears like a rolling broadside.

While she was looking around for someone she might know Bratian appeared with a blonde at least ten inches taller than himself who seemed to be under the impression that being his friend of the moment involved her in the duties of being his hostess as well. After Bratian had introduced her, she said to Lucy, "Now be sure to meet the guest of honour. He's over there by the piano, but he seems pretty busy."

Lucy looked in the direction indicated and saw a tall man standing with his back to the room making sculptural motions with long brown hands before Bratian's Rouault.

"He's terribly clever. He's an Englishman and he helped plan the invasion."

"He's a stupid bastard of an Austrian and he wants to sell me a new picture," Bratian said. To Lucy he added, "I haven't seen you in city clothes for over a year. You look like a million."

"But Carl," the girl protested. "I *know* there's an Englishman somewhere."

"There are several, darling." He put his hand under the girl's elbow as though displaying her to Lucy. "Myrna wants me to get her a job with Harry Luce. Do you think it would make any difference?" He gave Lucy another long and approving look as the blonde drifted away. "Well, my dear?"

"Well, Carl?"

"I'm glad you changed your mind. It was the smart thing to do. Suppose you make your own way around the room. Half the people here don't know each other and most of them would hate each other if they did."

He moved toward the door to greet a newcomer and Lucy turned to face the sea of spring hats with men's heads sticking up among them like islands. Small clusters of people were talking intimately around the fringes of the room.

"Martini, manhattan, daiquiri, or whiskey sour?"

The senior Filipino in Bratian's service was smiling before her with a tray held elbow high. She took a martini, sipped it, moved on with it in her left hand, and was immediately confronted by a distraught young man who informed her he was an expert on Czechoslovakia.

"For ten minutes I thought I was talking to the editor of *Foreign Affairs*, but do you know who he turned out to be?"

"No."

"I don't either. Why are all these people here?"

He moved on, leaving Lucy with the feeling that she had been asked a question of some profundity. She began to sort the faces, separating those who were familiar from those she had never seen before. There was no sign of Stephen.

"I tell you," a large man in a grey suit was saying to another who looked like his twin, "it's all a matter of know-how. Either you've got it or you haven't. Were you ever in Russia? You were? Then we're talking about the same thing."

She passed them unseen to starboard and then she was blocked by a group surrounding a young major with two rows of ribbons on his chest. She gathered from a question somebody asked him that he was just back from Europe and from the expression on his face that he wished he were still there. "But you'll love it in Washington," a young woman with hyperthyroid eyes was saying to him. "It's the purest Kafka!"

A woman with a vaguely familiar face spoke to Lucy. She had a mountainous bosom and would have looked like an earth mother if her face had not been lifted and she were not discussing Rorschach tests. A fresh-cheeked boy with a crew cut nodded to her and she remembered him as one of the bright college graduates who had moved from Yale into the agency; now he was in a captain's uniform and he was hobbling stiffly on a cane. Behind her the Austrian was gesturing truculently to a meek little woman in a ribald hat who nodded her head to his every sentence.

"The red dots on the forehead – there is from Rouault the attitude to pain. In America you have pain, but to it no attitude. So in America, no tragedy – no? In America you think that pain is something for foreigners only. Here you think to reform the pain in us, but this you cannot do." He looked at the woman accusingly. "For the next ten years there will be more pain in America than for the last hundred."

Lucy left the vicinity of the Austrian. Now her eyes were moving quickly from face to face. Which one of these women was the girl Stephen had found? Whoever she was, Lucy guessed she would not be discovered in the nondescript crowd in the centre of the room.

As her eyes turned to the stray groups clustered near the windows she saw Stephen appear through the door leading to the pantry. He had a glass in either hand and as he entered the room she pulled back into the lee of a large man who stood between them. But Stephen was not looking about the room; his eyes shot directly to the window nearest the bookshelves in the far corner. Lucy saw his face break into a smile as he went over and handed one of the glasses to the girl who was standing there alone. A single glance told Lucy that young as she was, she was the smartest woman in the room; a second glance that she was not beautiful or even particularly good looking. She was short, with wide shoulders and a slim figure. An almost Slavonic width of cheekbones increased the look of depth in her grey, intelligent eyes. As she said something to Stephen and followed it with a quick laugh, Lucy received an impression of tremendous vitality.

The room went out of focus and gradually cleared again. Lucy felt the need of steadying herself but she stood quite still where she was. Physical jealousy might come later; at the moment her mind was too alert for her senses to feel empirical pain. Across all the people between them she heard Stephen laugh, saw him turn with a glance of intimacy and fondness to which the girl responded. He looked very well this afternoon. The grey streaks in his tawny hair served to enhance the vitality he always radiated when he was happy or excited. Both of them, she thought, had questing faces.

For only a fraction of a moment Lucy watched them, yet it was time enough to make an inevitable comparison between this girl and herself. How dull and stale his wife must seem to Stephen now, all her lights and shadows explored, all her feelings and responses known, nothing left but his dread of hurting her. Lucy turned to look for Carl, saw him coming toward her through his thronging guests, and skirted a knotted group to join him.

"Your parties haven't fallen off in colour since I've been away," she said. She was pleased at the cool sound of her own voice. "I'm glad I came. And now I'm going, thank you."

Bratian looked at her closely. "Not yet," he said. "You're the most attractive woman in the room and I want you to meet some more of my guests."

He was looking over her shoulder and she knew that Stephen had seen her and was coming toward them. Carl was still talking to her but she had no idea what he was saying. Then she heard Stephen's voice. "Hullo, Lucy! I thought you'd turned Carl down on this party!"

She turned around. "I changed my mind." She was smiling with bright animation. "I had to get some things for the children that I couldn't find in Princeton. I called the office and they told me you were already here so I came along for half an hour before the next train."

The girl had followed Stephen across the room and now she was at his elbow. Without turning around he knew she was there.

"Lucy," he said. "I don't think you know Gail Beaumont?"

Gail extended her hand, and Lucy taking it learned that it was short-fingered, well-kept, and capable.

"I've heard a great deal about you from Carl." The girl's voice was warm, as Lucy had known it would be. "He's one of your great admirers."

Lucy smiled.

"It's a rare compliment, you know." She had a natural and very attractive laugh. "He thinks all the rest of us are phonies."

"As you are," Bratian said.

"There are lots of people here you know," Stephen said to Lucy. "Come along and talk to them."

"I've been talking to all sorts of them. Right now I'm talking to Carl." She turned to Gail Beaumont and smiled again. "I've been away from New York so long I'm finding this fun for a change."

Stephen was restless and Carl was watchful but the girl was completely at ease.

"Your husband has just been telling me about some of the things advertising could do if it ever grew up," she said. "And I've been telling him the same about radio. Such wishful-thinking for a Thursday afternoon in Beekman Place."

Stephen cut in, "You remember Leo Emerson, don't you, Lucy? I had lunch with him today. He's left OWI and he's going in with Jack Mansfield. As they say in the trade, when Leo builds something by himself it's the biggest thing since the Crucifixion, but when Leo and Jack get together you'll have to go back to the Immaculate Conception to beat them."

Lucy wished he would stop, for his own sake. She saw the familiar sardonic expression begin to form about Bratian's lips and then Stephen suddenly stopped talking as two men joined them. They were friends of Gail's, they were introduced, and conversation became general, with Gail the centre of attention. She talked well, with a light touch Lucy envied, mainly about her work and the people she knew. She called Norman Corwin and Orson Welles by their first names and Archibald MacLeish and E.B. White by their nicknames.

As Lucy listened to her, feeling tongue-tied and incompetent, she saw Gail Beaumont as a sort of end-product of all the battles for improvement in the lot of the female sex which had been waged over the past half-century. A generation ago a woman with her mind and lack of conventional beauty would have resigned herself to a career. But Gail had been brought up to believe she could have her cake and eat it too. She was too young to be a member of the well-meaning generation; here was none of the gay desperation which made Marcia so vulnerable. Gail had always known precisely what she was doing. She knew that in an age like her own, her morality would be judged by the kind of opinions she held. She knew how unsure most men had become, and as a concomitant, that vitality and confidence were worth more in a woman than any degree of beauty. Gail was one of a new species, a woman who took it for granted that she was as much superior to the average female in bed as she was better than the average male across a desk.

But even as her mind drew these generalizations, Lucy knew that it made little difference to her what Gail Beaumont was like in reality. The only thing that counted was what she seemed to be to Stephen, and his beliefs depended on his state of mind.

She heard Bratian say, "Why don't you stay in town for the night, Lucy?"

"I'd love to, but I promised the children I'd be back by nine."

"What's more, you also promised Shirley. But you can phone her. Tell her to stay all night. We can have dinner as soon as this mob clears out. For that matter, we can go away and leave them."

"Thanks just the same, Carl, but I can't manage it this time. Are you coming home tonight, Stephen, or staying in town?"

"Damn it, I've got to work tonight."

Did she only imagine that a smile touched Gail's mouth? She said goodbye to Carl and thanked him, smiled once again at Gail and the men who were standing just behind her, and passed through the room, knowing that Stephen was following her. The elevator opened into a private foyer and while they waited for it Stephen put his arm about her waist.

"You're looking swell. You ought to come into town more often. If you'd told me you were coming in today I'd have made arrangements for you to stay the night."

"What difference would it make if you have to work?"

"It's a hell of a life we lead, isn't it?" He dropped his arm as he heard the sign of the rising elevator. "How are the kids?"

"They're fine."

The elevator stopped, the door opened, and he followed her into it. As it began to descend he handed her a copy of *The Reader's Digest* which he had been carrying in his pocket.

"You might like to read this on the train. It's got the article on Myron Harper – the one you helped me with." A frown rutted his forehead. "Things are jamming at the office. We're working harder than ever but everyone of us knows that the minute the war ends the Harper account will go with it. Of course, the Privateer has definitely shortened the war, and if it hadn't been put inside the public imagination – well, the harder you work the surer you are of putting yourself out of a job."

They stepped onto the marble floor of the entrance hall surrounded by wallpaper that represented a hunting scene on the banks of the Hudson a century ago.

"I liked the girl you introduced me to," Lucy said, not looking at him. "What was her name – Gail Beaumont?"

"She's all right, isn't she? Only twenty-four and she's had several original shows on the air already. She worked up the continuity and sound effects on the program we did for Harper last fall, too."

The air in Beekman Place was warm and fresh. A taxi rolled up to the canopy and stopped in answer to Stephen's signal, he kissed Lucy as he held the door open for her, she stepped in, and he told the driver to go to Penn Station. Lucy waved to him as the car drove off, then leaned back in the shadows of the tonneau and closed her eyes.

How had it come about that she was part of a situation so stale, so ridden with clichés? A set routine had been outlined for it long ago. All four of them – Carl, Stephen, Gail, and herself – had played their parts automatically. They had been so civilized, so modern. They had said or done nothing to break the smooth acceptance of a primal injustice so vast no woman since the beginning of time had ever been able to remove it. A man could act as Stephen was acting now and be fairly sure of losing nothing so long as he stayed within the accepted pattern. If his wife wished to retaliate she would lose everything she had left merely by trying.

The taxi worked its way across town in the early evening traffic. When it came to a stop behind a line of cars held up by a red light on Fifth Avenue Lucy leaned forward and asked the driver to let her out. The man clicked off his meter, she got out, leaving *The Readers Digest* on the seat, fumbled in her bag, paid him, and walked away.

Now she was alone in New York; for almost the first time since leaving Grenville she felt she was alone in a foreign city in a strange land. She crossed the street and drifted northward. Couples were moving on the avenue, so glad to be alive and together their gladness filled the air. There were more single men and women on the street than couples, but she saw only those who were together. She turned into the mall at Rockefeller Center and saw that the blue hyacinths and yellow forsythia were back for another spring. She walked through the mall, skirted the sunken pond and went into the R.C.A. Building, down the stairs to the telephones, and there she called home to tell Shirley she would be back on a later train. Shirley didn't want to stay.

"Please do it this time," Lucy said. "I'll pay you overtime and you can have Saturday off this week."

Shirley agreed to stay.

Back in the street again Lucy began to wander with the air cool on her cheeks, hardly knowing where she was or what she was doing, knowing only that she was unfit to go home and talk to John and Sally as she always did before they went to sleep.

She found herself in a line that was forming up for the Music Hall and she stood passively while people continued the line behind her. Images shot through her mind like bursting lights. Stephen's voice was in her ears repeating to Gail the same words he had so often used to her. With diabolical clarity she saw the expression that would appear on his face as he made love to the girl, and for a moment her imagination became so violent it made her whole body quiver as it built up a montage of scenes, natural as health were she a part of them, obscene and terrible and unjust when they were of Stephen and Gail.

She slipped out of the line and walked rapidly around the whole of Radio City until she was back again in the plaza. Again the eternal couples were moving in the spring evening, but now their happiness was intolerable. She crossed Fiftieth Street and made her way to the Embassy Theater where she sat for half an hour watching newsreels. She saw a Japanese soldier leaping like a human torch from a gun pit with flames ripping the flesh off his naked shoulders and she saw the helmet and back of the Australian soldier who continued to spray him with burning oil. She saw Russians fighting over the rubble of a German town, the peasant faces and wide buttocks, falling and shooting, rising and shambling forward, and then all of them blotted out by a mortar burst which blasted rock and earth into the camera's lens. She took her eyes away from the screen and looked at the people sitting around her. Practically all of them were men. And why not? Why shouldn't men come to see the logical result of their activities? A group of Polish women replaced the Russians on the screen and the camera panned their faces: faces worn by age-old primitive work were here torn with agony as they fulfilled the function appropriate to them, for their slaughtered children lay in shapeless bundles at their feet. Even for this kind of tragedy there was a prescribed routine. Civilization had reached the point where its own death agony could be used as entertainment in a theatre.

She got up and left the movie house, and when she came out into the air it was almost dark. She looked up and tried to see the sky but found only a reflection of neon lights overhead. She was back in the place from which she had tried to escape, back in Rockefeller Center with its eternal couples and the solitary ones, while from high in the tower above the hyacinths and forsythia, Thursday night radio programs were leaping into space to make the nation laugh. A solitary man passed. Two soldiers walking together. A soldier and a girl. Then with a warm feeling of irrational pleasure she saw an airman with a Canada shoulder-flash looking into the window of a bookshop in the mall. She went to stand beside him, looked into the window herself, then turned and smiled.

"I'm a Canadian too," she said. "I hope you like New York."

He turned, another of the uniformed children. "It's wonderful, ma'am. People are certainly swell to us down here."

"Are you a long way from home?"

"All the way from Alberta. You wouldn't know the town. It's a pretty small one."

"I'm from a small town, too. Grenville, in Ontario."

He grinned at her. "Well, I certainly know Grenville. I trained at the R.C.A.F. camp near there."

She said something else to him and then she was suddenly alone again. Had she sent the boy away? Or had he thought she looked too old to be interesting, said something polite the way the young do to older people, and slipped off? She realized now that she was homesick, homesick with a deep inner pain. She had often missed Grenville but she had never felt like this before. She wondered how Jane was tonight. It was Thursday and Jane would be alone in the old house. It would be cold up there, colder than here. Rotted ice would still lie in the ponds and the earth and trees would be bare and stark, the sun warm in the afternoons, while in the nights the cold air would suck down from the tundra and stiffen the softened earth in farms and gardens.

Could she ever go home again? To go back to Grenville would be a return to nothing. What had she ever done in Grenville but grow a garden? She had made nothing good of her life in Grenville and her life down here was over. So she had failed. But had she? For a while at least she had lived. Had any woman failed if she had two happy children? To love them, to tell them the truth as one knew it, to keep them till they wanted to leave – and then to sit back, to withdraw from their lives, to let them make their own mistakes while one grew old knowing one's importance was over. And then to watch the same process repeated again by them, each adding something to the sum their parents had accumulated, the town where they lived slowly growing into a wider graciousness, the generations dependent on one another as the seasons of the year are dependent. Without such a surety where was a woman's value or dignity?

She watched the water streaming in a repeated series of silver curves from the mouths of the dolphins among the hyacinths. She looked back and up to the R.C.A. Building, clean and cold as a sword. What century did she think she was living in? No wonder Stephen had gone to Gail! His wife was an anachronism. Why try to hold a family together when the best brains in the world were working night and day to rip families apart?

Water continued to stream from the dolphins, as cold as the silver bracelets on her arms that Marcia had given her last Christmas. What had Marcia been talking about the last time they met? A Christmas party at a school where Marcia had gone with one of her friends. Marcia had used all her talent for mimicry as she recounted a dialogue she had overheard between two children during the reception in the school gymnasium.

"But you called him your daddy!"

"I know, but he's not my real daddy. My real daddy's over there with Betty's mother, but he's not Betty's real daddy even if he is Betty's mother's husband. He's just her new daddy."

Lucy turned and began to walk rapidly out of the mall onto Fifth Avenue. Oh, no, she whispered, not that! John and Sally must never be allowed to think such a thing as that. She stood at the curb and hailed a cab, and this time remained in it until she reached Pennsylvania Station. She walked through the concourse and found a seat in a coach just before the Philadelphia train pulled out.

Her mind was cooler now, it was back at the old female job of sorting out the gains and the losses. If she made an issue with Stephen over the Beaumont girl, what would be the good of it? If she let him see that she knew, she would hurt his pride, would make him feel less confident than ever, and Gail would immediately become all the more necessary to him. It was his pride, she told herself again and again. His male pride, exasperated by the continued frustration caused by the war and his business. If it hadn't been Gail it would doubtless have been someone else. He was forty, and in the accepted pattern he felt his youth slipping away. Perhaps all he wanted was a fling, a woman who could take him lightly for a time and give him a new sense of himself as a man.

She would be a crowning fool, Lucy decided, to let him see that she knew about this affair. One of the things he already resented in her was the fact that he felt she knew more about him than he knew himself. No, she told herself! No! A woman was a fool if she assumed that her marriage was wrecked the first time she discovered that her husband had committed adultery.

And yet Lucy knew as surely as she breathed that it would be impossible for her to live long in a state of suspense and dishonesty.

The train moved out of the tunnel into the factory wasteland, a million lights twinkled like stars in a sky turned upside down. A strange and unnatural lightness replaced the desperation Lucy had felt when she was alone in the city. At Newark the coach began to fill and the other half of her seat was taken by a soldier whose medal-ribbons proclaimed him a veteran from Europe. She had no wish to talk to him when he asked her a casual question, but he was too eager to share his excitement with someone to notice her withdrawal. He told her he had just returned to the United States that day on leave and was on his way home.

The train crashed through a station without stopping and a queer look crossed the soldier's face.

"Metuchen!" he muttered. "Were you ever in that town?"

"Never, I'm afraid."

"Isn't it a funny thing? You go over this line maybe three hundred times but you never know what kind of a place Metuchen is." He laughed. "Did you ever hear of a place called Saarlautern in Germany?"

"I think so. I'm not sure."

"Well I was there about a month ago for a couple of hours – we were working the streets, see? I got cut off and I sure thought I was going to stay in that Kraut town for keeps. Do you know what I kept telling myself all the time? I kept telling myself that if I ever got home alive the first thing I was going to do was to go and see what Metuchen looked like. Can you beat it?"

"Do you still want to see it?"

"No. It don't mean a thing any more."

The train banged across a set of points and rushed into thick darkness. It was bright as they went through New Brunswick and then it was dark again, and the soldier kept on talking and Lucy scarcely listened. As they neared Princeton Junction he got up and stretched his arms to the duffle bag he had put on the rack overhead.

Lucy looked up. "Getting off here?"

"Yes, ma'am, this is home." He swung his bag to the floor of the aisle and leaned against the seat. "And my folks don't even know I'm back in the country. I got a lucky break and came over in a B-24. This time yesterday I was in England."

The soldier's long body swayed under the yellow lights as the train slowed to a fast stop. Lucy rose and slipped the strap of her bag over her left shoulder.

"If nobody's meeting you perhaps I could drive you home?" she said. "My car's in the parking lot."

"That's mighty nice of you, but it's farther out of your way than you think. My folks live outside of Princeton. It's Hunter's farm, off the Trenton pike."

Lucy smiled at him for the first time. "How nice! Your father happens to be one of my best friends, and you're Jim, of course."

As they drove along Nassau Street and out the Trenton pike the sky was filled with stars and a young moon was setting in the trees. Lucy turned into the Hunter farm and drove away again before Sam and his wife could see her and be forced out of politeness to let her intrude on the boy's homecoming. As she closed her own garage door on the station wagon some of the strange lightness was still with her. She spoke briefly to Shirley who was sitting by the door with her scarf tied around her head and was gone before Lucy could do more than thank her for staying.

On her way upstairs Lucy heard a sound in the darkness and knew John was sitting up in bed in the nursery.

"Mummy, you promised you'd be back by nine," he said as she opened the door.

"I know, dear. But New York's such a big city I got lost for a time."

"I got lost this afternoon, too, but only for a little while."

"Did you? Well, go back to sleep now and in the morning I'll tell you something wonderful."

"Tell me now."

"Well, maybe just a little bit of it now. I met Mr. Hunter's son on the train, and –"

"The one that's in the Airborne?"

"I suppose that's what he was in. Anyway, I drove him home. He'd just come all the way from England in an airplane. Yesterday he was in England and now he's home on the farm."

"Did he come in one of Daddy's planes?"

"I'll tell you all about it in the morning."

"Promise, Mummy?"

"Promise."

She touched her fingers to his lips, looked into Sally's crib and saw she was sleeping quietly, then closed the door of the nursery and went into her own room. Where were they now, she wondered. In Stephen's apartment or in Gail's?

THE days passed somehow and grew warmer. It was the spring for which more than a billion people had been waiting for over six years. Any hour now American and British armies would make contact with the Russians in Germany. The nightmare created by a generation of technicians in temporary collusion with a madman was nearly over, and for this little while the world seemed to be wide awake, like a fever patient between dreams.

Lucy found herself thinking back to the early days of the war when Canada was in it and the United States was not. She remembered the weeks of the London Blitz, the feeling of exposure it had given her, as though the solid floor of her own spiritual past had collapsed and left her dangling over a void. She remembered the jolt to perspective when she discovered that Americans had come to think of England as an outpost, the way the British, only yesterday, had thought of Poland and even of France.

Alone with the children in Princeton, Lucy began to wonder if one of the causes of her failure to hold Stephen's love might not simply be the fact that he was an American and she was not. The war did queer things to everybody, made them exaggerate themselves, made them take an unnatural view of strangers. Had she as a Canadian, raised in a small country which once had believed the United Kingdom to be the centre of the world, failed to understand what this terrific spectacle of rising American power meant to someone like Stephen Lassiter? A man could be conscious of it without being a politician. The sense of this power was everywhere. During the Depression it had slept like a hibernating animal grunting and tossing in its cave, but now it was striding forth, darting its eyes backward and all around, insensately loud and proud in exact proportion to its haunting knowledge that the greater it grew the more certain it was to lose forever the freshness of its youth and the very innocence which had made America unique.

But Stephen was her husband. What was manufactured nationalism compared to all they had shared together?

Yet there was definitely some place where she had made a mistake. There was her longing for stability, which meant little or nothing to him. She had come slowly to realize that contentment, which would have meant everything to her, was boring to Stephen, and she wondered if almost any American woman would not have been able to accommodate herself better to his inner restlessness. To Lucy it often seemed a hard thing to be an American; harder than to be anything else. In a small country, contentment was easier to achieve because there were always limits. In America there were no limits, or none that Stephen had ever recognized. Apparently he had always expected something new around every corner and had been reared to consider himself a failure unless he found it: more money to make, more ideas to try out, more women to sleep with, more rules to smash, more impossibilities to make commonplace. Part of her failure lay simply in her incapacity to keep him amused, in not being able to feel enthusiastic about the kind of success he had made, in not sharing the same values. And yet – what did Stephen really want now? She didn't know. Worse still, he didn't know either. From what was he trying to escape? From his own inner sense of failure? But failure to do what?

In the middle of the week following her trip to New York, Stephen surprised her by coming home to spend a night. She found him much quieter than usual and his manner cautioned her to forget her half-formed idea of talking things out with him and perhaps reaching something approaching an understanding. He took only a short drink before dinner and then insisted on going upstairs to put Sally to bed. She left him alone with the child in the nursery while she worked in the kitchen. After dinner he spent half an hour on the lawn behind the house tossing a football to John, teaching him how to hold it if he wanted to throw a forward pass and how to catch it by taking it against his chest and clasping it there with his hands and forearms. Stephen was quieter and more patient than usual when John made mistakes, and John was excited and proud because his father had come home, so he thought, especially to play with him. They came into the house glistening with sweat and Lucy sent John to take a bath before he went to bed.

Afterwards when the house was quiet Stephen sat in his long chair and for twenty minutes said nothing while Lucy sat at her desk and worked on her account books, hardly conscious of the figures her pencil made. She knew he was watching her, and once she looked up and smiled at him, but he seemed not to see her. She finished making entries, put her papers into a drawer, then picked up a book and moved to another chair. Stephen was still watching her.

As she opened the book to find her place he said, "You remember Austie Phillips, don't you?"

"Yes, of course." Austin had been a classmate and close friend of Stephen's. She remembered him as a scientist of brilliance, with wonderful eyes and a happy laugh.

"He was killed day before yesterday. In the beginning of the war he refused to work on a scientific job. They wanted him to develop a new fluid for flame-throwers. He pulled wires until he got into the army and I don't think he was physically A-1, either." He stared straight ahead. "In town they're already talking about another war. What's the matter with us?"

There was another long silence and finally he got up and filled his pipe, moved across the room, lifted the silver cigarette box he had won in a tournament nearly twenty years ago, held it to the light, and set it down again.

"Everything seemed so damn simple when I was playing for that."

He returned to his chair; and his restlessness, unaccompanied by any nervous gesture, was like a third person in the room. Lucy tried to hold his eyes, to ease his tension with a reassuring smile, but he refused to look at her unless she was looking at something else. So she went back to her book.

With a sudden movement he laid down his pipe and picked Lucy up in his arms, his forearm under her thighs, his hand under her hip. He kissed her fiercely and her arms went about his neck and stayed there as he carried her upstairs. In silence, and for the first time in weeks, he made love to her, holding her with a muscular fierceness so unlike him that it frightened her. Taken by surprise, she responded with a sort of blind desperation, her head thrown back, her eyes closed, her thoughts exploding in the darkness like sparks from a scattered fire. Afterwards he lay breathing heavily, separate from her, breathing as if his whole spirit had been poured out. She could feel the marks on her flesh where his hands had gripped her.

"Lucy?" he said in a heavy voice. And then, "Oh, Lucy!"

She reached out a hand to touch him. "Yes, darling – what is it? What's the matter? You're so unhappy." Her fingers followed the lines of his forehead, trying to smooth them out. "No matter what it is," she said simply, "don't ever forget that I love you."

She tried to draw his head against her breast, but he got up as if in pain and left her, put on his dressing gown and went downstairs while she continued to lie as she was and watch a patch of moonlight on the window-sill. From the sound of his steps she knew he was in the dining room. Then he moved to the living room and then there was silence.

She was in the nursery when she heard him start back up the stairs. She pulled a coverlet closer about John's chin, turned out the night-light, and tip-toed back to the door. Stephen's forehead was still wrinkled as he looked up at her from the landing.

"Everything all right?" he said.

"Yes, of course."

There was no intimacy in his voice, no hostility, nothing. He turned and went downstairs again, she heard the clink of a bottle against a glass and then his slippers shuffling toward the living room.

After a moment she went back to bed and turned out the light and lay in the darkness.

The following weekend Stephen did not come home at all. On Monday morning she called the office and the girl at the switchboard, recognizing her voice, put her through to him at once.

"Oh, Lucy!" he said, his voice showing his surprise. "I meant to call you Friday. I'm sorry, but –"

Not knowing why she did it, she hung up without speaking to him and sat still before the telephone, her hands and knees quivering with illogical anger. Now she let herself think about their last night together. It was as if he had come home to give her a final try-out, had gone back to New York and compared her with Gail, and then had tossed her into the discard. Not with calculation – oh no, not deliberately. When in his whole life had Stephen ever done anything with deliberation? The telephone rang in her face while she sat looking at the instrument and she let it ring. It rang again while she was upstairs making the beds and she let it peal through the house. In the void of the following silence she had a recollection that the same thing had happened once before in her life. Or had it happened only in a dream? No, it was a pattern repeating itself. Seven years ago in Grenville the doorbell had pealed and echoed through the house while she sat in her father's chair in the living room, unable to make a move to answer it.

When she returned in mid-afternoon with the two children in the station wagon, her arms full of groceries, she found Stephen walking about the garden. She sent Sally with John to play at Sam Hunter's and then she entered the house, left the packages in the kitchen, and went up the stairs.

In the dining room Shirley could hear Stephen's voice overhead, explaining something over and over again. From Lucy she heard not a sound. In a few minutes Stephen came downstairs and phoned for a taxi and then strode out of the house, leaving the front door open behind him. Shirley went to close it, but before she did she watched him walking up the road to meet the taxi on the pike – a lonely, puzzled middle-aged man.

AT ANY moment now the war in Europe might end, and it was clear that it was not going to end as a human mission fulfilled but as a technical feat performed. The great voices, one by one, were beginning to fall silent. Roosevelt was gone, Churchill soon to retire from Downing Street by a will other than his own; these last great human voices which had been tempered in the sunshine of warm valleys no longer warmed the people or gave them a sense of fellowship with an older, richer, and mellower age. In the new tones arising was the chill of the ice-cap.

On the first Saturday afternoon in May, Marcia and Lucy were sitting in garden chairs behind the house with the sun warm on their faces while Sally played in a sandpile in a corner of the garden and in the centre of the lawn a robin hunted for worms. John had gone to the Hunters' farm.

Marcia knew Lucy had heard scarcely anything she had said for the past half-hour, but she kept on talking just the same. "– and the puritans made us *live* with our guilt. They shamed us with our own humanity. For three hundred years we've lived on this continent in that same puritan tradition without ever knowing ourselves forgiven, and that's why we've become so callous and hard and rebellious. Even when we no longer believe in the God of our ancestors, the old guilt-habit stays. That's the trouble with Steve and I know it's the trouble with me – trying to run away from ourselves, not by finding something better but just trying to escape. Three hundred years of unspent pleasures in the bank, and every one of us thinking we had the combination of the vault."

She watched Sally throwing sand at the robin. "Sondberg showed me all the reasons why I'd made such an awful mess of my life by letting my subconscious bring it all to the surface. Finding out was supposed to cure me, but my analysis didn't work out that way. I felt as though I'd been passed through a wringer, saturated with perpetual burning sweat, and finally dropped with a thud in a cold, wet room. What good did it do me to find out I'd wrecked my life because I'd been resentful of my father for being a bully and hated my mother for the way she always got what she wanted out of men by flattering them? I longed to have men like me, too, and at the same time I subconsciously hated them. You know the way it works." Her eyes kept straying off to Sally as she talked. "And the times we're living in don't help much, either. When history acts like a Rotarian on a drunken jag, how can anyone sublimate his impulses in constructive work?"

Lucy turned to look at her sister-in-law and Marcia thought perhaps she had begun to listen.

"What I couldn't reconcile myself to was the waste. Suppose Sondberg had cleared up all my complexes – still there was the waste. More than thirty years wasted. God, Lucy – thirty years of nothing but harm! Some psychoanalysts still believe in religion, but he doesn't. He told me any religious impulses I had were simply a residual desire to return to the security of my mother's womb, and I told him that was the very *last* place I wanted to go. So I asked myself, if a psychoanalyst is as much a materialist as his patient, what's the good of going to him? It's like being sick from a drop of prussic acid and trying to cure yourself by swallowing the whole bottle. Sondberg left me with the unpleasant knowledge of the contents of my subconscious, and nothing else. If a man drives his car into a brick wall it doesn't help him to be told afterwards that his brake-bands were no good."

Sally toddled into the centre of the lawn with two fistfuls of sand which she tried to throw at the robin. The bird flew away and the child stood looking at it with round eyes, then looked at her mother, and went back to the sandpile.

"Then I went to work in the hospital. Every single patient in the wards was far worse off than I was and yet they seldom pitied themselves and sometimes they got well simply because they had to, for the sake of their families. You see, they had an aim. And I loved them for their dignity." She looked at her sister-in-law. "The same kind of dignity you have, Lucy, though yours shows itself in different ways. Are you listening to me? I wish you would."

She waited and the cessation of her voice made Lucy turn and look at her. "I haven't told this to anyone else and I think it's rather important," Marcia said.

Lucy's head was resting against the back of the chair and her eyes seemed engrossed by a great white cloud that was floating across the sky.

"I met Father Donovan in the wards," Marcia went on, speaking more quietly. "He's such a tough-looking man, apart from his eyes. His eyes are wonderful. You'd have thought he'd despise someone like me, but he didn't."

She knew Lucy was listening now. "I remember the first time I met him. I was in the military hospital then and Father Donovan had come to give a boy who was dying the last rites. It was a Sunday and I went to church that evening for the first time in years and years. It was an Episcopalian Church. I don't know why I happened to choose it unless it just happened to be near. Ordinarily I don't like Episcopalians – they seem so neat and respectable and far from the people. But that night something happened to me. They read that Psalm from their Prayer Book – 'But no man may deliver his brother, or make agreement unto God for him.'"

She stopped talking and waited until Lucy met her eyes. "I knew God was talking directly to me," she said. "And I knew the trouble with all of us is that we're trying to save ourselves by denying that simple fact. No *man* may deliver another from evil – only God can do it. And all of us keep right on killing ourselves by the sin of pride, all of us claiming we have a monopoly on deliverance – communists, socialists, democrats – all of us playing at being God."

Her voice was almost a whisper when she went on. "After that night I began taking instruction from Father Donovan. And last week I was admitted into the Church."

Lucy was studying Marcia now. In her expression she saw genuine contentment. "I'm so glad," she said. "It's good to have one of us happy at last. I'm really very happy for you."

Tears showed in Marcia's eyes and she blinked them away. "It's no good telling Stephen. He'd only mock me. But I wanted to tell you. I thought, somehow, I might be able to help you. Only you're so – so proud and Protestant. Father says that the only morality Protestants understand any more is pride in being able to take it. You know, like Humphrey Bogart or Alan Ladd. And that's so barren – that good old American virtue of being able to take it on the chin. If you'd only let yourself go, Lucy! Let your emotions flow out and God will understand even if nobody else does. You've been hurt and you're bitter and you're too proud even to allow yourself to cry or talk about it."

Lucy let her gaze go to a green copse on a distant rise of land. As Marcia went on talking her mind began forming another picture: three hundred years ago in a Suffolk village the first American ancestor of Marcia and Stephen, plain and hard-handed, refusing to doff his cap to the squire, obsessed by the conviction that if he allowed any authority to stand between himself and his God his soul would be irrevocably lost, going down by night to the tidewater with a few other stubborn, proud men like himself, secretly boarding the tiny, worm-eaten vessel, with scurvy and months of the Atlantic and years of the wilderness before them – but in the mind of that ancestor the beacon words which had brought Martin Luther face to face with Charles the Great and had fired a handful of peasants and craftsmen to open and break a new continent" – "Here I stand alone. So help me God, I can do no other!" And now after three centuries, as though a fire which had lighted the world had suddenly gone out, Marcia had renounced all that her forebears had stood for by going back to incense and authority and the high altar, led by an Irish priest from the streets of New York.

Turning her eyes back to Marcia's face, Lucy knew that her act had been inevitable, for Father Donovan was the only person Marcia had met in her whole life who had given her hope.

"I can't bear to have you grow bitter," Marcia was saying. "When you first came down here, and especially after John was born, you had something I've never found in anyone else. If it hadn't been for you I don't think I'd have been ready to listen when I met Father Donovan. You have a quality in your nature that I can't help thinking of whenever I try to understand what the Church means when it talks of grace."

But Lucy was no longer with her and Marcia knew it. Still, she had to finish what she had come to say.

"Steve's a fool and he's weak and he's acting like a heel, but he's a lost man if you don't stand by him, because you're the only decent thing he's ever had in his life. At least he recognized the goodness in you when he met you. And perfect people don't need help, Lucy."

A wistful expression appeared to cross her face. "You know, you have to be very wrong, you have to wound yourself and be completely lost and abandoned and then forgiven before you can see God. When you're in the depths – when the very thought of yourself disgusts you – when you feel yourself trapped at the bottom of a deep, slimy well – that's when a miracle can happen. You see a patch of light a long way off and the light spreads and becomes golden and the sun rises and you look around and suddenly you realize it's a beautiful morning." She hesitated and her voice was like a schoolgirl's. "You know – I used to be far worse than Stephen."

But Lucy was still incapable of talking about Stephen to anyone, even to Marcia who had become her best friend.

"It's not that I've stopped loving Stephen," she said. "It's just that he doesn't want me. It's as simple as that and I haven't yet found a way to live with that fact."

"I don't believe it, you know. He still loves you as much as he ever did."

"He's afraid of hurting me. And that's not the same as love."

"Has he asked for a divorce?"

Lucy gripped the arms of her chair and closed her eyes. "No. He just doesn't come home any more. I stay here with the children because I don't know what else to do."

"If he doesn't come home it's only because he's ashamed of himself. He's accustomed to women who throw hysterics and tell him loudly and specifically what they don't like about him. Mother was that way and so was Joyce. Your silence makes him more ashamed than they ever did or ever could."

"Please, Marcia – l don't want to talk about it. I know I've failed him, somehow, but I can't change my own nature, any more than he can change his. Yet if I knew what the real trouble is I'd do anything on earth to help get rid of it. Sometimes I think he's just fallen mechanically into the routine so many men of his age follow in New York. Sometimes I think there's a drive in his subconscious that makes what he's doing now a real necessity to him. If that's so, I'll have to learn to live without him. But I'm not sure. I'll have to be sure before I'll know what to do."

Marcia looked at her closely. "You'd be sure if you'd known Mother. Steve's been hunting female approval ever since he left home. He got it there, but only on and off."

"Do you really believe it's as simple as that? Because I don't."

"Look at that gang he works with! Steve's the kind of man who has to be liked by everyone around him, and the only way to make a heel approve of you is to be more of a heel than the rest of the crowd." She answered Sally's wave by raising her arm over her head.

"Damn us Americans! Why do we have to insist on everyone's liking us no matter what kind of people they are?"

Sally came across the lawn toward them, a snail held out on the palm of her hand. It was moist, pinkish white with a blob of wet earth on its shell. She presented the snail to Marcia with a smile, and Marcia explained what it was and how long it took a snail to move from place to place and what its shell was for. Sally listened intently and then returned to the sandpile, taking the snail with her.

For several minutes neither woman spoke. Then Marica's face brightened. "Do you remember the time your friend from Grenville, Bruce Fraser, came to New York?" she asked.

Her choice of a change of subject made Lucy smile, made her think, too, that Marcia's essential nature had changed less than Marcia believed it had.

"You mean that night we all went to dinner and he drank too much?"

"Did he? It was such a heedless night. My second-last night as a practising pagan. Bruce helped me, you know. But that wasn't what I was thinking about. I was remembering that it was the night he fell in love with you."

Lucy felt laughter rising in her throat, and surprisingly it was warm and good. "With me? But Marcia, Bruce has known me all his life!"

"What if he has? That night he fell in love with you. I saw it happen."

"He was excited at being in New York, that was all. Every thing Bruce feels shows in his face."

Marcia looked down at her hands; they were no longer milk-smooth and cared for, but hard and competent as a kitchen maid's. "I saw him the next night, too, you know. And being the bitch I was, I seduced him."

Lucy accepted the confidence with no outward emotion. "Did you? I'm rather glad for his sake. Do you ever hear from him now?"

"No, I'd be the last person in the world he'd write to. I spoiled something for him. I spoiled the way he was thinking about you and then he blamed himself rather than me. Strange people you are – both of you. Are you all like that where you come from – shy and self-critical and under the surface as passionate as hell? How old is he now?"

Lucy thought a moment. "Thirty-one."

"And he's the kind of man who could never possibly be converted to the Church."

Lucy laughed again. "You're right about that."

"Oh, well, I wasn't serious. He's thirty-one and I'm thirty-six and don't I ever look it!"

She did look it. The excitement and lost sleep of her twenties had recoiled on her, and the war work and long hospital hours had added further marks of their own. Her black hair was no longer glossy and there were lines about her eyes and mouth, though she was still a handsome woman. Lucy thought the most noticeable change in Marcia had taken place when she stopped dressing to attract attention.

She got up from the white garden chair and stretched in the sun, holding her arms wide as if to clasp the whole garden and countryside within their circle.

"We should see more of each other," she said. "You and I get on so terribly well. It's a grim world when people who like each other never see each other any more and those who loathe each other can't get out of sight. I'll tell you what let's do – you never use half your gas ration. Let's take the station wagon and go over Washington's Crossing and up the other side of the Delaware. We can have tea or something in Lumberville. I used to know a lovely place there. We can get back by dark. Let Shirley give the children their supper."

"All right," Lucy said. "That sounds a fine idea."

She went into the house for the car keys, came out, and spoke to Sally and handed Marcia a light coat. It seemed strange to be going off on an impulse like this; for days she had stayed close to the house in the hope that Stephen might call again.

As she opened the door of the garage Marcia looked at her strangely. "Tell me something," she said. "Do you ever hear from your older sister? She's still living in your old home, isn't she?"

"Yes." She hooked the door back against the wall and went in to the car. "I had a letter from her only a few days ago. It was the first she's written since I was married except for the letters she always sends at Christmas."

After Lucy had backed out, Marcia got into the car and slammed the door on her side. "Do you miss her very much?" she said.

Lucy made no answer as she swung the car about and headed up the road. Finally she said, "It must have been telepathy that made her write now. I've been thinking about her a lot lately. As Stephen says when I get on his nerves, the Scotch are a funny people."

Looking at the line of Lucy's jaw, Marcia thought she could imagine how Stephen must have felt about her sometimes. But while she looked, the lines of Lucy's face softened and her expression changed.

"I think Jane really wants to see my children," Lucy said.

RAIN was falling in New York. It was slapping the windows and washing off pavements into gutters, and as the Madison buses hissed to a stop at every other corner black clusters of people darted out of arched doorways of office buildings to crowd into them. In the Village the cobbles glistened darkly under the lights and a small fume of steam drifted over the open counter of a Riker's stand in Sheridan Square.

Stephen walked out of Gail Beaumont's apartment building and turned up his collar against the rain. His face looked haggard as he stopped under a light and struck a match to a cigarette. He flicked the match away, walked a block to the subway entrance, then tossed away his cigarette and descended. The platform was silent and empty and his wet feet made marks on the cement as he walked up and down waiting for the train. A hard rumble of moving steel poured out of the tunnel at him, he saw the lights of the train growing, and deliberately stood within two feet of the platform edge as it crashed by. The doors gaped open, he stepped in and slumped onto a wicker seat. It was a slack hour and the car he was in was almost empty. He laid his dripping hat on the seat beside him and looked up the car to a tiny old man asleep in the far corner. He wondered if the man were riding the subway simply to keep out of the rain.

Stephen leaned back and closed his eyes. Christ, of all the nights for Gail to run out of liquor! The train crashed onward uptown. Half a dozen people got out at Penn Station but Stephen did not open his eyes.

Was it Monday or Tuesday? It must be Monday. Then it was eight days since he had seen Lucy, and he couldn't have gone home over the past weekend if he'd wanted to. Without warning Myron Harper had summoned him to his place in Maryland on Friday and he'd phoned Lucy to tell her where he was going, but nobody answered the phone. Well, what difference would it have made if she had answered it? In her place he wouldn't have considered the Maryland story a likely one.

The noise of the train drowned out the sound of his heavy breathing. Why did a man always have to make his discoveries too late? This was his second marriage and it had taken him seven years to find out what was wrong with it. Lucy wasn't like Joyce. Joyce was a bitch and he'd been nothing more than a kid when he married her. Lucy was different. She was too good for comfort. And somehow or other she had worked her way right into his mind and there she sat watching, knowing what he was about to do even before he knew it himself, caring too much, wanting too much of him. And why?

The train slowed down for Times Square and he opened his eyes and got to his feet. No matter what he did, no matter how he lived, Lucy would have to learn to stand on her own feet and not pin her entire happiness onto him. No man could stand a burden like that. No man. Could he help being the kind of man he was? Was he worse than anyone else he knew?

The train stopped and he threaded the maze to the Grand Central shuttle. Ten minutes later he was riding up to his office in the elevator, joking with the operator, feeling a sudden lift of spirit as he realized that for three hours he would be alone, solitary with his work.

He unlocked the door of his private office, switched on the light, hung up his wet hat and coat, took off his jacket, loosened his necktie, and slumped into the chair behind his desk. Before him were piled the papers he had left there in the afternoon, reflecting light from a horizontal lamp.

He was glad to be alone.

He pulled open a drawer and took out a half-empty bottle of bonded bourbon. After unscrewing the cap he remembered that he had no glass and went out to the water cooler for a paper cup. He came back with three in each hand, the set in his left hand filled with water, each cup to within an inch of the brim. He poured himself a drink and tossed it off, refilled a cup and set it beside him on the desk. A warm glow began to radiate through him.

For three hours, broken only by the moments when he refilled a paper cup with whiskey and water, Stephen worked. His mind seemed to him to be clear and decisive, but when he finished the job he had set himself he felt drained. It was forty minutes past midnight. He rose and stretched, poured himself another drink and replaced the bottle in the drawer. The rain was still washing the windows and it still felt good to be alone. To hell with the war and to hell with everyone! Let them huddle like beetles in doorways to keep out of the rain. When you were alone you didn't care. That's what Carl was always talking about – he'd learned it young. When you were alone you were free. Only one night-shift elevator operator was in this whole building now, besides himself. To be alone, to be bound to nobody, to do what he liked and not have every swing counted for a strike-out!

He went out to the files in the outer office, hearing his shoes loud on the linoleum of the big room, and returned with a pile of back numbers of his own displays. He laid them on the desk and drank the whiskey that was left in the cup while he leafed through them, trying to recall the feeling of excitement that each one, at least at one stage of its development, had given him. It was strange that someone like himself could have turned into an able man at this kind of job. Carl insisted that no man chose his job; the job chose the man. But advertising wasn't his real job. He hadn't been selling the Privateer through his skill and ingenuity. Hitler had been its real salesman. He had merely been its celebrator, showing America what it meant to have citizens and techniques which could produce a plane of such power.

As Stephen continued to examine his past work a sense of disenchantment grew. These displays with their balanced legends, their over-simplifications, were an insult to the genius and mind-breaking work that Myron Harper and his men had put into their plane. He remembered the room in the Maryland plant where models of every fundamental part of the Privateer were laid out on plastic shelves and tables in order that engineers could pick them up and study them at will. Whenever there was a discussion involving the improvement of any part of the plane, Harper insisted on having a model of the part on the conference table. "Unless you can see and handle a thing," Harper said, "you can never understand it. You can never see how simple the problem is or how difficult it is. My business is making things, and things aren't made with ideas. They're made with hands or with the machines men have invented to take the place of their hands."

If only he had met a man like Myron Harper when he was twenty!

Stephen's mind veered back as it inevitably did to his part in the war. Well, there were others who had done less. It was something to have given the public at least a crude idea of what Harper had done for engineering and his country. No single aircraft in the United States Air Forces except the B-29s and the earlier Forts had become so well known as the Privateer and that was largely because of work done in this office. He loved those shark-nosed, deadly, beautiful instruments. And he knew them so well he could almost make a blueprint of one from memory. He knew how a good pilot would feel about his Privateer.

As he returned the displays to the files he wondered for the hundredth time what was going to happen to the account. The Privateer was already outmoded and Harper was talking about jets.

Maybe the real question was not what was going to happen to the account but what was going to happen to Harper himself. Give him another ten years like the past five and he would be producing guided missiles which could be sent from Maryland to Tokyo in a couple of hours. But the government would have to come through with some solid subsidies, or Harper would be finished just at the moment when he was ready to show the world what he could really do.

Well, no matter what happened to Harper, this account, bred of excess war profits, was living on borrowed time. When it was closed, could he stand working at the agency on a routine luxury account? He closed his eyes and yawned. Even the thought of it made him sick. What about the Shasta Dam job Lucy had wanted him to take? And leave New York? Exchange Shasta for Gail? What was the matter with New York, for Christ's sake? Was it his fault if Lucy hadn't been able to adjust herself to life down here? The United States set the pace for the world. The world could take it or leave it. He had to take it himself, didn't he? Gail had to take it.

God damn it, a hundred and forty million Americans took it – and liked it.

As he put on his hat and coat and snapped off the lights he knew he was tired and he also knew he would not be able to sleep for hours. He stepped into the elevator, dropped to the ground floor, and walked out into the rain. A few taxis were swishing up Madison and their sound made him think how wonderful New York could be on a rainy night when you were alone with the buildings in the long empty streets. He felt good again, eager to go somewhere and do something. What? It was too late to go back to Gail, for she was sure to be asleep already. He caught a taxi cruising downtown and gave the driver an address in the Village.

Was that actually where he wanted to go? It was a little place Gail had discovered, where Povey Bartt played the piano, with Eddie Soper on the clarinet and Sol Gold on the drums. The real music never got loose there until after midnight. Gail said Bartt's was a new kind of jazz – a genuine white man's jazz, she called it, close to the New Orleans idiom, but under Bartt's hands it came out differently. Stephen had been down there only once before and had annoyed Gail by talking while Bartt played. She insisted the man was as important an artist as anyone you could hear in a season at Carnegie Hall. And maybe she was right. Anyway, it was a good place to go now, a place to sit and be alone and have nobody bother him.

He paid the driver, went in, checked his coat at a hole in the wall where a dark face emerged from a faint yellow glow, and found a table near the band. The room was nearly dark, bare, ugly, and more than three-quarters empty on account of the rain. While he waited for his drink and a sandwich, a Negro improvised on the piano, playing an imitation Basie not quite good enough to pass for the original. Gail called this one of the places where the musicians worked for love and marijuana.

The Negro finally slid away from the piano and the white men came in one by one, settled themselves at their instruments and began to play, taking their time, feeling their way into the music. A waiter appeared with a drink and a sandwich, put them on the table, and Stephen began to eat, noticing little change in the music since the coloured man had left, apart from the support of the clarinet and drums. And then, so gradually it was something he felt in the pit of his stomach, felt it lying there alive and moving, the loneliness began.

He could hear it in the high trilling in the treble of Bartt's piano, the right hand poised like a five-beaked vulture over the same group of keys, endlessly poised while the left spent an infinite brooding patience as it beat out the rhythm, exploring fantastic harmonies which always promised to be something new but which always – cruelly, relentlessly, logically as fate – came back to where they had started as Bartt stripped away the delusion of hope and revealed that nothing had changed at all.

Stephen stared up at him, saw the man's eyes bright with marijuana, saw how he needed it, the relapsed ease it gave his whole body, saw how he used it and made it work for him, how with the drug he could accept what he was doing and love it.

The loneliness jetted out in piercing personal agony on Soper's clarinet. It was visible, it was something you could touch in the posture of Sol Gold crouched among his drums like a sharp-nosed animal confident in danger, the flaring lapels of his striped double-breasted jacket pointing upward to his narrow shoulders, the shoulders marking time in contemptuous nonchalance, vast Asiatic eyes deep and softly smiling on either side of his great hook of a nose.

Stephen finished his drink and beckoned the waiter for another one. He was mindless; the music had saturated him. Now every whorehouse and station hotel and backroom from Utica to Flagstaff was present in that half-dark box of a place, was displayed as if under glass in the arc-lighted bareness of Stephen's mind, every whorehouse, station hotel, and saloon in the dead hours of the morning when time stops and the continental night pales before the morning stars and the whistles of freight trains wail from town to town across the American plain. Cones of light shine down over the green baize of the crap game. Cones of light make the poker table a phantasmal altar. Rows of bottles brood behind the bar under the mirror that reflects *Custer's Last Stand* from the opposite wall, while the hard-faced men, every face with its own variety of the same expression, sit above shirt sleeves and loosened collars in organized disorder. They have been there for hours. A single waiter shuffles about soundlessly refilling their glasses, the dice rattle in the box, flash white on the green and stare up at the light with black eyes.

The cards shuffle, the spittoon splashes over. Upstairs the springs of three brass beds jingle steadily while a brakeman, a telegrapher, and a traveller in women's hosiery silently fornicate three girls whose names they do not know except by the framed pictures which hang above each bed – *September Morn, Rosebud, Salome.* Downstairs there is a roar as someone is given the hotfoot, a loose laugh, and through the light-cone at the card table a voice snaps, "Pipe down you sonofabitch." The door leading upstairs opens and the brakeman comes in; he looks relaxed and easy, pushes back a cowlick from a moist forehead and grins knowingly as he slumps over to the bar. His pants tighten across his fat buttocks as he sets his elbows.

Stephen closed his eyes and clutched the glass in front of him, lifted it and poured the rest of the drink down his throat, opened his eyes again and beckoned to the waiter. Then he stared straight ahead at the musicians as the waiter went off with the empty glass.

It is three o'clock in the morning. Where is it three in the morning, aside from a worn old song? Everywhere. The loneliness is all there is, Bartt's piano has captured it all and translated it into Stephen Lassiter's soul. It is three o'clock in the morning and suddenly the wooden timbers of the back room begin to tremble as a freight on its way from Evansville to St. Louis crashes through the town, the whistle wails four times for the crossing where the Ritz Cafe faces across Main Street to Hergesheimer's hardware, the empties rattle out of town and silence again, silence creeping like white mice out of the plain into the open streets of the wooden town. And at that moment an American boy looks up from the crap game with his hands in his empty pockets and a dream in his eyes. No words, he never needed them and he never will, only the dream in his eyes as he listens to the train and wishes to God he were with it, wishes he were out of this town and guesses it's time for the road again, maybe St. Louis, maybe Chicago, who knows but maybe New York itself, maybe this is the break, the apartment high above the Christmas-tree lights of Park Avenue and the limousine waiting below, the girl, and the top of the world.

From the piano Povey Bartt tells it all because he has seen it all already: the American boy with the dream in his eyes. Bartt sees him thirty years from now with the pouches under his eyes, without the dream but still with the hope, here in the same backroom on the fringe of the light-cone where the tobacco smoke is rising. And Bartt knows the skill of all these men and loves them for it: their skill with cards, with electric wires, with jumping pistons and turning wheels, their skill with anything lifeless their hands can touch, and he sees that their skill is part of the vastness of the continental loneliness that bred itself into the seed their fathers and grandfathers carried about from town to town along with the knowledge that there is nothing they or anyone else can do about it, nothing but what the freight train does, go on and on and on until it stops in another town exactly like the one it left. And Bartt loves them. He knows them and they know him, for he is with them and always has been, and without him where is their meaning? He was with them when the Conestoga wagons rolled westward out of Council Bluffs, he was down in the Lehigh Valley when Lil met Sawed-off Pete, he was in San Francisco when the earth trembled under the cribs. When the cops come in to break it up he will be there, his left hand weaving the heartbeat of the bass to the shrill pain of the quivering right, and his rhythm will continue as long as America does, for when he dies, another will be there in his place.

One close look at Povey Bartt shows he is dying now. He is small, hollow-chested, with high cheekbones and a flush over the bones, black hair parted in the middle but still stiff and untamed, his face a white and smiling triangle over the keys, over the gentle, wise brooding hands with the signet on the fourth finger of the left.

"Waiter, what time is it?"

"Four-twenty. It's four o'clock in the morning."

Stephen got to his feet and rubbed his eyes, staggered and leaned his head against the side wall. The beating in his head – was it the liquor or his blood pressure? Or was it that goddam music that never stopped?

LUCY lifted her head as she heard the carillon ringing in the tower of the Graduate College and she smiled because she recognized the tune it was playing, one of its old standbys – *The British Grenadier*.

She ran downstairs and turned on the radio to listen. The war in Europe was over. Hitler was dead.

"John!" she called. "John!"

He came running in from the kitchen. "Yes, Mummy?"

"Get Sally and come and listen. The war's over in Europe. Isn't it wonderful? It's a day you'll always remember."

In a few minutes John was back holding Sally by the hand, and they sat in front of the radio while Lucy listened to a news report. The network took them to London, to Paris, and back to Washington. Sally had no interest in what the voices were saying, but she watched John and her mother, and tried to imitate their rapt attention. A senator gave a patriotic address, a band played martial music, and in all the time they listened nobody mentioned the name of Canada.

"We always win, don't we, Mummy?" John said.

Lucy was startled by the significance of the pronoun, and her answering smile was for herself. Of course Americans always won and of course John was an American.

"Will Daddy come home today?"

"I don't know, dear. Perhaps he'll telephone. He's still very busy, you know. The war isn't over in the Pacific yet."

When John grew bored and Sally followed him out to the garden to play, Lucy felt an insistent longing to talk to someone. This was no day to spend alone. She wondered if it would be an impertinence to walk over to see the Hunters, but the moment she thought about it she realized they would be somewhere on Nassau Street by now. Should she get the children and drive into Princeton, too? But surely Stephen would come home, or at least call her on a day like this!

She telephoned Marcia and had to wait for nearly twenty minutes for the call to go through on the crowded switchboards. When she finally got the hospital she was told Marcia was not there.

"John!" she called at the side door. "Sally! Come on in and wash your hands. Let's go into town and see what's happening."

The children tumbled after each other up the stairs and she heard John talking excitedly in the bathroom while she brushed her hair in the bedroom. They all went down the stairs together and the two children climbed in beside her in the station wagon. As they drove out to the pike they met three soldiers on the corner and she stopped to offer them a lift. They were only boys, she realized when they clambered into the back seat, far more interested in talking to John and Sally than they were to her.

Even before she reached the war memorial she saw that Nassau Street was going to be crowded. She let the boys out and then had to drive more than a block down Alexander Street before she found a place to park. She walked slowly back toward Nassau Street through the campus with John and Sally following behind. An excited young naval ensign appeared in her path and threw his arms about her neck. He began to kiss her exuberantly as John and Sally stopped with their mouths open to watch. When he saw the children he drew back abruptly.

"Are these *yours?*"

"Yes." She smiled at him as she took one of the children by each hand.

He bowed with extreme dignity. "If I may say so, ma'am, you're very deceptive for the mother of two."

He accompanied her as far as the street, where he recognized a friend and left her.

Stephen ought to be here, she thought. Today of all days he should have come home. He'd love this. Will his not coming home today mean that he doesn't intend to come home at all?

But here on Nassau Street, surrounded by so many eager Americans united by common feelings and memories, Lucy began to feel herself an outsider, a stranger in a country she hardly knew at all. She began to wonder how Grenville was behaving today. The United States had passed through three and a half years of war. Canada had endured nearly six. Yet she knew as clearly as though she were there that the mood of Canada on such a day, no matter what its outward manifestations, would be different from the mood here. It would be more private. Canadians were probably the only people in the world who neither envied nor resented the United States. They knew that in the eyes of a powerful neighbour, a small country such as theirs seemed very much as a poor man seems to the rich. If he manages his own affairs and keeps quiet, he is dull; if he doesn't, he affords an opportunity for charity. The only possible way for a poor man or a small country to appear interesting is to commit a crime on a scale calculated to impinge on the rights of the rich. Lucy smiled to herself.

"Mummy, can Sally and I have an ice cream soda in Renwick's?"

"If we can get in we'll all have one."

She worked her way down the sidewalk, holding Sally by the hand while John darted ahead, but her mind was still far from Nassau Street. She could see Jane at the console of the organ in St. David's, striking the first chord for a "God, Our Help in Ages Past." She could hear Dr. Grant's voice recording the end of Hitler in cosmic terms: "O Lucifer, Son of the Morning, how art thou brought low to the ground!" She could see the veterans of the old war marching to the memorial, each with sons in Holland or Germany, each remembering personally those awful and legendary names which would always be a part of the texture of Lucy's childhood in Grenville – Vimy, Arras, Saint-Julien, Lens, Cambrai, and Passchendaele. At home today everyone in the church would know exactly what each family had gained or lost by the war, as people in a small place always do, and on a day like this some of their suppressed warmth would overflow. Princeton was a small town, too, but since the war it had become a town of strangers – the university filled with naval men from every state in the Union, houses filled with commuters who had been unable to find apartments in New York.

They reached Renwick's and managed to find seats near the door. As Lucy sat down she noticed one of Stephen's friends at the fountain. When he saw her he got up and came over.

"Where's Steve?" he said. "We're going to celebrate. Tell him to give me a call."

"It looks as if he got caught in New York and couldn't get out."

"Well, there's plenty of liquor in New York, but he's missing something if he doesn't get out here. This is a wonderful place, you know. If I could earn a living here you couldn't drag me into New York."

When they went out to the street again they stood on the curb and watched the crowds. A group had started to sing; and soon a whole section of Nassau Street was singing with them. This remarkable, unpredictable country, Lucy thought. It can change like lightning from cold and ruthless efficiency to open-hearted laughter and never consider itself inconsistent in the process.

With a child by either hand she began to thread her way across the street. Halfway across, a strange man picked up Sally and lifted her to his shoulder.

"On a day like this," he said, "there's nothing I'd sooner do than carry a little girl. Wish I had one just like her. Besides, she can see better up here."

He kept her on his shoulder all the way across the campus to the car on Alexandria Street, then touched his hat, and went back the way he had come.

"What shall we do now?" Lucy said to the children. "Drive around to the other end of town or go home?"

"Let's go home," John said. "Maybe Daddy will telephone to us."

She was preparing their lunch when the reaction set in. Suddenly she was depressed and lonely and some of her depression infected John while they were eating. She tried to smile and make him laugh, but John was so sensitive to the moods of his parents that concealment was of little use. What would happen in a year, or for that matter in a few weeks or months when he found out for himself the true situation in his own house?

For an hour after lunch Lucy occupied herself with the usual dreary routine of housework while the children took naps in the nursery. Her hands were in dishwater when she looked up and saw her face in the mirror that hung over the sink. The expression she encountered shocked her, and when the shock wore away she realized that she had reached her limit. Slowly and carefully she emptied the dishpan, cleaned the sink, and dried her hands.

"This is impossible," she said aloud. "It's stupid and degrading. What's the matter with me? I'm ashamed of myself."

As though the song she had heard the crowd singing in Nassau Street were still ringing in her mind, calling it forth from the numbness of the past weeks, clearing her thoughts for action, she was able to stand apart and look at herself with fresh understanding. A suggestion of a spontaneous smile moved over her lips. She stacked the dishes on a rack, poured steaming water over them, and walked out of the kitchen. She stood still in the hall for a moment, then went upstairs. In the bedroom she opened a drawer in her dressing table and took out a billfold. Nearly all the month's housekeeping allowance was in it still. Then she went into the nursery. John was sitting up in bed looking at a picture book and Sally was just waking out of her sleep.

"How would you like to go for a long drive?" she said, smiling at them. "A drive that would take maybe two whole days."

"Where, Mummy?" John dropped his book.

"How would you like to go up to Canada? You've never seen your Aunt Jane and she'd very much like to see you. We could leave this afternoon if we're quick about it. And drive up in the station wagon. Aunt Nina might even be there if she's out of the Navy. You'll like her."

"Will we see the lake? The one you told us about?"

"We'll live right beside it, almost."

"Is it really and truly bigger than Lake Carnegie?"

"It's so big you can get into a ship and sail straight out from Canada and sail for hours and hours before you even see the United States on the other side."

John looked dubious and Sally laughed because she thought his frown was funny. "It would be the sea if it was that big," he said.

"Shall we see how quick we can all be?" Lucy said. Sally began to sense that something was going to happen. "John – you go down and put your wagon in the garage while I dress Sally. Then I'll pack while you get dressed."

As John started downstairs he stopped abruptly on the top step. "What about Daddy?"

"Oh, he'll be all right. Perhaps he'll come to see us in Grenville."

"Will he know how to get there?"

"Yes. He was there once before – before you were born."

"He might forget," John said. "That was a long time ago."

For the next hour she worked with her usual concentrated speed at packing, remembering which clothes the children would need, answering their questions, listening for the telephone. It occurred to her to wonder why an otherwise temperate individual must leave the only two homes she had ever had with such precipitation. She remembered the expression on Bruce's face that Saturday afternoon seven years ago when he had asked her if she had any conception of the kind of life she was diving into. The recollection brought her no pain. She had refused nothing. She had lived. Seven years ago, apart from the immature boy Bruce then was, she had been completely alone. Now John and Sally were with her. Now at least she was a whole woman.

The children were standing at the foot of the stairs waiting for her when she came into the house after putting the last piece of luggage into the back of the car. She went to her writing table and wrote a brief note for Stephen, put it into an envelope, sealed it, wrote his name on the envelope, and laid it on the table in the hall. She called Shirley's mother to say that she wouldn't need Shirley for some time, but would send a cheque for the remainder of the month. She made a last round to check the doors and windows and sent the children out to the car. Then she stood in the hall fighting off a rising panic as she tried to imagine Stephen's emotions when he returned to an empty house. She took one step toward the telephone and stopped; then she picked up the note she had written and slipped it into her purse. She walked out into a late afternoon sun, closed the door behind her, heard the lock click, and joined the children in the car. They were sitting gravely on the front seat, solemn as mice in their best clothes. She opened the glove box and took out a road map and spread it on her knees.

"Look, dears, where we're going." She pointed to a red line. "We'll spend the night in Stroudsburg and tomorrow we'll go up into the Mohawk Valley. We'll go through Utica and Watertown and then we'll cross the Saint Lawrence at the Thousand Islands. We'll see the greatest river on the continent from the International Bridge and then we'll be in Canada. After that we'll have a lovely drive along Lake Ontario and pretty soon we'll be in Grenville. That's my old home. Isn't it going to be fun?"

She backed the car and turned it, and just as she was changing gears she heard a faint sound from the house. The telephone was ringing.

Lucy sat motionless behind the wheel while John and Sally turned their heads to look at her. They had not heard the telephone; perhaps it was only her imagination. Suddenly she cut the engine and hurried up the flagstone walk to the front door. The phone was still ringing as she fumbled in her bag for the door key. It rang once more as she entered the hall and she dropped her bag and ran to it. But then she picked up the instrument all she heard was the dial tone. She replaced it and stood in the dim hall feeling the weight of her disappointment. At that moment she felt as though she were standing alone in an unfurnished house, a house with no personality, no suggestion of an owner, no past and no future.

She picked up the instrument once again and dialled long distance. When a girl answered, "Bratian Advertising Company," she asked for Mr. Lassiter.

"He's not here," the frustrated voice answered sharply. "Nobody's here. The office is closed for the day. He's not in his hotel either. I just tried to get him there."

Lucy drew a deep breath, then picked up her bag, heard the lock click behind her once more, and returned to the car.

"Was it Daddy?" John asked as she started the motor.

"No, dear. I just thought I heard the phone. There was nobody on the line."

FIVE

THE ELM TREES OVERHANGING Matilda Lane were silent and dense with leaves on this warm July evening. As Bruce Fraser left his father's house, walked down to the common and across it to the shore, he thought how this short stretch of barely a hundred yards had changed in length since he could first remember having run away from home to cross it at the age of three.

In length, but not in aspect. All of us in childhood discover a special walk which leads us directly to the edge of the world. We reach a point where we can physically go no farther, but our thoughts leap and then for a few moments we are on our way toward becoming Everyman. Such a place can never be completely real to us again because all that is valuable in it has become part of ourselves, and it changes with ourselves, becoming empty or full, wise or meaningless as we grow old.

During the years of his teens this was the walk that Bruce had invariably taken whenever he was in trouble, or very happy, or merely longing to be alone. Whenever he returned to Grenville from a journey he had always found an excuse to walk out of the house and turn toward the common within the first few hours, to keep going until he found himself standing once again on the sand. It took him less than two minutes to cover the distance now, though once it had seemed to take two hours. Yet he tended to measure all space in his mind's eye by this stretch of a hundred yards and he always would.

The sun was down and in the gathering twilight the lake was almost as great a source of light as the sky. Saffron and shrimp-coloured clouds shredding out of the west were floating eastward down the water. Two ships were in sight several miles from the shore; the smoke of a third trailed along the southern horizon and lost itself in the mauve gloaming which rose like a presence out of the invisible United States. The lake was as still tonight as water in a bowl, not a leaf stirred, and the small sounds of Grenville pulsed at his back. Somewhere a door was closing, a woman calling her child in for the night, steps crossing the gravel path near the band-stand, a multitude of crickets chirping, a muted blast rising from a motor horn on the King's Highway.

Bruce was tired. He knew why and he knew he would soon be fresh again and eager to work, but tonight he was simply tired. He breathed deeply and smelled the flat odour of fresh water that has been lying still under the sun.

Had he come back to Canada and settled into a civilian job after the operation on his eye, he might by now be feeling as fresh and hopeful as the majority of the boys who were pouring back into the country on every trooper from England. Like himself, they had dis-covered Canada only after they left it three years ago and now they were eager to find out first-hand how good it was. But instead of leaving the war when his own battles were over he had returned to it as a spectator, had trained himself to analyze and to analyze ruthlessly, to consider escapism the lowest degradation to which a man could sink. And now this tough attitude of which he had been so proud was showing wide gaps. A wry, not even bitter sense of humour was causing him to mock himself and to tell himself that if he continued to develop the way he had started he would soon be like the reformer who got picked up in a brothel, or the psy-chiatrist who committed suicide. The insanity of the times was so pervading it could even appear to turn intellectual integrity into a vice. In lush seasons there was a certain bullying self-flattery about a harsh determination to be realistic, but what was the good of it now? The best men of his time had believed that the way to reform evil was to expose it, and to that end they had thought about evil constantly. The most famous books of the century swam in evil, all of them, right down to puny imitators like himself, swallowing the whole materialistic fallacy which maintained that to dissect evil is the same as to practise good.

Now that he was back in Grenville the humiliating thought had occurred to Bruce that no matter how you slice it, the food a man eats turns into the man himself. The early Christians had apparently believed this, for when they revolted against the materialism of Rome they had not considered Nero worth more than a few lines of scripture. Bruce grinned at his own thoughts. What a godsend Nero would be to the rough-paper magazines today!

As he started back across the common he realized that an elderly man coming toward him was deliberately walking into his path. Bruce passed a hand over his imitation eye, thinking he must be more tired than he had thought. The man stopped and waited for Bruce to reach him, and he saw it was Matt McCunn.

"Well for God's sake!" Bruce said. "When did you get home?"

"Hullo, laddie! I could ask you the same."

"Last night. I came in on the late train."

The two men drifted toward a green bench.

"Going to stay a while?" McCunn asked, looking across the common carefully before he allowed the seat of his pants to touch the wood.

"A month. Maybe more. I've got plenty of time to think things over. I've been offered a job in Toronto and another in Vancouver. Haven't decided yet which I'll take."

"Don't take either," McCunn said. He reached in his pocket and drew out a blackened old pipe which he took some time to fill. As Bruce watched him he realized that the man had aged at last. McCunn's hair had always been white, but white like a premature frost. Now his posture suggested the kind of repose that comes only with age and a willing acceptance of it.

"I've been home no more than three weeks myself," McCunn said between puffs of his pipe. "The last time I hit Liverpool after I got out of Trieste I shipped out for Halifax and came straight back here. And, by God, here is where I stay from now on!"

Bruce laughed and once again put his hand over the scar which crossed one cheek from temple to chin. It was a habit of which he was unaware. "What in hell were you doing in Yugoslavia?" he said.

"Getting myself a liberal education, for one thing. It turned me into a Presbyterian again, for if original sin don't account for what goes on there, nothing else does." McCunn pulled on his pipe. "But they were mighty nice to me. I got pneumonia and some of them would come back from a massacre – at least that's what they claimed they'd been doing – and be as good to me as if I was their own father. They'd laugh like kids and show their teeth, and they've got teeth so good a dentist would starve to death if he had to live among them, and tell me what they'd been doing and what a fine country they were going to have when they'd killed everyone they didn't like." He turned to look at Bruce. "I heard you had a bad time yourself."

"No, I don't think so. I was one of the lucky ones."

"Maybe you're right. For the troops, this wasn't as bad as the last one. But it was damn queer. I thought it was a pretty good war at first, but it piled up slowly and before it was over it really got me."

Bruce leaned back against the green slats of the bench and watched the fading light on the lake while McCunn went on talking. He wondered why the sort of inner humour of a man like McCunn – humour that wasn't funny but which seemed to mitigate everything unpleasant in life for those who had it – had apparently skipped his own generation. For instance, what kind of reports would a man like McCunn have written from the San Francisco Conference? Bruce had an odd feeling that in their way they would have been more accurate than his own. Because he had been called back from Europe to cover the conference and had been commissioned to write a magazine article for *Maclean's* to explain its significance for Canada, he had taken it very seriously indeed. The article was still only half-finished, but in it he had established the premise that Canada, in more or less settling her old disharmony between the French and English within the country, had at last responded to the challenge peculiar to her nature and therefore had finished the war fresher than she had entered it. She was hopeful, eager, ready to start. The problem he must go on to state concerned how much chance the big powers were going to give her, for they had established at San Francisco the principle that the wisdom of a nation is in exact proportion to its size. Given the article to finish, what would McCunn do with it?

At a break in the old man's monologue Bruce said, "What did you think of the San Francisco Conference? I've got to write an article on it for *Maclean's*."

"Balls," McCunn said. "All balls!" And went on to urge him to get out of newspaper work and put his mind on something pleasant.

"You know," he went on, "I've always considered myself a pretty smart man, if you take my definition of smartness. When I was sick in that cave in the worst goddam mountains I ever saw, like heaps of iron with flour dusted over them, I decided exactly what I wanted to do when I got back to Grenville. It was better than wondering if I ever would get back, which seemed pretty unlikely."

"What was it?"

"What I'm doing. Right now. I'm in charge of this common. I rake up leaves and mow the grass and keep the benches in order and I'm going to put in some flower beds this fall. I felt pretty good about persuading them to let me do that. The Chamber of Commerce's got a new booklet printed that says there's more ozone in the air in Grenville than any other place in the world but one. They don't say where the other place is. So I said, what's the use of ozone if you can't smell anything better than an occasional whiff from the Ceramic Company? You should have heard me talking to Wes Muchmore! You're too young to remember but I was a damned good preacher once. I had the gift."

Bruce laughed and felt his scar again. And after a moment McCunn added, "I've been hunting rotted manure all over the countryside for three days. Plenty of horse for some reason, but I can't find enough cow."

Bruce crossed and uncrossed his legs and tried to keep his mind on what McCunn was saying. The nearest of the ships out on the lake had broken out her riding lights and behind them darkness was filling the common, growing like a substance between the boles of the trees. Somewhere out of it came the sound of a girl's laughter. Bruce and Matt McCunn talked for a while longer in sparse sentences broken by long periods of silence. Then McCunn broke his peace.

"Have you seen Lucy yet?"

Bruce felt his throat tighten. "For a few minutes this afternoon. But not to talk to."

"Funny thing," McCunn said. "I never thought I'd see them all together in that house again. Hear Nina's getting home soon too."

After a few more idle sentences Bruce got to his feet, said good-night, and left McCunn on the edge of darkness between the trees and the water, with his pipe glowing occasionally as he drew on it.

On his way home Bruce saw the lights in the Cameron house and wondered how he could stand living next to Lucy all summer unless he could get over feeling as he did now. During the years in England he had convinced himself that the emotion he had felt about her in New York had been nothing more than the product of his own burning imagination. Now he knew how wrong he had been; the emotion had lain dormant like a buried plant and its returning growth was riving him. He had seen her coming out the door of the Cameron house that afternoon and when she looked up toward his window and found him standing there, she had waved. But after returning the gesture he had left the window abruptly and spent the rest of the afternoon indoors thinking of something else, a feat which years of discipline had made possible.

Then his mother had brought Lucy into his mind again at supper, this time in a startling new aspect. "I believe she's had trouble with her husband," his mother said. "I wouldn't dream of asking questions, of course, but she's been here quite a while, you know. Since about the middle of May. And Jane never speaks of her husband when she talks about Lucy at I.O.D.E. meetings and other places I usually see her."

"Jane wouldn't be likely to speak about him under any circumstances," Bruce's father said.

"No, I suppose not. But she's so happy lately. Jane is, I mean."

"Never thought she'd come back to Jane after leaving the way she did!" Dr. Fraser said.

Bruce had changed the subject.

Now his mother was waiting for him when he returned from the common and she met him in the hall as he started up the stairs.

"You've been gone such a long time," she said.

"Have I? I didn't think it was more than half an hour."

"No – I mean, nearly five years. Wouldn't you like to come in and talk to your father and me this evening? There's such a lot you haven't told us yet."

"Yes, of course," he said automatically and came down the two steps to stand beside her. "But I'm really awfully tired tonight. If you wouldn't mind waiting for another day, I'd be better company." He looked at her with affection and knew that no matter what words might pass between himself and them, the conversation would be painful for them all because they still clung to their old idea of him and he had not yet discovered a way of making himself seem like the son they thought they knew.

"All right," she said, as complacent as she had always been with him. "Let's make it tomorrow night then. I'll explain to your father."

He kissed her forehead and then her cheek. "Do you mind if I take a bottle of beer and sit in the dark in the garden for a while? It's still pretty hot upstairs and I've got to think of some ideas to finish an article I'm doing on the U.N.O."

"Yes, of course. Only – Bruce dear, you shouldn't work all the time. You need a rest. Goodness only knows your father was never one to encourage you not to work, but even he's beginning to worry about you." She smiled up at him. "It will be nice for you when Nina gets home. Jane says she's due sometime this week. She's such a nice girl and you and she used to be such good friends."

"Nina?" He tried to keep the irony out of his voice, but he was startled by the implications of the suggestion. So they were beginning to worry because he wasn't married! He smiled down at his mother and put his arm about her shoulder.

"It's awfully dark out now," she said. "Surely you can't do any work in the garden at this time of night!"

One more attempt to coax him into the living room and then she would give up. What could she know of the nature of darkness? How could he hope to tell her a fraction of the thoughts that had cataracted through his mind in the darkness of these past years? It was in darkness that you sat and fought down your fear on the way to the target. It was out of darkness that you leaped naked and indecent for your frenzied minutes in the slashing lights over a flaming town. It was back to darkness that you returned after perpetrating your action, a darkness velvet-soft and lovelier at such a moment than any woman you had ever dreamed of. And the death in the darkness you had left behind was the reason why you felt spasms of hysterical omnipotence as you gabbled over the intercom and watched the glowing instrument panels as you flew home over the North Sea and listened to all the motors humming steadily.

His mother's smile hid her disappointment as she returned to the living room. Bruce took a bottle from the ice box, removed the cap, and went out the back door with the bottle in one hand and a glass in the other. The stars were visible as he rested in a garden chair, but he closed his eyelids and did not see them. The bottle was three-quarters empty when he heard a movement on the other side of the hedge. Someone besides himself was sitting in the dark tonight.

He got up silently. And for how many nights before this? He waited for several minutes but there was no further sound. Then he walked across the lawn and paused at the gap in the hedge.

"Lucy?" he said half under his breath.

"Yes?"

"May I come over?"

"Please. I've been waiting for you."

Then she was in his arms and he felt her lips soft under his own. For just a fraction of a second he felt her body come in against his with instinctual hunger, then she had broken away.

He saw a group of chairs under the apple tree and when she returned to one of them he sat down beside her, partly facing her at an angle. Deliberately he lit a cigarette and watched her face in the flare of the match. When the match went out their outlines were still visible to each other, and he remembered that on a clear night it never became totally dark so close to the lake.

"It's good to see you again," Lucy said a trifle breathlessly.

Half an hour later they were still sitting quietly under the apple tree, each separate, and though neither had mentioned anything of importance, there was less restraint between them than there had ever been.

"One thing I can't understand," Bruce was saying. "If Jane never wrote to you, if she'd never really relented from that day you left here years ago, how could you bring yourself to come back here?"

"I didn't bring myself," she said. "I just went crazy one day in Princeton and left with the children and began driving north. I didn't even telephone to Jane until we'd crossed the river and reached Gananoque and I knew we could reach home that day. Then I was scared to death and I chattered like a half-wit to the children to prevent them from seeing it."

"And then?"

He could hear her take a deep breath in the darkness. "We came into Grenville in the late afternoon and when we passed that idiotic sign on the edge of town about Grenville loving its children, John leaned out the window – he can read quite well, you know – and said, 'Mummy, does that mean they'll love us too?' I couldn't answer that one, but we were already through King Street and passing the Ceramic Company and coming to Matilda Lane. When I turned the car this way John looked ahead and caught a glimpse of the water. I said we were going to live at the end of the street and he said, 'Mummy, is this going to *our* lake, the one you told us about?' And then I stopped the car in front of the house."

She paused and he heard her laugh quietly, almost ruefully. "There's no sense in ever planning anything, Bruce. If I didn't know it before, I learned it that day."

He waited and presently she went on. He noticed then that her voice sounded a little older than the way he remembered it, and her use of words more confident.

"Jane opened the door before we could get out of the station wagon. She must have been waiting, all ready with something to say, for hours before we came. As I went up the walk she just stood there staring at me with no expression on her face, taking in every line of my face and clothes. There was a child on either side, but for ten seconds I honestly don't think she even saw them. Then John piped up and said, 'Hullo, Aunt Jane!' and she looked down and saw him standing there in his best clothes with his hand held out."

She paused again and Bruce lit another cigarette, watching Lucy's face emerge in the temporary light of it.

"I'll never know what went through Jane's mind in that moment and I don't suppose she ever will, either. Suddenly she smiled – at John, not at me – and told us to come in. And the next thing I knew her back was to me and she was doing something with a handkerchief. When she turned around she said quite briskly, as though she'd seen me only last week, 'You can have your own room, Lucy. The children can share Nina's room until she comes back. I've put a cot in there beside her bed. You'll find the sheets and blankets in their usual place.'"

Lucy stopped and Bruce blew a stream of smoke toward the stars.

"Grenville!" he said softly. "This is quite a place!"

Silence fell between them without separating them. Over the top of the hedge Bruce could see that the light in his parents' bedroom had gone out.

"That was in May," he murmured as if to himself. "And you've been here ever since! How does it feel to be back – for day after day?"

"It feels different ways – day after day. June was a cold, long, wet month, and I hated every minute of it."

He waited before his next question. "What about now?"

And it took her some time to answer. "The children love it," she said at last. "Lake Ontario delights them, as though it were a private swimming pool, and John seems to have discovered all the queer characters in town, including Uncle Matt. Children are wonderful at changing and adjusting themselves. The only thing I can't do anything about is the way they miss their father."

For Bruce, the mood which lay between them was broken. "I was thinking about you, Lucy."

"I know you were, Bruce dear. And I know you weren't really asking if I liked Grenville, either."

He thought about her own capacity for change, in the sense that she had never, since he first became aware of her, ceased to grow. His mind began to grope for the significant point in her otherwise commonplace experience. Failing to find it, he felt a sudden bitter indignation that Lucy should have become involved in this routine sequel to the modern American love story.

"Forgive a straight question," he said. "What's going to happen now?"

"I don't know."

"What about Stephen?"

She made no answer.

"Are you still in touch with him?"

He saw her hands move in the dark. "It took him about two weeks to guess where I was and then he telephoned. He called four successive nights. Then the calls stopped."

"Asking you to go back?"

"Yes."

Bruce waited, then went on. "And you told him?"

"Simply that I had to have time to think things out. My mind seems to be made of cotton wool and I haven't yet been able to work my way through it."

Bruce got to his feet, his thoughts at war with his feelings. "Why doesn't he come up here? Why doesn't he come to you instead of asking you to go back to him?" His voice took on a note of unconscious malice. "One doesn't settle things like that by telephone."

He saw her face turned up to him, a pale blur in the dark. "Bruce, if I could talk to anybody about Stephen I could talk to you, but I can't."

"I know, Lucy. I know." And suddenly recalling Lassiter's face, his powerful, good-natured self-confidence, Bruce burst into an angry generalization. "What's the matter with Americans of our age? They usen't to be this way. What gives them this damnable new mixture of hardness and softness?"

"Please, Bruce –" Her voice was firm, almost warning. "Thinking and talking like that gets none of us anywhere."

He stood poised on the dew-wet grass, trying hopelessly to discover her face in the darkness. It occurred to him that there was no use staying with her any longer feeling as he did, for suddenly there was nothing more to say. He reached down and took her hand and she came to her feet. For an instant they stood face to face in the darkness, and then he murmured something unintelligible and went back through the gap in the hedge. His toe hit the bottle of beer he had left beside his chair and knocked it over, but he passed into the house without stopping to pick it up.

He was a fool, he told himself; a fool to believe that because both of them had come back to Grenville, they had also both come home.

AS JULY advanced in a long procession of lovely days – hours on the sandy beach with the children, picnics and canoeing at Granite Mere, the first peas out of the garden, the King's Highway alive with hitch-hiking veterans, evenings of talk and gramophone music with Bruce, Jane's piano marking out the hours of the day just as it had always done – it seemed to Lucy that her spirit, like the climate itself, was taking a holiday.

And then a morning came when she woke up looking forward to the day. After weeks of feeling more solitary than she had ever felt in her life, she realized that she was no longer quite alone, nor washed back on precisely the same beach from which she had once escaped. Bruce's admiration, his desire for her which he so painfully tried to conceal, conspired with Jane's renewed fondness to restore some of her battered pride. The children were happy, Jane was satisfied, even Grenville seemed more lighthearted than she had remembered it. She discovered that happiness, like misery, is infectious.

In the third week of July, Nina returned from Halifax and Jane and Lucy met her at the station. She got off the train looking official and impersonal in her Wren's uniform, and after supper she announced that she could get her discharge almost as soon as she wished. Jane watched her steadily as she talked, asked questions about Halifax and her work there, and seemed eager to know what she planned to do. As Lucy watched them both she felt sad to hear the lifelessness and lack of interest in Nina's voice. Nina said she supposed she could get another secretarial job in Toronto, at all events she wouldn't stay in Grenville, and almost anything would be better than Halifax. At twenty-six, she spoke as if all her growth lay behind her. But she came down to breakfast next morning looking very pretty in one of her old summer dresses, and the moment she discovered that Bruce Fraser was back in town her face lightened and became vivacious.

"Well, at least I can have *some* fun this summer," she said.

THE days following her return seemed to Bruce the most irritatingly unreal he had ever spent. He wanted only to be with Lucy, but Nina was now between them. He would lie on the sand watching Nina, golden in the sunshine, splashing up from the water and tossing her hair back from her eyes in her old defiant gesture. He would glance at Lucy's calm profile, wonder what thoughts lay behind it, and wish to God her younger sister had been transferred to Australia, even while he admitted to himself that he liked her better than he had ever liked her before.

Yet the most unreal thing about this summer was Grenville itself. Calm, sure of its point of view, it had already contrived to reach the middle of the twentieth century without losing the smallest part of its innocence. On warm days he would lie on the beach with the town behind him, hearing the clack of McCunn's lawn mower moving over the surface of the common and occasionally the scream of a cicada. And always coming to the surface of his mind were scenes he had witnessed over the past years, throbbing, exploding, and obliterating the present. The night missions, the day the infantry finally cracked the Germans at Caen, the dead bodies floating in Dutch canals, the look on the faces of the first German civilians in Emmerich, the doublebreasted jackets of statesmen at San Francisco – what could one man's brain do with them? Then he would look at Lucy and ask himself what significance a woman's personal un-happiness could possibly have compared to the misery he had seen in a single half-hour in the Bremen railroad station? Once Europe had been as peaceful as the shore of Lake Ontario, he would tell him-self. Only a few years ago the problems of Europeans were individual problems, too. And surely it was out of their refusal or incapacity to solve their individual problems that they had robbed themselves of the right to be considered as individuals, letting themselves be-come DPs of history itself, cannon fodder for Nazis, raw material for Communists, columns of statistics for the mushrooming bureaus. He knew now why he had been so eager to get out of Europe; had he stayed even a month longer he might well have lost forever the one priceless thing his own experience of war had given him – a tempered confidence in the ability of plain human beings to make the most of themselves if they were given a chance.

Even with such thoughts in his mind he would jump up from the sand and go out into the water with John, laugh with him and support him under the chest while he taught him the rudiments of a flutter kick. And then he would become aware, with an added sense of unreality, of the microscopic tensions newly rising between Lucy, himself, and Nina.

Once he heard Nina say to her sister, "Well I notice that even when he's pretending to play with John he keeps looking up to make sure you're noticing him!"

A moment later he left John and came up the beach to join them.

"Bruce," Nina said. "What are you going to do when the war's over?"

He glanced from one to the other. "Write a book about food and win the Nobel prize."

Lucy gave him a mocking smile but Nina had no idea what he was talking about.

"Everybody's become so terribly old!" she said. "Nobody's fun any more. What good does it do you to worry about politics all the time?"

"None whatever, so far as I can see."

"Do you think it will be any better in Toronto after the war than it was before?"

The question opened still another door in Bruce's mind. That was how it worked now: open one door and you saw the corpses of Belsen, open another and you met a lovely girl laughing in the sun, enter one country and you saw a perverted mass of humanity living in a hell they had made for themselves, enter another and you found a people just discovering a life of its own and eager to live it.

Lucy, he could see, had quietly withdrawn herself, as she was doing now whenever the three of them were together. The tart remarks Nina made to her no longer bothered either of them, but Bruce continued to be uncomfortable as one of the trio they made. He wanted to talk to Lucy, to bring her forth again from her mood of inner absorption, to see her return to the transitory mood of lightness which had supported her through the first weeks of July. Today for the first time since his return she seemed much older than himself; older in the sense that she had become impregnable in her own inner reserve and more capable of weighing and balancing the pros and cons of any situation in which she might find herself. He knew intuitively that this was exactly what she was doing now. She was thinking about her life with Stephen Lassiter in the United States and balancing it off against the life she might expect to lead if she divorced him and lived with the children in Canada.

"It's going to be better all over Canada after the war," he said, trying to answer her thoughts, though his words might sound like a direct answer to Nina's last question. "When the San Francisco Conference was over I went up the coast to Vancouver and came back on the Transcontinental. God, what a land to live in! When the train was crawling up that colossal grade under Cathedral Mountain an American in the observation car said to anyone who would listen to him, 'How the hell did Canadians manage to break a country like this without anybody shooting his mouth off about it?'"

"What did you tell him?" Nina said rather archly.

"I said I'd no more known what Canada was really like than he did. For years before the war this whole country –" He looked at

Lucy, then back at Nina. "Well, you know what it was like. We seemed to think it was shameful to be pleased with ourselves."

Lucy broke in. "Maybe we were preparing ourselves for the future without knowing it."

"Maybe," he replied. "But talk to people on the roads everywhere in Canada today and listen to what they say. We're just beginning to discover ourselves. Americans had that excitement fifty to a hundred years ago. Ours is beginning now. Have you ever stopped to think what it means that this is the only country on the face of the earth where people are happier – happier inside themselves – than they were twenty years ago?"

Looking down at Nina's blue eyes, fixed so attentively on his own, he realized that she had stopped listening. His own fault, he thought. She must have sensed that he was talking to Lucy all the time.

"I don't know whether you're merely healthy-minded," he said to her, "or –"

"Or what?"

"Don't make me say it."

Only a few years ago her boredom would have annoyed him, but now he felt he had come to understand her. At some point during the war he had ceased to judge people by their intelligence. Nina seemed neither cheap nor ludicrous to him now because her only interest lay in getting married. As he looked at her figure, at once slimmer and more mature than he remembered it, he told himself that all she needed was a man to love her, and realized with something of a start that if Lucy were not here he might easily choose the part for himself.

After that day on the beach a full week went by without his seeing Lucy, for now she was withdrawing herself from him as she had already done from the others. She hadn't deliberately refused to see him; she simply wasn't around where he and Nina and the children were. And the procession of fine days continued. A few spindly phlox, last survivors of Lucy's original garden, bloomed among the weeds she had made no attempt this summer to remove. But the beans and beets matured in Jane's Victory Garden in such profusion that three-quarters of them had to be given away.

Finally a rainy evening came when Bruce, restless and thinking it was about time to end his holiday and begin work again, troubled by his inability to do anything about the situation in which he found himself with Lucy, went over to the Cameron house simply to see her, although he knew that with Nina and Jane in the room no conversation would be possible. As an excuse, he took some flowers from his mother's garden and Jane went to the kitchen to find a vase for them. Lucy was making a frilly dress for Sally, and though she kept on with her work, he felt she was glad to see him again. Nina had been reading, but now she turned on the radio and began twisting the dial as she searched for dance music. She picked up a Toronto station, heard a man announcing the news, and was about to dial off when Bruce jumped from his chair and caught her hand.

"Wait!" he said, his face with its long scar looking frozen. "Let's hear that."

They listened while the announcer, using the measured, cool tones of all Canadian news reporters during the war, described the destruction of Hiroshima.

The voice went on, repeating itself as though repetition could make the appalling real. No one in the room spoke and no one moved until Bruce snapped off the radio again. Then they were aware that Jane had been standing in the door of the living room all the time the announcer had been speaking, a vase full of bright flowers in her hand. Her voice was as measured as the announcer's when she broke the silence.

"The Americans were bound to do something like that one day," she said.

THAT night Lucy was unable to sleep. She lay in bed with all her nerves tense while her ears heard every sound in the night. She heard each truck and car pass the head of Matilda Lane and each riffle of breeze in the leaves of the elms outside her window. After midnight the breeze became steady and the air was filled with the constant wash of waves.

She remembered Bruce's face as he had talked about what tonight's news was going to mean. His quick, poetic imagination had raced off into the future, drawing one deduction after another, and now he was almost certainly awake in his own bed next door, trying to find some hope in a world his reason told him had reached the position in a crime story of the criminals' confederate who knew too much to live. She knew what he was thinking because his mind was too much like her own. The kind of world he wanted to live in was too much like the kind she wanted. Even the judgments he uttered were statements of ideas she herself tried to suppress. It was bad enough having to live with her own thoughts these days, without having their weight doubled by Bruce's problems.

Tonight, more acutely than on any night since she had left Princeton, Lucy found herself longing for Stephen. First for his arms around her, for his sheer physical strength and the peace his body gave her. But far more than that she missed the way his factual engineer's mind, totally different from her own, had stood between her and this world the engineers had made. She remembered his words, spoken years ago in Grenville before they were married, "Some day they'll do it – they'll go faster than sound, they'll rocket clear off this planet."

Whatever else Stephen might feel, he would feel no shock or angry bewilderment at the appalling information they had received tonight. The frame of mind which had produced this bomb was the frame of mind in which he had been born and raised. The skills which had made it were the only skills he really valued. And the tensions produced by those skills, the tensions arising in hundreds of thousands of men driving constantly forward, committing themselves and everyone else again and again to the risk of living with the results of their skill, were the tensions he had been trying so desperately to escape.

She knew tonight, clearly for the first time, in what she had failed him. She had not sufficiently understood the tensions, she had given him no adequate release for them. When she could lie alone with this realization no longer, she got out of bed, put on her dressing gown and slippers, and tip toed downstairs.

It was two-forty by the clock in the hall. She looked at the phone and tried to think of the consequences of carrying out her impulse to call Stephen at his hotel in New York. She tried to picture the scene at the other end of the line. What likelihood that he would even be in his room? He knew where she was; he had known it for months. If he still needed her, he would have called long ago; he would – as Bruce had said – have left New York and come up to get her.

She opened the front door and stood on the threshold while the cool breeze off the lake fanned her cheeks. Where was he now? What was he doing? With whom was he sharing his plans – if he still had any?

"What's the matter, Lucy? Aren't you well?"

She turned and saw Jane on the landing of the stairs.

"I'm all right." She stepped back into the hall and closed the door behind her. "I couldn't sleep. Sometimes it helps to move about."

Jane came down, an old dressing gown held close about her, and turned on the light in the hall. *The Death of Nelson*, grey and precise, assumed its place above the table to the right of the hat-rack.

"I'll fix you something hot to drink," Jane said.

They went out to the kitchen together, and after pouring milk into a pan, Jane looked up and remarked, "I wonder when Bruce will get over his habit of upsetting people? You can't blame it on the war, for he was always like that. What do you think will become of him?"

Lucy picked up an unopened tin of Ovaltine, took the top off, and set it on the table.

"Whatever else you do," Jane went on, "you mustn't brood. It's not as if you have anything to blame yourself for. If I were in your position, I wouldn't care what somebody else had done to me, so long as I knew I hadn't done anything wrong myself."

She was standing over the electric burner, looking down at the milk in the pan. The overhead light showed the grey streaks in her dark hair, which even now, after several hours in bed, managed to look fairly neat.

She turned off the switch and carried the pan to the table. While pouring the milk into two glasses, she went on, "I forgot to tell you I was talking to Mr. Armitage this morning. He's looking forward to having John start school in September. He said he was sure he'd make a good pupil because you were so good when you were his age. It's a very fortunate thing for John to be here, for it means he won't be spoiled. Mr. Armitage was telling me the American schools are filled with this new progressive nonsense. It's even spreading into Toronto and Montreal, he says. So long as he's principal, we're not going to have any of it here." She finished stirring the Ovaltine into the milk and handed Lucy her glass. "Next week I'll look into getting his books and scribblers. Falconer's has them in stock already, for I've seen them in the window. What's the matter?"

Lucy turned to hide a convulsive movement of the muscles of her throat.

"This is your home now," Jane said. "And the children have become quite accustomed to it. You must stop thinking about him."

The eyes of the two sisters met, but this time it was Jane who looked away.

NAGASAKI was destroyed and the Japanese war was over. There was dancing on the main cross street off the King's Highway in Grenville, and a huge raft was built and heaped with oiled logs, towed into the lake from the dock of the Ceramic Company, and lighted after sunset. It burned for hours. When Lucy went to bed that night the last glow of red-hot ashes was still visible on the water.

For days afterwards she did her best to hide her restlessness. She felt that the purposes of everyone she knew were pulling in opposite directions. Jane came back from shopping in King Street with a set of school books for John, a box of yellow pencils, and a carton of crayons. Bruce went to Toronto and after two days he was home again with the news that he had accepted a job on a large newspaper and would begin work immediately after Labour Day. Nina wrote to her old employer in Toronto and was told by return mail that she could have her job back whenever she wished it, the sooner the better. Jane began her new schedule of music lessons and the sound of scales being played on the piano filled more hours of every day.

THE roar of unheard, unfelt, unsmelled explosions thundered through Stephen Lassiter's brain as he lay clamped by the inland heat of an August night to the soft mattress of his hotel bed. A thousand Privateers formed themselves into a relief map of the town they were destroying, they covered it like a coffin lid in the most exact operation ever conceived, the bombs dropped like a carpet, each one precisely placed, the blast of each bomb so calculated in advance by specialists that a single salvo would obliterate all life below in the split of a second. The planes swept through Stephen's brain over the town, the church steeples disappeared in the boiling dust, then the planes droned away into the lean face of Stephen Holt

Carson, into the faces of his own New England ancestors hanging on the walls of his mother's house in black walnut frames.

His heavy muscles stirred. Suddenly a great tongue of darkness writhed down from a red sky as hot as the turmoil in his tired, middle-aged stomach and licked him in the face, licked him so that his skin revolted from its texture, horrid and wet and senseless as the tongue of a cow.

He groaned and heaved his body upright. Where was he?

Eyes sore in the darkness, mouth like sour dry wool from too many cigarettes, he groped for the light, turned it on, and saw a telephone book and a bottle of whiskey and a glass. The bottle stood on a Gideon Bible and it was nearly full. He remembered now. It was a strange hotel in a city he had never lived in before and he was not drunk. Even before going to sleep he had known that whiskey was no longer any help. Again the tongue of darkness licked down into his brain. God, how many other men in the world were lying in the darkness dreaming of bursting bombs and town-smashing inventions?

He lay on his back in the darkness stripped to the waist, his chest heaving. The window was a visible shape in the room, steel coloured at the upper part, dark grey where it was open. He felt the sweat cold on his forehead and chest, warm on his stomach.

Why should he be in a fix like this? What had he done that hundreds of thousands of others hadn't done? Christ, it wasn't as if he hadn't worked hard all his life!

He surged up, rolled sideways out of bed, lurched to the window, and thrust out his head, sucking in gulps of the hot night air. It was a terrible city in summer when the wind came in from the prairies. At half-past four in the morning his eyes ached with the dry heat.

He sat down in a high-backed chair before the window, his big body motionless. Hog butcher for the world. Even cities had their slogans now. He saw the lights of widely spaced cars travelling along the Outer Drive, and beyond it the lake broadening out into a plain that seemed to grow more visible as he watched it.

Where were the people in those cars going at this hour of the morning? And they might ask the same of him. What was he doing sitting in this particular window in this particular hotel room at the bad end of a hot night. At the moment the only reason he could think of for being here was his memory of a winter in school when his mother had written to him on the stationery of this same hotel and he had told himself that some day he would stay there, too. But there were other reasons. He was here because Myron Harper had gone all the way to the top from being a minister's son in a little Ohio town, a bigger man than any four-star general in the army, and just at the minute when he was ready to show the world there were no limits to what he could do, the government had taken away his contracts.

Harper's face confused itself with Bratian's in Stephen's mind. Carl had said, "Why worry, Steve? You'll fall on your feet. You ought to buy a book. Life begins at forty, you know."

Bastard!

His head and shoulders were a solid mass, ominous and powerful in the pale frame of the window. What was happening? What in God's name was the matter with him? Had the whole world suddenly become populated by faceless people? You thought you knew them, you thought they loved you, and then –

Gail Beaumont's voice, cool, competent, deliberately sealing in the eager vitality he had thought so unique, freezing him away from any touching of that vibrant body: "It's no use, Steve. You're too immature. If there's one thing I can't live with it's a man with a guilt-complex. If you won't go to a psychiatrist and get rid of it –"

Bitch! Did she really believe there was a patent remedy for everything?

He drew back his right fist and smashed it against the stone that jutted beyond the window. He drew it back and smashed it again and again, then let it lie on his thigh, the skin broken and bleeding, the flesh swelling.

His eyes closed and he felt the pain throb up from his hand into his brain. At least the pain was positive. It was better to feel pain than to feel nothing.

And then, sharp as a New England barn etched against the snow in winter, he saw the face of his mother's old friend, S.H. Carson. When had that been? A week ago? How long? Carson's voice had matched his face, a face that carried in its lines the story of generations of self-denial. "And now you've deserted your wife – well, it amounts to the same thing – and you've come to me because you're no good to advertising any more." So much power in the quiet shake of a head like that. "Where's your integrity? Come and see me again when you've pulled yourself together. You're very like your father, you know."

The long splendid curve of the lakefront emerged slowly out of the east. A light wind sprang off the water and for a moment drove back the heat. Stephen picked up a blanket from the floor at the foot of the bed, wrapped it around his shoulders, and resumed his place at the window. Again the stern faces of his ancestors swam around him, each in its walnut frame. Side by side they hung on the wall, adding up to so much more than the sum of their parts. Side by side they stared at him, all accusing, all self-confident, not a single glance of mercy in the eyes of one of them, nothing but hard, faultless arrogance.

What sense did it make? What were they all trying to say to him? On one side were Carl and Gail and all the agency crowd in New York. They had turned him out because he was no good to them any more, because he didn't measure up to their standards in spite of how hard he had tried. On the other side were Carson and Lucy and his ancestors. They had turned him out, too, disapproved of him and found him wanting. What did it mean?

He got to his feet and threw the blanket to the floor, crossed the room and went into the bathroom. He took off his pajamas and stood under the shower and turned it on full force; first hot, then tepid, then cold. He stood there under the cold jets of water, forcing himself to take it without a grimace. Then he turned the water off and towelled himself and stood naked in front of the long glass. His right hand was still bleeding. He wrapped a linen towel around it and then flexed his muscles. They bunched heavily as they had always done. What if he was forty? What if they all thought he was a failure? They cancelled each other out, didn't they, since their ideas about what was good were diametrically opposed.

But where did that leave him? Where – except dangling between them?

He put on the trousers of his pajamas again, picked up the blanket, and sat down in the chair by the window. He could take it. Whether they thought so or not, he knew he could. Only he'd have to figure out somehow where he stood – who he was going to try to please.

The lake was bright in the dawn now, but the breeze had died and it was hot again.

Take a boat, take a white boat with a yawl rig and sail up the lake all the way to the straits of Mackinac, starboard down the South Channel past Cheboygan into Huron, past Sarnia down the St. Clair, past Detroit and Windsor into Erie, up through the Welland into the first lake the Frenchmen entered when they paddled the river and portaged the rapids on their way to China. Let the sheets run out through the blocks while the south wind blows her to the northern shore. An hour from now Sally would be awake and crying to be fed. But no, it was a long time since Sally had wakened at dawn; now she clung to her sleep till John or her mother wakened her.

When the children grew up, when John and Sally got into difficulties, would they know what had happened to them and where it had all begun? Would they find anyone to tell them that wanting to be liked, wanting to be admired for doing a good job was so much too little in this world?

He breathed slowly, evenly, his great chest sucking in the clean air off the lake. He heard the rumble of a train, but he couldn't decide whether it was in Grant Park or an elevated on its way to the Loop somewhere behind the hotel. The clouds over the lake were flushed along the edges and already it was bright enough to see a gull in the sky. Lucy loved the dawn. Lucy always knew why she liked something and why she didn't. But could she really tell the difference between sunset and dawn?

At one time during the war Myron Harper had worked for three weeks without once leaving the wing of the plant where his office was. He had worked in a room without windows, air conditioned, with indirect lighting and sound-proofed walls. Suppose the electricity had failed and the clocks had stopped and he had emerged from that office at a certain moment of dawn or sunset – could he have known whether it was going to be night or day?

Stephen's face was heavy as the light caught it, heavy lines were marked in the flesh and dark circles lay under his eyes.

Dear Lucy, I didn't mean to hurt you. How could I tell it would matter that much to you?

For a while his mind emptied and he stopped thinking about anything. Perhaps he slept for a while in the chair. Then he heard trucks and buses on the avenue below and he felt the pain in his hand.

I must get this straight, he said to himself. I'm hanging halfway between them, and it's not a place any man can stay for long. He tried to put his mind on a backward look over his life and he could see nothing but a long, twisting empty road. He had worked hard, he had tried to do what the best of them did, and now he might just as well have done nothing at all.

And then in a rushing sweep of comprehension the full shock of what he had done to Lucy smashed against his brain. What thoughts must have passed through her mind before she took the children and left the house in Princeton to go back to the place where he had found her? The only reason he had felt her silence to be a matter of sitting in judgment was because he knew it should have been. Yet Lucy had never judged anyone in her life except herself. Years and years before he met her she had come to terms with herself.

He closed his eyes and again the tongue of darkness menaced him out of the red sky. He opened them again, fighting back this time. Did other men have nightmares while they were awake?

What can I do? What can I do to make up for what I've done? And again: What can I do?

He was completely alone. Maybe all the rest of them were alone, too. Maybe that was how those grim men in the walnut frames had fixed things in America – the minute you stopped to think where you were you found yourself alone. All right. Lucy had learned to live alone because he was the one who had shut her out, not the other way about. Now maybe he could learn to live alone, too. It was the only way to keep from dangling in the middle. What the hell difference did it make what anyone else thought about him, so long as he knew what to think about himself?

The noises of another work-day morning grew louder in the streets below. Slowly, very gradually and slowly, Stephen's features steadied into firm lines almost Roman in their sombre dignity. Somewhere there was an answer to all this. A man couldn't let himself be a punching-bag forever.

IT WAS the last Friday in August that Lucy came back from shopping one morning and found a letter from Marcia lying on the table in the hall. She dropped her packages in the kitchen and took the letter out to the garden to read it, knowing that Marcia wrote only when she had something to say. The tinkling sounds of a beginner at the piano drifted through the kitchen door. Before she opened the letter she looked about, and then she remembered that John and Sally were being watched by Uncle Matt.

What Marcia had to say was there in the second line.

Stephen has left New York. When Harper dropped the account Carl let Steve go. He'd left town several days before I heard about it, indirectly as a matter of fact, and when I phoned Carl to find out what it was all about I gathered there'd been a terrific row.

All I've been able to find out for sure is that he was registered at the Blackstone in Chicago up to three days ago. Inference is that he and the Beaumont gal are washed up too because she's still around, and not alone.

Sorry to send you news like this, but I'm not sure it's all bad. I only hope he hasn't decided to go on a long, long drunk. Carl implied that he had another job already, but he was too glib about that and I'm afraid I didn't believe him. I'd like to hope he was right.

Try to remember what I said to you in Princeton. I'm not excusing Steve. But I think I understand him. It's not entirely his fault that he tried to make sex take the place of religion, for most of our generation at one time or another of our lives has tried to do the same.

If you ever see Bruce Fraser again and I hope you do, remind him of a conversation he and I had one night years ago in a New York restaurant – about the well-meaning generation. He'll know what I'm talking about.

I'm still at the hospital and if I could get off I'd come up to see you sometime, inimical as I might be to your life in Grenville.

Bless you! Give John and Sally special hugs for me.

Lucy lay back in the deck chair, looked up, and saw the first flush of colour in the apples overhead. Above the dark leaves of the tree, clouds were running like shaggy white horses across a sapphire sky. The wind was making a warm turmoil in the leaves, rushing humidly off the lake, and even here in the garden she could hear the waves volleying against the shore.

She looked down at Marcia's letter, held in one hand against her thigh. And suddenly she became frightened, and a feeling of blind helplessness seemed to paralyze all her limbs. Then she was on her feet looking over the hedge into the Frasers' garden where Bruce had set up a table and was making corrections in the script of the article he had finished at last. A pile of papers lay on the left side of the table under a heavy stone and he was bending over the remaining sheets with a pencil in his hands.

"Bruce!" she said, surprised at the sound of her own voice.

He looked up, stared at her a moment, then put the remainder of his script under the stone and rose. "Hello!" he said. "Anything the matter?"

She slipped through the gap in the hedge and joined him. "I can't keep still this morning," she said. "Will you come for a drive with me? No place in particular – so long as it's out of town."

"Love to. Just wait until I take this stuff into the house."

A minute later he joined her in the lane on the far side of the house where the station wagon had been parked all summer. She turned the car around and drove up to the King's Highway and then out of town, and as soon as she reached the open road she raced the car at seventy while her hair caught snatches of the wind. From time to time Bruce looked at her in quiet surprise. Finally she turned down a side road and stopped the car near an open stretch of the beach.

"I'm crazy today," she said. "But I couldn't stand it any longer at home."

They left the car and walked the beach to the water's edge. The waves were pounding in heavily and the wind whipped the spray in their faces and spattered their clothes. Brilliant sheens of sunlight as wide as fields tossed and flickered on the lake.

"We'll get soaked if we stay here any longer," Bruce said. He turned and walked back about twenty-five yards to rising turf, she stayed a moment longer by the water's edge and then joined him, careful when she sat down to be on his good side. Above their heads a gnarled pine sang in the wind.

She reached into a deep pocket on the front of her linen dress and handed him Marcia's letter.

"I'd like you to read this. I suppose I've been waiting for something like it all summer. It may explain why I – why I've been so difficult for you."

He turned from the wind as he read the letter, then handed it back, gave her a quick glance, and stared out at the tossing water.

"What do you hear from Stephen himself?" he said.

"Nothing."

"What in God's name is the matter with him?" Bruce kicked so hard with his heel that sand spurted out from under it. "Why should you be involved in this – this insensate American pattern?"

"Never mind that," she said. "So much of what has happened to Stephen is my own fault."

"I'm afraid I don't get it."

"I let myself be too proud. I let myself be hurt too easily. When he seemed to be drawing away from me, I drew away too. I shut him out when he needed me most, and my – my silence must have driven him nearly insane. You see – Stephen never had a religion – just as Marcia says. He isn't even able to get above a situation by thinking about it, the way you do. He has to deal with it. He has to – to feel it in his hands. Women are more necessary to him than they are to you, even though you're a poet and he's an engineer."

She lifted her head as the wind caught her hair; inner passion was plain on her face, and Bruce wondered why he had never realized she could be so formidable.

His jaw set hard. "Don't be such a damn fool!" he said. "There's nothing you've got to blame yourself for. The divorce rate in the United States is one to four. What else does that mean except that –"

"No, Bruce," she said quietly. "No."

He looked down at the sand.

"Marcia was divorced three times. Did you feel she was commonplace?"

He flushed. "Of course not."

"Stephen and Marcia aren't small people, Bruce. They're both used to taking long chances."

What does she want of me, he thought. Why has she brought me out here? To get me to put a period after the conclusions she's already reached?

"Stephen and I have different needs," she said. "He gave me what I needed. I failed to give him what he required." Her body seemed to contract as she drew up her knees and clasped them with her hands. "Stephen taught me not to be afraid of my own feelings. He unfroze my heart. He made me see that what counts is not what you keep yourself from doing, but what you *do*. And what did I give him in return? All I could do was to love him, and he needed so much more than that."

Bruce made no reply.

"The other night after we heard about the atomic bomb I began to think of the Americans the way you do – like a great mass of people and not as individuals. I saw them moving in a vast swarm over a plain. They had gone faster and farther than any people had ever gone before. Each day for years they had measured out the distance they'd advanced. They were trained to believe there was nothing any of them had to do but keep on travelling in the same way. And then suddenly they were brought up short at the edge of a precipice which hadn't been marked on the map. There they were with all their vehicles and equipment, jostling and piling up on the front rank. For of course the ones behind didn't know the precipice was there and couldn't understand why the ones in front had stopped advancing. The pressure from behind kept increasing on the front ranks and they were all shouting at each other so loudly nobody could hear anything." She gave a quiet laugh, unclasped her knees and turned to look at him. "And there was Stephen himself, heaving and pushing without realizing the significance of what he was doing, in a rank not very far from the front."

The wind drummed past their ears and tangled Lucy's hair. Bruce passed his hand over his scar and rubbed his forehead. An unspoken hope, an expectation with which he had lived for years, never quite admitting it nor quite rejecting it, had finally resolved itself, become sharply visible, and now had disappeared.

"What are you going to do?" he said quietly.

She smiled as she looked at him. "I didn't know when I asked you to come here with me, but I do now. I'm going to him."

Bruce got to his feet and with a quick movement she rose with him.

"I walked out on him," she said. "And there's no reason why he should come to me."

Her eyes hadn't left Bruce's face. "Forgive me," she said. Gently she kissed his lips, and then she added, "I know I've been unfair to you."

He stood looking at her, his face naked as she had never seen it. "No, you haven't. I've known all along how you felt."

He followed her up the bank toward the car. "A precipice," he repeated to himself. "Does she think the Americans have a monopoly on that, too?"

LUCY'S train reached the LaSalle Street Station shortly after seven-thirty in the morning. She checked her suitcase, walked out to the Van Buren Street entrance to get a taxi, and felt the dry heat reach for her lungs. Her first thought was for the ugliness of the section of the city before her eyes. Her next thought was for the people on the streets; they looked beaten by the hot air that had been lying in the Loop for days.

"The Blackstone Hotel," she said to the taxi driver when she got in his cab, but he was either too tired or too surly to acknowledge having heard what she said. The cab started with a jerk and she fell back on the warm leather seat. Bronze-coloured light filtered slant-wise through the overhead trestles of the elevated tracks onto the tops of trucks and cabs pressing solidly up and down Van Buren. Since she had never been in Chicago she had no idea how long a ride she might have, and she began to wish she had eaten breakfast on the train. They crossed Wabash, the trestles turned and went off in another direction, and the sky seemed to open up ahead. When they reached Michigan Avenue the whole world opened wide. Sunshine flooded the avenue and the rest of the city seemed to drop off behind them in shadowy space.

She paid the driver and went through the glass doors of the hotel into the lobby and the cool dignity of the building enfolded her. She was glad Stephen had chosen to stay in a place like this. But was he still here? That was the only thought in her mind at the moment.

When she asked at the desk and was told he was still registered she found herself smiling at the clerk, hoping he didn't know how suddenly light-headed she felt.

"I'm Mrs. Lassiter," she said. "But he's not expecting me. I've just arrived from Canada. I –" She stopped because she realized it was barely ten minutes to eight and Stephen was probably not awake yet. In any case it was too early to talk to him. Nobody likes to be surprised before breakfast, Stephen as little as anyone. He always woke up hungry, and he was always inarticulate and short-tempered before he had eaten.

She smiled again while the clerk watched her. "I'll go into the dining room," she said. "I'll have you ring his room later on."

In the high-ceilinged, high-windowed restaurant she was shown to a table covered with a stiff, shining white cloth. She took off her gloves, inspected the menu on a smooth white card that was placed before her, and wondered how she was going to hide her nervousness. What if Stephen happened to walk in while she was eating? Would he be angry, as though she had been spying on him? She had no plans for meeting him, no set words to say. She had decided on the train to improvise from moment to moment once she found out where he was.

She took her time over breakfast, trying to read the newspaper that had been placed beside her plate but looking up whenever a newcomer entered the room. But by nine-fifteen there had been no sight of Stephen. She paid her check, left the dining room, and went back to the desk.

"Will you ring Mr. Lassiter's room now, please?"

She waited while another clerk held a receiver to his ears. Finally he said, "The room doesn't answer. I believe Mr. Lassiter has already gone out."

"Oh!" She stood there trying to decide what to do. "I'll wait here for him," she said. "You wouldn't know when he'd be back?"

"He didn't leave any message."

She took a deep breath. "When he does come in, will you tell him I'm waiting in the lobby?"

"Certainly, Mrs. Lassiter."

She picked up a copy of the *Tribune* and found a chair from which she could watch the door. The minutes ticked by as she turned the pages. A woman had been murdered. American officers had surveyed the ruins of Hiroshima. Yugoslavia was threatening the United States. The *Tribune* was threatening England. Great Britain was not to be trusted. The Cubs had won another ball game. When Lucy reached the back page of the paper she laid it down and looked around the lobby. No one had walked through without her eyes finding him. She went to the newsstand, looked over the paper books, and bought a copy of *The Late George Apley* which she had been meaning to read for years.

Elevators opened and people came out, doors opened and people came in, but none of them was Stephen. She was the only one sitting for any length of time in the lobby. Bellboys and a house detective were aware of her presence now. And her eyes still lifted automatically every time anyone entered the revolving doors.

At ten-fifteen she put the book down, unable to concentrate on print of any kind any longer. She tried to think what Stephen would look like when she did see him. What kind of a suit would he be wearing in such heat? A new one, or an old familiar one? What kind of a hat? Or no hat at all? Now she found herself in sudden panic as she tried to recall his features. She had a sense of having forgotten entirely what he looked like. She could bring the image of Jane to her mind, of Bruce and Nina and John and Sally, but not Stephen. Why hadn't she taken a photograph with her when she left Princeton so hurriedly that day? If she had to sit here all day long and search the face of every strange man who crossed her path she would be a gibbering fool by evening.

And then shortly before eleven o'clock Stephen came through the doors from the street. Just for a moment she saw his face, and the sense of familiarity was like seeing herself in the glass after days of being ill in bed. He went straight to the desk and began to talk to the new clerk who had come on duty at ten o'clock. She sat quite still as she was, watching.

All the good things his face had ever meant to her began swarming into her mind – the way he had laughed in the falling snow that December day when they had first tried to ski, the expression of pride and anxiety when he was allowed in her room after John was born, his consternation over the first turkey he had had to carve on Thanksgiving, his adolescent grin when he stripped off his clothes and flexed his muscles for her admiration and appreciation, the set of his jaw as he used his strength and self-confidence to stand like a triple wall between herself and all the things that had bewildered her in a strange country in the first few years of their marriage.

He was still talking to the clerk, leaning sideways, his elbow on the desk, his profile toward the lobby while the clerk made a note on a pad. She saw then that many things had happened to Stephen's face since she had seen it last. More grey hair was visible along the temples, the lines about his eyes and mouth were deeper. He was tired, but above everything else she saw that it was a sad and thoughtful face, far less diffuse than it had been six months ago.

She got to her feet and walked quietly toward the elevators. If the clerk at the desk did tell him she was waiting, she couldn't bear to have him turn around and find her there, in the sight of so many strangers and the house detective. This was a moment for which she had made no plans, but she hadn't meant it to take place in a hotel lobby. The suggestion of dramatics in what she was doing made her shudder.

As he turned away from the desk she realized that the clerk had not delivered her message. Stephen was crossing the lobby toward the elevators, his head slightly bent, his mind busy with its own thoughts. She stood there, undecided what to do next, when an elevator door opened, three people got out, and Stephen stepped in. She followed him, but another man had moved in between them and still Stephen didn't look up, still preoccupied.

The elevator stopped at the third floor after the man called his number, the man got out, and the doors closed again.

"Ten," she heard Stephen say.

She could touch him if she reached out an arm. She took a deep breath, kept her voice low, and said, "Hello, Stephen."

His head came up and turned with a startled jerk. He saw her smiling shyly up at him, his eyes opened wide.

"Good God!" he said, and one hand went out to lean against the wall of the cage.

The elevator slowed quickly to a stop and the doors swung open.

"Ten," the operator said.

Stephen stepped aside and let her precede him and the door swung shut behind them. The hall was perfectly still. One of his hands, she saw, was bandaged across the knuckles. The other went under her elbow and she could feel it trembling. He guided her down a hall, their feet soundless on the thick carpets. They turned a corner and she stopped while his key scraped in the lock of a door.

This is too barren, too impersonal a place to see him for the first time in four months, she thought. How hateful to be like millions of other couples, working out our destiny in a hotel bedroom!

The door opened and he stood back while she went in, and then she was glad they were where they were. Perhaps it was the best kind of place in all the world to be meeting him, without the weight of a personalized background familiar to one or the other, a strange hotel in a strange city, bare of reminders of the past, either good or bad. Besides, it was a charming room for a hotel bedroom. The eastward-facing windows were bright with sun and a view over Lake Michigan. There was an air of the past in the furnishings, of dignity and spacious comfort. The furniture might be no better than imitations in the best manner of Grand Rapids, but they were at least imitations of an era of graciousness. Before she arrived in Chicago the Blackstone had been no more than a name to her; unconsciously she had dreaded the thought of having to talk to Stephen in a room filled with streamlined furniture and aseptic walls, a room lighted indirectly with an overcast of blue, a place that would remind them of Bratian's apartment or their own original furnishings, of Madison Avenue agencies, of the places where Marcia had once liked to eat, of the kind of rooms Gail Beaumont probably kept in New York. What, she thought, would the hypothetical survivors of this century make of the character of people who chose to live with chrome and steel and blue glass when they encountered replicas of such rooms in museums? Exactly what we make of ourselves – cocktail parties, hangovers, childlessness, psychoanalysis, and divorce.

She stood still and looked at the soft colours of wall paper and draperies and rug while Stephen pulled a chair of Georgian design toward the window.

"I like it here," she said, and he seemed grateful for the naturalness of her first remark.

"It's not a bad room," he said. "I've been here over two weeks. Mother used to stay in the Blackstone. I suppose that's why I did too."

As she dropped her purse and gloves on the bed and sat down she saw the pain in his face as it caught the light, but his eyes met hers when she faced him. His self-control made him seem so much older than she remembered him. She knew that he might be as glad to see her as she was to be with him, but a moment like this would be hell for him. Yet he gave no signs of wisecracking or shrugging it off. In no other way did he show her so clearly that much had been happening to him.

"How did you know I was here?" he said quietly, sitting on the edge of the bed.

"Marcia told me."

For the first time she saw the trace of a smile touch his face. "I needn't have asked. I came out to see Carson about that Shasta job. He's been here for more than a month." His voice was heavily controlled. She had the feeling that he was not so much warding her off as keeping his distance, being scrupulously careful to presume nothing from the fact of her presence.

"It's good to see you again," he said. "Very good." He looked out the window. "But Lucy – why did you come?"

There was no defensiveness in his voice and no pretense. It was the voice of a man who had lost something he knew he could never replace. His youth was gone, but whether he had gained anything to fill the vacuum she didn't know.

"Because I wanted to see you," she said.

He searched her features with the expression of a man who has discovered, late and painfully, that only a few words of the thousands he hears in the space of each day can be believed. He looked down and saw that his own hands were trembling. He got up and moved the draperies farther from the window to let in more air, then sat down heavily again. Finally he looked up at her, held her eyes, then with a slow movement he put his head in his hands.

"I'm so ashamed."

"No, Stephen," she murmured. "No!"

She sat down on the bed beside him and he made a movement to ward her off. She touched her fingers to his cheek, felt the warm, familiar, tough, male skin. Then she got up and went back to her chair. As if from a long time and a long distance his voice came to her again.

"Why did you come?"

This time she had no answer.

"I suppose Marcia told you why I left New York?"

"Yes."

"I'd hoped I wouldn't be a trouble to you again."

"Stephen –" She was on her feet, wanting desperately to have him take her in his arms, to stop talking, to see that words were useless. "Come on back to Grenville with me. We can forget all about the past two years. As though –" Her hands made a motion of brushing unseen objects aside. "As though they never were. As though –"

He looked up. Slowly, with deliberate emphasis he said, "But they *were*, Lucy. They happened exactly the way you remember them. The way I remember them, too."

Her mind lurched wildly as she wondered how Bruce would have behaved in a situation like this, and she knew in the next instant that he would never let himself get in a situation like this, and that if he did, his imagination would distort it. But Stephen was still an engineer, trained never to argue with facts.

"I'm not drinking now. I cut it out before I left New York, except for the first night here and that was nothing to speak of. I don't think I ever drank enough to do anything more than lower my efficiency, so I can't blame – what I did on that."

The whir of tires on Michigan Avenue seemed to grow louder in the noon heat. Thank God, she thought, I didn't come here with any set phrases or plans in my head.

"A big guy like me!" he said. "How did you stand it so long? Lassiter thought he could have everything both ways. He tried –"

"Stephen, dear – don't!" She saw that her hands were clenched and she put them behind her back. "Don't punish yourself like that!"

"Facts are still facts, Lucy. You've faced most of the ones that came your way. It's my turn now."

Suddenly she smiled. "You don't have to be quite so headstrong, darling."

The last word surprised him; Lucy had never thrown endearments around the way Marcia did; its implied familiarity broke the grimness of his mood and she took advantage of the break.

"You must listen to me. Just this once, Stephen. Please listen! I've been making discoveries of my own these past months, too. I've learned where I stand on all sorts of things. Stephen, dear – please listen! There's not a single thing that makes my life worth living that you haven't given me. You're the only real strength I have in the world."

He stared at her. "Strength? You're not talking about *me*?"

She closed her eyes, opened them, and her face was as bare and beautiful as he had ever seen it in passion.

"I love you now more than I've ever loved you before."

He got to his feet, blundered to her almost blindly, and she felt his arms come about her. Then his muscles tightened and he forced her away. She leaned heavily against the dresser and watched him move to the window and stare out.

"Stop trying to believe the best," he said. "Listen! Listen and I'll tell you."

There was a long silence during which he continued to stare at the lake while she resumed her place in the chair and studied the carpet.

"How are John and Sally?" he said.

"They're fine. They've had a lovely summer. John's grown a full inch since spring."

The whir of tires on the avenue was as steady as her breathing.

He turned around and looked at her for a long time. "It would be easy to say I've been crazy these past two years. It would be easy to say I was only one of hundreds of thousands of other men in New York. You knew I wasn't unacquainted with women before I married you, or before I married Joyce. But the facts are still there." He returned to the edge of the bed. "I never stopped loving you or the children. If you can believe that you can believe the rest of what I've got to say. In spite of loving you I practically moved in with another woman. I stayed with her while you knew about it. I stayed with her after you'd taken the children to Canada. I stayed with her until Harper stopped the account and Carl fired me. I stayed with her until even she got wise and kicked me out. And all that time –" His eyes forced her to look at him. "I never stopped loving you."

Lucy's eyes held his. "Then I came to Chicago to see Carson about another job," he went on, "because I heard he was going to be here for a few weeks. But my reputation got here first. He just looked at me over his desk and said, 'What's happened to your integrity?'"

Stephen got up again and began to prowl about the room. "It took me quite a while, but I found the answer. I didn't have any."

He was standing over her. "That's the kind of man I am now."

Her chin lifted. It was an old gesture of hers; it highlighted the bone structure of her face and let the unbreakable quality in her nature dominate it. Six months ago it had seemed accusing and intolerable to him. Now he accepted it gratefully.

"No man is the kind of man you think you are if he can bring himself to say what you've just said."

For the first time that morning she saw a light of hope appear in his tired face; it appeared for a second and then it was gone, and she knew that the nature of her problem had changed with its going. Stephen had reached the end of the same road Marcia had taken, had followed to the source most of the marsh-lights which had appeared to his generation like rising suns. And at some time during the past fortnight he had found himself staring in horror at his own face in the glass.

It took all the discipline at her command to prevent pity from driving her into his arms and destroying the ultimate dignity of his despair. The fact that she and John and Sally still loved him was no final answer to his need. She learned then that there are moments when human love is no more help to a man than the sight of friends beckoning across a bottomless chasm.

"I think I know what to do, Lucy. But I've got to be alone."

Six months ago she had believed him powerless to check his own deterioration. Now he had reached the yawning edge of the precipice and he knew it was there, he knew the map he had followed was no longer of any use.

"I'm forty years old, you know."

She heard him, but she made no answer. Into her mind floated a scene from her childhood in Grenville, her father reading the morning prayers: "And by grace are ye saved through faith, not of yourselves; it is a gift of God."

The walls of the room in this strange hotel in a foreign city seemed to slide soundlessly apart to leave her looking outward into infinite distance. The walls which had encompassed her all her life, the walls of a puritan tradition, were there no longer. But Stephen, even when drunk and in bed with another woman, was more of a puritan than she herself had ever been. In defeat, his judgment of himself was identically the same as Jane's. Behind them both was the same bleakness, the same terror of appearing weak, the incapacity to recognize the difference between a fault and a sin, or a sin and a crime, the same refusal to believe that Christ had meant what he said when he stated that the kingdom of heaven belonged to the poor in spirit. In Stephen's self-condemnation she could hear the authentic ring of her sister's voice, and she knew that both of them, Jane deliberately, Stephen by a sort of inheritance in his own subconscious, had spent their lives trying to keep the door shut between their own inner solitude and the mystery of life itself.

"I'm going away," she heard Stephen say.

But instead of listening to him she heard Jane's voice, the voice which for more than a century had been driving the bold and generous ones out of a thousand Grenvilles all over North America, driving them away to cities which had lost all touch with the towns, driving some into a transplanted Asiatic luxury they could never understand, launching others into a rootless technology in which they could never do enough to appease the unknown monster on the other side of the door, leaving them unforgiven and longing helplessly for the purity and safety of a childhood to which none of them could ever return.

She listened to his words. He was telling her that only this morning he had taken a job in northern Minnesota. He was going to drive a truck for a contractor who was building a new road. He wanted to work with his hands. Perhaps later – he didn't know – he would try for an engineering job again.

Lucy could feel the aching, empty pain in him as she watched his face. She moved away from the dresser and put both her hands on his cheeks, raising his chin until his eyes met hers.

"Stephen dear – how long are you going to let dead men make you ashamed of yourself?"

He stood there quietly under the touch of her hands and Lucy wondered if the trembling she felt was in herself or in him.

Had he heard her? Did he know what she meant?

Driven from his father to Bratian, all his life he had been taking upon himself a devious, useless punishment for a useless, ancient guilt.

She saw him in the construction gang in Minnesota – sweating, unhappy, working with men he did not like, trying to persuade himself that by being miserable he would somehow render himself immune from blame. Was punishment the only thing in which he could still believe?

His eyes were searching hers. He made an indecisive movement as if to turn away. Then, as though compelled by a new and unrecognized force, he took her quietly into his arms.

"What have you done to me, Lucy? What did you say?"

"Nothing, darling. You've been listening to yourself."

It's the beginning, she thought. Once again, it's a beginning.

~~~